DESPERATE FIRE

Professionally Published Books by Christopher G. Nuttall

Angel in the Whirlwind

The Oncoming Storm
Falcone Strike
Cursed Command

ELSEWHEN PRESS

The Royal Sorceress

The Royal Sorceress (Book I)
The Great Game (Book II)
Necropolis (Book III)
Sons of Liberty (Book IV)

Bookworm

Bookworm
Bookworm II: The Very Ugly Duckling
Bookworm III: The Best Laid Plans
Bookworm IV: Full Circle

Inverse Shadows

Sufficiently Advanced Technology

Stand Alone

A Life Less Ordinary
The Mind's Eye

TWILIGHT TIMES BOOKS

Schooled in Magic

The Decline and Fall of the Galactic Empire

HENCHMEN PRESS

DESPERATE FIRE

ANGEL IN THE WHIRLWIND

CHRISTOPHER G. NUTTALL

Text copyright © 2017 by Christopher G. Nuttall

Published by 47North, Seattle

www.apub.com

Amazon, the Amazon logo, and 47North are trademarks of Amazon.com, Inc., or its affiliates.

ISBN-13: 9781612185064
ISBN-10: 1612185061

Cover design by Ray Lundgren

Cover illustrated by Paul Youll

Printed in the United States of America

DESPERATE FIRE

PROLOGUE

"I refuse to believe," Lord Cleric Eliseus snarled, "that we are losing the war."

Speaker Nehemiah kept his face carefully blank as the Lord Cleric ranted in front of the entire Speakers Council, the nine men who ruled the Theocracy, accusing an unfortunate intelligence officer of everything from making up figures to outright heresy and unbelief. The Lord Cleric didn't want to accept what he was being told. None of them did. The thought of losing the war, the war which had begun with such promise eighteen months ago, was unthinkable. But they had to face it squarely.

"Enough," Nehemiah said sharply.

Eliseus spun around to face him. "Speaker, do *you* believe that we are losing the war?"

Nehemiah looked back at the Lord Cleric evenly. Eliseus was a fanatic. There was no one more determined to uphold the Theocracy and the True Faith than himself. And Nehemiah would be the first to admit that fanatics had their uses. But when contemplating the cold hard numbers—and the possibility of losing the war—fanatics were nothing more than dangerous liabilities.

The Speaker ignored the question. "Continue," he ordered the intelligence officer. "Summarize the data for us."

"Yes, Your Holiness," Commodore Durkheim said.

He swallowed hard and continued. "Over the last eighteen months, the Commonwealth has switched its economy onto a war footing and commenced mass production of warships, gunboats, freighters, and everything else necessary to sustain a war. Despite our best efforts, we have been unable to impede their production to any significant extent. In addition, they have recruited vast numbers of starship crews and soldiers from their subject worlds, ensuring that their manpower shortage is a thing of the past. We had hoped that integrating so many personnel from so many worlds would cause them problems, but they appear to have coped with them admirably."

Nehemiah kept his face still even as he felt a flicker of discontent. The Commonwealth *had* been having problems as it struggled to integrate so many worlds into its political and economic union, but the war had pushed those problems aside. In hindsight, the Theocracy had made a mistake by moving to the occupied worlds as soon as possible. There might be strife between the Tyre-born and the colonials, but both sides knew that they had to work together or be destroyed. The Theocracy wouldn't give them a peace they could live with, and they knew it.

"Our own economy is on the verge of imploding," Durkheim continued. His voice was carefully flat. He did *not* look at the Speakers charged with overseeing the economy. "Our war production has shrunk remarkably in the last six months; production of everything from starships to missile warheads has declined sharply. Indeed, we only managed to launch four superdreadnoughts since the start of the war; the enemy, damn them to hell, has launched *twenty*. And, thanks to enemy raiding parties operating behind our lines, we have problems getting supplies to the war front. We simply cannot afford to keep losing freighters at this rate."

"The crews are treacherous," Speaker Adam snapped. "They cannot be trusted!"

"They're unbelievers," Nehemiah said. "What do you expect?"

He rubbed his eyes tiredly. The Theocracy had poured resources into its battle fleet, building up the largest military machine it could . . . but it had neglected the sinews of war. Supporting the vast fleet hadn't been easy before the war; now, it was almost impossible. The Commonwealth's tactic of raiding transport convoys was paying off for them. Either the Theocracy recalled ships from the front to escort convoys, thus weakening the defense lines, or the freighters were blown out of space. The Commonwealth won either way.

And hiring outsiders to transport our supplies has backfired, he thought. *They start planning to leave as soon as they get a good look at our system.*

Durkheim kept talking. "Our sources within the Commonwealth agree that the enemy intends to begin a major offensive within the next three months," he said. "They will start by evicting us from the occupied worlds, followed by a thrust through the Gap and into Theocratic Space. I do not believe that they have grasped our current weakness, or just how far ahead of us they are, but they will find out when they begin their offensive. We are in no state to keep them from achieving their goals and stabbing deeper into our space."

He paused. "The war will soon come to an end."

"No," Eliseus snapped. "Our men will fight . . ."

"And they will lose," Durkheim said.

Nehemiah held up a hand before Eliseus could say a word. "Explain."

Durkheim bowed his head. "Our forces are weakening fast," he said. "We have significant shortages of everything from spare parts to missiles and other weapons systems. Worse, we have been unable to run basic maintenance cycles. As a result, too many of our remaining superdreadnoughts are not at full combat efficiency and won't be without a long stay in the yards. There have been accidents—long *strings* of accidents—that have cost lives and destroyed morale. Our forces are brittle, Your Holiness. When the enemy attacks, and they will, our forces will break."

"Impossible," Eliseus snarled.

"The figures speak for themselves," Durkheim said. He spoke like a man who had nothing left to lose. "We cannot counter hard numbers with faith."

He leaned back slightly. "We could kill ten of theirs for every one of ours," he added, "and we would still lose."

"The Commonwealth is *weak*," Eliseus said. He turned to Nehemiah. "They could not endure such losses."

"Assuming we could inflict them," Nehemiah said.

"We *can*," Eliseus insisted.

Nehemiah ignored him. The war had been intended to be short and victorious. Instead, it was turning into a long war of attrition . . . a war they couldn't hope to win. Already, rumors were spreading through the Theocracy, rumors that couldn't be stopped no matter how many unbelievers were purged. The population outside was starting to doubt their leaders . . . and resent the demands placed on them by the war effort. And there were rumors of resistance cells on planets that had been quiet only two years ago.

And we can't even send additional troops to reinforce the occupying forces, he thought. *We don't have the shipping to transport them any longer.*

He closed his eyes for a long moment as the table started to babble. The fanatics, like Eliseus, would demand that the war be continued, despite the cost. Their faith in ultimate victory was unshakable. But others would be considering their own futures. They'd profited hugely through their positions, and they wouldn't want to lose them.

Speaker Adam leaned forward. "Perhaps we should sue for peace."

"Impossible," Eliseus roared.

Nehemiah allowed the council to finish shouting its outrage, each man practically competing to denounce the idea as loudly as possible, then looked at Durkheim. "*Can* we sue for peace?"

Durkheim grew even paler. "Your Holiness, they will not accept peace on any terms we would consider acceptable," he warned. "They want to ensure that we will no longer be a threat to them."

And we don't have any leverage to convince them otherwise, Nehemiah thought. *Or do we?*

He thought rapidly as the table erupted once again. Now that the suggestion had been made . . . it could not be withdrawn. The thought of ending the war on any terms other than total victory was unthinkable—no, it had *been* unthinkable. Now . . . Nehemiah would be happy to end the wretched war and return to the *status quo ante bellum*, but the Commonwealth would not. And why should it? The Commonwealth was on the verge of winning the war.

Unless we can force them to pay a high price for victory, he told himself. The idea was gelling in his mind. It was a gamble, but they had nothing to lose. Besides, God was on their side. *And if the price is too high, they might accept a compromise peace.*

He cleared his throat, bringing the argument to an end. "We have to convince them to agree to a truce," he said. The members of the council would listen to him, in the end, because they were desperate. The war *had* to be ended on acceptable terms. "This is what we're going to do."

CHAPTER ONE

"Transit complete, Captain," Lieutenant Matthew Gross said. "We have entered the system."

"No enemy contacts detected," Lieutenant Commander Cecelia Parkinson added, studying her console carefully. "I'm not detecting any starships within sensor range."

Captain Sir William McElney sucked in his breath. HMS *Thunderchild* had slipped out of hyperspace on the very edge of the system, where there was no reason to expect to encounter enemy warships on patrol, but it was *just* possible that the Theocrats might have installed extensive deep-space monitoring arrays. They were immensely expensive, even by the Commonwealth's standards, yet the Theocracy *needed* them. Hebrides was right in the middle of the war front.

"Take us into cloak," he ordered quietly. The tactical display updated again. A handful of freighters were making their way to and from the system's largest gas giant, but otherwise the system appeared to be empty. He knew it was an illusion. "And then set course for Hebrides."

"Aye, Captain," Gross said. "Course laid in."

"Take us there," William ordered.

He leaned back in his command chair as the starship picked up speed. Hebrides had never had the industrial base of Tyre. His home-world had been a stage-two colony before the Breakaway Wars, but his people were industrious. The loans and equipment the Commonwealth had offered them, during the first few years of membership, had been used to establish a whole network of mining stations and industrial nodes. They'd even produced a second cloudscoop to match the one the Commonwealth had installed years ago. But now the system was as cold and still as the grave. The installations his people had produced were gone.

They wouldn't have let them fall into enemy hands, he thought. The battle for Hebrides had been savage, but the outcome had been preor-dained from the start. *They'd have destroyed everything that couldn't be removed before it was too late.*

He couldn't help feeling a wave of nostalgia mixed with an odd sense that he no longer fit in on his homeworld. *Decades* had passed since he'd left, decades since he'd joined the Royal Navy . . . he'd thought about retiring and going home but never very seriously. Only a hand-ful of his family remained alive on the barren rock—his only surviving brother, Scott, had left too—and he hadn't been very close to any of them. He'd hated the planet's leaders with a passion . . .

. . . but they didn't deserve to be occupied by the Theocracy.

No one does, he thought. *The bastards couldn't even bother to wait for the end of the war before they started converting the population.*

He shuddered at the thought. He'd seen the recordings from Hebrides, from Cadiz, from a dozen other unfortunate worlds that had been occupied by the Theocracy. And he'd listened as countless refugees told their stories, warning the Commonwealth's population of the fate that was in store for them if they lost the war. The entire planetary government would be slaughtered, along with all military and religious personnel; men would be expected to learn to pray, women would be forced to remain in their homes, children would be educated in

Theocratic schools . . . *even if Hebrides was liberated tomorrow,* William thought, *the damage to her society would take generations to fix.*

But my people are tough, he thought. *They will resist.*

The Office of Naval Intelligence *insisted* that Hebrides was still resisting the Theocracy. And, while William had learned to take ONI's pronouncements with a grain of salt, he had to admit that Hebrides was definitely well prepared for a long-term insurrection. The population was composed of stubborn men and women, most of whom had weapons and knew how to use them. And while other planets might be cowed by the threat of orbital bombardment, Hebrides had few population centers that could be threatened. There would be a planet-wide resistance, William was sure, but such a movement couldn't hope to do more than sting the Theocracy without outside help.

Which is why we're here, he reminded himself. *It's time to drive the bastards out of the system, once and for all.*

He couldn't help feeling a surge of very mixed emotions. He *knew* the Commonwealth had needed time to build up its navy, he *knew* the Commonwealth needed to protect the stage-four and stage-five worlds ahead of the others . . . but he still couldn't help feeling as though his adopted government had left Hebrides to suffer. Hebrides had nothing, save for location, and realistically, it didn't have *enough* of a location to make up for its other defects. Liberating his homeworld had always been a very low priority.

But we're coming now, he thought.

The hours ticked by slowly as *Thunderchild* slipped towards the planet. William cursed under his breath as new icons flickered to life on the display: two enemy superdreadnought squadrons, holding station in high orbit. They didn't seem to have many flankers, he noted; there were only five destroyers and two ships that resembled converted freighters. But then, the Theocracy was running short of escorts. They probably hoped the superdreadnoughts could take care of themselves.

Which is careless, William thought. *Every missile taken out by a flanker is one that won't threaten the superdreadnought itself.*

He rose and paced over to the tactical console. "Analysis?"

"They're not in good shape, Captain," Cecelia said. She tapped an enemy icon on the display. "They're running constant near-orbit scans, but their sensor emissions look a little ragged; I'd say they're trying to keep their system constantly ramped up and some of their components are burning out. And this ship"—she pointed to a second icon—"has some very odd fluctuations in her drive fields. I'd bet good money that she's lost at least one, perhaps two, of her nodes."

"No bet," William said. "And the freighters?"

"They've got mil-grade drives," Cecelia said. She sniffed rudely. "It's impossible to be sure, Captain, but I think there's a very real risk they'd rip themselves apart if they brought their drives up to full power."

William wasn't so sure. The Theocracy's starship designers were inferior to the Commonwealth's, but they weren't *stupid*. They wouldn't have put such a drive in a freighter unless they were *sure* she could handle it. And that meant . . .

He stroked his chin, thoughtfully. "What do you think they are?"

"I'd guess they were Q-Ships," Cecelia said after a moment. She looked up at him thoughtfully. "But they're a bit obvious for Q-Ships. They *might* be gunboat carriers."

"Perhaps," William said. He'd bet on the latter. Unless the Theocracy was trying to intimidate potential raiders . . . but really, the raiding parties that had been sent into enemy space wouldn't be particularly intimidated. Capturing enemy freighters was all very well and good, yet the Commonwealth's objectives would be served just as well by blowing the suspect vessel out of space from a safe distance. "Keep a sharp eye on them."

"Aye, Captain," Cecelia said. She smiled thinly. "My overall analysis is that both squadrons are in trouble," she added. "I think they really need a few months in the yard."

William nodded. As a general rule, a starship, particularly anything as big as a superdreadnought, required at least three months in the yard per year. Even in the Commonwealth, where engineering crews knew what they were doing and why they were doing it, the ships needed to spend time in the yards. But the Theocracy was running its fleet ragged. William had a feeling that his opposite numbers aboard the enemy ships were just waiting, biting their nails, to see what failed *next*.

And to think I thought Uncanny *was bad*, he thought. *These ships are in worse condition.*

"See if you can pick out any specific weaknesses," he ordered. "If you can, add them to the tactical matrix."

"Aye, Captain," Cecelia said.

William felt a flicker of pride as he turned and walked back to his chair. He'd never been a father, but he couldn't help feeling a certain paternalistic pride in the officer Cecelia had become. The young midshipwoman he'd met on *Lightning* had turned into a confident, capable woman who would probably be on the shortlist for a command of her own after she served a term as Executive Officer. And she'd probably do a good job of being an XO too.

He sat down and studied the report from the analysis department. The team largely agreed with Cecelia's conclusions, although there were a few refinements. The enemy ships seemed to be permanently on combat alert, even though the Commonwealth hadn't raided the system in months. William had no idea if the enemy was being paranoid or merely trying to make a good show, but he knew pushing themselves too hard couldn't be good for their equipment . . . or their crew. No crew could remain on alert indefinitely. By now, the poor bastards would be worn down so badly they'd probably be falling asleep at their stations.

And getting flogged when they're caught, he thought. He'd heard enough about what passed for discipline in the Theocratic Navy to be very glad he didn't serve in it. *The poor bastards are treated like shit by absolutely everyone.*

"Captain," Cecelia said. "I have an update on the planet itself."

"Show me," William said.

He felt an odd pang as a holographic image of the planet appeared in front of him. Hebrides was a greenish orb. Unusual for a life-bearing world, most of her surface area was land rather than sea, patches of greenery broken by towering mountains that reached up towards the skies. He remembered climbing some of them as a child, back before the pirates had started to raid his homeworld. Even now, there were mountains that had never been successfully climbed by anyone. But they'd claimed dozens of lives as people tried . . .

"A number of settlements have been destroyed," Cecelia said. "And the enemy appears to have installed a couple of Planetary Defense Centers near Lothian."

"That's bad," William said. Two PDCs couldn't hope to defend the planet alone, not without the fleet, but they could make life difficult for the landing force. "Can you determine their current status?"

"No, Captain," Cecelia said. "They're not emitting any sensor radiation."

William shook his head. Task Force Hebrides had more than enough firepower—and marines—to deal with two PDCs, even if the defense centers *did* put up a fight. The real danger lay in the enemy superdreadnoughts, but they would still be massively outgunned. In their place, William would retreat the moment Task Force Hebrides showed itself. Nothing was gained by sacrificing two squadrons of superdreadnoughts in a futile attempt to keep a useless world. Hell, he wasn't sure why the Theocracy hadn't cut its losses years ago. Hebrides wasn't going to pose a threat to its rear.

He leaned back in his chair. If there were any other enemy ships or installations within the system, they were very well hidden. But they were also irrelevant. Hebrides was the sole prize . . . and besides, the opportunity to crush two squadrons of superdreadnoughts was not one to miss. Task Force Hebrides had more than enough firepower to smash them.

"Helm, take us to the first waypoint," he ordered. "Tactical, start preparing to deploy the first set of sensor platforms."

"Aye, Captain," Gross said. A low quiver ran through the light cruiser as she altered course. "ETA seven minutes."

William kept a sharp eye on the display. The recon platforms were heavily stealthed—he knew from experience that they were almost impossible to detect, even at point-blank range—but *Thunderchild* would never be more vulnerable than when she was deploying the platforms. A vigilant sensor officer might *just* pick up something that would alert him to *Thunderchild*'s presence, and, if his commanding officer took him seriously, he might dispatch a couple of destroyers to sweep local space. William had no doubt he could avoid contact long enough to make a clean getaway, but the enemy would be alerted. They'd *know* the Commonwealth was planning an offensive.

And they might have a chance to capture one of the platforms too, he thought sourly. *That would get us all in deep shit.*

His face darkened at the thought. The Theocracy was unlikely to be able to reverse engineer anything they captured, at least quickly enough to matter, but there were other multistar political entities out there. ONI had warned, in considerable detail, that certain powers were negotiating with the Theocracy, trading weapons and supplies for samples of Commonwealth technology. William wasn't sure *just* how seriously to take the reports, but he had to admit they were a valid concern. The Commonwealth-Theocracy War was the first true interstellar war fought between peer powers. *Every* naval force worthy of the name would be frantically studying the conflict and trying to determine what lessons could be learned from it before they too had to go to war.

Starting with not allowing a complete idiot to take command of a major fleet base, William thought, feeling a flicker of cold amusement. *If Admiral Morrison had done his fucking job . . .*

"Captain," Gross said. "We have reached the first waypoint."

"Very good," William said. The enemy squadrons didn't *look* to be any more alert, but it was impossible to be sure. He wondered if the enemy ships would decay into complete uselessness if left alone. "Deploy the recon platform."

"Aye, Captain," Cecelia said.

William tensed. He would have preferred to deploy the platform much farther away from Hebrides, but his briefing clearly stated that they needed the platform as close to the planet as possible. It wasn't *just* a recon platform, not really. Many of the details were classified well above his pay grade, but he'd picked up enough hints to know that the platforms connected to a whole new weapons system. And if it worked . . .

Another good reason to test the system here, he thought. *No one will notice if the system fails.*

"Platform deployed," Cecelia said. "No sign of enemy reaction."

William wasn't reassured. In *his* experience, a crew needed time to convince a commanding officer to investigate a potential disturbance . . . longer if the commanding officer needed to speak to *his* commanding officers. And if the enemy commander decided to play it smart, he might be careful not to do anything to warn William while the enemy ships readied themselves for action. But there was no time to wait and see what the enemy did.

"Establish the laser link, and then move us to the second waypoint," he ordered. "Do *not* lose contact with the platform."

"Aye, Captain," Gross said.

William had to smile at the flicker of indignation in Gross's voice. He was a *very* good helmsman. But then, stealthed platforms *had* been lost before, and while there was an omnidirectional radio beacon mounted on the platform, triggering the beacon would alert the enemy to *Thunderchild*'s presence. The platform would have to be destroyed instead of recovered.

"Laser link firmly in place, Captain," Cecelia reported.

"Reaching second waypoint," Gross added.

"Deploy the second platform," William ordered.

He kept a wary eye on the enemy ships as *Thunderchild* deployed the remaining platforms, one by one, but the enemy showed no hint that they were aware of his ship's presence. They didn't even seem to be exercising, although that proved nothing. The vast majority of shipboard functions could be practiced through simulations, even though there was no true substitute for a live-fire exercise. But if half his suspicions were accurate, the Theocratic ships were in no state for anything. A live-fire exercise might end in tragedy.

Just like it nearly had for Uncanny, he mused. The thought of his first command caused him a pang, even though the heavy cruiser had died well. *And they don't have the ships or men to spare.*

"Captain!" Cecelia snapped. "One of the superdreadnoughts just fired on the planet."

William swung around to stare at her. "At what?"

"A town, five hundred kilometers from Lothian," Cecelia said. Her voice was tightly controlled. "They dropped at least seven KEWs, midsized weapons."

Bastards, William thought. Seven kinetic energy weapons would be more than enough to utterly devastate the town. If anything, such a move was massive overkill. *What are they doing down there?*

He had a feeling he knew the answer. The Theocracy's theology insisted that anyone who resisted, anyone who did not cheerfully accept the True Faith as soon as they heard it, was nothing more than a devil-spawned heretic. Unbelievers weren't just wrong, they were *willfully* wrong. William didn't care to follow the logic—or the complete lack of it—but he didn't *need* to follow it to know where it led. Anyone the Theocracy classed as a heretic could be enslaved or killed at will.

And there will be an awful lot of heretics on my homeworld, he thought. *We don't give in that easily.*

The assault looked bloodless on the display, falling icons touching the planet and flickering out of existence. But he knew what it was like to be under enemy weapons when they struck the surface. The entire town would have been smashed flat, anyone unlucky enough to be inside was killed before they realized that they were under attack. And enemy kill-teams would follow up, sweeping the surrounding area to catch anyone who might have managed to escape. He knew, all too well, what they would do to anyone caught. Or, for that matter, anyone unlucky enough to live too close to the blast zone.

We're coming, he promised the planet silently. *You will be free soon.*

"Take us back into deep space," he ordered. There was nothing they could do now, but once they linked up with the remainder of the task force . . . the Theocracy was in for a nasty shock. "We'll slip back into hyperspace once we've crossed the system limits."

"Aye, Captain," Gross said.

Ten hours later, HMS *Thunderchild* departed the system as stealthily as she'd arrived.

CHAPTER TWO

If there was one advantage of being promoted to commodore, Kat Falcone considered, it was that she had a truly palatial suite onboard HMS *Queen Elizabeth*. Her compartment on the superdreadnought was still smaller than her rooms in the family mansion—and she couldn't help feeling as though she was rattling around like a pea in a pod—but there was plenty of room for two people. And hardly anyone cared if the task force's commander was sharing a bed with her Marine CO.

She sat upright in bed, turning her head to look down at Patrick Davidson. It was rare, very rare, for her to wake without disturbing him, but he barely even stirred as she moved. She smiled as she studied him, fixing his features in her mind. Dark hair cut close to the skull, a shaved face, muscular body . . . before Pat, she'd never met anyone who made her feel *safe*. But then, she hadn't been looking.

They made an odd couple, she had to admit. There was definitely something *rough* about Pat—Kat's sister had called him ugly, back when she'd been trying to set Kat up with someone more aristocratic—but she didn't care about his appearance. She, on the other hand, was tall and thin, almost willowy. Her long blonde hair hung down until it stroked the top of her breasts. And yet she was damned if she was letting him go. She'd learned enough about politics, ever since becoming a teenager, to know that a true friend and lover was worth his weight in gold.

Which isn't that much these days, she thought wryly. *Asteroid miners produce thousands of tons of gold every month.*

She reached for her terminal and checked for updates. Task Force Hebrides was still holding station in hyperspace, two light-years from its destination. There wasn't much risk of being detected, but she'd been careful to keep the squadron off the shipping lanes as much as possible. The last report had stated that at least one squadron of enemy super-dreadnoughts was orbiting Hebrides, utterly unaware she was coming. And she didn't *want* them to know she was coming until she actually arrived. After spending so long matching herself against superior enemy firepower, having the decisive advantage herself would be a breath of fresh air.

And besides, she told herself, *destroying an entire squadron of super-dreadnoughts is a worthwhile goal in itself.*

Pat stirred, his eyes opening sharply. "What time is it?"

Kat made a show of glancing at the terminal. "You were meant to be in Marine Country two hours ago," she said in a deadpan. "And there have been no less than five official complaints filed already."

"I hope not," Pat said. He elbowed her as he saw the terminal. "I've still got an hour."

"Yeah," Kat said. She let out a long breath. "*Thunderchild* hasn't returned."

Pat sat upright and wrapped his arm around her shoulders. "Sir William is a good man," he said. "And he has strict orders to avoid all enemy contact. He'll be back."

Kat snorted. Only an idiot, or a politician, would imagine that *Thunderchild* could carry out her mission without *any* prospect of being detected. She had to slip right up to the planet, for crying out loud! *Thunderchild* was a good ship, far better than *Uncanny*, but her cloaking systems would have problems compensating for the moment she deployed her recon platforms. William might have real problems escaping the system without engaging the enemy, if they caught a whiff of his presence.

She swung her legs over the side of the bed and stood. "I'm going for a shower," she said. "Ask Lucy to send in some coffee, would you?"

Pat nodded. "And breakfast?"

Kat smiled wanly as she strode across the compartment and into the shower. Being a flag officer in the navy was like staying at an expensive hotel with a giant bed, immense washroom, and room service. But no one staying at a hotel had the same responsibilities as a flag officer on active duty. She might no longer be in command of her own ship—she'd had to resist the temptation to peer over Captain Fran Higgins's shoulder—but she was responsible for the entire task force. Fifty-seven ships, eighteen of them superdreadnoughts . . . she was responsible for them all.

And yet, she would never know them. They would never be truly hers.

She turned on the water and sighed in relief as it ran down her body. It was hard *not* to worry about *Thunderchild*, let alone the other ships and crew under her command. Her promotion hadn't been a surprise, but she would have refused it if that had been an option. She cared too much about her ships and crew, she knew. She'd handled squadron command before, yet this was different. A single superdreadnought would take over a thousand spacers with it if it were blown out of space by enemy fire.

The captains have their job, she told herself firmly. *And I have mine.*

She finished washing herself and turned off the water, feeling oddly guilty for using so much. The water was recycled, naturally, but none of the lower decks had the time to just luxuriate under the flow. They'd already be heading to their duty stations as the shift changed, after catching enough sleep, she hoped, so that they'd be in tip-top condition for the coming battle. She couldn't have tired men and women manning her ships. Exhaustion had killed more spacers than anything else outside an actual engagement.

"Coffee on the table," Pat said. "And a full breakfast, which you are going to eat."

"Yes, mother," Kat said, dryly. She'd never found it easy to eat before a battle, although the genetic improvements spliced into her DNA ensured that she didn't put her ship at risk through starvation. "I'll see how much of it I can choke down."

"Try choking down marine rations," Pat said as he climbed out of bed. "If you can stomach those, you can stomach anything."

Kat stuck out her tongue childishly. "I thought that was why you had your stomach modified?"

"It was," Pat said.

He turned and walked into the shower. Kat watched his nude body for a long moment, wondering if this was what it was like to be married. To be with someone, to *relax* with someone . . . her parents had been married for over sixty years, but she knew they didn't always spend time together. But then, family politics would never let them divorce, even if they had grown to hate one another.

But they still seem to like one another, she thought as she sipped her coffee. *How do they do it?*

Lucy Yangtze, her steward, had outdone herself, Kat decided as she tucked into the scrambled eggs and bacon. The food was the same reconstituted crap everyone else ate, but that of flag officers got special flavorings to make it almost completely indistinguishable from the real thing. Or so Kat had been told. She might have grown up among the aristocracy, yet she'd never developed the gourmand tastes of some of her relatives. *Their* lives were meaningless. They'd never accomplished anything on their own, ever. And they knew it.

She glanced up as Pat stepped back into the compartment, a towel wrapped around his waist, then nodded to the covered plate on the table. Pat sat down and began to eat, wolfing down the food in a manner Kat knew would earn the highest levels of scorn and disdain in aristocratic society. *She* didn't care much for fine dining, but at least she knew how to comport herself at table. Yet she didn't blame Pat. He'd been taught, time and time again, better to eat quickly, whenever one had a moment, rather than risk being caught by surprise. The thought of a platoon of marines having a formal dinner under enemy fire . . .

Pat glanced at her. "What's so funny?"

"A random thought," Kat lied. "I . . ."

The intercom bleeped. "Commodore, this is Gaston in Tracking," a male voice said. "HMS *Thunderchild* has returned to the fleet. She's copying her files over now."

"Understood," Kat said. "Inform the commanding officers that I am calling a general meeting in"—she glanced at the chronometer—"twenty minutes. They are to attend via hologram."

"Aye, Commodore," Gaston said.

Kat closed the connection, feeling a surge of warm relief. *Thunderchild* had returned! She hadn't run into trouble or been blown out of space. But now it was time to go to war. Kat took one last swig of coffee, rose, and hastily started to dress. The meeting might be holographic, but they'd be heading straight for Hebrides in less than an hour. She doubted she'd have time to go back to her cabin and change.

"Here we go, then," Pat said. He rose and dressed with lightning speed. "Do you want me to attend in person?"

"If you would," Kat said. "Or do you have to go back to Marine Country?"

"Not yet," Pat said. "I'll have to give them the final briefing after we download the recordings from *Thunderchild*."

They shared a grin, and then Kat turned and led the way out of her cabin, down towards the flag bridge. Stepping into the compartment felt odd after spending so long in command of her own ship, but she knew she'd probably never command her own ship again. Shaking her head, she took one look at the tactical display as she walked by and into the conference room. A handful of ghostly holographic images were already present, waiting for her. More were blinking in all the time.

She took her seat and smiled. She'd known admirals who'd insisted on everyone attending in person, something that caused all sorts of delays and irritations for their subordinates. She could see the value, she supposed, but it was a pain in the ass when time was pressing. There was no way to be *entirely* sure *Thunderchild* had escaped without detection, and even if she *had*, the enemy ships might change their positions anyway. It was what Kat would do if she'd been charged with defending a useless planet.

But I wouldn't try to defend the planet in the first place, she thought. *It contributes nothing to the war effort.*

"Gentlemen, be seated," she said, once the last of the holographic images had flickered into existence. "Sir William?"

William's image took a step forward. "Commodore," he said. A tactical display blinked up, hovering over the conference table. "As you can see, the enemy fleet is numerically strong, but there are excellent reasons to believe that their ships are not in good condition."

"They look like *Uncanny*," Captain Hemlock Jones said.

"Worse," William said. "We suspect that two of the superdreadnoughts cannot move under their own power."

Kat studied the display for a long moment, flicking through the more detailed reports William's staff had put together. Finding a *second* superdreadnought squadron orbiting Hebrides was a nasty surprise, but if the analysts were right, Kat still had a crushing advantage even without the new weapons. Indeed, there was no logical reason to *keep* the superdreadnoughts at Hebrides unless the enemy couldn't put them to use elsewhere. She would have expected them to be pointed straight at the nearest Commonwealth world.

Because tactical retreats don't seem to be included in their tactical manuals, she thought wryly. *All they want to do is attack, attack, attack.*

"They look like easy targets," Captain Smith said. "Is it a trap?"

"If so, it's a very odd one," William said. "We detected no hints that there were any other ships in the system, save for the ones on the display."

Kat knew better than to take that for granted. Space was *vast*. Every starship in the entire galaxy could be hidden within a single star system, as long as elementary precautions were taken. But William was right. It *was* a very odd trap. If nothing else, she could be relatively sure of getting her ships back out of the system if indeed three or four *more* superdreadnought squadrons *were* lurking in the interplanetary void.

"The presence of a second enemy squadron changes nothing," she said when William had finished giving the briefing. "We will proceed as planned."

She waited for an objection but heard none. Her officers *wanted* to go on the offensive; they *wanted* to give the Theocracy a bloody nose. They were sworn to defend the Commonwealth, but they had failed to keep the Theocracy from occupying the system and landing a colossal force on Hebrides. And besides, they *knew* they had a decisive advantage over their foes. Even if the new weapons failed, they still had plenty of other tricks up their sleeves.

"We will engage the enemy ships as quickly as possible," Kat continued. "We don't want them trying to escape into hyperspace."

"Fat chance," Captain Jones muttered.

Kat was inclined to agree. The Theocracy *rarely* ran, even when the odds were stacked against them. And they might assume that two squadrons of superdreadnoughts had a reasonable chance of inflicting serious harm on *another* two squadrons of superdreadnoughts, even if some of their ships were in poor condition. But Kat knew that didn't matter. There were so many new warships coming off the slips now that she could lose her entire fleet without inflicting any harm on the enemy . . . and it wouldn't matter. The balance of power would remain firmly on the Commonwealth's side.

Unless they come up with a new weapons system of their own, she thought. *But that isn't likely either.*

"Once we have secured the high orbitals, we will commence bombardment of enemy positions while landing the marines," she said. "If the enemy attempts to surrender, we will of course accept it, but we cannot assume that they *will* surrender. The marines will land around Lothian and ready themselves for an advance on the PDCs. Hopefully, we will link up with resistance forces on the ground during the advance."

They weren't a very specific set of instructions, but she knew better than to micromanage her subordinates. There was no way to *know* what would happen on the ground, at least until the marines landed. Pat would be in command. *He* knew his objective; Kat might have issued the orders, but *he* would be the one to determine how the mission would be carried out. There was no way Kat could hope to steer events from orbit.

"Assuming the enemy does surrender, we will make certain to separate them from the civilian population as quickly as possible," she added. "Enlisted men will be separated from officers, the latter transported to orbit for interrogation before they are sent to a holding camp. Those charged with war crimes will be put on trial after the war is over. The remainder . . . we'll have to see what happens, after the war."

She shook her head bitterly. Too many atrocities had been committed over the last two years for anyone to be enthusiastic about treating prisoners gently. She knew, all too well, that some politicians had even proposed simply executing every POW without bothering with the formality of a trial. And her own darker side found it tempting. What was the *point* of being the good guys, of trying to treat prisoners well, when one's own personnel were treated barbarically? Wasn't retaliation enshrined in the laws of war?

But that assumes that the other side gives a damn, she thought. *The Theocrats wouldn't care if we tortured their captured personnel until they were in permanent agony.*

"We move out in thirty minutes," she concluded. Thankfully, her ships and crews were ready to move with ten minutes' notice. "And we'll give the enemy hell."

A low rumble of agreement ran around the chamber. The Commonwealth had been on the offensive before, raiding deep into enemy space, but this was different; the first thrust aimed at liberating an enemy-held world. And it would be the first of many. Kat had seen the plans drawn up back on Tyre. The Theocracy would be smothered ruthlessly, crushed under the colossal weight of Commonwealth war production. The fight wouldn't be fair, but she couldn't even *begin* to feel sorry for the bastards.

"Good luck to us all," she said. "Dismissed."

The holographic images winked out, leaving her alone with Pat. She glanced at him, then looked back at the display. Hebrides hung in front of her, surrounded by twenty-five red icons. Perhaps it was her imagination, but they seemed to be glaring angrily at her. They *knew* she was coming for them.

"Try and protect the civilians," she said without looking at him. "Please."

"I wish that were possible," Pat said. "But they put most of their bases close to civilian population centers."

Kat gritted her teeth. The Theocracy had killed thousands of civilians, and she was about to kill thousands more. But Kat had no choice. The enemy could *not* be allowed time to go underground. The Commonwealth would need years to root them all out, even with the locals helping. She didn't have the time.

"Good luck," she said. She turned and gave him a tight hug. "Come back to me, all right?"

"I will," Pat promised.

He kissed her once, then turned and strode out of the compartment. Kat looked back at the display, silently considering the more detailed reports. The enemy ships *did* seem to be in very poor condition. But *Uncanny* had seemed in poor condition too.

But they'll want to intimidate us, she thought coldly. *Looking like wounded gazelles will merely invite attack.*

She dismissed the thought as she turned and headed for the hatch. It no longer mattered. She'd find out the truth, sooner or later. But now . . . ?

Now was the time to make war.

CHAPTER THREE

"I have the latest reports from *Saladin*," Commander Farad said. He held out a datapad, the report glowing on the screen. "Her commander *insists* the ship can handle her duties."

Admiral Ashram took the datapad, struggling to hide his displeasure. He'd grown to hate Hebrides over the last two months, ever since he'd been assigned to replace the previous officer. *That* worthy had been brutally murdered in a local brothel, the whore who'd killed him vanishing into the underground before the Inquisitors could catch up with her. Ashram had no idea how the underground had even managed to slip someone *into* the brothel, but he had to admit the unbelievers were very good at exploiting the Theocracy's weaknesses.

"Let me see," he said. "Does he really feel he can take his ship into combat?"

He groaned under his breath as he scanned the report. The super-dreadnought had lost two of her four fusion cores, ensuring she could barely limp back to the shipyard. There was no way she could take on an enemy ship, even something as puny as a light cruiser, with a reasonable hope of victory. In a sane universe, she would be dispatched back to the yards for a total refit, along with a third of his other ships. But the Theocracy didn't have time. He'd been asking, begging, for permission to take some of his ships out of the line of battle, yet he'd always been refused. The demands of the war came first.

We're on the war front, he thought, turning his gaze to the greenish orb floating in the main display. *And we're nowhere near ready to fight.*

He glowered at the orb, feeling a surge of naked hatred. Hebrides was *tough*, tougher than any other world the Theocracy had overrun. Its population was stubborn as hell, resisting his forces when and wherever they could. Even in the more civilized places, the handful of cities, the unbelievers were just waiting for a chance to harm his men. And all of the usual means of social control had failed. There wasn't a boy or girl on the planet who didn't know how to forage for food, even if the farms were occupied or destroyed; outside the cities, controlling the countryside was a nightmare. The occupation forces were fighting with holy zeal and barely holding their own. They would lose, and lose fast, if they couldn't call on his ships for support.

The Inquisition believes the locals would make good Janissaries, he reminded himself. *And they're probably right . . . if we could trust them.*

Gritting his teeth, he returned the datapad and stalked over to the planetary display. The Inquisition had reported dozens, perhaps hundreds, of rumors flowing through the ranks despite harsh punishments for anyone caught breathing a word of dissent. It was becoming harder and harder to conceal the gulf between official pronouncements and reality . . . and his men were growing increasingly aware of it. The insurgency had been proclaimed dead so many times that it wasn't funny anymore. And then there were the newcomers from Ahura Mazda, a handful of men with orders so highly classified that he, the local commander, hadn't been allowed to see them. All Ashram knew was that he had to give them whatever they asked for, without question.

Hebrides was *worthless*, he knew. The planet's industrial base had been destroyed during the brief struggle for control of the high orbitals and its population was too fanatical to be trusted with anything more complex than hewing wood and drawing water. The Theocracy gained nothing by committing so many troops to the surface, or two entire squadrons of superdreadnoughts to the high orbitals, but the high command was reluctant to abandon an occupied world. They'd been *proud* of capturing Hebrides . . .

An alarm sounded. "Admiral, long-range sensors have detected a gateway opening, two light minutes from the planet," a voice said. "We're picking up a small enemy fleet."

And what, Ashram asked himself silently, *aren't you detecting?*

He turned and strode back towards his command chair, sitting down as the tactical display updated rapidly. The gateway was far too large for anything other than an enemy fleet, probably including at least one squadron of superdreadnoughts or assault carriers. Either one would pose a serious threat, perhaps a terminal one. His squadron was in no state to fight off a major offensive. But his orders were clear. He was to stand and fight—and die, if necessary—in defense of the planet.

"Bring the fleet to full alert," he ordered. His crews had been pressing their sensors too hard over the last month, ever since intelligence had begun warning of a major enemy offensive, but hopefully they would endure. "And order the courier boat to ready itself to leave orbit."

"Aye, sir," Commander Farad said.

Ashram sucked in his breath as the enemy fleet took on shape and form. The sensor readings weren't entirely clear, thanks to enemy electronic countermeasures, but there were at least fifty ships advancing on his position. And there was something odd about their formation. He stroked his chin gently as he contemplated the situation. Enemy forces had come out of hyperspace too far from the planet to have any hope of taking him by surprise. Had they messed up their calculations? Or did they have something nasty in store?

"The fleet is at full alert," Commander Farad reported. "The tactical datanet is fully functional."

"Make sure the net stays up at all times," Ashram ordered. Such a move ran the risk of allowing the enemy to identify his flagship and target her for destruction, but he saw no other choice. Too many of his ships had no fire control at all. They wouldn't be able to do anything apart from shoot blind without the datanet. "Order the forces on the ground to brace themselves."

He cursed his superiors under his breath. If he ordered a retreat . . . his family would suffer for his crimes. He would have cheerfully accepted his own death by execution if he'd managed to save the ships and crews, but such an act would not save his wives and children. His adult sons would be killed, his wives and daughters parceled out to whoever wanted them . . . better to fight and die than condemn *them* to such a fate. No doubt his bravery would go down in history as a valiant last stand against overwhelming odds.

"Picking up a message, sir," Commander Farad said. "They're calling on us to surrender."

"Do not reply," Ashram said. Surrender? There was no way he could surrender! "Order the courier boat to leave orbit now."

He leaned back in his chair as the enemy fleet continued its advance. He was about to die, but at least he'd have a chance to hurt the enemy before he perished. Who knew? Perhaps his death wouldn't be meaningless after all.

And my family will survive, he thought numbly. *That, if nothing else, will give my life meaning.*

◆ ◆ ◆

"Commodore," Commander Bobby Wheeler said, "there has been no response to our hail."

Kat wasn't surprised. The Theocracy rarely surrendered. Even if the enemy CO *had* tried to surrender, she wasn't sure she could have trusted him. The Theocracy seemed to regard attempts to surrender as just another way to gain a tactical advantage. Hell, Admiral Junayd, the lone senior defector from the Theocracy's ranks, had confirmed that the Theocrats wanted to make sure that none of their personnel were allowed to surrender. They didn't want them to think that there was any hope for a better life on the other side of the hill.

"Prepare to flush the external racks," she ordered. "Ready missiles."

There was a pause. "Missiles ready," Wheeler said. "Tactical combat links ready and waiting."

"Good," Kat said. She wondered absently what the enemy CO was thinking. He *had* to be wondering if she'd made a mistake. *And* he had to believe he still had time before the two fleets entered missile range. "Flush the external racks."

Queen Elizabeth shook as she fired a barrage of missiles. Kat leaned forward, never taking her eyes off the display, as the other superdreadnoughts flushed their own external racks. The new missiles might be too large to be fired from a standard tube, but there were still enough of them to give the enemy a very nasty surprise. And while targeting was often a problem at such long range, the recon platforms *Thunderchild* had emplaced could provide real-time data to the command missiles as they closed in on their targets.

And the missiles are faster too, she thought as her fleet plunged onwards. *The enemy won't have time to react.*

♦ ♦ ♦

"They fired," Farad said in disbelief. "All those missiles . . . wasted."

"Don't count on it," Ashram growled. The Commonwealth wasn't stupid. Their commanders wouldn't have fired upwards of three thousand missiles unless they had a reasonable expectation of scoring hits. And *that* meant that the missiles probably wouldn't burn out before they reached his ships. "Ready point defense, prepare to engage."

He braced himself. "And launch a spread of antimatter missiles," he added. "Configure them for detonation within the enemy missile swarm."

Farad looked shocked. "Sir . . ."

"Do it," Ashram snarled. Antimatter missiles were expensive, true, and the squadron only had a handful of them after his ships had been stripped bare to support the last offensive, but they had to use them now or lose them. "Fire!"

"Aye, sir," Farad said.

◆ ◆ ◆

"The enemy is launching missiles," Wheeler said.

Kat nodded. The tacticians had worked their way through a number of prospective enemy responses to the new missiles, looking for ways the Theocracy might seek to tip the balance back in their favor. Using their own missiles to swat the incoming weapons out of space . . . it was certainly possible, if they thought of the maneuver in time. And besides, the tactic would waste more of their missiles before her ships closed to engagement range.

But their desperate gamble wasn't going to be enough, she noted, as the first antimatter warheads began to detonate, one by one. Hundreds of her missiles were blown out of space, but hundreds more survived. And even though their command network was disrupted, they were still drawing tactical data from the recon platforms. One by one, the missiles selected their final targets and closed in for the kill.

"Their point defense is oddly sporadic," Wheeler reported. "I'd say we grossly overestimated their efficiency."

"It looks that way," Kat agreed. The enemy ships weren't coping very well with the missiles, even though they'd had plenty of time to prepare. The enemy datanet seemed to be in a terrible state. And a quarter of the point defense fire they should have had was missing. "Ramp up our speed."

"Aye, Commodore," Wheeler said.

Kat watched with grim satisfaction as the first of the missiles struck home. The drives and sensors weren't the only things that had been improved, she knew; the antimatter warheads had been enhanced too. Enemy shields flickered, flared, and failed as they were pounded out of existence, the remaining missiles slamming into unprotected hulls. Seven superdreadnoughts were destroyed, blown out of space with all hands; five more were badly damaged, leaking atmosphere and plasma as they struggled to survive. Kat remembered the final minutes of HMS *Lightning* and shuddered. It was unlikely the crews of the damaged ships would manage to escape, even if their commanders ordered them to abandon ship . . .

She winced as another enemy ship exploded. The enemy didn't seem to be trying to escape, even though she knew their ships had life-pods. Were they that scared of being taken prisoner? Or were their commanders refusing to allow them to escape? The enemy ships couldn't win the battle unless a relief fleet arrived in the nick of time. And Kat doubted, very much, that the Theocrats would make the effort.

Should have recalled both squadrons before they could be attacked, she thought. *It isn't as if they were doing any good out here.*

"The remaining enemy ships are continuing their advance," Wheeler reported.

Kat made a face. What had the enemy crews *done* to deserve such a commander? He'd signed their death warrants without a second thought. What had they *done*?

But there was no time for sentiment. "Signal all ships," she ordered. "They are to engage the enemy as soon as they enter missile range."

"Aye, Commodore," Wheeler said.

◆ ◆ ◆

"Keep us on course," Ashram ordered. "Prepare to engage the enemy."

"Aye, sir," Farad said.

"And order all ships to fall in behind us," Ashram added. "We are to do everything in our power to get within energy range."

He kept his face impassive even though he knew he'd lost, and lost badly. Eight superdreadnoughts gone, four more so badly damaged that they couldn't hope to keep up with the remainder of his ships. He had six superdreadnoughts left, against eighteen. Ashram had no hope of doing more than scratching the enemy's paint before he died, taking his ships with him. But there was no alternative.

The range was closing rapidly, the enemy tacitly accepting his challenge. Whoever was in command over there didn't seem inclined to try to keep the range open, even though such a strategy favored him. Ashram's opponent wanted the battle to end as quickly as he did. There was nothing subtle about his tactics, no desire to be clever . . . he'd brought a very big hammer and used it to smash Ashram's squadron. Whoever was in command of the other side had set out to win, and he'd done it.

"The gunboats are being launched now," Farad said.

"Finally," Ashram snapped. He would have ordered the immediate execution of the unfortunate commanders of the two makeshift carriers if he hadn't been sure the enemy would take care of that for him. But the modified transports hadn't been *designed* to serve as carriers. "Order them to provide cover for the fleet as long as possible."

"Aye, sir," Farad said. He paused. "We could send them against the enemy ships . . ."

"They're not ready for it," Ashram snapped.

And they never will be, he added silently.

◆ ◆ ◆

"The enemy ships are launching gunboats," Wheeler said. "I count forty-five craft, Type-II."

So that's what those ships were, Kat thought. *I wonder why they didn't launch them earlier.*

She pushed the thought aside as the range closed sharply. The enemy ships hadn't flinched, even though they might have been able to escape if they'd opened a gateway and slipped back into hyperspace. Instead, they were pushing their drives so hard that they were on the verge of overloading one or more of their drive nodes. They were determined, truly determined, to hurt her as much as they could before they died. And she was equally determined that they wouldn't have the chance.

"Launch our own gunboats," she ordered. "And then prepare to launch missiles."

"Entering missile range in two minutes," Wheeler said. "Missiles ready; targeting programs laid in."

"Fire as soon as we enter missile range," Kat ordered.

She watched as the gunboats zoomed away from her fleet, closing rapidly with the enemy ships. Their gunboats fought back desperately, but clearly their pilots hadn't had enough training. The Type-II gunboats had been outdated as far back as First Cadiz, yet they could be handled significantly better by skilled pilots. The Theocrats definitely didn't know how to get the best out of their crafts. And *her* crews had received months of intensive training to hone their skills.

Good, Kat thought savagely. *Let the bastards die.*

"Entering missile range," Wheeler reported. He tapped a switch on his console. "Missiles firing . . . *now.*"

◆ ◆ ◆

Ashram cursed under his breath as the enemy ships opened fire, each of his vessels targeted by two or three opponents. The barrage of their missiles seemed unstoppable, his missiles nothing more than a pitiful stream that evaporated as they flew into the enemy's point defense network. He prayed, with a fervor he hadn't felt since his first command, that *something* would survive long enough to reach the enemy shields and do damage, but God wasn't listening. Or perhaps He wasn't on the Theocracy's side after all.

His ship shook violently as a string of missiles struck home. Superdreadnoughts were built to soak up damage and keep going, but *his* ship was suffering from four months' worth of poor maintenance. Red icons flashed on the displays as components overloaded and failed, some exploding within the ship itself. Ashram spun around in alarm as a console exploded, something he'd never seen outside bootleg movies. A crewman stumbled backwards and hit the deck, his uniform on fire. And then the shields failed . . .

My family will be safe, he thought, closing his eyes. *And that is all that matters.*

◆ ◆ ◆

"The enemy ships have been destroyed, save for one," Wheeler reported. "She appears to have lost power completely."

"Give her a wide berth," Kat ordered. Normally she would have sent a marine recon team to board the enemy vessel, but right now she didn't have time. They'd investigate the hulk later. "Take us straight to the planet."

"Aye, Commodore," Wheeler said. "We will enter high orbit in seven minutes."

Kat barely heard him. The Theocracy was terrifyingly ruthless, but this was a new low. The enemy had thrown away twenty-five ships for nothing . . . she'd lost four gunboats, a loss that would barely be noticed during the post-battle assessments. Would it have been so bad to withdraw before they were overwhelmed and destroyed? But instead the enemy ships had gone on a death ride with only one possible outcome.

"And pass the word," she added coldly. "As soon as we enter orbit, begin bombardment and insert the landing force."

"Aye, Commodore," Wheeler said.

CHAPTER FOUR

"Sir, the enemy fleet is entering orbit!"

"Open fire," General Barak snapped.

He cursed Admiral Ashram savagely as his officers struggled to carry out their orders. If the wretched bastard had done his bloody job . . . there were only two PDCs on the planet's surface, both positioned within five kilometers of Lothian. Their force shields were strong enough to stand up to enemy bombardment—unless the enemy decided to wipe the planet clean of life in a desperate attempt to crack the defenses—but their ground-based weapons couldn't shoot *through* the planet. There was nothing stopping the enemy ships from lurking on the other side while they landed ground troops to retake the wretched shithole.

And here we are, stuck under a PDC, watching helplessly, he thought. The command center had very little to command. *They have us on the ropes and they know it.*

"The enemy fleet is engaging our bases with KEWs," the officer added. "Sir . . ."

"Order the ground troops to take up positions near the rubble," Barak snarled. "Do it!"

The command was already too late, he suspected. He'd never *dreamed* that Admiral Ashram could lose the battle. The Theocratic Navy was always bragging about its invincibility. But now they had lost control of the high orbitals, and the KEWs were raining down. Base after base, from the giant supply centers to the local garrisons, was being wiped out, their occupants unable to retreat in time. And he could do nothing to remedy the situation.

"Deploy our remaining forces to hold Lothian," he said. He had no illusions about their chances of ultimate success, but he could bleed the enemy as long as his men were covered by the PDC's force shield. "And prepare to fight to the last."

He glanced at the two men in the corner of the operations center, both wearing featureless black uniforms. They'd arrived three weeks ago, carrying papers that ordered him to provide them with anything they wanted—and warning him not to ask questions. They could take command at any moment, he knew, yet they had done nothing but watch as the fleet was blown out of space. And yet he still didn't dare ask any questions.

"Enemy shuttles are entering engagement range," an operator warned.

"Target them," Barak ordered sharply. Standard procedure for an orbital assault called for the capture of a shuttleport, which would then be used to bring in more and more supplies from high orbit. "And then order the troops on the shuttleport to destroy the base before withdrawing."

"Yes, sir," the operator said.

◆ ◆ ◆

"Thirty seconds," the jumpmaster barked. "Twenty seconds . . ."

Colonel Patrick James Davidson moved forward as the last seconds ticked away, then jumped out of the shuttle and plummeted down towards the ground far below. His suit's sensors reported a flurry of activity, from ground-launched missiles and energy weapons to Electronic Countermeasure drones trying to soak up as much enemy fire as possible. The Theocrats would never have a better chance to inflict mass damage on his men than when they were in their shuttles, terrifyingly vulnerable. And they knew it too. He cursed under his breath as two shuttles vanished, one taking two platoons of marines with it, then he pushed the thought aside savagely as the spaceport came into view. There would be time to mourn later.

His suit's antigravity compensators kicked in a heartbeat before he hit the ground, slowing his fall so sharply that he felt nothing when his armored feet finally set foot on the planet's surface. Pat brought up his rifle and looked around, searching for targets as the remainder of the lead platoon landed around him. The enemy had done a great deal of damage to the spaceport, he noted as he led the way towards the nearest building, but hadn't managed to destroy it. Spaceports were huge, designed to soak up a great deal of damage and keep going. The terminal's Air Traffic Control systems would have been smashed, but that hardly mattered. A single shuttle could bring in everything his staff needed to coordinate the remainder of the landings.

He darted to one side as a stream of plasma fire leapt out at him. His men hit the deck, returning fire with their own weapons. The Theocrats had chosen to make a brief stand in one of the towers, but they hadn't realized just how determined Pat was to take control of the spaceport as quickly as possible. The tower was blown to rubble within seconds, bodies lost somewhere within the pile of debris. The marines fanned out, half searching the damaged buildings while their comrades secured the roads leading down to the city. Pat could see smoke rising from Lothian. The city had apparently risen against the occupying forces.

"Bring down the shuttles," he ordered. "And order the ground forces to prepare to advance."

He allowed himself a moment of satisfaction. The enemy had to be running short of missiles, judging by the sheer number they'd hurled against the first assault force. Even if they weren't, the shuttles could enter orbit well out of range and then fly low to their final destinations. Pat would have been surprised if there were many surviving enemy air defense teams outside Lothian and the PDCs. The bastards who hadn't been blasted from orbit would be lynched by the locals. Pat wouldn't waste his time feeling sorry for them. He'd seen the results of their handiwork far too often.

The next flight of armored marines landed, immediately fanning out to join the forces securing the approaches to the spaceport. Pat watched them deploy, checking and rechecking his Heads-Up Display for any sign of an enemy counterattack. He would be astonished if the Theocracy wasn't already planning its next move. The spaceport wasn't the only place he could land troops and their equipment, but it was certainly the most convenient. And the Theocrats would realize that.

"Incoming!"

Pat glanced up sharply as red icons flared in front of him. Mortar rounds, fired from somewhere just underneath the PDC's force shield. He silently congratulated the enemy on their timing as he locked his suit into the datanet, allowing it to draw on his weapons to pick off the shells before they hit the ground. If the Theocrats were lucky, they might just take out a shuttle as it came in to land, crashing down on top of his position.

But it won't be enough to stop us, he thought.

Civilians might expect battles to be bloodless—or, at least, not to lose any of the *good* guys while slaughtering hundreds of *bad* guys—but anyone with genuine military experience knew better. Even the most effortless of campaigns produced losses, some owing more to inexperience or incompetence than enemy action. Pat acknowledged quietly that *he* could be one of the casualties. If it happened, it happened.

He'd steeled himself to face the possibility of his own death way back in boot camp.

"The shuttles are coming in to land now," Captain Rogers bawled. "Sir?"

"Get the point defense systems set up," Pat ordered. "And then bring in the second flight of shuttles!"

They'd practiced the operation time and time again, but he was still awed as a seemingly endless line of shuttles landed, unloaded their cargos, and then returned to orbit to pick up the *next* load of marines from the giant troop transports. The enemy shot down four shuttles, but he'd calculated the probability that his forces would lose nearly a third of their supplies and had arranged for spares to be held in orbit. And as more and more troops landed, he directed them down towards the city. According to reports, the Theocracy was clearly under attack from within as well as without.

And that led to a problem. If he attacked the PDCs, he could take down the force shields and allow the orbiting starships to flatten any remaining enemy positions within the city. But that would give the enemy more time to slaughter the city's population. Hebrides might have a heavily armed citizen militia, but Pat doubted the remaining civilians in the city had enough weapons to put up a real fight. They'd certainly not have any *heavy* weapons . . .

He gritted his teeth. "The 1st and 5th Regiments are to move against PDC One and PDC Two," he ordered finally. "The 6th Regiment is to do what it can for the city."

♦ ♦ ♦

"The enemy are on the move," an officer reported. "They're advancing towards the PDCs."

Barak nodded, unsurprised. The Commonwealth might be soft, but it wasn't stupid. Lothian was important, yet the city wasn't the key to

Hebrides. Taking out the PDCs would allow the Commonwealth time to recover the planet and hunt down the remainder of the occupation force at will.

"Move our own forces to block their advance," he ordered. Thankfully, Admiral Ashram hadn't bothered to forbid him from drawing up contingency plans. "And then destroy all sensitive material in the datacores."

"Yes, sir."

The display fuzzed. Barak cursed under his breath. The Commonwealth had always been better at electronic warfare than the Theocracy. Now, with two years of experience with what worked and what didn't, the Commonwealth could do a great deal of damage to his communications. The network he relied upon to direct the troops was already starting to collapse, while the landlines had been badly disrupted by the bombardment. But enough of them had survived for him to issue *some* orders.

"Tell the troops to hold out as long as they can," he said. "Reinforcements are on the way."

And that, he knew, was an utter lie.

◆ ◆ ◆

Pat wasn't sure what he'd expected from William's homeworld, but he couldn't help feeling that there was something . . . *primitive* about the lands surrounding the spaceport. A handful of buildings popping out of cornfields and fallow cropland; lines of trees marking the boundaries between one set of farmland and the next. Lothian, looming to the north as the marines marched towards PDC One, looked more like a vision from the past than a modern city. Indeed, compared to Tyre City, it was tiny. The files stated that only fifty thousand people lived within its confines.

But Lothian was at war. His sensors picked up an endless rattle of gunfire, punctuated by loud explosions and brief moments of silence.

Reports from the forces probing the edge of the city were grim, warning that the Theocrats seemed to have dug in along the boundaries and were refusing to shift. They'd have to be starved out or evicted, the latter practically guaranteeing that a chunk of the city died with them. The enemy was gunning down everyone in sight.

And it's worse elsewhere, he thought. The resistance hadn't made contact with the fleet, but orbital observation confirmed that the occupation force was on the run. *There'll be a slaughter if we don't put an end to this in a hurry.*

He ducked as a hail of shellfire crashed down to the south. The enemy had dug in, turning a small town into a strongpoint. Pat gritted his teeth as counterbattery fire rained down in response, shattering the town beyond repair. He could only pray that the locals had been able to flee before the Theocrats arrived. The Theocrats clearly hadn't been dislodged, even by the heavy shellfire. They were dug in too well to be shifted easily.

"Order the tanks to advance," he said. Ideally, he would have preferred to isolate the town and let it die on the vine, but he didn't have time. "We'll move in behind them."

A low roar echoed through the air as the first hovertanks advanced towards the town, their force shields deflecting a hail of bullets and plasma blasts. Pat allowed himself a moment of relief that they'd brought the tanks along—the road network was so bad that he doubted ordinary tanks could handle the trip without turning the roads into powder—and then watched as the tanks cruised onwards, firing burst after burst of plasma fire into the town. Building after building was engulfed in flames, brilliant surges of white fire crackling from target to target. The flames were so hot that unprotected men wouldn't stand a chance.

"Go," Pat ordered.

The marines advanced, weapons at the ready, meeting no resistance as they ran through the flames and out to the other side. Pat had half expected to see the enemy running for their lives, but instead . . .

nothing. They'd all been caught up inside the town and incinerated, wiped out effortlessly. Their leaders had sacrificed them for nothing.

Bastards, he thought.

"Run additional security patrols through this sector," he ordered as he reorganized his forces to resume the advance. "And keep the tanks in reserve."

The fighting grew more intense as the marines pressed towards the PDC. Enemy forces popped out of nowhere, firing savagely until they were killed by the marines. A handful of armored vehicles in hiding, built more for crowd control than heavy fighting, fired on the advancing tanks until they were destroyed. Both sides shelled the other relentlessly. Pat kept a silent tally of the dead and wounded, even though he knew better. Casualties weren't something to dwell upon in the midst of battle.

"6th Regiment is breaking through into the city itself," Captain Haines reported. "The locals are lynching the remaining enemy soldiers and their converts."

Pat cursed under his breath as another hail of shells fell near his position. Of *course* the Theocracy would have converts. *He* had difficulty imagining why anyone would want to convert, but drowning men would clutch at any straws. No doubt they'd assumed the Theocracy would win the war and wanted to please their new overlords. Or perhaps they'd planned to betray the Theocracy in time. Right now, it didn't matter.

"Separate the converts from the POWs, but protect them from the locals," he ordered. "Their cases can be considered after the war."

"The locals are insistent," Haines said.

"Use all necessary force to keep the converts safe," Pat ordered.

Haines coughed. "Sir?"

"Those are your orders, Captain," Pat snarled. "And you can have them in writing, if you wish."

He put rigid controls on his temper. A marine captain shouldn't be questioning his orders. But then Haines was in one hell of a spot. Protecting the converts wouldn't win the Commonwealth any friends on Hebrides. The diplomats would have a fit. But he was damned if he was allowing a lynch mob to run riot over the planet. Besides, if the converts had no reason to expect anything else, they probably wouldn't surrender. Hebrides might be the first planet to be liberated, but it wouldn't be the last. There was no point in making the task harder than necessary.

"Yes, sir," Haines said stiffly.

Pat gritted his teeth in annoyance. Haines had a distinguished war record, but he hadn't seen the Theocracy in action. He certainly hadn't been attached to the marines on Cadiz or Verdean. He'd heard stories, of course, and seen the data records, yet nothing had the same impact as seeing the devastation for himself here on Hebrides. Now . . . now Haines wanted to kill every last Theocrat. Pat didn't blame him, but his troops *needed* to convince the Theocrats and their converts that they *could* surrender without being brutally murdered.

Although I'm damned if I know what we're going to do with the converts, he thought as a flight of missiles roared overhead. A moment later, an icon blinked up, warning him that a supply convoy had been hit. *Ship them to a penal world or transport them all the way to Ahura Mazda?*

He pushed the thought out of his mind. Both PDCs were about to come under siege. If the Theocrats refused to surrender after their final defenses had been obliterated, the PDCs would be destroyed, putting an end to the battle. The marines could worry about the aftermath when it came.

"Bring up the reinforcements," he ordered. "And ready the forward units for the final advance."

◆ ◆ ◆

The end, Barak thought, could not be long delayed.

His forces had fought like lions, he admitted; they'd delayed the enemy longer than he'd thought possible, given how little time they'd had to prepare for the engagement. And they'd hurt the enemy, taking out dozens of their marines along with several of their tanks and other war machines. But the effort hadn't been enough. Now the enemy was pressing up against the PDC's inner defense line. If they couldn't break through, they'd use a nuclear charge to finish the job.

And we have no sign of reinforcements, he thought. His forces were on the ropes, the handful of survivors being systematically hunted down and killed. There was no hope of anything but a quick death and a rise to paradise. *We lost the moment Admiral Ashram got himself killed.*

"Ready your communications network, General," a cold voice said. Barak looked up to see one of the black-clad outsiders. "We have a message to send."

"There's no one to reply," Barak said. The certainty of death made him flippant. What could the outsider *do* to him before the PDC was destroyed? "Unless you want to surrender?"

"Ready the network," the outsider repeated sharply. His hand dropped to the pistol at his belt. "Now."

Barak nodded to the communications operator, who started to tap commands into his console. The message seemed pointless. The radio signal would be heard across the planet, but who was going to listen? And the signal itself . . .

His eyes widened in horror. It was an activation code. "What are you doing?"

"Scorched earth," the outsider said. He looked up. His voice rang with fanatical determination. His eyes glittered with rage. "May God defend the right."

The world went white.

CHAPTER FIVE

"Nuclear detonation," Cecelia snapped. "I say again, *multiple* nuclear detonations!"

William snapped out of his command chair as new icons, icons he'd never seen outside training simulations, blossomed to life on the display. Nuclear strikes, dozens of them, on a planetary surface! No one had nuked a planet-side target since the Breakaway Wars, when Earth's surface had been blasted clean of life. Even the *Theocracy* had declined to nuke civilian populations . . .

. . . until now.

"At least fifty blasts," Cecelia said. She sounded badly shaken. "All on or near population centers. Preliminary sensor readings suggest the blasts were highly radioactive."

William felt as if he'd been punched in the gut. Nuclear weapons hadn't been radioactive for *centuries*, ever since straight fusion warheads had entered service. But the Theocracy wouldn't have any trouble designing weapons that produced vast clouds of radiation as well as slaughtering thousands and tearing up the landscape. Anyone who survived the blasts might well wind up wishing they hadn't. The atrocity . . .

He struggled to comprehend what he was seeing as the last of the blasts faded away, the enemy force shield over Lothian flickering out of existence a moment later. Both PDCs were gone, wiped out by suicide charges. If any enemy presence remained on the planet, it had gone to ground . . . although, with so much electromagnetic distortion washing through the air, the orbiting starships had no way to be sure. But perhaps it didn't matter. He knew what would happen to any Theocrats unlucky enough to be caught by his people. Somehow, he found it hard to care.

"Order sickbay to prepare for an immediate deployment to the surface," William said finally. He struggled to keep his voice composed, let alone issue orders, but he had no choice. "Raise the flag. This has just become a rescue mission."

He forced himself to sit down as his crew hurried to carry out their orders. Rescuing the crew of an asteroid settlement or a small lunar colony was one thing, but saving the population of an entire planet? The task force had brought emergency supplies, yet they'd never *dreamed* they would need to bring enough supplies to save *everyone*. His head swam as he struggled to come to terms with what had happened. He'd loved his homeworld, even as he'd disdained its society and disliked its leaders. And now it was effectively gone.

There were nearly half a billion people down there, he thought numbly. He couldn't grasp the sheer scale of the atrocity. *And how many of them are left?*

◆ ◆ ◆

Pat hit the ground instinctively as a flash of white light caused his helmet to darken automatically. Something that bright could only be a nuclear weapon. The shockwaves struck seconds later, followed by a sleet of radiation that caused emergency icons to blink up in his HUD. Anyone outside and unprotected would need medical treatment within hours or be condemned to a truly horrific death. The ground shook repeatedly, then quieted. Gritting his teeth, he forced himself to stand and peer towards the PDC. Now, it was shrouded in a massive mushroom cloud.

Shit, he thought.

"Sir!" Corporal Jack said. "The city!"

Pat swung around and stared in horror. A mushroom cloud—a *second* mushroom cloud—was rising over Lothian, its sheer brooding mass hiding the horror within. He imagined, just for a second, a demonic face within the cloud, laughing at him . . . he shook his head, dismissing the thought. The offensive had come to an utterly unexpected end.

"Sound off," he snapped. The communications network was in disarray. Had there been a nuke buried under the spaceport? If that was the case, bringing in emergency supplies and evacuating the wounded had suddenly become much harder. "Now!"

His men sounded off, one by one. No one appeared to be harmed, although one of the hovertanks had been picked up by the blast and tossed over and over until it had crashed to the ground. Pat wasn't sure precisely how *that* had happened, but it hardly mattered. His suit's sensors reported a gradual increase in radiation levels. The marines were safe inside their armor, unless the levels rose to *truly* unbearable levels, yet the locals had no protection.

Dear God, he thought. *What did they* put *in those warheads?*

Just for a moment, he found himself unsure of what to do. There was clearly no point in heading onwards; their targets, the PDCs, were gone. The force shield had collapsed immediately after the blasts. But the marines had lost communications with the starships in orbit, which meant that calling for pickup was impossible . . .

"Get a laser link to orbit," he ordered finally. He'd never seen so much distortion, not outside training exercises. Thankfully, the tanks could use communications lasers to make contact with the starships, given time. "We'll head back to the spaceport, then go onwards into the city."

He contemplated the situation as the marines turned and started to jog back the way they'd come. A nuclear weapon—a *standard* missile warhead—wouldn't be radioactive, but if they'd all been groundbursts, there was a very good chance that they'd sucked up thousands of tons of soil and turned it into nuclear fallout. The sleet of radiation the marines had already detected suggested that the warhead had been *deliberately* designed to be as dirty as possible. Theocratic forces hadn't just slaughtered a large chunk of the city's population, they'd literally rendered the local area uninhabitable. They clearly didn't have any intention of rebuilding the city in the near future.

And how long, he asked himself, *will it take for the radiation to fade away?*

"Shit," Jack breathed. "Sir, the spaceport!"

"It hasn't been nuked," Pat said sharply. "Be grateful."

It *was* a mess, he had to admit. The blast wave had clearly washed over the spaceport—a number of vehicles had been knocked over; a pair of ground-based missile launchers had been destroyed—but the complex was largely intact. And yet he knew that some of the ground crews wouldn't have been wearing armor. He hoped, prayed, that Kat would think to send down emergency teams as fast as possible. The local radiation levels were too high.

His radio buzzed. "Colonel," a familiar voice said. "Report."

"Commodore," Pat said. He couldn't call Kat by her first name, not when they were both on duty. "We were nearly at the PDC when the nukes detonated. 1st Regiment is largely intact; 5th and 6th are still out of contact."

And 6th had been headed down to the city, he thought grimly. Marine combat battlesuits were tough, but they would have been right on top of a nuclear blast. *They may all be dead.*

He pushed the thought aside. "Radiation levels at the spaceport are alarmingly high," he added. His suit would already be forwarding its data to the orbiting ships. "We need urgent medical support, but they have to wear proper armor and bring stasis pods."

"Understood," Kat said. She paused. "Colonel, Lothian wasn't the only place to be nuked."

Pat blanched. "Where else?"

"Everywhere," Kat said. "They hit the entire planet. There were at least fifty blasts."

". . . Shit."

Pat's throat was suddenly very dry. He swallowed hard. Hebrides wasn't the most heavily populated planet in the Commonwealth, but millions of people had been on the surface. The population *was* spread out, thankfully, yet that number of nukes would have injected so much radiation into the biosphere that the planet would likely become uninhabitable. Hebrides had been condemned to a slow and agonizing death.

The Theocracy must be out of their minds, he thought. *They must know we'll retaliate.*

"I'm going to take a preliminary team down to Lothian," he said softly. The question of retaliation would be decided well above his pay grade. "Major Garth will take command at the spaceport."

"Understood," Kat said. She hesitated, just for a second. "Be careful."

Pat nodded to himself, then started issuing orders to his team. The mushroom cloud was slowly dispersing, revealing fires blazing across the remains of the city. Everything flammable within the blast radius would have been lit by the heat wave. His mind quietly catalogued the other effects as he led the way to the gates, walked through the barricades, and headed down to the city. The light of the explosion would have blinded anyone looking at it, the blast wave would have smashed hundreds of buildings, the radiation would have been overkill . . .

Lothian had been surrounded by a forest, he knew, broken only by a motorway that encircled the entire city. Now the forest was blazing brightly, hundreds of trees crashing to the ground as flames destroyed their roots; the road was barely recognizable, covered in burning trees and cars. The intense heat would have killed him if he hadn't been wearing the suit. Sweat seemed to trickle down his back as he trudged onwards. It had to be his imagination, he told himself firmly, but it felt real nonetheless.

"The fleet's launching recon drones," Jack said quietly. "They'll peer through the cloud."

Pat barely heard him as his team crossed the road and entered Lothian itself. The barricades they'd noted during their preliminary recon of the city were torn and broken, the bodies of their former defenders missing in action. He hoped that meant they'd been destroyed by the blasts, but he feared the civilians, upon liberation, had been mutilating the corpses and thus would have been caught in the open when the nukes detonated. Outside the immediate blast range, someone who took cover would have a reasonable chance of survival . . .

Not here, he reminded himself. The radiation seemed to be growing stronger, far stronger. *If the blast hadn't gotten them, the radiation would.*

He saw something moving just inside a damaged building; he motioned for his men to stay back, then moved forward himself, weapon at the ready. But there was no threat inside the building, just a handful of dying men and women, their bodies practically melted . . .

Pat felt his gorge rise in his throat, despite all his training, as he realized the citizens were doomed. The Commonwealth could do nothing for them, even if they were somehow teleported to a hospital on Tyre. The damage was just too great.

I'm sorry, he thought. He hefted his rifle and shot the first man in the head, then moved on to the next and the next. He could do nothing but make the end quick. *I'm sorry.*

He turned and forced himself to walk out of the building, feeling utterly wretched. He'd been trained to protect civilians, not kill them. He'd put his life on the line, time and time again, to defend the Commonwealth. And yet, all he'd been able to do for these dying men and women was kill them himself. A quick death was a mercy, but it didn't *feel* like a mercy.

Damn me, he thought.

The damage grew worse as the troops probed the center of the city. More bodies were discovered amidst the ruined buildings, including a handful wearing cracked and broken battlesuits. His men, Pat knew; he took their ID tags and then left the corpses for later recovery. They'd be shipped home if their bodies could be decontaminated. If not, they'd have to be fired into the sun. The wind picked up, blowing dust and ash towards the marines as they reached the giant crater at the heart of Lothian. The planetary government's offices were gone, as were the Theocrats defending it . . . and his men, caught by the blasts as they were pressing against the defenses. They had all died for nothing.

He wanted to sit down and curse the enemy, but he had too much work to do. The radio kept crackling alarmingly, even though a flight of drones now served as communication relays. More and more shuttles were landing, bringing with them emergency supplies . . . emergency supplies that wouldn't, that *couldn't*, be remotely enough to save the entire planet. He shuddered as he led the small patrol on a long and winding path through the remains of Lothian. Even if every starship in the Commonwealth was dedicated to evacuating the planet, it couldn't be done in a reasonable length of time. The wind was already dispersing the fallout all over Hebrides. Millions had died . . . millions *more* were going to die.

And repairing the planet might be impossible, he thought. Terraforming programs, particularly the brute-force project the United Nations had used to terraform Mars before humanity had learned how to enter and navigate hyperspace, were hugely expensive. And he didn't think any such project had ever been carried out on a radioactive world. *We might have to abandon the planet altogether.*

He shuddered as he peered into a building. It might have been a schoolhouse, or a church, or even a family house; now, the interior was so badly scorched that he had no way of determining what the structure had been. The Commonwealth had enough problems coping with the hundreds of thousands of refugees who'd fled Theocratic Space; this, the entire surviving population of a dead world, was an order of magnitude worse. And the evacuation would have to be done *quickly*, before the radiation slaughtered the remaining population.

Perhaps that was the point, he told himself. *They wanted to slow us down before we pressed into their territory.*

He made a note of the thought for later contemplation, then led the way back out of Lothian and up to the spaceport. If any more survivors remained within the city—and he doubted it—there was nothing he could do for them. Hundreds of shuttles flew overhead, dropping medical supplies and other pieces of equipment; thousands of stasis pods, hastily removed from the transport ships, were already in place on the landing strips. But they needed hundreds of thousands, perhaps *millions* of pods.

And we don't have them, he thought. *We never anticipated needing them on such a scale.*

Major Garth saluted as Pat approached. "Sir," he said. "Seventeen marines from 6th Regiment have returned from Lothian."

Pat grimaced. 6th Regiment had been the smallest of his formations, but it had still deployed 1,500 marines. They couldn't all be dead, could they? And yet he'd seen the blast crater. Anyone caught within the blast, battlesuit or no, wouldn't have stood a chance. There might be other survivors, he told himself. The entire regiment wouldn't have been committed to the final offensive. But unless his men returned to the spaceport under their own power . . .

We will sweep the ruins, he told himself. *But when?*

"Understood," he said. "And the ground crews?"

"A number were wounded and they all took pretty nasty doses of radiation, sir," Garth reported shortly. "I've had them all put into stasis for the moment."

"Very good," Pat said. It *wasn't* good, but it was the best they could do. Military medicine had advanced in leaps and bounds over the last two centuries. Given time, anything that wasn't immediately fatal could be repaired. But it might be months, years perhaps, before anyone had the time to actually give the victims proper medical care. "And the newcomers?"

"All suited, sir," Garth said. "The medics are already establishing a secure hospital for emergency cases. We're bringing in additional doctors from the starships too."

Pat winced. "Make sure they know not to take risks," he ordered firmly. "We're going to need every medic we can get."

He gritted his teeth. Confusion was likely to cost lives. Marine combat medics knew the score, but starship doctors weren't used to working under fire. Or, for that matter, in a poisonous environment. Radiation levels were still increasing as the wind blew fallout towards the spaceport. The marines would have to establish a long-term base somewhere safer, if there *was* such a place on Hebrides.

"Yes, sir," Garth said. "Do you want to send recon patrols to the PDCs?"

"I don't think there's any point," Pat said. Both PDCs had destroyed themselves. He doubted there were any survivors. "They were blasted to rubble too."

He groaned as another flight of shuttles flew overhead, landing neatly on the runway. Armored crews hastily removed another set of stasis pods, carrying them over towards the medical tents and placing them neatly by the others. It looked like he had enough pods to cope with any crisis, but he knew the massive collection was merely a drop in the ocean. Even assuming a mere *tenth* of the population survived and a fifth of those needed emergency attention, he didn't have enough pods.

"Ask the fleet to strip out their pods and send them down to the surface," he ordered. The fleet *needed* a handful of colonist-carriers, which carried hundreds of thousands of pods, but the closest one he knew of was back at Tyre. And they didn't even have a StarCom to call for help. "We're going to need them."

"Yes, sir," Garth said. "Regulations . . ."

"To hell with regulations," Pat snapped. The Rear Echelon Mother Fuckers on Tyre might have decreed that a starship couldn't remove more than half of its stasis pods, but the bean counters had never had to deal with a planet-wide crisis. "There are people *dying* down here."

He forced himself to calm down. Kat would ignore the regulations and send them all down, but a few hundred more stasis pods wouldn't make much of a difference. They needed *millions* of the damn things. Hell, they needed more than they had in the entire Commonwealth. The scale of the disaster was beyond comprehension. There hadn't been anything like this since the outbreak of plague on Williamson's World, seventy years ago.

But this was not a disaster, he told himself sharply. *It was an atrocity.*

And the Theocracy, he promised himself silently, would pay for what it had done.

CHAPTER SIX

"Captain," Crewwoman Shannon Foster said, "are you sure you want to land here?"

William swallowed the angry response that came to mind. The landing zone he'd designated was over seventy kilometers from the nearest nuclear detonation, but the radiation in the air was already alarmingly high—not enough to cause him real problems, thanks to gene-splicing, medical nanotechnology, and booster injections, yet enough to be worrying. Some of the locals might survive, but their unborn children would pay a fearsome price.

"Yes," he said shortly. "You see that croft over there? Put us down next to it."

"Aye, sir," Shannon said.

The shuttle touched down with nary a bump. William made a mental note, as he donned his long coat, to ensure that Shannon received a commendation for her flying, and then he headed for the hatch. Flying hadn't gotten any easier in the seven days since his homeworld had been nuked, he knew; the weather had become dangerously unpredictable, great gusts of turbulence battering shuttles and knocking two of them out of the sky. The radiation and radio distortion only made matters worse.

I shouldn't be here, he thought as he stepped out of the shuttle and took his first breath. The atmosphere tasted odd, a faint hint of burning hanging in the air. And yet, the smell of cows and sheep *also* hung in the air, bringing back memories of a childhood that had been a decidedly mixed experience. *I don't belong here any longer.*

He strode towards the croft, his feet squishing through the muddy ground. He'd expected that someone would have taken the croft, since William and Scott had left their homeworld, but it was seemingly deserted. The door was open, allowing him to step into his childhood home. Much of the furniture had been taken, probably by their neighbors; the remainder, what little there was of it, rotting from disuse. His father and grandfather had *crafted* much of the furniture, rather than ordering pieces from an industrial production node. Making their own chairs and tables had been a simple task.

Removing the flashlight from his belt, William switched it on, illuminating the darkened croft. His parents had slept in the living room before their untimely deaths, their double bed still fixed at one end of the room. He'd joked with his brother that whichever of them wed first would take the bed, but in the end neither of them had married. Scott's prospective bride had been given to the pirates, while William had joined the Royal Navy. And now . . .

He shone the light into the bedroom. The two little beds he remembered were gone, but the carvings his father had placed on the wall were still there. Losing the beds didn't anger him, not after so long. Abandoned crofts were always stripped of everything their neighbors might find useful if the homestead was abandoned for more than a year and a day. He hoped that whoever had taken the beds was making good use of them.

William felt, as he walked back into the living room, as if he'd stepped into a shell of his former home. His father's armchair, the sole luxury in the house, was gone; the handful of books, ranging from a Bible to a pair of historical fiction novels, had vanished long ago. He wondered absently if they'd been put to good use or if the local vicar had tossed them into the fire. The Kirk had never been keen on people reading anything more than the Bible; indeed, William had often suspected they'd ban people reading the Bible too, if they could. Their objections had caused no end of problems before the pirates had arrived. Now . . .

The Commonwealth was changing everything, he thought. *Just having access to the datanet changed the world.*

He sat down on the double bed and put his head in his hands. The radiation levels were still rising, wind sweeping the fallout across the planet. The last set of projections indicated that the entire planet would be uninhabitable within a year as the radiation wiped out large chunks of the biosphere. God alone knew what would happen when the survivors were moved to refugee camps elsewhere, when they were exposed to other cultures and societies. The Kirk's grip on their minds would be shattered.

Not that it was that strong a grip, he told himself. *We were too stubborn to let the Kirk dictate to us.*

It had been a hard life, he recalled, and yet there had been something oddly satisfying about living in the croft. He'd never known a time when he could relax and enjoy childhood; he'd been put to work, doing household and farming tasks, almost as soon as he was old enough to walk. His schooling had been very limited, long hours in the schoolhouse during winter, almost no education at all during the planting and harvesting seasons. He'd been pulling his weight on the farm before he entered his second decade, then co-running it with his brother when their parents died. No one had ever thought they couldn't handle the work. Even the vicar had been helpful to the two young orphans as they struggled to keep their family's farm in their hands.

And we did, William thought.

He shook his head slowly as he rose. Children on Tyre didn't know how lucky they were, even commoner children. They were surrounded by luxury as soon as they first drew breath, luxury so commonplace they never noticed it. The terminal at his belt held more e-books than every library on Hebrides put together; a child's terminal, loaded with movies, games, and other interactive entertainments, would have seemed a fantasy to him back when he'd been a boy. And yet, there was a *hardness* about his peers that was lacking on Tyre, a grim awareness that the world could turn hostile at any moment. They would survive anything that didn't kill them outright.

His terminal bleeped. "Captain," Shannon said, "the drones report four people making their way up the track towards the croft."

"Understood," William said. The shuttle would have been seen as it descended. *Someone* would come to investigate. "I don't think there's any need to panic."

He walked back outside and peered down the long track. The fields were heavily overgrown; the stone walls his family had used to mark their property almost invisible. He smiled as he saw the orchard, spotting the telltale signs that children and teenagers had been taking apples from the trees. The abandoned croft had probably served as a courting place for young couples, he thought, feeling an odd hint of nostalgia. Young men and women both knew the rules of courtship and understood the consequences if they were broken. His cousin had needed to marry her boyfriend in a tearing hurry after going a little too far and ending up with child.

And her father gave her boyfriend a black eye, William thought as a small group appeared at the bottom of the track. *But he was still a good husband and father.*

He sobered. He'd been taught that he would marry a good woman, perhaps someone from the next town, bring her back to the farm and give her children, eventually passing the croft on to his eldest son. But that had never happened and never would. The young boy he'd been was restless, unwilling to settle down; the old man he'd become didn't fit in on his homeworld any longer. Even if the world hadn't been poisoned, he couldn't make a go of the farm any longer. Better to leave it for a new family.

There won't be a new family, he reminded himself bitterly. *The entire planet is doomed.*

He held up a hand in greeting as the newcomers came into view. An old woman, a middle-aged woman, and two young men, all carrying hunting rifles. The old woman, he reminded himself, might well be the same age as himself, merely worn down by the hardships of the desperate struggle to survive. All four of them would be good shots too; they'd probably been practicing on the occupying forces.

The old woman studied him for a long moment and then froze.

"William?"

William stared at her. Could it be . . . ?

"Morag?"

"William," Morag said. "You look *very* much like your father."

"Thank you," William said. Morag had been a year younger than him, back when he'd lived on the croft. He'd tried to court her, but her father had been flatly against the match and refused to allow his daughter to walk out with him. "It's been a very long time."

"It has," Morag agreed. Her voice turned ruthlessly practical. "What *happened?*"

"The planet has been poisoned," William said flatly. "You'll have to leave."

Morag didn't look impressed. William didn't really blame her. She didn't have the background to understand what had happened. For all he knew, she might not have *seen* the occupation force for herself. She lived forty miles from the nearest enemy base. Her world was limited to the farm, a handful of nearby communities, and little else. She couldn't even begin to comprehend how far William had traveled since he'd joined the navy.

One of the men leaned forward. "What do you mean, *poisoned?*"

"The Theocracy detonated a number of *very* dirty nuclear weapons on the surface," William said. He kept his voice calm with an effort. Hadn't they heard the radio broadcasts? But then, they might not even have radios! "The poison is already spreading through the biosphere. You'll need to prepare for evacuation."

If we can evacuate them, he added to himself. Kat had sent a courier boat to the nearest fleet base for emergency supplies and as many transports as they could scrape up, but the logistics of evacuating an entire planet were nightmarish. *We might have to sit and watch them die.*

"You'd better come speak to the vicar," Morag said, finally. "Do you remember the way?"

"You'd better show me," William said. A stranger in uniform . . . he might end up being shot by his own people. "Let me speak to my pilot first."

He called Shannon to tell her where he was going, then allowed Morag to lead him down the road towards the small town. It hadn't changed much, he noted; the fields were still full of cows and sheep, the roads nothing more than muddy tracks . . . the only real change was a handful of prefabricated buildings on the edge of Kirkhaven itself. The town was tiny, so small that it would barely pass for a hamlet on Tyre. A single church, a handful of houses, a schoolhouse, and a town hall . . . little more. Most of the nearby farmers cared little for the town's government, such as it was. Even the vicar had little power over his flock.

But he didn't need it, William thought as they walked towards the church. *We kept ourselves in line.*

It wasn't a pleasant admission. He'd learned the value of freethinkers during his time in the Commonwealth, although there was little room for them on starships. To have people who questioned, to have people who constantly sought new answers . . . they were a necessary part of a growing society. But Hebrides had tried its hardest to remain firmly stuck in the past. If the pirates hadn't shown up, the planet would probably have declined Commonwealth membership when it was offered.

He shook his head slowly. The church hadn't changed either: stone walls; wooden carvings of Joseph, Mary, and Jesus; pews he *knew* had been designed to be as uncomfortable as possible. A handful of young women sat to the left, their heads covered with white cloths; their mothers, sitting behind them, turned their heads to stare as Morag led William into the building. The male side of the church was deserted, save for the vicar himself. William felt a flicker of dislike, which he ruthlessly suppressed. The vicars weren't *evil*, not like the pirates; they were just intensely conservative, ready to order the shunning of anyone who questioned their authority.

And that could destroy the strongest mind, William reminded himself.

Morag spoke briefly to the vicar, then nodded to William. "William?"

William nodded to the vicar, studying him thoughtfully. He was tall and thin, his head shaved bare; he wore a long black robe, completely unmarked. Some vicars were corrupt, but it was rare to encounter one away from the major towns. The farming communities never tolerated corruption in their vicars.

"It's been a long time," the vicar said. "I am Father Larry."

"Pleased to meet you," William said. He rather doubted the vicar was old enough to remember him. Life in the vicarage wasn't *just* preaching and praying. *Everyone* was expected to help with ploughing the fields and harvesting the crops. "You have to prepare to evacuate."

The vicar stared at him in shock. William explained, as best as he could, but he knew the vicar wouldn't understand more than one word in ten. Vicars had been the only people, before the planet had joined the Commonwealth, to get any form of further education, yet it had been solely focused on religion. The vicar probably didn't know that matter was made up of atoms, let alone that they could be split. Explaining what a radioactive cloud *was* took nearly an hour.

"I must pray," the vicar said, finally. "I . . ."

"You have to start preparing the town for evacuation," William said. He glanced down at his terminal. The radiation level had increased, slightly, since the time of his arrival. "You don't have a choice."

"We can't leave," one of the mothers objected. "Where can we go?"

"I don't know yet," William said. It was possible, he supposed, that protected habitats could be established on the planetary surface. The marine engineers were already considering the potential options. "But if you stay here you're going to die."

He ignored the muttering sweeping through the church as he turned back to the vicar. "I'll have a proper radio shipped to you," he said firmly. "Make sure you stay in touch with the evacuation committee."

Shaking his head, he turned and left the church. His mother had always sent her children to Sunday school with a coin for the vicar, but his father had had his doubts. William tended to agree with his father. He saw no point in giving money to the Kirk when the family needed every last penny to survive. Besides, the Kirk was rich enough already. *And* it played a role in keeping things precisely the same, year after year.

But now change is forced on the community, he thought as he looked around the town. Word was already spreading, thanks to the mothers ordering their daughters out of the church and straight back to their homes. *And who knows where it will lead?*

He shuddered as he looked towards the empty schoolhouse. It hadn't changed a bit, not on the outside; he'd bet half his monthly salary that the interior hadn't changed either. The masters had been tyrants, ready to apply the rod to any students who misbehaved; he couldn't help wondering, deep inside, just how many of the masters had been trained to *dull* the impulse for learning, rather than encourage it. If asking a question could get someone in trouble . . . it wouldn't be long before they stopped asking questions.

And the parents tended to agree, he reminded himself. Would his life have been different if his parents had lived longer? *They didn't want children who put on airs and graces, but children who could inherit the farms when the parents died.*

Morag caught up with him as he reached the bottom of the track. "William," she said, "are you married?"

William had to laugh. "*That's* your first question?"

"I have a daughter in need of a husband," Morag said. "She isn't the only eligible girl around town, but she does come with a good dowry."

"Oh," William said dryly. "And why isn't she married now?"

Such affairs struck him as silly to worry about when the entire planet was doomed, but he could see Morag's perspective. If William accepted the offer, he'd be obliged to look after a wife, no matter what else happened. Morag might not know *precisely* what would happen after she and her family were evacuated, yet attaching themselves to William might give them their best shot at navigating the uncertain waters ahead.

"She's picky," Morag said. She shrugged expressively. "And her father indulges her."

"Good for him," William said. He had no idea who Morag had married, but he didn't really want to know. Probably one of the other young men in the region. Maybe a townsman, if he was genuinely indulgent. "Right now, you have other problems."

He turned to look back at the gray town. There was something oddly tranquil about the settlement, despite the men and women running through the streets, but he knew the peace was an illusion. The entire region was in deep shit, even if the radiation levels didn't rise any higher. They just didn't have the resources or mindset to cope with the impending doom. Even the Commonwealth would have found it almost impossible to cope.

"I know," Morag said. She cocked her head. "I was serious."

"I know," William said. He looked down at her, knowing she wouldn't understand. "But I'm not interested."

The flicker of embarrassed anger that crossed her face almost made him reconsider. Her offer would have been a *good* offer, he had to admit, if he'd wanted to come home for good. A wife young enough to bear strong children, a set of very well-connected relatives . . . it *was* a good offer. But it wasn't one he wanted, not any longer. His life was bound to the navy.

"Tell your family to prepare to evacuate," he said instead. "And make sure they understand just how serious this is. They may not get a second chance to leave."

CHAPTER SEVEN

"I think you need to go to sleep for a week," Kat said as Pat entered her cabin. "You look ghastly."

"I was sleeping in the suit," Pat said. He *did* look tired, his face pale and wan; his eyes dull, almost lifeless. "It wasn't very pleasant."

Kat nodded as she gave him a tight hug, wrinkling her nose at the smell. Pat and her flag captain had threatened to handcuff her to her command chair if she tried to go down to the surface herself, but she knew she'd only get in the way. The last ten days had been chaotic as her marines and their support crews had struggled to cope with a humanitarian crisis on an unimaginable scale. It would be months, she suspected, before the fleet could truthfully say that they had the situation under control. God alone knew how many people would die before then.

Pat drew back slightly. "Tell me there's help on the way."

"I've called every ship and medical crew in the sector," Kat assured him. "Hopefully, most of them will come."

"It won't be enough," Pat predicted.

Kat was inclined to agree. They'd built up vast stockpiles of supplies—medical supplies, humanitarian supplies—for the liberation campaign, but the atrocity on Hebrides had made a mockery of their careful planning.

Even if they kept the Theocracy from bombing other planets again and again, they'd still have to save as many people as they could from the planet below. And she knew the resources to do that simply didn't exist.

"They wanted us to suffer," Pat said. "They could have used antimatter if they wanted to sweep the planet clean of life."

"I know," Kat said. Her analysts had reached the same conclusion. The Theocracy had wanted to ensure that the Commonwealth was tied up rescuing as many people as possible from the radiation. The bastards had succeeded. "And what's to stop them from doing the same to the other occupied worlds?"

"Nothing," Pat said. "What's to stop them from doing it to Tyre?"

Kat winced. Tyre was surrounded by extensive deep-space tracking networks. It was unlikely that anyone could get a missile, even a *c*-fractional projectile, through the network without having the missile intercepted and destroyed before it struck the surface. But *unlikely* wasn't the same as *impossible*.

"I don't know," she said. The Commonwealth could do the same to Ahura Mazda and every other Theocratic world too, if it wanted. She'd assumed, they'd all assumed, that deterrence would be enough to keep the Theocracy from committing mass slaughter. They'd been wrong. "I don't know."

She looked up at her lover, feeling a twinge of sympathy. Pat liked to have tasks he could accomplish, objectives he could reach. He wanted, he *needed*, to feel there was something he could do. But there was nothing he could do for the planet below. His marines had worked themselves to the bone, recovering survivors and shipping them to orbit, but their valiance wasn't enough. It would never be enough.

"Go get a proper bath," she said, nudging him towards the washroom. "Take as long as you need."

Pat merely nodded. The lack of any suggestion that she join him—or mock irritation at her suggestion he needed to wash—bothered her more than she cared to admit. If what he'd seen on the planet below had broken him . . .

She watched him walk into the washroom and close the door, silently cursing the Theocracy. To her, the horror the enemy had unleashed was abstract; to him—and William—it was all too real.

She sat down at her desk and scanned the latest report. Nearly a hundred thousand survivors had been pulled out of the blast zones, almost all in urgent need of intensive medical treatment. The stasis pods were already full, even though thousands more civilians would die if they weren't put in stasis. Her medics were frantically triaging the patients, trying to ensure that the ones with the greatest chances of survival were given the best treatment . . . but it wasn't enough. It could *never* be enough.

And the planet's population seems torn too, she thought. *Not all of them believe us when we tell them they have to go.*

The situation was an utter nightmare. Some towns and villages had accepted the warning with good grace. Others seemed to believe that it was all a plot to steal their land . . . or that there was no difference, at base, between the Commonwealth and the Theocracy. They killed enemy prisoners and fired on Commonwealth shuttles without hesitation. She had no idea how she was going to get through to them, but she had no choice.

We have to keep warning them, she told herself. *But they won't listen.*

Her intercom bleeped. "Commodore, a courier boat just dropped out of hyperspace," Wheeler said. "She's transmitting a recorded message, your eyes only."

"Understood," Kat said. She'd hoped for more than just a courier boat, but Admiral Christian would probably have sent it ahead of 6th Fleet. "Download the message to my terminal, then order the courier boat to hold position."

"Aye, Commodore," Wheeler said.

Kat waited for the message to blink up in her terminal, then pressed her hand against the sensor, allowing the terminal to query her brain implants and check her identity. A moment later, Admiral Christian's face popped up in front of her. He looked grim.

"Commodore Falcone," he said. "I'll make this brief. We have received your report and forwarded it to Tyre. For the moment, significant reserve elements have been ordered to Hebrides to assist in the relief efforts. Once those elements arrive, you are ordered to take your task force and rendezvous with 6th Fleet at McCaughey."

Kat blinked. He expected her to *leave* Hebrides?

"I appreciate that this decision may cause you some problems," Admiral Christian continued, firmly. "Therefore, you are authorized to transport as many stasis pods and evacuees as you can cram into your ships to McCaughey. The planetary authorities have been informed and are already preparing holding compounds and medical centers. However, I must reiterate that I expect you to depart your current station and make your way to McCaughey. This is not an opportunity for creative disobedience."

He smiled humorlessly. "As you can imagine, the decision of just how to react to the atrocity will be taken at the very highest level," he added. "I suspect, however, that 6th Fleet will be called upon to . . . express our displeasure to the Theocracy. You and I will play a role in that expression. I'll see you in two weeks."

The image froze. Kat stared down at it for a long moment, then swore out loud. He expected her to abandon the planet? Even if she pushed her life support to the limits, she couldn't hope to cram more than a few tens of thousands of evacuees into her ships. There would be uncounted hundreds of thousands, perhaps millions, left behind.

She keyed her terminal. "Bobby, I want an all-ships conference call, captains only, in twenty minutes," she said. "Spread the word."

"Aye, Commodore," Wheeler said.

Kat rose and strode over to the washroom. Pat was lying in the bath, half-asleep. "Stay here," she said. "And try to get some rest."

She felt a shiver of rage as she hurried out of her cabin and into the conference room. She couldn't begin to comprehend just how many people had died. A single death was a tragedy, as her instructors had taught her, but millions of deaths were a statistic. It was simply impossible to grasp such figures as anything other than cold numbers. She knew, intellectually, that the dead had all had lives, that they'd had people who loved them . . . but it was so hard to believe. They were all just numbers. But Pat had seen the dead and dying . . .

And this is William's homeworld, she thought. The conference room was already starting to fill with holographic images. *How is he taking this?*

She made a mental note to have a private talk with her former XO, then took her seat and waited for the rest of her captains to take their places. They'd all been little more than helpless spectators, waiting for an attack none of them believed would materialize. Theocratic forces had nothing to gain by attacking Hebrides now, not after they'd poisoned the entire world. But then, they'd never had anything to gain by taking the planet. Hebrides just hadn't been important enough to make invading and occupying the surface worth the effort.

"We have new orders," Kat said once the last captain had joined the group. "A relief force has been dispatched. Once that force arrives, we will be departing orbit and heading straight for McCaughey . . ."

"Fuck that," Captain Apollo Hansen said. "Commodore, we should be here."

"This is not up for debate," Kat said, sharply. She had a sneaking feeling that Admiral Christian hadn't issued the orders. He'd merely passed them on. "You may register a formal protest in writing, if you wish, but I expect you to have your ship ready for departure once the relief force arrives."

Or be relieved of command, she added silently. She appreciated debate among her subordinates, but there were limits. *These aren't my orders.*

"We will be loading as many active stasis pods as we can over the next few days," she added, "followed by as many evacuees as we can cram into our hulls. You are authorized to redline life support for the next three weeks, giving us time to take as many people as possible. This will not be easy, but I expect you to handle it."

There was a long pause. No spacer worthy of the title would play games with life support. Doing so could get everyone on the ship killed. In theory, her warships could easily support double or triple their personnel; in practice, a single fault at the wrong time could condemn hundreds or thousands of spacers to death. She wouldn't have blamed her captains for protesting in a body. They understood, better than any civilian, just what was at stake.

"I think we can handle it," Captain Higgins said. "But if we run into trouble . . ."

"We'd better hope we don't," Kat agreed. The odds of encountering anything more dangerous than a handful of raiders were low, but if they did . . . coming to battle stations with the corridors crammed would be difficult. "Once we arrive at McCaughey, we can offload the evacuees as quickly as possible."

William looked up. "And then what?"

"I don't know," Kat said. "The politicians will have to decide how we respond to the atrocity."

"By blowing one of their worlds into dust," Captain Hansen said. "We cannot let them get away with it!"

"Except they don't give a damn about their own lives," Fran said. "Their damned religion says that anyone killed in battle goes straight to heaven. We blast a world out of space, and the fuckers will *thank* us for it!"

"We would also be slaughtering countless innocents," Captain Kurt Connors said. "Can any of you look me in the eye and say the entire planetary population of Ahura Mazda is guilty of anything more than being born on the wrong world?"

"With all due respect," Captain Hansen said, "we don't have any other choice. If we let them think they can get away with it, they'll do it again and again!"

Kat tapped the table sharply. "The decision to retaliate or not will be made back on Tyre," she said. "We cannot influence the decision, one way or the other. And I expect you all to remember that."

She pressed on before anyone could object. "Start preparing your ships for taking on evacuees and stasis pods," she ordered, keeping her voice level. "We'll leave orbit once the relief force arrives. Any questions?"

"Some of my medical staff have requested permanent reassignment to the planetary surface," Captain Rebus Jakes said. "Can I grant them permission?"

"As long as you keep a third of your medical staff on your ship," Kat said. She rubbed her forehead in annoyance. A predictable request she hadn't anticipated. "And the same goes for your marines."

She cleared her throat. "William, remain behind," she ordered. "Everyone else, dismissed."

"That wasn't what I meant," William said once the remainder of the images had blinked out of existence. "About what happens next, I mean."

Kat studied his image for a long moment. He looked tired, as if he hadn't been sleeping; she would have wondered, under other circumstances, if he'd been drinking. But then, she supposed he had a reason to crawl into the bottle for a few hours. His homeworld had been effectively destroyed, its society shattered beyond repair. She had no idea how she'd cope if Tyre was destroyed. Badly, she suspected.

She leaned forward. "What *did* you mean?"

"The evacuees," William said. "What's going to happen to them?"

"I don't know," Kat admitted. "There will be holding centers on McCaughey, but after that . . . ?"

She had no answer. The Commonwealth had done a fairly good job resettling refugees from the Theocracy, but no one had anticipated a sudden deluge of evacuees from Hebrides. Hell, there would be enough of them to maintain a distinct culture even after they were resettled somewhere farther towards Tyre. God alone knew what the locals would make of the newcomers. They might be better off being sent to a world of their own, or one so sparsely settled that there was plenty of room to go around. And yet, it would still be a crisis.

"They're not going to like it," William warned. "Being shipped around like cattle."

"No," Kat agreed. "But do we have a choice?"

She'd read the preliminary reports from the engineers. Building radiation-proof settlements on Hebrides would be simple enough, but actually repairing the damage to the planet itself within a reasonable timescale would be damn near impossible. Anyone living within the settlements would be *stuck* in the settlements, unable to leave, unable to expand . . . all the disadvantages of an asteroid colony without any of the advantages. Getting the remaining population off the doomed world, no matter what happened to them afterwards, might be the only way to guarantee that something of their society and culture survived.

But that might not be a good thing, she thought morbidly. *It wasn't the best of cultures.*

She sharply pushed the thought aside. "Are you all right?"

"I often thought about going home," William said. He smiled humorlessly. "And when I do go home, I find I don't fit in." He looked down at the deck. "And my homeworld is doomed," he added. "That does tend to concentrate the mind."

Kat nodded. "How are they taking it? Your family, I mean."

"I don't have any immediate family left," William said. "Save for Scott, but . . . well, you know."

"Your smuggler brother," Kat said. She'd never met Scott and doubted she ever would. "No others?"

"I have a few cousins, or had, I should say," William said. "A couple died, apparently. The others married onwards, leaving us behind. My father's brother was the closest relative we had, and he died before I left for good."

"I'm sorry to hear that," Kat said. She had nine siblings and plenty of relatives. But then, the cost of raising children on Tyre was relatively low. "Are you going to be fine?"

"I should probably put in for a session with the headshrinkers," William said with a flash of the old humor. They shared a smile. No captain in his right mind would *voluntarily* walk into a shrink's office. "I'll just have to cope with it, just like everyone else. It isn't ideal, Kat, but . . ."

"Let me know if you have any problems," Kat ordered. She'd depended on William throughout her first captaincy. He'd more than earned a command of his own, but she'd missed him deeply during the ill-fated mission to the Jorlem Sector. "And if you want to talk, you know where to find me."

"Your young man would probably complain," William said dryly. He gave her a rather droll smile. "I wasn't born on Tyre, Kat."

Kat blinked. "I know," she said. That had been literally the first thing she'd learned about her first XO. "I don't understand the point."

"My people are raised to suck up misfortune and keep going," William said. "Losing any chance to return to my home is unfortunate, but the people down there have it far worse than me. They have to leave their homes, the plots they've worked for generations, and set sail to an unknown destination, dependent on the charity of others. They are not going to enjoy living in a holding camp, particularly when there's no hope of going home."

Kat nodded again. The refugees from other worlds had been given a flat choice between remaining in the camps and waiting for a chance to go home or integrating into the Commonwealth's society. Most of them, particularly the youngsters, had chosen the latter. They barely remembered their birthplaces and, even if they had the chance to go home tomorrow, probably wouldn't take it. The older refugees, on the other hand, clung to the past.

"We may be able to settle them permanently on a pastoral world," she said. Several suitable planets were within Commonwealth space, all with plenty of unoccupied land. "It won't be the same, but . . ."

"That's the point," William said. "It won't be the same."

"Nothing will be," Kat agreed. "But we will do our best for them."

But she knew, all too well, that their best was unlikely to be good enough.

CHAPTER EIGHT

As prisons went, Admiral Junayd thought, his apartment on Tyre was remarkably pleasant.

He hadn't been sure what to expect, but he'd been surprised by the sheer level of luxury the Commonwealth was prepared to offer him. The apartment was huge, with a giant bath, an entertainment complex that allowed him to explore popular culture, and room service that brought him the finest foods and drinks. There was nothing like it on Ahura Mazda, not even for the Speakers. And to think such accommodations were commonplace on Tyre! The lowest of the low on the Commonwealth's homeworld lived a life far beyond the imaginations of even the highest on Ahura Mazda.

And all such luxury cost him, he reflected, was answering a few questions.

He'd long since lost any qualms he might have about aiding the enemy. He'd quickly realized that the Theocracy's calculations of the Commonwealth's industrial potential were grave underestimates. The only hope for victory had been an immediate drive on Tyre and that had failed, disastrously. Junayd knew he'd been lucky to escape execution for his role in the catastrophe, even though he'd been reassigned to interior security after Second Cadiz. And then he'd taken advantage of an opportunity to defect.

And I may have a role to play in the postwar government, he told himself as he sat and sipped his tea. The apartment came with a generous supply of alcoholic drinks, but he'd resisted the temptation to experiment. *My family is back on the homeworld.*

It was a pleasant thought to pass the time, although he had to admit that he wasn't too keen on returning to Ahura Mazda. There was nothing there for him, save for a family who could easily be brought to Tyre instead. Indeed, the Commonwealth's intelligence officers had promised to do just that at the earliest possible moment. *That,* Junayd knew, would be a while. Even with his training and advice, it was unlikely the Commonwealth could slip an extraction team down to the surface without detection. Ahura Mazda was the most heavily defended world in the Theocracy. And intruders, assuming they reached the surface, would stick out like sore thumbs.

He heard a knock on the door. Junayd rose, silently appreciating the *politeness* his handlers showed. Theocratic intelligence agents would have opened the door and walked straight in just to make it absolutely clear that Junayd was in their power. The Commonwealth's ONI officers, on the other hand, saw no reason to make a fuss. They and Junayd both knew who was in charge and who had to sing for his supper.

He opened the door and blinked in surprise as he saw Commander Janice Wilson and Lieutenant Harry Grivets standing outside. He had been astonished to discover that Janice outranked Grivets, although he'd known intellectually that women in the Commonwealth were expected to be more than just mothers, daughters, and wives. He'd been quite uncomfortable talking to her at first, which might have been the point. Talking to another man's woman in the Theocracy was an insult at best, a challenge to a fight at worst. And the poor woman would suffer . . .

"Admiral," Janice said. There was an edge in her voice that bothered him. "May we come in?"

Junayd stepped back, silently inviting them to enter. It was easier, at times, to think of Janice as just another man, despite her tight uniform. She would have been whipped on Ahura Mazda for wearing something that revealed her curves, let alone forgetting to cover her hair with a scarf. Her short brown hair, almost mannish, would have incurred further disapproval from her male relatives. A woman should not dress and act as a man.

Things are different here, he reminded himself sternly. *And you are dependent upon her.*

"Please, take a seat," he said as he closed the door. "Can I pour either of you a drink?"

"No, thank you," Janice said. *That* was odd. Offering someone a drink was basic etiquette in the Commonwealth. And refusing it was an insult of sorts. "We just received word from the front."

Junayd sat facing them. "What happened?"

"Two weeks ago, we dispatched a task force to liberate Hebrides," Janice said. "The two squadrons of superdreadnoughts defending the planet were rapidly smashed, allowing us to land ground forces. However, as we were advancing on the PDCs, the defenders detonated a number of very dirty nuclear bombs. The planet is now heading rapidly towards complete disaster."

Junayd felt a chill running down his spine. "They wouldn't."

"They did," Grivets said sharply. "Millions of people have already been confirmed dead."

They can't have, Junayd thought, stunned. *They can't have.*

But Janice wouldn't lie to him. She had no motive to lie. And that meant . . .

His head swam. Mass slaughter was sinful. Even the Inquisitors understood that mass slaughter only ensured that countless souls, souls who had never heard of the True Faith, were doomed to burn in eternal hellfire. Bombarding planetary targets and killing those who resisted was one thing, but slaughtering an entire planet's population? Unthinkable, utterly unthinkable.

But it had happened.

He swallowed, hard. "What are you going to do?"

"That has not yet been decided," Janice said. Her lips thinned. "And my invitation to the high-level planning sessions went missing."

Junayd wasn't sure if that was a weak joke or not, so he chose to ignore it. "They've gone mad."

Grivets leaned forward. He'd never seemed to like Junayd, although Junayd wasn't sure if the man's dislike was professional disdain for a defector or anger over a relative who'd been killed in the fighting. Or maybe Grivets's job was to *act* as though he didn't like Junayd, to force him to take steps to prove himself. Junayd, in all honesty, didn't care.

"You were privy to their planning sessions," Grivets growled. "Was this ever discussed?"

"No," Junayd said flatly. "It would have been rejected out of hand."

"If that's true," Janice said, "what's changed?"

Junayd contemplated the problem for a long moment. The Theocracy had always rested on a knife-edge between the hardline extremists and those who took a more flexible view of the universe, although the Commonwealth would have happily classified both sides as extremists. One simply did not rise in the Theocracy without a constant and public show of devotion to the True Faith. Even the "liberals" in government were terrifyingly aggressive by the Commonwealth's standards. *None* of them would have accepted Janice's dress without screaming for her to be publicly flogged.

"The extremists might have finally gained control of the government," he said. Such a feat wasn't too likely, but losing so many ships over the past year might have upset some of the undecided Speakers. Or the extremists might have managed to launch a coup. "Or they may simply be desperate."

Janice lifted her eyebrows. "Desperate?"

"You are winning the war," Junayd said coolly. "Your forces have held the line over the last year, preventing them from advancing farther into your space. You have struck deep into *their* space, forcing them to devote scarce resources to countering your blows. You have blocked their plans to take control of the Jorlem Sector and recruit spacers and freighters to support their war effort. And now you are planning an offensive to liberate the occupied worlds and invade the Theocracy. They have reason to be desperate."

"True," Grivets agreed. He cocked his head. "Does that bother you?"

Junayd hid his irritation with an effort. "My family is at risk," he said. "The longer the war continues, the greater the chance that *someone* will realize that I defected and take their fury and frustration out on my relatives. And they will, if they discover the truth."

"Lovely people, your government," Grivets said.

"They will see the string of defeats as a sign they are not pure enough to deserve victory," Junayd said sharply. Grivets didn't understand. How could he? "They will probably have started purifying themselves now, purging everyone suspected of questioning the faith from the body politic. The Inquisition will have free reign to throw anyone it doesn't like into the fire, torturing them to death."

"How nice," Grivets said.

"They believe that sin taints the soul," Junayd said. He'd believed it too, when he'd been younger. It had taken constant exposure to the highest levels of Theocratic government to shake his faith. "But pain *cleanses* the soul. A willing penitent will beg to be flogged, just to remove his sin. That is the way they *think*, Lieutenant. They will do everything in their power to root out the unbelievers and destroy them."

"Madness," Grivets said.

"It makes perfect sense," Junayd assured him dryly. "If, of course, you accept the True Faith."

Janice cleared her throat. "If we were to retaliate against one of their worlds," she said, "how would they react?"

"Poorly," Junayd said.

He took a breath. "I don't know what they were thinking at the time, but surrendering territory goes against everything they believe in," he added. "They could be determined to make sure you recover nothing more than dead lands and countless bodies."

"Shitheads," Grivets said.

"They're following the True Faith," Junayd pointed out. "Hebrides was occupied for eighteen months, correct? During that time, the inhabitants had plenty of time to hear about the True Faith. Those who accepted it are assured of heaven; those who willfully *rejected* it are irredeemable unbelievers condemned to hell. Slaughtering everyone on Hebrides simply doesn't have the same connotations to them as it does to you."

"So they might not try to strike at Tyre," Janice mused. "This world was never occupied."

"I suspect they will manage to justify anything, given time," Junayd said. Learning how easily scripture could be manipulated had disillusioned him more than he cared to admit. "I believe there are copies of all of the holy books on your planetary datanet, right? They could claim that you *have* had a chance to accept the True Faith."

"That makes no sense," Grivets protested.

"Of course it does," Junayd said. "The Theocracy believes that the *truth* of the True Faith is so strong that no one except a completely irredeemable unbeliever will fail to accept it at once, the moment they *hear* it. A person who doesn't accept it at once is not just *wrong*, he is *willfully* wrong. They're wrong in the same sense that someone who insisted that you were actually a woman would be wrong. The evidence is all against you.

"Logically, insofar as you can apply logic to religion, a person who hasn't heard the truth cannot be blamed for not hearing it," he added.

"Killing that person would be morally wrong. But a person who heard the truth and rejected it . . . yes, that person deserves to die, and die quickly, before he infects others."

He gave him a tight smile. "Do not make the mistake of assuming the Theocracy's leaders will follow their rules," he warned. "They are perfectly capable of twisting rules to suit their purposes."

"Of course," Grivets said. "That's what religions *do*."

Junayd winced. One of the advantages of being on Tyre was that he had access to history records that *hadn't* been carefully sanitized by the Inquisition. He'd known, of course, that the Theocracy's official history was a lie, but he hadn't known just how badly history had been warped and perverted to serve his former masters. The original Theocrats hadn't been madmen with dreams of galactic conquest. They'd been men and women who'd merely wanted to be left alone. But the dream had been perverted into a nightmare during the years of persecution and exile. The men had been enslaved by their leaders, bound in chains of faith and fear; the women had been turned into baby-machines, their bodies modified to ensure they brought dozens of children into the world. And none of the modern-day Theocrats knew the truth.

But they will be starting to suspect it, he thought. Just as he'd found it hard to rationalize the difference between what he'd been told and reality, and he had, the commoners on Ahura Mazda would be feeling the same way. They'd be quiet about their feelings, knowing that the Inquisition would be out for blood, but discontent would be spreading. *And who knows what will happen when the commoners are pushed too far?*

He shuddered at the thought. He had no way of knowing what was happening on Ahura Mazda, but his former masters *would* know. Word would be spreading, passed down from soldiers and spacers to their civilian relatives. And those who couldn't be kept ignorant of the outside universe, the engineers and shipyard workers, would know that something was badly wrong. Who knew what would happen when discontent snowballed into a critical mass?

Janice gave him a searching look. "Is there any way we can deter them from slaughtering the population of another planet?"

"You'd need to threaten the leadership themselves," Junayd said.

He met her eyes, somehow. "I don't think you understand just how little the average commoner on Ahura Mazda knows about the universe," he added. "There aren't many people who own computers, let alone have access to the datanet. The radio and television stations are run by the government. Rest assured, each and every program they produce is vetted by the Inquisition before it is broadcast."

"I've watched some of their broadcasts," Grivets said. "It was awful."

"They're not trying to entertain their population," Junayd pointed out. "They're trying to brainwash people."

Grivets was right. The vast majority of television programs on Ahura Mazda *were* genuinely awful, even the ones meant to be entertaining. His people were beset by tales of heroic Inquisitors who strove mightily to weed out unbelief wherever they found it, facing enemies who were ludicrously incompetent. Junayd couldn't help wondering if the shows actually made it easier for people to consider rebelling, if they believed that the Inquisitors were incompetent too. But the heroes always won in the end.

And besides, they wouldn't want to show too much detail, he thought. *It would be far too revealing.*

Those shows weren't even the worst, he recalled. Hours upon hours of religious instruction, hundreds of clerics babbling on and on about the right way to behave; government warnings and notices encouraging the population to watch for heresy and unbelief, even urging children to report their parents for sedition. And far too many people took them seriously . . .

"You think we should threaten the leaders," Janice mused. "Why them?"

"The leadership is unlikely to be moved by threats of mass slaughter," Junayd pointed out. "Those who actually believe the crap they spout will claim that the dead will go straight to heaven, those who don't will not give a damn about them. You need to make a credible threat against *their* lives, something that will convince them that they can and will be killed if they destroy another planet."

Grivets snorted. "Like what?"

"Bombard Ahura Mazda," Junayd said simply. "Or even merely destroy the Tabernacle."

"Both of those options would kill millions of civilians," Janice pointed out. "Your family would be at risk."

"Yes, they will," Junayd agreed. He cursed his own words. He had no idea where his family was currently hiding, but they wouldn't survive something that burned the entire planet. "I just don't see any other option."

"I'll pass your words on to my superiors," Janice said. She looked around the apartment. "Is there anything else we can get you, while we're here?"

"Just an updated intelligence brief, if you have one," Junayd said. He liked knowing what was going on. "There's nothing else I want right now."

Grivets smirked. "Not even a walk outside the complex?"

"There's nothing to see outside," Junayd said untruthfully. He'd spent enough time on starships to overcome whatever hints of claustrophobia he might have suffered. "And I doubt the population wants to see me."

"They wouldn't recognize you," Janice said.

"No, thank you," Junayd said. The last thing he wanted was for someone to make a note of his presence. He'd warned the Commonwealth that the Theocracy still had a spy network on Tyre, although he didn't know any details they could use to find the bastards. "I'll stay here until the end of the war."

"Start looking at ways we can try to find out who is in charge on Ahura Mazda," Janice said, rising. It was an order. "And we'll see you soon."

Junayd watched them leave, then turned to click on the terminal. The news had recently broken, clearly. The local news channel was ranting and raving about the attack on Hebrides, showing endless scenes of horror as the relief crews struggled to cope with the aftermath. Every channel was showing the same thing, with presenters demanding everything from an immediate end to the war to a full-scale strike on Ahura Mazda. Junayd had no idea which way the Commonwealth would jump, but he had to admit that the war had just taken a turn for the worse. No one had destroyed an entire planet since Earth had been attacked in the closing days of the Breakaway Wars.

And even then, it caused problems, he thought. *Now . . .*

He turned off the terminal and paced over to his desk. Janice knew she had given him an impossible task. Everything he knew about the Theocracy's government was nearly a year out of date. And the average commoner on Ahura Mazda wouldn't be told anything about his government, not even the name of the man in charge. The commoner couldn't know how things had changed, let alone why.

If they're desperate, that's one thing, he told himself. Desperate men could be talked down, if necessary. The Commonwealth might waive the right to hold war crimes trials if the Theocracy surrendered. Dumping the former government on a penal world would be almost as good as putting them in front of a firing squad. *But if the extremists have taken control, that's quite another thing altogether.*

He shivered, despite the warm air. *They won't surrender easily . . .*

CHAPTER NINE

"Entering hyperspace now, Captain," Lieutenant Gross said.

"Local hyperspace appears clear," Cecelia added. "There's nothing here but us chickens."

"Good," William said. The odds were against the Theocracy waiting in ambush, but the possibility couldn't be discounted. The task force, its corridors crammed with evacuees and its life support redlined, was in no state for a fight. "Keep us in formation."

He sat back in his command chair and forced himself to relax. Cold logic told him he could do nothing more for his homeworld, but he didn't believe it. He'd been sorely tempted to request permission to remain behind, along with the other volunteers, yet he'd known permission would never be granted. *Thunderchild* and her sisters were needed to flank the task force as she returned to the fleet base. And then . . .

Perhaps we go on the offensive, he thought. The last courier boat to arrive had included updates stating that the entire Commonwealth was outraged at the atrocity with little detail on how the government planned to respond. *Or perhaps we make peace.*

The thought was horrific. Even before his homeworld had been blasted, blighted beyond repair, the Theocracy had committed an endless stream of atrocities. He had no idea how many people, military or civilian, had died in the war, but he was sure casualties were in the high millions. The populations of the other occupied worlds, the populations of the worlds the Theocracy had conquered before encountering the Commonwealth . . . they were suffering under the Theocracy's yoke. He couldn't bear the thought of leaving them in enemy hands, despite the risk of mass slaughter if the war continued . . .

And yet the government might think differently, he reminded himself. *They're responsible for the rest of the Commonwealth.*

His console chimed. "Yes?"

"Captain, this is Roach," Commander Christopher Roach said. He sounded irked, although he was making a brave effort to hide it. "We have a situation on Deck Four. Our passengers are requesting your intervention."

"Understood," William said. He had no need to ask who was causing the situation. Or, for that matter, who'd asked for his presence. "I'm on my way."

He rose. "Commander Parkinson, you have the bridge," he said. "I'll be on Deck Four."

"Aye, sir," Cecelia said.

William concealed his amusement at her eager expression as he turned and walked through the hatch, nodding to the marine on duty outside as he passed. Cecelia, like all ambitious officers, would do whatever it took to get more hours in the command chair, building up experience in the hope it would smooth her path to her own vessel. And she would probably find it easy to get promoted too, he thought. There were hundreds of new starships coming out of the yards, and she'd yet to blot her copybook beyond repair.

His ship smelled . . . *rank* as he walked down the stairs, despite the air filters working overtime to cleanse and recycle the atmosphere. There were only two hundred spacers on *Thunderchild*, but they'd been joined by over a thousand evacuees from Hebrides: men, women, and children. Cramming them all into the ship had been a nightmare; even now, with some corridors specifically left clear for the crew, the overcrowding was still a major headache. He'd asked his officers to share cabins just to clear more room for the evacuees.

And that hasn't stopped them from complaining, he thought, wondering just what *this* complaint was about. The food? The drink? The toilets? *They're just not used to being on a starship.*

Commander Roach was standing outside the hold looking tired. William had given him the job of organizing the evacuees, which had become something of a poisoned chalice under the circumstances. The things spacers took for granted, the safety rules that ensured their survival in a very hostile environment, were completely alien to the refugees. He hoped they'd avoid any nasty accidents, but he had a feeling that soon something very unpleasant would happen.

"They're in there," Roach said wearily. "Can't we just stun them for the trip?"

William shook his head firmly. Though the thought was tempting, stunning someone repeatedly risked brain damage—or worse. Besides, keeping the stunned bodies alive would be tricky without stasis pods. They wouldn't be able to eat or drink, let alone go to the toilet. And when they woke, they'd be understandably outraged.

"Stay here," he said. "And wait."

The smell of too many people in too close proximity grew stronger as he stepped into the hold. Several families were jammed together: four older women, three men, nineteen teenage girls, and at least thirty children running around despite the best efforts of their older relatives. Morag was sitting on the bed, her arms crossed under her breasts; Father Larry was sitting next to her, looking grim. Once, William knew, it was an expression that would have chilled him to the bone, promising a harsh punishment in the very near future. Now . . . now, it was merely annoying.

"Father," he said curtly.

Father Larry looked up at him. "Remove the . . . the computer terminals at once."

William barely resisted the urge to clench his fists. One did *not* dictate to a captain on his ship. Even an admiral would hesitate before trying to direct the inner affairs of a captain's vessel. Undermining the commanding officer was against both regulations and common sense. And for a *guest*, someone who was being saved from a gruesome death, to try . . .

If he'd spoken like that to my father, he thought, *he would have had his eye blackened . . . at the very least.*

William clamped down hard on his temper. "Why?"

"Our children have been using them," Father Larry said. "They are being exposed to bad influences."

William lifted an eyebrow. "And what influences are those?"

Father Larry reddened. "It doesn't matter," he protested. "All that matters is that the children are looking at them."

"You don't know," William said. He wasn't surprised. Father Larry and his ilk had never bothered to research the outside universe. They hadn't needed to know anything about the Commonwealth to condemn it. "Access to the datanet, at least the sections open to civilians, is a basic human right, laid down in the Commonwealth Charter. I cannot ban your people from looking at it without a very good reason."

"It will damage their minds," Father Larry protested. "Gayle was insisting that she could become a spacer too!"

William had to fight to conceal his amusement. "The Commonwealth allows women to work as spacers," he said deadpan. "I do recall women working in the field when I was a lad."

Morag covered her mouth hastily. Father Larry shot her a sharp look but didn't try to press the point. Women might be subject to their husbands on Hebrides, yet most of them worked in the fields and knew how to shoot. It was a rare husband who was stupid enough to try to break his wife. One who tried might end up dead, his body dumped in a ditch. And the wife might well escape punishment altogether.

"It isn't proper," Father Larry said.

"I suppose the culture shock will be quite significant," William agreed. Discovering that men and women bunked together *had* been a shock, back when he'd joined the navy. He had needed months to get used to sharing his living space with a woman. "But if she wishes to apply to join the navy . . ."

He paused. "How old is she?"

"Twenty-one," Morag said.

"More than old enough to make up her own mind," William said. He was surprised Gayle wasn't married yet. Girls rarely remained unmarried past the age of twenty. "If she wishes to apply, I will certainly forward her request to the proper authorities."

Father Larry glared at him. "It's not the only problem," he growled. "The cooks are refusing to serve food in here. We have to eat in the mess."

William allowed his irritation to show on his face. "So what?"

"So our girls are eating with men," Father Larry snapped. "Don't you know it?"

"It isn't a problem," William said.

"They cannot eat with unrelated men," Father Larry insisted. "I demand—"

William cut him off sharply. "You *demand*?"

Father Larry met his eyes. "Yes. I—"

"You are in no position to demand anything," William said, keeping his voice icy cold. "We are doing our level best to get you to McCaughey alive and well. Right now, the ship is crammed to the gunwales. We do not have the space to isolate you from everyone else. I suggest you get used to it."

He paused. "And you will *not* punish anyone for talking to the crew," he added. "If you do, you'll spend the remainder of the trip in the brig."

"You can't do that," Father Larry protested.

"I can put you in the brig at any moment, if I wish," William said. "I won't even have to come up with an excuse for the logbook. Now . . . do you have any *reasonable* complaints?"

He shook his head when Father Larry remained silent. He couldn't blame the crew for looking at the young women, perhaps even flirting. He wouldn't care, as long as the interaction was consensual. Who knew? Perhaps Gayle wouldn't be the only one interested in a naval career. Hundreds of young men had already signed up for the groundpounders, according to the last report before departure. They wanted to continue their war against the Theocracy.

"I know this isn't going to be easy for any of you," he added, gentling his voice. "But it's better than remaining behind to die."

"If our home is truly dying," Father Larry said.

Morag put a hand on his arm. "Father, William wouldn't lie to us," she said. "He's a good man."

William blinked in surprise. A woman seeking physical contact with an unrelated man? *That* was a shock. Morag shouldn't have touched Father Larry, any more than he should have touched her. But she had.

He dismissed the thought. "Morag, walk with me a moment," he said. "Please."

Father Larry didn't say a word as Morag rose. William hoped, silently, that he wouldn't try to take his feelings out on the rest of his flock. He'd met too many people like Father Larry in his life, men who believed they had the right to issue orders and expect them to be obeyed, men who reacted badly when told they had to put up and shut up as though they didn't matter. But then, he had a great deal of faith in his people. If Father Larry started to throw his weight around *too* much, he'd get a fist in the face soon enough.

"This is an odd place," Morag said as they stepped through the hatch. "I know it's a ship, but I don't quite believe it."

"My home," William said. He smiled, rather tiredly. "You should see one of the mobile repair yards. They're truly immense."

"I believe you," Morag said. She looked down at the scruffy deck for a long moment. "It isn't easy, being here."

"I know," William said.

He tried to see *Thunderchild* as Morag saw her. A strange environment—metal floors, glowing lights, an ever-present hum echoing through the air—a place so *alien* there was no way to know what would happen if you touched one of the buttons. The warnings the evacuees had been given when they'd been herded onto the shuttlecraft would have intimidated men and women who rarely used anything more advanced than a tractor. They'd known how their tractors worked. A starship was so far beyond them that it might as well have come from a whole different world.

Which it did, he supposed. *There aren't many boats on Hebrides, let alone starships.*

"The children *are* talking to your crew," Morag added after a moment. "Can't you stop them?"

"Not easily," William said. "And why would I *want* to?"

Morag gave him a sidelong look. "Do you have any respect for the values of your family?"

"I chose to leave," William said. The remembered insult, Morag's father refusing to consider him as a potential son-in-law, suddenly hurt. "Does that answer your question?" He shrugged. "The crew knows the rules," he said. "But talking to guests isn't actually forbidden."

"I'm sorry about Father Larry," Morag said. "He's . . ."

"Feeling helpless and adrift," William said. "I do understand. I just don't have any sympathy. And it's not going to get any easier."

"I thought it wouldn't," Morag said. "Here we are, cast out . . . we didn't even get to bring most of our belongings."

"There isn't room," William pointed out stiffly. "This isn't a very big ship."

"We understand," Morag said. "But it still isn't easy."

William was tempted to ask if she wanted some cheese with that whine, but he resisted the nasty impulse. Morag and the other refugees had little beyond the clothes on their backs. Everything else, unless it could be carried by hand, had been abandoned back on their former homeworld. *Thunderchild* could supply enough food and clean water for the refugees but almost nothing else. By the time they reached their destination, their clothes would probably be rags. And their replacements would come from the fleet base's stores, stripping away another part of their identities. A long time would pass before their lives returned to something like normal, if they ever did.

"You'll just have to cope," he said. "It shouldn't take more than ten days to reach our destination. There'll be more room there."

"Good," Morag said. "Have you thought about my offer?"

William shook his head. "I'm not interested," he said. Something *clicked* in his head. "But if Gayle wants to be sponsored for the naval academy, I'll be happy to do it."

"Her father would object," Morag pointed out.

"I don't think it matters at her age," William said. He stopped and turned to face Morag. "I think it would be better to allow dissidents to leave peacefully, the way the Commonwealth does, rather than try to keep them trapped. They'll resent it for the rest of their lives."

Morag met his eyes. "Does that make you a dissident?"

"Perhaps," William said. There was, in truth, no *perhaps* about it. "But I like to think, in the end, that I am as ruthlessly practical as the rest of my people."

He escorted Morag back to the hold, then nodded to Roach. "There's nothing we can do about their problems," he said. "Not without a much bigger ship."

"I'll get the engineer to work on inflating the hull," Roach said cheerfully. "Pity we don't have any balloons left."

"They were needed back at Hebrides," William said. Dragging an inflatable habitat into hyperspace was asking for trouble, but they could serve as emergency housing for evacuees as long as they were carefully monitored. "And if we did have a bigger ship, we'd have to take on more evacuees."

He felt a flicker of sympathy for Fran and the other superdreadnought captains. Their ships would be absolutely heaving with evacuees, even though they might be called upon to fight at any moment. Their evacuees would include countless families, thousands of people who weren't related to one another. But there was no helping it.

His terminal bleeped. "The doctor wants to see me," he said. "Keep an eye on the situation here. Don't hesitate to send in the marines to intervene if all hell breaks loose."

"I won't," Roach promised.

William nodded, then hurried down the corridor and into Sickbay. The area was crammed with wounded, all with relatively minor injuries. A handful of medical staff moved among them, tending to their wounds. Nearly all the ship's supplies had been stripped out, save for the bare essentials. The bean counters would have a fit, he was sure, when they found out, unless someone pointed out that regulations had been superseded by necessity. But was there anyone who might say that on Tyre?

Kat's father will, he told himself. *He's not stupid.*

"Doctor," he said as Sarah Prosser appeared and beckoned him into her office. "You called me?"

"I just completed the basic medical checks," she said. "Most of the evacuees have all kinds of minor problems. They don't even have the broad-spectrum vaccinations they'll need before landing on a Commonwealth world."

"They'll have to be injected when we reach the fleet base," William said. "What other problems do they have?"

"Quite a few," Sarah said. She picked up a datapad from her desk and held it out. "The most common problem is malnutrition, but there are a number of hereditary issues that need attention. I think seven or eight of the girls are going to have problems bearing children in later life."

She paused. "One of the girls begged me, on her knees, not to tell her parents that she wasn't a virgin," she added. "Is that a problem there?"

"It can be," William said. "If a relationship broke up, the girl might be disgraced if it turned out she had sex with her former boyfriend."

"Barbaric," Sarah said. "I can restore her maidenhead, easily, but—"

"If you can, do it," William said.

"These people don't even know what's available," Sarah said. "Captain, there's a man with a scar I could remove in twenty minutes. And a woman with cancer . . . I could cure that with a pill!"

"Do it," William said. He recalled a man he'd known, back when he'd been a child, who'd lost an arm in a freak accident. Growing a new arm for him would have been simple with modern medical technology. "And then start telling them what other services can be offered."

"Aye, Captain," Sarah said. "It's going to be a long voyage, isn't it?"

"And it won't end when we reach our destination," William agreed. "Not for any of us."

CHAPTER TEN

Kat hadn't been to McCaughey Naval Base since 2416, when she'd been XO on HMS *Thunderous*. Then, the military buildup had barely begun and the naval base had been relatively small. Now, dozens of heavily armed fortresses protected a planet surrounded by mobile repair yards, industrial nodes, and everything else 6th Fleet needed for its grand offensive. Ten whole squadrons of superdreadnoughts, flanked by over two hundred smaller warships, held station above the defense network, while thousands of freighters and interplanetary transports powered their way in and out of the system. The whole sight awed her beyond words.

The Theocracy wouldn't dare attack us here, she thought as the task force reentered realspace and headed towards the planet. *They'd be obliterated with ease.*

"Signal from Admiral Christian," Lieutenant Darren Cobb reported. "He welcomes you to McCaughey and invites you to report onboard HMS *Hammerhead* at your earliest opportunity."

"As soon as possible, he means," Kat translated. "Lock us into the planetary defense network, then ready my shuttle."

"Aye, Commodore," Wheeler said. "What about the evacuees?"

"Check with Fleet HQ to see about holding camps, then start offloading them," Kat ordered briskly. Her crews had been lucky to avoid a life support failure on one or more of the ships, but she knew that had been a very close-run thing. "Make sure they take all their possessions with them."

And pray the Inspectorate General doesn't decide to inspect my ship, she added as she rose and headed for the hatch. She'd have to change into her dress uniform before shuttling over to *Hammerhead*. Admiral Christian wasn't the sort to care if she wore it or not, but she knew from experience that he probably wouldn't be the only one in the compartment. *We might be talking directly to Tyre.*

She changed rapidly, said her good-byes to Pat, then hurried down to the shuttlebay. Lines of evacuees were already forming outside the hatch as marines struggled to keep them under control, but they parted for her as she walked through and headed to her shuttle. She couldn't help feeling a stab of guilt as she boarded the craft, even though she was heading to a superdreadnought rather than the planet's surface. Outside, more shuttles were already closing in on her task force. System Command, it seemed, was equally determined to ensure that the ships were unloaded as quickly as possible.

"Commodore, we're being invited to dock at the captain's hatch," the pilot said. "Is that suitable?"

"It will do," Kat said. Inwardly, she was relieved. Landing in the main shuttlebay would probably have meant a formal reception, a ceremony she had grown to dislike. "Just get us there as quickly as possible.

HMS *Hammerhead* was two years older than *Queen Elizabeth*, but she was practically identical to Kat's flagship, a blocky hull crammed with missile tubes, energy weapons, and point defense systems. Kat couldn't help noticing that her engineers had added extra point defenses, based on eighteen months of lessons learned from actual combat. *Queen Elizabeth* and her sisters had enhanced point defenses themselves, but *Hammerhead* hadn't had time to return to the yards for a full refit.

But her crews would definitely be able to keep her in fighting trim themselves.

As long as she doesn't take heavy damage, Kat thought as the shuttle docked with the superdreadnought. *They'd have to send her back to the yards then.*

Her gaze fell on the orbital display as the hatch hissed open. Seven mobile repair yards orbited the planet, the largest starships built by mankind. They dwarfed even the giant colonist-carriers, although much of their bulk was taken up by docking slips rather than endless rows of stasis pods. Maybe Admiral Christian *wouldn't* have to send his flagship back to Tyre if she needed repairs, not with so many mobile shipyards attached to his fleet. The Commonwealth not only built starships faster than the Theocracy, but they also could repair them more quickly. And so the Commonwealth's fighting power waxed even as the Theocracy's waned.

Kat rose and stepped through the hatch, saluting the flag as she boarded the giant superdreadnought. An auburn-haired young woman, wearing a lieutenant's uniform, waited for her.

"Welcome aboard," she said. "I'm Lieutenant Elena Pettigrew, Admiral Christian's aide."

"Thank you," Kat said. She didn't recognize the name, but Elena certainly *sounded* as though she'd grown up in high society. "Please take me to the admiral at once."

Elena bowed her head, then led Kat through a maze of corridors until they reached a sealed hatch. The lieutenant keyed the console to open it, then motioned for Kat to step through into Admiral Christian's office. The space was huge, larger than Kat's office on *Queen Elizabeth*. A giant star chart hovered in the center of the room, glittering with tactical icons representing starships, fleet bases, StarComs, and ONI's best guesses about enemy dispositions. Admiral Christian himself was standing in front of the display, studying the latest reports from the front. He turned and smiled when he saw Kat.

"It's nice to see you again, Commodore," he said. "Congratulations on your promotion."

"Thank you, sir," Kat said. *She* might not be entirely pleased with it, but she knew better than to say that out loud. "And congratulations on your last set of victories."

"It's the gunboat pilots who deserve credit for the last one," Admiral Christian said. He looked at Elena. "Please bring tea and biscuits for my guest, and then that will be all."

"Yes, sir," Elena said.

Kat settled down on the sofa, allowing her eyes to drift over the display. The front lines—the seven worlds deemed to be under threat—were all heavily defended, surrounded by fortresses, automated weapons platforms, swarms of gunboats, and several squadrons of frontline starships. Taking even one of them would cost Theocratic forces dearly, while trying to bypass the planets and stabbing deeper into the Commonwealth would expose the enemy's rear and give the Commonwealth an opportunity to cut their supply lines. There were enough fixed defenses, now, for the Commonwealth to start reassembling the fleets and taking the offensive into enemy territory.

Assuming we decide what to do about the Theocracy's new willingness to kill entire worlds, she thought. She hadn't heard much before they'd departed Hebrides, but she was fairly sure the news would have caused absolute chaos. *There's no hope of bringing the war to an end without risking massive devastation.*

"I read your report carefully," Admiral Christian said once Elena had brought the snacks and departed again. "A number of your political enemies tried to blame you for the disaster, but it is my belief that you cannot be held responsible. The Admiralty and His Majesty appear to agree."

Kat nodded, relieved. She hadn't thought the attack would be a serious threat to her career, not when she'd had no warning at all before the first nuclear detonations, but she knew she had enemies who wouldn't hesitate to try to take advantage of the disaster. There hadn't been anything quite so horrific in human history since Earth had been turned to a bed of ashes. Perhaps even her enemies figured that trying to use the disaster to score political points would cause them problems in the future.

"Overall, though, it is a serious problem," Admiral Christian continued. "I've stripped the fleet base of personnel transports and medical supplies, but that's still only a drop in the ocean compared to what they need. Other bases will be sending their own supplies, yet . . ."

His voice trailed off. Kat nodded in grim understanding. No matter how desperately she worked and reworked the figures, at least a third of the survivors would die before they could be evacuated. And many of the evacuees had medical problems, far more than she'd ever anticipated. The Commonwealth would need years to cope with the sudden demand for supplies. She hated to think of what would happen if the process had to be repeated for another inhabited world.

"We need to end this war quickly," Admiral Christian added. "Our original plan may have just flown out the airlock."

"Yes, sir," Kat agreed. "There's no point in trying to liberate Delphi if they destroy the planet as soon as we drive them out."

She looked up at the star chart. The original plan had been for her to advance on Delphi as soon as the follow-up elements secured Hebrides. If she'd been lucky, she would have hit the system before the Theocrats realized she was coming. And then she would have moved on to her third target while 6th Fleet advanced on Cadiz, securing the shipping lanes for passage through the Gap and into Theocratic Space.

But the slow, grinding advance they'd planned had been blown out of the water.

If nothing else, she reflected numbly, *the bastards have more time to prepare.*

Admiral Christian glanced at his watch. "We are due to join a secure conference with the War Cabinet in an hour," he added. "Before then, we need to have a proposal to put to them."

Kat frowned. Hitting Delphi, or even Cadiz, struck her as dangerous now. She had no doubt that they could destroy the orbital defenses and land ground forces, but the Theocracy would just trigger their nukes and blight the entire planet. Nukes could be taken out with KEW strikes, unlike antimatter bombs, yet *finding* the damn things was almost impossible unless the enemy decided to make it easy. Drones might be able to locate enough of the nukes, but if they missed more than a handful . . .

Let's not kid ourselves, she thought. *Even a single dirty bomb is a major disaster.*

"The original plan is dead," she said, finally. "It's simply not workable any longer."

"Quite," Admiral Christian agreed.

"So we change the plan," Kat continued. "Instead of advancing system by system and world by world, we thrust straight at Ahura Mazda itself. We dare them to destroy their own homeworld."

"Ahura Mazda is the most heavily defended world in Theocratic Space," Admiral Christian observed. "Do you plan to charge straight in, guns blazing?"

"It would depend on what we encountered," Kat said bluntly. "6th Fleet is the most powerful formation in known space. We can pull in squadrons from 5th and 4th Fleet to back us up too. As long as we are careful, the first Theocratic forces will know of our approach only when we open gateways in the heart of their system. And then we just thrust straight at their homeworld and start landing troops."

"And meet fanatical resistance," Admiral Christian observed.

Kat had her doubts. She'd met a number of fanatical Theocrats, but she'd had the very definite impression, mainly from reading prisoner transcripts, that a great many Theocrats tolerated rather than embraced their faith. And while she was sure the Theocrats had been told they were *winning* the war, the arrival of a massive enemy fleet at Ahura Mazda would have to be a terrible shock. The invasion might just encourage them to question their leaders and step aside when Commonwealth troops finally landed.

"It would have to be handled," she said. They couldn't *count* on meeting no resistance. "But I doubt they'd be prepared to destroy their own homeworld, not if we offer them reasonable surrender terms."

"That won't go down well with the public," Admiral Christian said. "Right now, according to the latest polls, public support is three-to-one in favor of wiping Ahura Mazda clean of life, then sowing the planet with radioactive dirty bombs just to make sure no one can ever set foot on her again."

Kat shuddered. "Millions of innocents would be killed."

"Millions of innocents have already been killed," Admiral Christian reminded her. "And the public wants *blood*." He shook his head. "That decision is not ours to make," he added. "You propose to simply bypass Cadiz completely?"

"If the Theocrats surrender, we can recover the occupied worlds at a stroke," Kat said, carefully. "And if they refuse to surrender, we can deal with the occupying forces later."

"Unless they decide to commit suicide anyway," Admiral Christian muttered. "I don't trust fanatics."

"Neither do I," Kat said. "But the shock of seeing us turn up in their star system should concentrate their minds a little."

Admiral Christian nodded, then started tapping commands into a datapad. The star chart vanished, replaced by a complete fleet listing for 4th, 5th, and 6th Fleets. Kat was silently impressed as Admiral Christian started maneuvering forces around the system and deciding what could be ordered to join 6th Fleet. She'd known that hundreds of new ships were coming out of the shipyards, but seeing them displayed, right in front of her, brought it home. The Theocracy didn't stand a chance.

"We should be able to concentrate fourteen squadrons of super-dreadnoughts, perhaps sixteen if we can convince the Admiralty that Nova Roma doesn't need three squadrons of superdreadnoughts on guard duty," Admiral Christian mused. "That would also give us around fifty squadrons of smaller ships and over four thousand gunboats. Ahura Mazda is heavily defended, but we should be able to break down at least one of her PDCs and land troops on the surface."

He stopped for a moment. "We could probably also arrange for several marine and militia divisions," he added. "It'll be a smaller force than I'd be comfortable with. I'll discuss it with General Winters. He'll probably insist on bringing more troops."

"I wouldn't blame him," Kat said. "Hebrides had a relatively friendly population, Admiral. We didn't plan to coordinate with the resistance, but we could have done so. The population on Ahura Mazda is unlikely to side with us, at least not at first. Their . . . enforcers will probably try to shove them at the marines."

She winced. Pat had once told her, when they'd been comparing notes on who had the hardest job, that even a couple of thousand soldiers could vanish without a trace in a large city, unable to control territory that wasn't directly under their guns. Ten divisions of marines and militia, assuming they could be scraped up, would be around a hundred thousand soldiers, not all of whom would be frontline riflemen. And yet, they were talking about hitting an entire planet, a planet known to be heavily populated. Fighting their way to the Tabernacle would be a nightmare.

"General Winters can draw up the plan," Admiral Christian said. "And if he thinks it can't be done, it probably can't be done."

Kat made a face. The *original* plan had been to isolate Ahura Mazda, then wear her defenses down through a series of steady attacks. Any rational enemy would have surrendered upon understanding that they survived only at their attacker's sufferance. But now, they were talking about landing vast numbers of troops in a *coup de main*. The prospect for heavy casualties was terrifyingly high.

"And what," she asked quietly, "if it *can't* be done?"

"We'd need to find another solution," Admiral Christian said. His face darkened. "A political one, perhaps."

Kat rose and started to pace the giant compartment. The Breakaway Wars had been a series of relatively minor engagements; the handful of tiny conflicts since then resolved with a couple of battles and peace treaties. But the Commonwealth-Theocratic War was different. It had started with a surprise attack, then a series of engagements marked by staggering brutality and a whole string of horrific slaughters, culminating in the death of an entire world. There was no way they could return to the *status quo ante bellum*, no way they could just let the Theocracy get away with starting the war. If nothing else, they'd be refighting the war again in a couple of decades against an enemy that would have learned from its past mistakes.

"I don't see a way to stop short of utter victory," she said. "Do you?"

"No," Admiral Christian agreed. "But our political masters may feel they do."

Kat wasn't so sure. The aristocracy took the long view. Her great-grandfather, the CEO of the Falcone Corporation during the move to Tyre, had ensured that his children and their heirs married for talent, rather than money, looks, or love. And the tradition had continued, the highest elements of the aristocracy constantly engaging in genteel competition for power, place, and profits. The process ensured that the winners, those who dictated the future of the entire planet, understood how the universe truly worked. They were certainly unlikely to fold at the first hurdle.

But that's not true of the king, she thought. It felt like disloyalty to even *consider* it—she *liked* King Hadrian—but she knew it was true. *He didn't compete for his position.*

She shook her head. The king was powerful, that was beyond dispute, but he wasn't *all*-powerful. And he was smart enough to surround himself with capable advisors.

"I think they'll understand that we have to end the war," she said finally. Her father would, at least. The others would be just as stubborn and bloody minded. "And that we have to make sure the Theocracy cannot return to threaten us once again."

"Destroying their ships and shipyards would accomplish that," Admiral Christian pointed out dryly. "And surely their religion would have to engage in some . . . self-examination if they failed so badly."

Kat rather doubted it. She'd studied the early years of the Theocracy. Accomplishing as much as they had was nothing short of miraculous. But somewhere along the line they'd forgotten the underlying ethos of their faith and committed themselves to converting the rest of the galaxy by force. Once, they'd questioned everything, testing and retesting their doctrines until they'd developed a new way to live; now, questioning was utterly forbidden, even when fanatics should be able to understand that they were losing the war. They'd become a monster, a monster that had to be stopped.

And if the price for stopping the monster is my death, she thought, *it is a price I will gladly pay.*

CHAPTER ELEVEN

"All rise," the prime minister said. "All rise for His Majesty, King Hadrian."

Duke Lucas Falcone, Minister for War Production, rose to his feet as King Hadrian walked through the door and took his seat at the head of the table. The king was young, only two years older than Lucas's youngest daughter, but Lucas had to admit that he'd proven himself a reasonably effective war leader. And yet, the king's youth worried him. Kids, in his experience, were prone to making mistakes through simple ignorance of the world around them.

"Be seated," King Hadrian said.

He was a tall man, his short dark hair crowning a face that had been deliberately designed for strength of character rather than raw beauty. The geneticists had outdone themselves, Lucas admitted; King Hadrian *looked* trustworthy, as if he could make tough decisions. And yet he'd been thrust forward too quickly. His father hadn't been willing or able to make his heirs compete for power. King Hadrian simply lacked the experience Lucas had brought to the Dukedom when he'd succeeded his uncle.

But he doesn't have the urge to fight for every last fragment of power either, Lucas reminded himself. *That's a point in his favor.*

He kept his expression blank as holographic images of his daughter and Admiral Christian appeared and took their places at the far side of the table. Lucas wasn't sure *why* King Hadrian was showering so much favor on his youngest daughter, but he didn't think he liked it. Kat would benefit in the short run, he was sure, but there would be a political price at some point. He would have wondered if the king was courting his daughter if he hadn't known King Hadrian seemed interested in Princess Drusilla.

And that brings problems of its own, he thought. Princess Drusilla had escaped the Theocracy a month before the war had officially begun. He could see political advantages to the match, but he was sure it wouldn't win public approval. *Marrying her would certainly put the cat amid the mice.*

"There's no time for formalities," King Hadrian said briskly. "We all know why we're here."

A holographic image of Hebrides appeared, floating over the table. The planet looked surprisingly normal from high orbit, but icons and text boxes hovering beside the image showed destroyed settlements and radioactive clouds slowly drifting through the world's atmosphere. Lucas's staff had run the figures and calculated that cleaning up Hebrides would cost trillions of crowns. It would be a great deal cheaper, they'd concluded, to terraform three or four Mars-type worlds for the evacuees.

"Public opinion is demanding retaliation," the king added. "Do we retaliate?"

"That would be pointless slaughter," Lucas said before anyone else could say a word. He knew himself to be ruthless; he knew he had few limits when called upon to preserve his family's power and position, but pointless slaughter was beyond the pale. "The Theocrats would not be particularly concerned if we kill a few billion people."

"And yet the public is torn between a demand for retaliation and a demand for immediate peace," Israel Harrison said. The Leader of the

Opposition looked grim. Problems for the government were normally opportunities for the Loyal Opposition, but *this* one was a poisoned chalice. "There is a strong concern that the Theocracy could hit one of our worlds."

"Orbital defenses have been tightened," the First Space Lord said. "Right now, I don't believe a marble could pass through the sensor grid without being detected, tracked, and logged."

"A portion of antimatter the size of a marble could do real damage," Harrison pointed out, grimly. "And the public knows it."

"We appear to be caught in a bind," the king commented. "Striking one of their worlds will not deter them; *not* striking one of their worlds will *also* not deter them. We need the war to end."

He paused, then looked at Lucas. "You have seen the message from the Theocracy?"

Lucas nodded, grimly. It was an open secret that some communications links had been maintained, via StarCom, between the Commonwealth and the Theocracy. They hadn't been used, save for arranging the return of both sets of ambassadors. Now the Theocracy had reopened the links to send a message.

"They want to end the war now," the king said. A star chart appeared above the table, replacing the previous image. "They're offering to withdraw to the Gap, essentially a return to the prewar status quo. Cadiz will be left independent, without influence from either side."

He paused. "I think I speak for much of the population," he added, "when I say I find this unacceptable."

"Yes, Your Majesty," Lucas said. "We'll be fighting the war again in twenty years, as soon as they have rebuilt their fleets and learned from their past mistakes. We have to put an end to the war on our terms."

Harrison cleared his throat. "Are they indicating that they are willing to negotiate?"

"The message suggests not," the king said. "They want a return to the prewar situation."

"So they're not offering to surrender?" Harrison mused.

"No," Lucas said.

"But this leads to a very different question," Harrison said. "Can we win the war?"

King Hadrian looked at the First Space Lord, who nodded.

"I think we can safely say that we are outproducing them in almost every category," the First Space Lord said. "Our figures for what came out of their shipyards over the last eighteen months are little more than educated guesses, but it is fairly clear that their production is definitely not keeping up with ours. Their repair and maintenance system is clearly breaking down, as the recent engagement shows. I think there's a strong case to be made that they will soon lose the ability to carry on the war.

"In addition, our technology is superior to theirs right across the board . . . and the gap is only widening. Our stockpiles of the latest missiles are limited, as yet, but within six months we will have enough to take the offensive deep into enemy territory. Their ability to resist us will collapse and that will be the end."

"If we have time," the prime minister said quietly. "It won't be long before the peace offer, as flawed as it is, leaks."

Lucas made a face. The prime minister was right. No amount of government control would be enough to keep word from getting out once it leaked. And it *would* leak. Too many people knew about the offer for it to remain secret indefinitely. He was surprised that rumors hadn't already begun to creep onto the datanet.

"And the other occupied worlds must also be deemed at risk," the prime minister added. "Can we prevent the Theocracy from depopulating them too?"

"No, Prime Minister," the First Space Lord admitted. "We've been running simulations, but even under the most favorable conditions, we couldn't hope to guarantee the capture or destruction of every last nuke. A handful surviving long enough to detonate would be quite enough to do serious damage. Merely coping with Hebrides has pushed our support network to the limit."

"We anticipated having to rebuild the occupied worlds," Lucas said. They'd had plans to do just that ever since it had become clear that the Commonwealth was going to win. "But we never anticipated such destruction. Our stockpiled supplies are totally inadequate for the task at hand."

He paused. "Bear in mind that we expected to be rebuilding four worlds, including Cadiz," he added. "And we stockpiled with that in mind."

King Hadrian looked displeased. "Is that it? Stalemate? We dare not continue the war because they are holding entire planets hostage?"

He looked at Kat. "What do you think?"

Lucas pursed his lips in disapproval. There were three naval officers in the room and Kat was easily the most junior. Asking *her* opinion over her superiors' was a gross breach of etiquette, something that would be bound to cause her problems in the future. But then, he knew the king had chafed under the tutelage of his father's former advisors. Kat *was* only a couple of years younger than him, after all.

Kat's face looked impassive, but Lucas could easily read her concern. "The original plan is no longer practical," she said carefully. "However, Admiral Christian and I have been drawing up plans to take the war directly to Ahura Mazda. Sixth Fleet, heavily reinforced, would depart its current base, pass through the Gap, and head for its target. Once there, we would land ground troops and put an end to the Theocracy's central government."

"Interesting," King Hadrian said. "Admiral Christian?"

Lucas listened as Admiral Christian outlined the plan, a very bare-bones concept suggesting that neither Kat nor her superiors had had much time to outline their strategy. But then, everyone had known that the original plan called for a steady advance through enemy space, liberating and occupying every star system between Cadiz and Ahura Mazda.

The planners hadn't seen any need for a daring stroke that could easily end in disaster if the Theocracy saw it coming. The Commonwealth's preponderance of firepower ensured such a move wasn't necessary.

Until now, he thought.

The First Space Lord looked irked. "My staff will have to go through the plan in some detail," he said. "However, it occurs to me that the operation would not only draw on starships all along the defense line but also put them out of contact for upwards of four to five months. Recalling them if we ran into trouble would be impossible."

"We do have the mobile StarComs," Lucas pointed out.

"Drawing down the defenses would be a political concern," the prime minister said. "The mere *suggestion* that ships should be withdrawn would cause a political firestorm."

"The risk is minimal," Admiral Christian said. "I do not believe that the Theocrats are in any position to take the offensive. Even if they do, our fixed defenses and gunboats are more than enough to handle anything they might realistically throw at the defense lines. It would take their entire remaining fleet to make a serious impression on the naval base, let alone punch through and head to Tyre."

"And Tyre is heavily defended," King Hadrian observed.

"So is Ahura Mazda," the prime minister warned. "The losses might be staggering."

"They could be replaced," Lucas said.

"Lives *cannot* be replaced," Harrison said. He held up a warning hand. "I understand the concept, Admiral, but can you guarantee success?"

"There's no such thing as a solid guarantee of success," Admiral Christian said. "I do believe, however, that we could, at the very least, tear the guts out of their industrial base and isolate Ahura Mazda from the rest of the galaxy. The destruction of their StarCom network would effectively isolate the remainder of their systems, giving us the ability to coordinate our operations on a much greater scale. I do not believe the Theocracy would long endure such a battering."

He paused. "Losses may well be steep," he added softly. "Ahura Mazda *is* heavily defended, with both fixed defenses and mobile units. But we do not have time to stick with the original plan, not unless we find a way to keep them from destroying and depopulating a dozen other worlds."

"And we can't," the First Space Lord said. "The choice, it seems, boils down to either stabbing at their heart or coming to terms."

"And coming to terms with the bastards is unthinkable," King Hadrian said. "We have to put a stake through their heart." He glanced at his prime minister. "Do you believe we can hold the government together long enough to plan and execute the operation?"

The prime minister nodded. "I believe so," he said. "Israel?"

Lucas concealed his amusement. The Leader of the Opposition was in an odd position. As a member of the War Cabinet, he had a say in proceedings, but he could choose to leave at any moment, if he felt that the interests of the Opposition were not being respected. And yet, if his comrades thought he'd betrayed them, he could find himself kicked out of office, even if the problem hadn't been his fault. The wrong choice could be disastrous.

"I believe there will be no serious challenge, as long as we make it clear that we will be continuing the war," Harrison said. "But we *must* ensure that the population understands that we are determined to stay on the offensive."

"True," the prime minister agreed.

Lucas kept his annoyance under tight control. He'd had plenty of moments when he'd felt the impulse to just take off the gloves and hit back, even though it would have been catastrophic. The general public on Tyre wanted revenge, wanted to burn a Theocratic world to ashes, yet such an act wouldn't deter Theocratic leaders from continuing the war.

They might even be relieved if the world was rebellious, he thought. *And we know that resistance movements have been spreading through their space.*

"Then I believe that you should go ahead and draw up a more comprehensive plan for the operation," King Hadrian said. "Do you have a name for it yet?"

"Operation Hammer," Admiral Christian said. "We will require a major commitment of ground forces, as well as transports and missile haulers. Supporting the fleet so far from a major fleet base is going to be a headache."

"You'll get them," the king assured him.

Lucas resisted the urge to rub his forehead in irritation. King Hadrian had seemingly forgotten that thousands of transports had been hastily reassigned to evacuating Hebrides and shipping the remaining population to holding camps across the sector. They would need weeks, perhaps months, to assemble enough of a transport fleet to support the warships, let alone find the light forces necessary to escort them. Once the Theocracy realized what the Commonwealth had in mind, they'd do everything in their power to cut the fleet's supply lines.

It isn't as if we haven't been showing them how effective such a tactic can be, he thought, sourly. *They'll have definitely learned from their experiences.*

"It will take at least a month to assemble the fleet," Admiral Christian concluded. "With your permission, Your Majesty, I would like to start now."

"Granted," King Hadrian said. "And good luck."

He looked around the table. "This plan offers the greatest chance for outright victory within the next four months," he said. "I expect you all to support it."

"Of course," Lucas said dryly. "However, I must remind you that supplies of our more advanced missiles and warheads are very limited. We simply do not have time to rebuild our stockpiles."

He saw Kat wince. She'd fired off most of the first production run at Hebrides, using them to smash two entire squadrons of enemy superdreadnoughts. The missiles had more than proved their value, but neither she nor anyone else would have more than a handful of them by the time Operation Hammer kicked off. There was no way to get around the production bottlenecks so quickly. He'd had his staff looking into ways to increase production rates, but none of their proposals were workable in the short term. Too many industrial nodes needed to be revamped.

"We have massive stockpiles of the older missiles," Admiral Christian said. "If necessary, we will simply swamp their defenses with overwhelming force."

"Good," King Hadrian said. "Very good."

He smiled. "And do your best to make sure that the Theocracy doesn't know you're coming," he added. "The impact of a few thousand superdreadnoughts appearing in their skies will be lessened if they have time to prepare for it."

A few thousand, Lucas thought. *We have barely five hundred super-dreadnoughts in total.*

King Hadrian rose. "This meeting is now at an end," he announced. "I will talk to some of you later concerning the future."

Lucas frowned as King Hadrian turned and left the room. The king had definitely become more independent over the last eighteen months. But then, he *was* learning on the job. His father had never expected to die so soon, denying his son the chance to take up a career of his own. *Prince* Hadrian could have served in the navy or the marines or even the militia. *King* Hadrian couldn't leave the palace, except on special occasions.

Lucas rose and headed for the helipad on the palace roof. His assistant was waiting outside, falling into step beside him as soon as he emerged. Lucas listened to her stream of updates as they took the elevator to the roof and then boarded an aircar. A trio of gunships escorted them as they took to the sky and headed north.

"There are more protesters down there," Sandra warned. "Both for and against the war."

Lucas wasn't surprised. Civilians rarely understood the realities of government, let alone interstellar warfare. Protesters could express their feelings if they wished, but nothing would change until the next election cycle. By then, he hoped, the war would be over and the rebuilding could begin. And yet, if the conflict didn't end, he didn't know what would happen if an antiwar government was elected. Balancing the interests of the commons and the aristocracy would be impossible if they were at loggerheads.

"Keep an eye on the situation," he said. He didn't blame people for being concerned, not really. An entire planet being destroyed was truly horrific. And far too many people believed that it could easily happen to Tyre too. "Let me know if it looks like it's getting out of hand."

"Some people would say it has already gotten out of hand," Sandra said. "Your Grace, the mood on the street isn't good."

"Tighten up security," Lucas ordered. "And make sure that all the factories are covered."

"Yes, sir," Sandra said.

And hope that the war can be brought to an end quickly, Lucas thought. *All the old certainties died with Hebrides.*

CHAPTER TWELVE

"Thirteen of the girls have applied to join the navy," Morag said as she and William walked towards the shuttle. "And their parents are not happy."

"They'll stay in touch," William assured her. "And they'll certainly be very different when they get home."

"That's the point," Morag admitted. "And there isn't a home for us any longer."

William nodded. The flight to McCaughey had been nerve-wracking as the life support had fluctuated, constantly on the verge of a breakdown, while the evacuees and the crew struggled to cope with culture shock. He'd had to speak quite sharply to several of his crew; four young men for flirting with evacuee women, two young women for trying to convince evacuees that they'd have a better life in the Commonwealth. And while he didn't blame any of his crew, he knew their evangelism was a problem.

He stepped back as Father Larry led the older women and children into the shuttlecraft, muttering prayers under his breath. The old man hadn't coped very well with the trip and looked desperate to be down on the ground again, even if it *was* a holding camp. William knew Father Larry should be relieved that they hadn't flown too close to a hyperspace storm, but he doubted the vicar would understand if he explained. All that mattered was that they'd made it.

"You'll be fine," he said to Morag, silently praying that was true. Accommodations in a holding camp would be very limited, at least at first. The fleet base hadn't expected to find itself playing host to hundreds of thousands of evacuees, not until the first courier boat had arrived. "And I will try to stay in touch too."

Morag looked away. They'd talked every day during the voyage, but a vast gulf still existed between them. *Thunderchild* was his world, his home; to her, it was a strange and alien environment, seductive to the young and dangerous to the old. The two no longer had anything in common, despite being born in the same region on the same planet, despite trying to form a relationship. And he'd rejected her repeated offers of her daughter's hand in marriage sharply enough to drive a permanent wedge between them.

"Thank you," she said.

William stepped back and watched her stride into the shuttle, the crew closing the hatch moments later. He turned and walked out of the shuttlebay, not looking back as he heard the craft taking off and making its way out through the force field and into open space. The flight down to McCaughey was short, but the evacuees would find it more terrifying than two weeks on *Thunderchild*. Merely passing through turbulence alone would be enough to scare them shitless.

Poor bastards, he thought.

A trio of marines was standing outside the shuttlebay lock, guarding five evacuees in cuffs and shackles. The prisoners stared at William pleadingly, but he ignored them. They'd started a fight on his ship, with his crew; he'd ordered them imprisoned until the end of the voyage. He had no idea what the authorities on McCaughey would do with them, but they'd definitely be out of his hair. God alone knew what they would make of the holding camps.

Probably bitch and moan about new ideas being introduced to children, he thought as he strode along the corridor. The stench of too many unwashed humans hung in the air, mocking him. He'd been on pirate ships that smelled better. *Or find themselves returned to jail soon enough.*

Roach met him outside the hold. "Captain," he said. "It isn't pretty."

William nodded as he peered inside. The space was a hellish mess. Debris and rubbish lay everywhere, items that could be recycled mingled carelessly with items that needed to be fed straight into a trash compactor. The portable toilets were overflowing with human waste, a mocking reminder that his family would have thought nothing of using an outside toilet or simply relieving themselves in the fields. And a handful of books lay on the deck, some damaged beyond repair.

"Get a crew in here to move out the rubbish and wash the deck," he ordered tiredly. "Are the cabins any better?"

"I'm afraid not," Roach said. "I'd be worried about infection if we hadn't all been vaccinated." He glanced at William. "How can people *live* like this?"

"They have a very different culture," William said reluctantly. How many people would feel nothing but utter contempt for his people after seeing the mess they'd left behind? "They've also been through hell."

"You'd think they'd know not to live in squalor," Roach said. "Do they not know how to use toilets?"

"Indoor toilets are quite rare on Hebrides," William said. He'd had problems too, back when he'd joined the navy. But then, his first senior chief had been happy to hammer lessons into his skull with his fists if necessary. "Outside the bigger settlements, they are vanishingly rare."

He gritted his teeth as it struck him, once again, just how much the Theocracy had casually destroyed. For better or worse, Hebrides no longer existed. Her surviving population was suddenly totally dependent upon the charity of others, the most demeaning circumstance in his planet's culture. Everyone was expected to work to support themselves, even pregnant women and disabled men. To do nothing, no matter how simple, to support oneself was no life for a Hebrides man. Or a woman.

And when we did take charity, he reminded himself, *we were determined to pay it back as soon as possible.*

"Not the only problem," Roach said, breaking into his thoughts. "I kept the new recruits aside, as you ordered, but their parents gave them a pretty hard time. A couple changed their minds and went with their families."

"They didn't take the oath," William said. He'd been offered a cooling-off period after he'd joined, but that period had ended when he'd taken the oath and committed himself. "They can change their minds later, if they wish."

"If their families let them," Roach said. "Captain, I don't understand your people."

"Family is important to them," William said gruffly. He shook his head, dismissing the question. "Start cleaning up the ship as soon as we get the remaining evacuees onto the shuttles," he ordered. "Get all the life support filters switched out as well. I think they're in tatters."

"Too much filth on the deck," Roach said. "We look worse than we did on *Uncanny*, Captain."

"We survived *Uncanny*," William said. "We'll survive *Thunderchild* too."

He nodded, then strode down the corridor, silently noting the scuff marks on the deck and countless other signs that his ship had been overburdened with evacuees. Teaching the young men not to urinate in corners had been hard enough, although the problem had practically vanished after he'd given a gruesome description of electricity traveling up a stream of urine and shocking a poor bastard. He doubted anything like that had actually happened, at least outside a pirate ship, but the story had been enough to keep the men from pissing in the corridors again. But they'd found plenty of other ways to be annoying.

His steward met him in his office, holding out a mug of coffee. William took it gratefully and then sat down at his desk and thumbed through the list of updates from Tyre. Countless civilian ships had been scooped up and forwarded to Hebrides, although he knew it wouldn't be enough. The civilians were likely to have problems transporting evacuees anywhere, he suspected. They didn't have a trained crew and marines to respond to trouble.

And if they can't handle the evacuees, he thought grimly, *they'll start refusing to take them onboard.*

That was a bitter thought. Everything they'd done, everything the Commonwealth was doing even now, was only a drop in the ocean. Hebrides was dead. Her survivors would never return to their homes, never repair the damage to their culture and society. And a dozen other worlds would follow his homeworld into death if the offensive continued.

But the offensive has to *continue,* he told himself. *We cannot let the Theocracy get away with it.*

A message blinked up in his display. Kat Falcone had invited him to dinner the following night. William was tempted to refuse, even though he knew declining would be an insult unless he had a very good excuse. He wasn't sure he wanted to face anyone right now. But, in the end, he keyed his console, sending a positive reply. He couldn't afford to wallow in self-pity, not when his crew needed him. They'd be going back to the war soon enough.

And the Theocracy may try to retake the offensive, he reminded himself. *Who knows what they'll do next?*

♦ ♦ ♦

Pat wasn't sure what he'd expected from the holding camps, but he wasn't too surprised when he and his troops flowed out of their shuttles to discover that they looked like basic marine barracks. Someone had taken prefabricated buildings that had been intended to serve as temporary housing on a colony world and erected them inside a fence, creating a cross between army barracks and prison camps. Pat had been in worse places during his long service, but he doubted the evacuees would like the barracks, which would be cramped, uncomfortable, and completely lacking in privacy.

"Colonel," a thin-lipped man said. He wore a militia uniform and carried himself in a manner that proved, beyond a shadow of a doubt, that he'd never seen combat. His boots were far too shiny for Pat's tastes. "I'm Major Jarrow, Evacuation Control Officer."

"A pleasure," Pat lied. Jarrow was a REMF, plain and simple. "How do you plan to distribute the evacuees?"

"We have three barracks for women in this camp, two barracks for men," Jarrow said. "Kids will be allowed to stay with their mothers, as long as they are younger than ten. Older boys will stay with their fathers. All evacuees will be entered in the database as soon as they land, then assigned a bunk. We'll brief them on how we expect them to comport themselves later."

Pat cocked his head. "And do you anticipate letting them *out* of the camp?"

"It depends on how they behave," Jarrow said. "If they behave themselves, they can explore the outside world. If not, they can stay here until we know where they're going."

"They're *people*," Pat reminded him sharply.

"And so are the people on this world," Jarrow snapped back. "There's already been some angry muttering about accepting so many refugees. It'll get worse if something, anything, happens to *really* make the locals mad."

Pat turned away to keep from punching Jarrow in the face. The hell of it was that the REMF had a point. Civilians were often charitable, but their willingness to be charitable was often dependent on the recipients behaving themselves. No one liked to see their donations being wasted, let alone watch helplessly as their towns and cities were transformed into dangerous wastelands. And the evacuees he'd supervised during the long trip had been prideful asses, reluctant to admit any dependency on the Commonwealth. These close quarters were a recipe for disaster.

"Check the buildings," he ordered his men. The first shuttles would be landing shortly. "If you have any concerns, bring them to me at once."

"There's nothing else," Jarrow said. "There's no way we can billet refugees on the local population."

"Bastards," Pat muttered. But, again, the REMF had a point. People tended to be reluctant to take complete strangers into their homes, particularly on Tyre. Trying to *force* the locals to take refugees would cause political problems. And perhaps riots. "We'll have to see what else we can organize."

The impression of walking into a prison camp only grew worse as he stepped into the closest barracks. If anything, the building was *worse* than the barracks he remembered from boot camp, a soulless monstrosity so bland and colorless that it would drive its occupants mad. Someone had the wit to collect books and entertainment terminals, but a quick glance at the titles was enough to tell him that they'd probably be tossed out by the vicars. He'd had to imprison a couple of men for beating a third man back on *Queen Elizabeth*. Their victim had been caught watching a very racy period drama dating all the way back to Old Earth.

He shook his head as he glanced into the washroom, making a mental note to arrange for extra toilets and washing supplies. No one ever had enough water in barracks. He still smiled at the memory of the sergeants teaching the new recruits how to wash by the numbers, but the evacuees wouldn't have anyone showing them how to wash. And they'd probably run short of water very quickly. He doubted the holding camp was part of the planet's water distribution network, and they were too far from the nearest city to make the connection feasible in a hurry.

There definitely is not enough water here, he thought. God alone knew what the poor bastards were going to do for food and drink. *Do we have enough of anything here?*

The remainder of the staff had already arrived, lining up as the first shuttle dropped down from orbit and landed neatly at the edge of the camp. Pat hurried to take up position with his men as the hatches opened, the wind blowing the stink towards the staffers. He couldn't help smiling at their shocked reactions, although he knew the situation wasn't really funny. They'd probably be filing complaints with their superiors about the disgraceful conditions. And they'd be right too, if the task force hadn't been more concerned with getting as many evacuees as possible off the surface to safer accommodations. He rather doubted the bean counters would take that into consideration when they were screaming about the whole affair.

"Line up," Jarrow ordered, using a megaphone to ensure he could be heard over the shouts of dismay. The evacuees were united in horror at the sight of their new homes. "Your details will be taken, then you can go straight to the barracks!"

Pat frowned as the mood rapidly darkened. The evacuees weren't happy at all, pushing and shoving as rough lines formed. None of the staffers looked pleased either as they struggled to record every last evacuee, including a number of children. Some of the husbands didn't seem to be pleased about their wives talking to other men. Pat decided that it was only a matter of time before violence broke out.

A planet of paradoxes, he decided, bracing himself. *Women who are both strong and weak at the same time; men who are domineering and yet unable to dominate.*

Pat cursed as he realized he'd made a mistake not coming in full armor. The armor would have been unpleasant if he and his marines had to stop a riot, but the intimidation factor alone might have kept the riot from happening.

He cursed again as an evacuee husband punched one of the staffers in the face, sending the man falling backwards. Others started to lash out too, the fight rapidly sliding out of control. Pat barked orders, drawing his stunner and hastily sweeping the weapon across the closest fighters. They tumbled to the ground, their bodies twitching unnaturally. The remainder of the evacuees drew back, clearly shocked. They weren't prisoners, they'd been assured, but they were being *treated* like prisoners.

"Line up," Pat ordered calmly. Showing weakness, any kind of weakness, would be a fatal mistake. "The staffers will take your details, then you can rest."

He ordered his men to carry the stunned evacuees out of the way, then flexi-cuffed them for later attention. A special camp would be set up for unruly evacuees, a prison camp. Idly, he wondered how anyone could hope to tell the difference. The remainder of the evacuees went through processing with surprising speed, then hurried into the barracks. He didn't need enhanced ears to hear their dismay.

There'll be more riots, he thought glumly as another shuttle landed. Hundreds of others were already on the way, stacking up until they had a chance to land. *We might lose control of an entire camp.*

"Thank you," Jarrow said, glancing at the prisoners. "Those fuckers . . ."

"Are probably sick of being treated like prisoners," Pat said. He'd met plenty of people with bullying tendencies, people who'd often become broken when faced with vastly superior force. They prided themselves on being men, but they didn't understand what that actually *meant*. "This camp needs to be improved."

Jarrow gave him an incredulous look. "You *do* realize how many refugees there *are* on those ships?"

"I helped to load them," Pat said. Another pair of shuttles screamed overhead. "What's your point?"

"My *point* is that even providing the basics for so many people has pushed us to the limit," Jarrow snapped. "Food and water, clothing, and other equipment. They're all in very short supply. I've put out a call for donations, but it will be days, at least, before more shit arrives for them. Until then, we have to do the best we can with what we have on hand."

"Of course," Pat agreed. The Commonwealth was rich, but getting vast amounts of supplies to the holding camps would take time. "But you don't have to rob them of their dignity."

"I don't care about their dignity," Jarrow said. "All I care about is keeping them alive and out of trouble."

"Yes," Pat agreed sarcastically. "Because losing control of a camp will *definitely* keep them out of trouble."

"And losing public support for the evacuation will be utterly disastrous," Jarrow said. "This isn't a relatively small number of refugees, Colonel. There are hundreds of thousands on the way. The public doesn't like it."

He turned and strode off. Pat watched him go, resisting the temptation to make a rude gesture at Jarrow's back. The hell of it was that Jarrow was right. If public support vanished, the camps would be closed down.

And what, he asked himself, would happen to the refugees then?

CHAPTER THIRTEEN

"There's nothing we can do," Kat said. "Supplies are already being pushed to the limit."

She sighed as she sat back in her chair. She'd invited both William and Pat to dinner, but the discussion had rapidly turned political. She supposed the development shouldn't have surprised her, not after the destruction of an entire planet. The Commonwealth's best attempts to cope with the crisis were *still* proving woefully inadequate.

"The barracks are overcrowded," Pat said softly. "It won't be long before there's a full-scale riot."

"And everyone is stuck in the camps," William added. "They can't even join the navy!"

Kat took a sip of her wine. She didn't blame either of them for siding with the refugees, but the briefs her father had sent her were depressingly blunt. The Battle of Hebrides had caused no end of economic damage to the Commonwealth as stock markets plummeted and resources were diverted to assist the survivors. The analysts had noted that the knock-on effects were likely going to cause all sorts of long-term problems. If a freighter owner-captain could lose his ship because it had been diverted to Hebrides, thus breaking his contract to deliver goods and supplies to their original destination, what would *that* do, particularly if it happened to more than one or two ships? It would be years before the problem was sorted out, years of uncertainty.

And who will want to invest in your own ship, she asked herself, *only to lose her for something that wasn't your fault?*

"I think we definitely need to open the local training centers to evacuees," she said. She had no idea why recruitment had flagged. Everyone agreed that young men from Hebrides made good recruits. "But there's little else we can do."

"I know that," William said. He sounded surprisingly petulant. "But the evacuees don't."

Kat felt a surge of sympathy. If *she'd* been in William's place, with Tyre destroyed and only a tiny fraction of her population surviving long enough to escape their homeworld, she would have been desperate to help them too. But she knew the cold hard facts of life that made solving the problem impossible. There was nothing she could do to ensure that the evacuees received better medical care, let alone anything else they needed. All she could do was pray that they were hastily moved on to a final destination.

William glanced at her. "Did you hear anything from the diplomats?"

"About a new homeworld?" Kat asked. "Nothing particularly new. Some planets have indicated they'll take a few thousand refugees, but no more. A couple of stage-one colonies have offered to accept more, yet they insist on the refugees meeting certain criteria. One of them wants every newcomer to convert to their religion before landing."

"And the other wants women and children alone," Pat said. "Bastards."

"Absorbing so many newcomers would be an absolute nightmare," Kat pointed out. "There's enough of them to form a separate society in their own right."

"And that would eventually lead to civil war," Pat finished. "I've seen that happen before, with far smaller populations."

"Our best bet would seem to be one of the under-settled worlds," Kat added. "But negotiations are proceeding slowly."

William gently put his wineglass down. "And what happens when the Theocracy destroys a second world?"

"I wish I knew," Kat admitted.

She had a nasty feeling she *did* know. The second world would be on its own, with barely a handful of people evacuated. The Commonwealth would be unable to put together a second evacuation fleet in time to do any good. And even if there was a fleet, where would the evacuees go?

"Rumor has it that some poor world is going to be forced to take the refugees," Pat commented. "Is that true?"

"I hope not," Kat said. The idea was tempting but would blow the entire Commonwealth out of the water. Planets could set their own immigration rates, according to the Commonwealth Charter. Forcing someone, even a stage-one colony world, to take hundreds of thousands of refugees would fragment the Commonwealth. "But it has to seem appealing to politicians on Tyre."

"Hebrides would not have reacted well to the suggestion," William admitted. "Can you imagine any other world accepting such a directive without a fight?"

"No," Kat said. "But what other solution *is* there?"

William shook his head. "Can we win the war before another world is destroyed?"

Kat had no idea. The details of Operation Hammer had remained a closely guarded secret, but it had been impossible to hide the arrival of four entire superdreadnought squadrons and hundreds of smaller ships. *Something* was in the works, even though hardly anyone knew the details. Rumors, some of them alarmingly accurate, had been circulating for days. She suspected that some of the rumors were already on their way to the Theocracy.

"I don't know the answer to that question," she said, finally. "The alternative is accepting the peace missive they sent us."

"And giving in to blackmail," Pat snapped. "We can't end the war on such terms."

"No," William said. "But what else can we do?"

"Push on," Kat said. "And hope for the best."

She ran her fingers through her hair. Her father's briefs stated that public opinion was veering wildly between pleading for bloody revenge and a demand for immediate peace. Thankfully, plenty of evidence maintained that the Theocracy couldn't be trusted to honor any peace treaty or the political debate would have been a great deal worse. As it stood, the prospect of an *enforceable* treaty would probably have been enough to swing most of the government behind peace. But enforcing such a treaty was impossible without beating the Theocracy into submission.

There's no way we could trust them to keep the peace, she told herself. *They'll be at our throats again as soon as they rebuild their fleets.*

"I hope you're right," William said. He reached for his glass and took another sip. Kat wondered again, suddenly, if her friend might be drinking more than he should. "Did you manage to get your flagship cleaned?"

"Barely," Kat said. "Captain Higgins was most unhappy."

"I must go see her," William mused. "It's been too long." He cleared his throat. "Good thing the IG isn't planning any inspections anytime soon," he added. "We'd all be in the doghouse."

Kat grinned. The *Uncanny* disaster had shaken the Inspectorate General badly, what little of it that had survived Admiral Morrison and First Cadiz. She'd heard rumors that a number of inspectors had been ordered to resign or face court-martial for gross incompetence. And while she knew that strings had been pulled to keep the inspectors from taking a close look at *Uncanny*, she found it hard to feel sorry for the bastards. Every captain with half a brain dreaded an inspection. They did everything within their power to keep the inspectors as far from their ships as possible.

"We have a war to fight," she said. "The inspectors can go hang."

"So we are going to be taking the offensive," William said. He sounded pleased by the notion. "Anywhere special?"

"Ask Admiral Christian," Kat said. "Or wait until the formal announcement."

"You should watch yourself," William warned. His voice suddenly sounded a great deal steadier. "People have been noticing that you've been spending a lot of time with Admiral Christian."

Kat swore under her breath. Nineteen commodores were under Admiral Christian's command, commanding officers of superdread-nought or battlecruiser squadrons, but *she* was the only one involved with planning Operation Hammer. And she was also the youngest, the one with least seniority, even though the nine ships under her direct command were the most powerful in the fleet. She had, quite by accident, probably put a great many noses out of joint.

"I can't help what the rumor mill says," she said, irritated. "No one in their right mind believes the crap that passes for news these days."

She put her wineglass down before she accidentally broke it. Being born a Falcone had ensured that she would be a public figure, even if she wanted privacy. And her career had made her interesting even to eminently *sensible* men and women who didn't read tabloid rags discussing the lives of the aristocracy. Her name had been romantically linked with everyone from King Hadrian to Duke Rogers. She frowned, fighting to keep her anger under control. Duke Rogers was old enough to be her grandfather. The idea of marrying him . . .

"People will say what they say," she said. Her father had advised her to keep that in mind the day she'd discovered a reporter had written nearly three thousand words about the dress she'd worn to her sister's birthday party. "But reality is quite different."

"I know that," William said. He finished his wine and put the glass down on the table. "But you are causing comment."

"I'll survive," Kat said, bluntly. She didn't dare look at Pat to see how he was taking the discussion. It still puzzled her that none of the tabloids had realized they were in a relationship, even though he'd stayed at the mansion several times. Maybe they'd refused to believe such a romance was possible. Pat was depressingly boring compared to her sister Candy's love interests. "And we *still* have a war to fight."

William nodded. "With your permission, I'll go find Fran before returning to *Thunderchild*," he said. "It's been too long since I've seen her."

"Of course," Kat said. "I'm sure she'll be glad to see you."

She rose and gave William a hug, feeling the tension in his body. No *wonder* he'd been drinking, although she hoped he was smart enough to take a sober-up pill before going on duty. Commander Roach otherwise would have to relieve William of his command, something that would probably end with both men in front of a court-martial. William would definitely lose his command, but Roach would probably lose all chance of a command of his own too. The Admiralty tended to frown on commanding officers being relieved by their subordinates.

"Don't worry about it," Pat said once William had stepped through the hatch. "The rumor mill is full of nonsense."

Kat nodded, although she couldn't help feeling annoyed. She'd heard plenty of absurd stories passed on so many times that the grain of truth was buried under a mountain of bullshit. But a rumor that could cause damage to her career was a serious matter. She couldn't have people genuinely thinking she was sleeping with Admiral Christian.

Her expression darkened. Technically, the relationship wouldn't be *quite* against naval regulations. *Technically*. She might have been one of his subordinate commanders, but she wasn't under his direct command. And yet, she would have a major problem if Admiral Christian's *other* subordinates believed he was showing her favoritism. It didn't help that her career had *already* benefited from favoritism.

"I flew into a pirate lair, seemingly alone," she muttered. "And they *still* believe I didn't earn my rank."

"I think that most people got the message after you planned the escape from Cadiz," Pat said sardonically. He rose and walked over to stand next to her, wrapping his arm around her shoulders. "Captain Higgins hasn't given you any problems, has she?"

Kat shook her head. Fran Higgins had been XO on HMS *Defiant* back before the desperate flight from Cadiz. She'd risked court-martial by siding with Kat and William, knowing that Admiral Morrison would disapprove of any preparations to abandon the system. Thankfully, she'd been cleared of any plans to mutiny as the post-battle assessment uncovered just how badly Admiral Morrison had failed the Royal Navy. And she'd stayed in command of *Defiant* until she'd been transferred to *Queen Elizabeth*.

And she's still in command of her own ship, Kat thought. She couldn't help but feel a flicker of jealousy. *I won't be a commander ever again.*

Kat took Pat's arm and pulled him through the hatch into the bedroom. Lucy would clear up the mess, then put out coffee for the following morning. Pat seemed to move slowly, as if he were tired and depressed. Kat couldn't really blame him.

"Pat," she said quietly. "How bad *is* it down there?"

"Nightmarish," Pat said. "There just aren't enough accommodations for everyone, Kat. That's the blunt truth. The refugees are sharing bunks designed for one person, privacy is a joke, we've already had a couple of near-riots because of the water and food shortages. And it's only going to get worse."

"I know," Kat said. "The staffers down there are doing everything they can." She sat down on the bed. "I wish there was something more we could do," she added, "but what?"

"You're planning a major offensive," Pat said. He looked down at her. "We're going straight for Ahura Mazda, aren't we?"

Kat hesitated. She wasn't supposed to talk about Operation Hammer with anyone outside the planning cell, but Pat knew her well enough to tell if she was lying to him. Hell, merely hesitating had probably been enough to confirm that he was right. And she didn't want to lie to him.

"Yes," she said. She looked back at him. "That isn't going any further, understand?"

"Yeah," Pat said.

She closed her eyes for a long moment, silently cursing the Theocracy. What had happened to the marine who'd never hesitated to take her to bed whenever they could both find the time? The atrocity on Hebrides had stolen him, leaving a stranger with his face standing in front of her. She'd seen war take a toll on men and women before, leaving them torn and broken, but this was different. Pat had never been afraid to risk his life, yet watching hundreds of thousands of people forced to flee their homes had damaged him.

"No one is meant to know, not yet," she said. "How did you figure it out?"

Pat smiled, humorlessly. "General Winters is calling in troops from all over the sector," he said. "Training programs for forced landing and urban combat are being shoved into gear. I think every last marine in the sector will be here in a couple of weeks. That's a hell of a lot of troops to liberate a world, which suggested that we had a bigger target in mind. And Ahura Mazda itself is top of the short list."

He sat down next to her, looking oddly out of place. "I want to take the lead," he said. "I want to be in the first shuttle heading down to the surface."

Kat frowned. "General Winters will have to authorize it," she said. "But you're one of the most experienced officers in the corps."

She contemplated the problem for a long moment. It wouldn't be *difficult* to pull strings on his behalf. Admiral Christian would certainly listen to her. And General Winters would recognize that Pat had the skills and experience needed. But sending him into the fire wasn't something she *wanted* to do. She wanted to keep him safe.

But there's no safety in the military, she thought. She'd put her life at risk countless times, but the marines had it worse. Pat had never had a million-ton starship wrapped around him when he'd closed with the enemy. *And he needs to get to grips with the bastards.*

"We'll see," she said.

She turned her head and kissed him, hard. For a moment, he didn't respond . . . and then he kissed her back, as if something had suddenly been unleashed. He pushed her down on the bed and rolled over until he was on top of her, his lips hovering just over hers. She wrapped her arms around him, pulling him down for another kiss. His tongue flicked in and out of her mouth, teasing her as his hands pulled her shirt out of her belt and ran up to caress her breasts.

Afterwards, Kat held Pat tightly as he slept, feeling a strange mixture of satisfaction and concern. His behavior was odd, worryingly odd. And yet, there was nothing she could do about it. She knew all too well that his problems were something he had to work through on his own, that he wouldn't appreciate any help she might have offered.

And he wants to lead the landing party, she thought. *He needs to lead the landing party.*

She must have dozed off because the next thing she heard was an urgent beeping from the intercom. Pat had shifted in his sleep, one leg resting on top of her; she pushed it away and sat upright, keying the intercom sharply.

"Commodore," Wheeler said. He sounded reassuringly alert, even though a glance at her timer told her it was only 0702. "Admiral Christian requests your presence onboard *Hammerhead*. There have been developments."

Kat's lips thinned. "Developments?"

"That's what he said, Commodore," Wheeler said.

"Have my shuttle prepared," Kat said. She stood, hearing Pat sit upright behind her. "I'll be with him as soon as possible."

She glanced at Pat. "Duty calls," she said. Pat could stay in the suite as long as he wanted, at least until he had to go on duty himself. "Try and make sure you get plenty of sleep."

"I'll sleep when I'm dead," Pat said. He sounded more like his old self. She felt a flicker of amusement. Perhaps she should have just dragged him into bed instead of letting him get depressed. There were sex workers on Tyre who claimed that getting laid did wonders for one's morale. "Try not to let the rumors get to you."

"I'll try," Kat said. She grinned as he stood, remembering their night together. "And you know what? I'll succeed."

CHAPTER FOURTEEN

The giant auditorium on the orbital battlestation was easily large enough to hold every commanding officer attached to the fleet, Kat decided, as she followed Admiral Christian into the massive compartment. By tradition, every captain and commodore should have attended in person, but a good third of them had been ordered to remain on their ships, just in case the Theocracy picked exactly the wrong moment to launch an attack. It was unlikely that the enemy would risk an attack, yet it was better to be paranoid than dead.

She sucked in her breath as she saw the assembled rows of captains, then hurried down to take her place in the front row. Sixth Fleet had been the most powerful formation in the Royal Navy even before the reinforcements had arrived; now, she was the single most powerful fleet in space by a very large margin. She represented such a concentration of military power that her ultimate success seemed assured, no matter what obstacles the enemy might throw in her way. And Admiral Christian, her commanding officer, was one of the most powerful men in the galaxy.

Not that running the fleet is easy, Kat thought ruefully. Squadron command could be tricky at times; she had to issue orders while carefully *not* stepping on toes. The line between a commodore's responsibilities and a captain's could not be crossed. *As admiral of them all, Christian has all the problems I have and then some.*

She sat, knowing the burden of command was a great deal heavier for her Theocratic counterparts. She could hardly imagine serving as a captain with a religious busybody peering over her shoulder, questioning each and every order she gave . . . not that she'd have had the chance if she'd been born into the Theocracy. Princess Drusilla's debriefings had made that quite clear. In the Theocracy, aristocratic women were suitable for nothing more than marriage alliances, used to link various families together. They didn't get to say no. Princess Drusilla had been astonishingly lucky to escape, so lucky that some intelligence officers suspected a scam. But Kat had seen enough of the enemy's thinking to know that questioning orders, particularly orders from their leadership, was not recommended. A person with nerve could go a very long way just by citing nonexistent orders from the very top.

"Thank you for coming," Admiral Christian said as he took his place at the stand. The hatches closed and locked, sealing the compartment. Anyone who was late wouldn't be able to enter. "I don't think I need to mention that everything discussed in this meeting is to remain strictly confidential, but regulations require me to remind you anyway."

A low ripple of amusement ran through the chamber. Kat smiled, remembering just how many copies of the same security agreements and understandings she'd had to sign as she climbed her way towards her first command. ONI harped on security, reminding officers time and time again that loose lips sank ships. And they were right, she knew. A careless word in the wrong place could prove disastrous.

"As of now, McCaughey Naval Base is going into lockdown," Admiral Christian bluntly continued. "All messages intended to go out-system will be held in communications buffers, unless cleared by my intelligence staff. Messages flowing into the system will be distributed as normal, but replies—of course—may be delayed."

Kat made a face. *That* wasn't going to be popular. Spacers understood that communications could often be delayed, but her crews had grown used to sending recorded messages back home via StarCom. Relationships were going to be damaged, even though families should understand the realities of a naval career. She'd had to comfort a number of young officers back when she'd been an XO, either reminding them of the practicalities or consoling them after they'd received a "Dear John" letter. There had been times when she'd honestly thought that everyone who sent such a letter should be tried for treason. The missives always sent morale plummeting.

Of course they did, she thought sardonically. *Watching a crewmate receive a good-bye letter only reminded others that they too could receive such a letter.*

She sat upright as a giant star chart appeared, floating over Admiral Christian's head like a halo. Another murmur ran through the compartment as the officers took in the tactical outline, giant red arrows leading through the Gap and stabbing straight towards Ahura Mazda. Smaller arrows followed the main body through the Gap, but broke off immediately afterwards, heading in all directions. Clearly, every system possessing a StarCom was marked down for attention.

"Operation Hammer," Admiral Christian said. "The operation that will make or break this war."

He nodded to an aide standing before the front row. "Suzy?"

Suzy—a lieutenant commander, Kat noted—didn't seem too intimidated at being the most junior officer in the room. She took Admiral Christian's place and adjusted the display, focusing on the hundreds of tactical icons surrounding McCaughey. Fifteen squadrons of superdreadnoughts, with more on the way; three hundred and seventy smaller ships, ranging from battlecruisers to destroyers and troop transports. It was an impressive sight. Intellectually, Kat had known that, but seeing the entire fleet lined up brought its magnitude home to her.

"Operation Hammer is broken into four successive stages," Suzy said. Her voice was calm, very composed. The map updated as she spoke. "First, we will clear the minefields and punch through the Gap. Second, once we are in enemy space, smaller squadrons will be detached to attack and destroy the enemy's remaining StarComs while the remainder of the fleet advances on Ahura Mazda. Third, the space-based defenses of Ahura Mazda, including its mobile units, will be destroyed. Fourth, and finally, ground forces will be landed to secure and occupy the planet itself."

She paused. "A *rational* foe would surrender immediately after losing control of the high orbitals," she continued. "We cannot, however, count on the Theocracy doing anything of the sort. They may believe, somehow, that there is still a hope of final victory. Therefore, our landing elements include enough troops to take and hold territory on the ground, with or without orbital fire support."

Kat sucked in her breath. The Commonwealth had a great deal of experience with counterinsurgency deployments, but a full-scale planetary invasion? Historically, there had *never* been a full-scale invasion, not when orbital fire support ensured that any mobile enemy formations could be effortlessly smashed. The landings on Hebrides had been the closest the Commonwealth had come to a full-scale invasion, and *they* had ended badly.

But the Theocrats wouldn't be mad enough to blow up their own home-world, she told herself. *Would they?*

"We will, of course, attempt to convince them to surrender," Suzy said. "Surrender terms have already been worked out that will give the bad guys *something*, even as they ensure that the Theocracy will never be a threat to us or anyone else again. But we have to proceed on the assumption that they will not surrender, that they will never surrender until we have occupied every last square inch of their homeworld and captured or killed their leadership."

She took a breath. "Deployment orders are as follows . . ."

Kat leaned back in her chair as Suzy worked her way through the disparate squadrons and assigned them to task forces within the giant fleet. A number of commanding officers were looking pleased at the prospect of independent commands, even if they did have strict orders merely to destroy the enemy's StarComs and then break contact. Shattering the enemy's communications network was a risk, if only because the Commonwealth had no way to know what contingency plans the enemy might have drawn up, but there was no choice. One way or the other, the Theocracy was going down.

"The fleet train will consist of over a thousand transports of various classes," Suzy concluded. "Chief among them will be a trio of mobile StarCom units."

A low rustle ran through the compartment. Kat had to smile, knowing how *she'd* reacted when she'd heard the news. It was interesting to know that the Commonwealth had taken the concept and actually made it work, after she'd captured the first mobile StarCom unit from the Theocracy. Yet the announcement wasn't entirely *good* news. Being able to update Tyre constantly, in real time, about the progress of the campaign was one thing, but having Tyre constantly micromanaging was quite another. Admiral Christian might be the *last* admiral to enjoy a truly independent command.

And then the king and his cabinet will feel they can start issuing orders directly to the ships, she thought numbly. *Who knows what will happen then?*

"Their bandwidth does not, as yet, allow for real-time conversations," Suzy said. "As a general rule, their capacity for sending messages is roughly comparable to a Type-I StarCom unit. The engineers keep promising that they can improve and update the systems, but as yet they have produced no workable tech."

Which might be for the best, Kat thought. *But someone can micromanage through emails too.*

Admiral Christian nodded as Suzy finished her presentation. "Thank you," he said. "Are there any questions before we proceed?"

No one said a word. Kat wasn't too surprised. They'd need time to digest what they'd heard before they started asking questions. The planning cell had done its best to address all the potential problems, but she doubted they'd found *all* of them. Some problems would only become apparent, she knew from experience, when they actually took the fleet to war.

Even flying so many ships in formation will be tricky, she thought. *And we will be very detectable as we fly through the Gap.*

She looked up at the star chart, remembering long patrols before the storm finally broke over Cadiz. The whims of hyperspace had created two semipermanent energy storms between the Commonwealth and the Theocracy, forcing all starships intent on crossing from one to the other to pass through the Gap, the lone passage through the storms. The route wasn't nearly as bad as trying to slip past the Seven Sisters, but it was one of the few places in hyperspace that could be solidly mined. The Theocracy hadn't hesitated to take advantage of the opportunity to block the shortest passage into their territory.

And we're going to be punching through, she reminded herself. Clearing a normal minefield was easy, but picking their way through one in hyperspace would be much harder. *It might be time to write a new will.*

General Gerry Winters took the stand. "Once the fleet has cleared the high orbitals," he said, "we will attempt a landing on the planetary surface. This will be a very difficult task. Long-range scans indicate that the planet is heavily fortified. We do not want to get into a duel with ground-based defenses, particularly as we do not want to damage the planet itself. Once we have isolated a potential landing zone, we will send the first body of marines through the firestorm and establish a base camp, funneling in supplies and expanding our grip on the local settlements."

He paused. "I do not pretend that this will be easy," he warned. "The enemy will move at once to crush our landing parties before they can be reinforced. We expect them to deploy nuclear weapons, as a last resort, to obliterate our footholds. They may also deploy chemical or biological weapons, despite the risks to their own populations. Any failure to reinforce our forces may result in their destruction."

Kat shuddered. She'd seen the medical reports after the refugees from Ahura Mazda had been examined. They'd had no genetic improvements at all, not even the enhanced immune systems that were commonplace almost everywhere else. A biological weapon might be largely harmless to the groundpounders, but run riot among the Theocracy's own population? Billions of people could die.

Chemical weapons won't be any better, she thought. *They could poison their own world for generations to come.*

"Our current plan is to reinforce to the maximum possible extent, then advance directly on the Tabernacle," General Winters stated. "However, a great deal depends on the situation we find when we land. I am reluctant to commit ourselves to any definite operational plan when we may find anything from a disintegrating society to a fanatical refusal to give up any ground. Our plans may have to be updated or even dumped entirely at short notice."

There was a long pause. "Any questions?"

Captain Andrew Dawlish held up a hand. "What about the civilians?"

General Winters looked concerned. "It depends," he said. "We will not be landing trained Civil Affairs units in the first and second invasion waves. Ideally, we will tell the civilians to remain under cover and stay out of the way. Practically, we may see anything from millions of people trying to flee the war zone to thousands of fanatics doing everything in their power to steer the civilians towards us. The . . . issues . . . with feeding millions of civilians will be quite serious."

Kat nodded. Ahura Mazda was, if anything, overpopulated. Food was one of the many things in short supply, even though mass-producing ration bars wasn't exactly difficult. The Theocracy could have bought or stolen the technology years ago. But an invasion—and a full-scale war—would almost certainly disrupt food shipments so badly that entire cities would starve. The Theocracy kept its population under tight control, yet the threat of starvation would undermine the government's power. And who knew what would happen then?

"Our first priority is to end the war," General Winters said. "Taking care of their civilians . . . is very much a secondary priority."

"The media will love that," someone muttered.

"We're not here to please the press," General Winters said bluntly. "We're here to win."

Admiral Christian returned to the stand. "We will certainly do everything in our power to assist the locals, once the war is over," he said. "Until then, winning comes first."

Kat kept her face impassive through sheer force of will. She had no compunction about killing enemy fighters, even ones who couldn't return fire. They were the servants of the Theocracy, men charged with enforcing its will. But slaughtering countless innocent civilians, directly or indirectly, was something else. Rebuilding Ahura Mazda and putting its economy on a more stable footing would be an utter nightmare. And after everything the Commonwealth had suffered in the war, public support from Tyre would be minimal.

Rebuilding our own worlds comes first, she thought. *And any government that says otherwise is going to lose power very quickly.*

She listened quietly as Admiral Christian ran through the final details, including a grueling exercise schedule that would hopefully work all the bugs out of the system before the fleet departed for its final mission. Then, he dismissed the remainder of the officers. Kat watched, unsure if she should be pleased or concerned by being asked to remain behind. She'd played a major role in planning the operation, but it was now out of her hands. *Everyone* would be trying to add their own wrinkle to the final plan.

And we'll probably have to improvise when we find out what the enemy is planning, she thought as she joined Admiral Christian under the display. It was repeating the original plan, showing countless starships heading towards their targets. *They'll do everything in their power to throw us off their homeworld.*

"Kat," Admiral Christian said, "do you have any final comments on the plan?"

"Nothing I haven't already said," Kat told him. "We have enough firepower to accomplish our objective, and even if we don't, we can still accomplish our secondary objective."

Admiral Christian nodded. "I'm assigning our remaining stockpiles of the new missiles to the StarCom squadrons," he said. "They're going to need every edge they can get."

Kat nodded in reluctant agreement. Losing the missiles was annoying, but losing the opportunity to take out the enemy communications network would be far worse. They *couldn't* allow the Theocracy to keep a working StarCom. If nothing else, the Theocracy would shatter if its masters lost the ability to send messages from place to place instantly. The transmission delay would buy the Commonwealth time to start mopping up the other worlds one by one.

"Yes, sir," she said.

"I've had word from Tyre," Admiral Christian told her. They stepped through the hatch and into a smaller office. A steaming pot of coffee and a selection of pastries were already waiting for them on the desk. "First, they've approved my request to make you my second for the operation."

"Yes, sir," Kat said, again.

She had to fight to keep from showing any reaction. Fleet command at such a young age, even if she was merely the *second*-in-command . . . everyone would *know* it was nepotism. Add that to the rumors about

Admiral Christian and she being lovers . . . the appointment could cause problems. But she'd just have to overcome the problems. She'd proved herself often enough, hadn't she?

"Second, there's been a development," Admiral Christian continued. "ONI has, for reasons of its own, strongly suggested that we take Admiral Junayd with us. They believe he might be able to rally support on Ahura Mazda."

"They *believe*," Kat said. She wasn't sure she wanted Admiral Junayd anywhere near her ship. "Do they have any *reason* to believe it?"

"They insist they do," Admiral Christian told her. "He'll be traveling with a pair of handlers. I'd like him to remain on *Queen Elizabeth*."

It was not, Kat knew, a request. And yet she wanted to argue. Admiral Junayd had come far too close to blowing her and her ship out of space. *And* he'd planned the attack on Cadiz that had started the war. His defection didn't change the simple fact that he'd fought as hard as he could for the other side. He couldn't be trusted completely.

But she knew it was definitely not a request.

"Yes, sir," she said, reluctantly. "I'll make him comfortable."

CHAPTER FIFTEEN

"Sir! Enemy sniper!"

Pat hit the ground as a bullet cracked over his head. Cursing, he crawled into cover as a hail of machine-gun fire split the air, slashing through the sniper's estimated position. A body fell off the building and plummeted down to the ground, striking the solid concrete with an audible thud. Pat rose to his knees, hastily scanning his surroundings for more enemy soldiers before getting to his feet and slipping forward. Remaining still in an urban environment was just asking to get killed.

He tongued his voder. "Bring up the reinforcements," he ordered. "We're going to need them."

"Yes, sir," the sergeant said.

Pat shook his head as he surveyed the scene. Countless apartment blocks, so primitive they didn't even have plastic or glass windows, let alone hot or cold running water; dozens of ruined cars and vans surrounded by piles of foul-smelling rubbish. The stench of burning hydrocarbons hung in the air, a mocking reminder that Ahura Mazda didn't have fusion power cells in common use. It wasn't something he'd smelled on any of the Commonwealth's worlds.

Poor bastards, he thought. *Growing up in a place like this.*

He led his men forward, feeling the prickle at the back of his spine that suggested they were being watched. There were just too many open windows, too many dark corners that could be used to hide a sniper . . . or worse. His eyes scanned from side to side, hunting for prospective threats and targets. Intelligence had warned him that the enemy had a terrorist cell operating within the sector, but intelligence had been wrong before.

A movement. He swung around just in time to see a young girl shuffle into view. She couldn't be any older than ten, not on Ahura Mazda. The Theocrats would have insisted that she be veiled if she'd been old enough to bear children. He stopped, just for a second, at the helpless look in her eyes. Her clothes were rags; her body was thin, so thin that he doubted that she'd live long enough to make it to adult-hood. And then he saw the bomb on her back.

He threw himself into cover a second before the bomb detonated. A wave of heat passed over his head; he rolled over hastily, bringing up his rifle as fire poured down at them from both sides of the street. He snapped a pair of shots back towards a visible enemy soldier, then dug into cover and glanced back at his squad. Two of his men had been caught in the blast and killed, three more had been badly injured. And there was nothing left of the girl who had carried the bomb.

Pat felt sick as he removed a grenade from his belt, slotted it into his grenade launcher and prepared to fire it into the nearest building. There was something unbearably filthy about a fighting force that was prepared to use children to carry bombs, pointing them at their tar-gets like a self-guiding missile. The girl hadn't understood what she'd been carrying, he hoped; they'd sent her to her death without a second thought. And the attack would make his people more paranoid, more willing to shoot at every shadow without verifying their targets. The enemy had plumbed new depths of horror.

He fired the grenade into the nearest window, then launched two more, readying a fourth as the first three detonated in quick succession.

Billowing explosions tore through the building, sending it toppling inwards and collapsing into a pile of rubble. Great clouds of dust drifted up from the remains, floating northwards as the wind changed. Pat allowed himself a moment of surprise—he hadn't thought the structures were *that* fragile—then led the way into the other building. Two enemy soldiers, hastily rigging another bomb, were shot down before they had a chance to react. The rattling sound from upstairs suggested that there were more enemy soldiers on the way. They *had* to know the marines had broken into the building.

"No grenades," he snapped. If one apartment block was so fragile, the others were probably in no better state. "Guns only."

He shot the first man plunging down the stairs, his body falling the rest of the way and landing badly. The bastard was wearing civilian clothes instead of a military uniform, he noted. No doubt he'd hoped to blend into the crowds and escape. Two more followed, only to be gunned down in turn. And then the entire building shook violently, pieces of dust and plaster dropping from the ceiling. Pat cursed and ordered his men to leave, taking one last look at the lower floor before following them out the door. How could anyone live like this?

Simple, his own thoughts answered. *They don't have a choice.*

The building creaked behind them, then crumbled into another pile of rubble. Pat saw a body within the debris, twitching helplessly before it was hidden behind the dust. The poor bastard didn't stand a chance. Pat gritted his teeth, allowing himself a moment of relief as reinforcements arrived, spearheaded by five light tanks. Compared to most of the weapons the defenders were using, the tanks were effectively invulnerable.

The marines took a moment to catch their breath, then advanced again. The tanks had left a hell of a mess in their paths, using plasma cannons to clear buildings of enemy snipers. Their blasts had left the buildings burning brightly, incinerating anyone unlucky enough to be trapped inside. Pat kept his distance from the flames, keeping a wary eye on the jumping shadows. The enemy might not be able to match the tanks face to face, but they'd certainly try to get behind the advancing forces and take them from the rear. They'd know the tanks couldn't be everywhere.

But the tanks are making a hell of a mess, he thought as the colossal machines crushed their way through a barricade, sending enemy fighters scurrying in all directions. *It takes a brave man to stand up to an unstoppable tank.*

He froze as he saw the car, parked on the other side of the barricade. The tank was driving right past it . . . he tongued his mouthpiece to sound the alert, but it was already too late. A giant explosion shook the ground, picking up the tank and hurling it end over end into a building, which promptly collapsed on top of the vehicle. Moments later, mortar shells started landing around the advancing forces, two clearly smart enough to seek out the remaining tanks. Both tanks ground to a halt, one so badly damaged it would have to be dragged back to the repair yard. Pat snapped orders as a line of enemy fighters appeared, rushing towards the marines as if they expected to drag them down by sheer force of numbers.

He couldn't help feeling a surge of horror as he saw their faces. Most of the advancing enemy fighters didn't *want* to be there, didn't *want* to be throwing their lives away. Many of them weren't even armed with anything more dangerous than kitchen knives! But the red-clad men in the rear were driving them forward, using neural whips to encourage any stragglers not to dawdle. Pat snapped orders, instructing his men to target the Inquisitors, but he knew it was *far* too late. The pressure of the men behind them would force the ones in the front to keep going.

"Call in a gas strike," he snapped. "Knock them out!"

His men opened fire, trying desperately to keep the crowd from getting any closer. Hundreds of bodies fell to the ground, each bullet striking two or three people. And yet they kept coming, climbing over their comrades' bodies to get to his men. Grenades fell among the mob, blasts killing dozens. It didn't slow them. He swore as his rifle clicked empty, then desperately prepared to fight as the enemy reached them.

"End program," a quiet voice ordered.

The scene froze. Pat allowed himself a long breath, then turned to face General Winters. The "dead" men stood up, staggering slightly as they headed for the edge of the training zone. Pat watched them go, silently grateful for the mixture of holographic images and robots that allowed him and his men to train so thoroughly. It was better to make mistakes in a training simulation, rather than on the battlefield. And yet, the image of the dead girl threatened to haunt his dreams for the rest of his life.

"General," he said. "That could have gone better."

"It could," General Winters agreed. "Losing pretty much the entire company is not a good thing."

Pat nodded, not bothering to deny the statement. The whole disaster wouldn't have happened if his men had been in armor, but the exercise planners had insisted on deploying without armor, claiming that being unarmored would give the marines a better understanding of their surroundings. Pat had to admit they had a point, yet things had gone spectacularly to hell. But he kept that to himself. General Winters would not be impressed by anything that sounded like whining.

"We underestimated their willingness to use their own people as expendable assets," Pat said instead. He'd have thumped any marine who dared suggest using a *child* as a mobile bomb delivery system. The sheer horror was beyond him. "And we underestimated their willingness to soak up losses just to draw us into a trap."

"All our reports suggest that our planners may be underestimating their willingness to expend their own people," General Winters said. He turned and strode towards the edge of the zone, motioning for Pat to follow him. "They've certainly shown no hesitation to risk lives in the past."

Pat nodded. No one joined the Marine Corps to be *safe*. His commanders had known, no matter how little they'd wanted to admit it, that there might come a time when they would have to sacrifice some of their men to save the others. But they'd never wantonly thrown lives away. If nothing else, each marine represented a year's worth of expensive training that shouldn't be wasted lightly. And the experience marines gathered, after a few deployments, was worth its weight in gold.

But most of the civilians are worthless to the Theocrat leaders, he thought, glancing back at the pile of bodies. The exercise coordinators would take great pleasure, he was sure, in telling them *precisely* how many civilians they'd killed. *The Theocrats don't care about their own people.*

"The planning for the operation continues apace," General Winters continued. "Based on your experiences, do you have any suggestions?"

"Only that we try to get as large a force down to the surface as possible," Pat said. "And ideally we should attempt to establish a landing zone well away from a spaceport."

General Winters didn't look pleased. Landing and unloading the fleet of shuttlecraft would be a great deal easier if they had a spaceport. But the Theocracy had had plenty of time to rig a nuclear demolition charge under any of their facilities. Pat wouldn't put it past them to *let* the marines land, then blow them to hell as soon as the spaceport started receiving shuttles. The trick would be enough to defeat the entire operation.

"That won't be easy," General Winters said. "But I take your point."

He shrugged. "And it does, of course, raise the question of precisely *where* we land."

Pat understood. He'd read every last intelligence report on Ahura Mazda that he could find, but none of them had been particularly detailed. Ideally, the landing zone should be within easy reach of the Tabernacle, yet far enough from any enemy garrisons that they could get down on the ground and dug in before the first enemy counterattack materialized. Spacers and government officials rarely understood that planets were *big*. A landing on the other side of Ahura Mazda might go unopposed, but it would take months to march around the planet to reach their final destination, giving the Theocracy plenty of time to prepare its countermoves.

"We may have to wait until we get there to make a final decision," he said. "Do you have a prospect in mind?"

"I have five," General Winters said. "But the facts on the ground will determine just how we proceed."

"We simply don't have enough data," Pat agreed. "Do we have any infiltration units handy?"

"Just a few," General Winters said. "But we don't know how well they'll fit in with their surroundings."

Pat couldn't disagree. The refugees had been more than willing to discuss the ins and outs of Ahura Mazda, their words making it very clear that nonconformity rarely went undetected for more than a few days. Homosexuals were sniffed out and executed; women were kept uneducated—even teaching one's daughters to *read* was against the law. And yet some women seemed to rise high in the science fields. It was a contradiction he couldn't even begin to unravel.

Maybe they're less concerned about enforcing the law on upper-class women, he thought. *It isn't as if the scum at the bottom know how their betters live.*

"They'll do the best they can," he said.

"Of course," General Winters said.

He paused, turning to face Pat. "I understand that you requested the honor of leading the first landing force?"

Pat hesitated. "Yes, sir."

General Winters studied him for a long moment. He was an experienced officer, one of the most experienced in the corps. Pat knew, without a shadow of a doubt, that General Winters would have rejected him out of hand if Pat *hadn't* been able to do the job. And yet, even *with* experience in landing on hostile worlds, General Winters might not want to bow to any form of political pressure. That would set a bad precedent.

"You'll have it," General Winters said finally. "I just hope it doesn't kill you."

"Thank you, sir," Pat said.

"Thank me when you get home," General Winters said. "Not a moment before."

He turned away. "I expect a detailed plan for the landing by the end of the week, one that can be modified, updated, or scrapped at a moment's notice," he added. "You understand, better than anyone else, the importance of getting a large force down as quickly as possible. Make sure you get the logistics officers involved immediately. They'll tell you what you can get down without a spaceport."

"Yes, sir," Pat said.

"And don't fuck up," General Winters added. "It'll get a lot of people killed."

Despite the awesome responsibility that had been dropped in his lap, Pat couldn't help a flicker of anticipation as his superior strode away. Landing on the Theocracy's homeworld, taking the first step towards ending the war—he couldn't resist the challenge. And yet, failure would be disastrous, personally and politically. The only consolation was that he probably wouldn't be alive to see it.

He walked out of the training zone and straight towards his office. Hundreds of newly arrived militiamen were running around the race-track or carrying their rifles to and from the firing ranges. He could hear an endless stream of gunshots in the distance as the newcomers sighted their weapons and then practiced their aiming. They'd be going onto the main training field in a few days, he knew, once they were ready. For most of them, the giant facilities on McCaughey would be their first true taste of combat.

Or as close to it as possible, Pat thought. He'd been in *real* engagements that had been less violent than some of the simulations. But hard training tended to lead to easy missions. *And when they're ready, they'll be boarding the transports for their first target.*

He paused as the sound of shooting grew louder. Those taking accounts would be furious when they realized just how many millions of rounds had been shot off in the last few weeks, although the giant industrial nodes orbiting McCaughey hadn't had any trouble keeping up with demand. Bullets were relatively cheap, after all. They were certainly cheaper than militiamen. Better to expend thousands upon thousands of bullets preparing each unit for war than risk losing the entire unit because it didn't know how to handle itself in battle.

Pushing the thought out of his mind, he stepped into the building and made his way to the office he'd been given. It was a featureless cubicle, barely larger than a midshipman's cabin, but he didn't need anything more. The corps tended to frown on luxury, even to the point of banning photographs of one's family. But then, a photograph could be captured by the enemy and used to break prisoners. And who knew *what* could be learned from something so seemingly harmless?

He sat down and keyed his terminal, bringing up his personal database. As he'd expected, copies of the preliminary order of battle and other important details were already waiting for him, marked for his personal attention. He'd be charged with securing a landing zone, then getting two entire divisions of marines to the surface as quickly as possible. At that point, someone more senior would take command. He wondered just how quickly General Winters would wrangle a trip down to the surface. The older man had clearly not been happy behind a desk.

But we couldn't have him killed by the enemy, Pat thought. *It would be devastating.*

And yet, General Winters would know the dangers. They all knew the dangers. And if he *were* killed, there would be a successor waiting in the wings. The marines couldn't afford a dispute over command in the middle of the war. There was *always* a clear chain of command.

And that will be true of the militia too, he promised himself. *We'll be ready for anything when we land.*

But he knew, deep inside, that they might still be surprised when they finally touched down on Ahura Mazda.

CHAPTER SIXTEEN

Admiral Junayd had expected an uncomfortable trip from Tyre to McCaughey. He'd never served on a courier boat, but he'd spent a good percentage of his time as a commanding officer shuttling from place to place in a tiny ship, and he'd expected nothing better. Instead, he'd been pleasantly surprised—and yet dismayed—by the sheer extravagance of the naval liner that had carried him to McCaughey. If the Commonwealth could afford such a luxurious ship merely to move its admirals from place to place, how large a war fleet could it afford?

He saw the answer as *White Swan* dropped out of hyperspace and glided towards the waiting fleet. There were *thousands* of warships surrounding McCaughey, backed up by dozens of giant orbital fortresses and entire swarms of gunboats and automated weapons platforms. He didn't even *want* to imagine just how many PDCs might be mounted on the planet's surface, ready and waiting to engage anyone foolish enough to claim the high orbitals. Details were sparse—he hadn't been given more than basic access to the sensor feed—but he was sure he was looking at a fleet with more firepower than the entire Theocratic Navy. The sight humbled him, even as he welcomed it. The sight was proof that he'd joined the right side.

Assuming they fight to the finish, he thought.

It wasn't a pleasant thought. Public opinion meant nothing in the Theocracy. A crowd of protesters could expect to be gassed, beaten, and then shipped to the work camps, assuming they survived the experience. Brutal repression was the order of the day, a repression enforced by millions of spies and self-righteous monitors. Anyone who put a foot out of line could expect to have it chopped off.

But the Commonwealth was different. He'd had real problems following the terms of the debate simply because such dialogue was completely alien to him, but the prospect of peace seemed very attractive to a large part of the population. And they were just being allowed to have their say, without anyone stopping them. No sense at all. What sort of leader would allow his people such freedom? But their freedoms seemed to have worked out for the Commonwealth, he had to admit. The giant fleet in front of him was proof of that.

"Admiral," Janice said. She and Grivets had traveled with him, although they'd generally left him in his cabin while they'd been elsewhere. Junayd didn't mind. The liner had plenty of delights, and he'd sampled as many of them as he could. "We will be shuttling over to *Queen Elizabeth* in five minutes."

Junayd nodded. A lesser man would have objected to leaving the comfortable liner, but *real* power would always rest with the warships. His comfort was less important than doing everything he could to build up influence, influence he could turn into power. He rose, picked up his knapsack, and followed Janice through the hatch. There was nothing else in the cabin he cared to take with him.

He wondered, as they walked down to the shuttle hatch, why they hadn't simply docked with the giant superdreadnought. Docking would have been easy, particularly when the liner was so much smaller than the superdreadnought. But he assumed they had their reasons, even if they didn't make sense to him. Navies often collected traditions that didn't make sense to outsiders.

"You'll be meeting Commodore Falcone," Janice advised him. Grivets followed them into the shuttle, banging the hatch closed behind him. "I suggest that you stay on your best behavior."

Junayd nodded, not trusting himself to speak as the shuttle detached from the liner and headed for the superdreadnought. He'd faced Captain Falcone in battle, several times, but they'd never actually *met*. The Commonwealth's propaganda had made a big song and dance about how the mighty Theocracy had been defeated by a *girl*; the Theocracy, in response, had smeared her as the puppet of her male XO and hinted, loudly, that she'd only risen so high because she'd offered her body to her superiors. And yet, he'd read her record when he'd been granted provisional access to some files. Woman or not, she'd snatched a limited victory from the jaws of a crushing defeat and gone on to ruin his career. Kat Falcone had never met him, but she'd played a major role in his life.

He pushed the thought aside as the shuttle flew through a force shield, shuddering slightly before landing neatly on the deck. It didn't matter if he liked her or not, if he wanted to be near her or stay as far from her as possible. All that mattered was taking what few cards he had and playing them to make sure his position remained secure. And if that meant being polite to someone who'd ruined his career, he could do it.

The hatch opened. A gust of warm air blew in. Junayd wrinkled his nose, reminding himself that all starships smelled different. He followed Janice out of the hatch. The gravity seemed to flicker around him, something he *knew* to be purely imaginary and yet impossible to dismiss completely. And then he looked up. Three people, two of them women, were waiting for him. Behind them, there were four men who were very clearly armed guards.

Junayd pulled himself up to his full height and saluted the flag and then Kat Falcone. She was instantly recognizable: tall and blonde, her hair framing a heart-shaped face that was the height of fashion in the Commonwealth. Her white uniform couldn't hide the contours of her body, even though she was decently covered. He couldn't escape the sense she was younger than his daughters, if only because her face was completely unmarked. But her DNA had been extensively modified to grant her a long lifespan his daughters would never know. He had to clamp down hard on the flash of bitter envy. The Theocrats had never told their people what they were leaving behind on Earth.

"Commodore," he said, extending a hand. "It's a pleasure."

"Admiral," Kat said. She took his hand and shook it, firmly. It felt odd to touch an unrelated woman, even for a mere handshake. "Welcome aboard."

She didn't look pleased to see him, Junayd noted. His wives and daughters had become *very* practiced at hiding their thoughts and emotions over the years, a survival skill for women in the Theocracy. Kat Falcone was surprisingly transparent compared to his relatives. But then, she hadn't spent her early years being told that she was good for nothing, apart from bearing and raising the next generation of children. And she wouldn't have been thrashed to within an inch of her life every time she stepped a millimeter out of line.

"My flag captain, Fran Higgins," Kat said. "And my aide, Bobby Wheeler."

Fran looked several years older than Kat, Junayd thought, although he couldn't be sure. She had a thinner face, with long dark ringlets of hair that fell down to her shoulders, and eyes so dark he felt he could lose himself in them. Her body was stockier too, as if she hadn't been given so much enhancement during her early years. Behind her, Bobby Wheeler looked alarmingly bright-eyed and bushy-tailed, his eyes studying Junayd with frank curiosity. No Theocrat would be willing to obey a woman, Junayd knew, but Wheeler didn't seem to care that he had two female superiors. Junayd wasn't sure if that was a sign of weakness or strength.

"A pleasure," Junayd said.

"My crew will show you to your quarters," Kat said, nodding to the men behind her. Junayd had no trouble recognizing them as soldiers, *experienced* soldiers. "We'll discuss the future after you've had a chance to freshen up."

"Of course," Junayd said. He nodded to Janice. "I assume there are quarters for my escorts too?"

Kat gave an odd little smile. "Right next to yours," she said. "We'll speak soon."

Junayd bowed. "Of course," he said again. "I look forward to it."

◆ ◆ ◆

Kat had asked, several times, if she could visit Admiral Junayd after his defection from the Theocracy. ONI, who'd taken him into custody, had always turned down her requests, citing security concerns. They still hadn't quite forgiven her for some of her decisions during Operation Knife, although they'd refrained from trying to file any official complaints. But she knew they hadn't kept their mouths shut for her own good, but for theirs. An official complaint would have required a public discussion of facts ONI wanted to keep hidden.

She wasn't sure what to make of her adversary, now that they'd actually met face to face. He was statuesque and slim, an inch or two taller than she, his arms and legs not particularly muscular even though she'd been told the Theocracy prized physical strength among its commanding officers. Beating crewmen for stepping out of line didn't come easily, after all. And, even after defecting, he had a commanding presence that surprised her. But then, he needed to keep as much credibility as he could.

And he looks crafty, she reminded herself. Junayd had sworn blind that Admiral Morrison hadn't been working for the Theocracy, but he'd certainly taken advantage of Morrison's weaknesses.

She dismissed Fran and Wheeler and then looked at Pat. Three of his marines were escorting Junayd to his quarters, just to make sure he didn't get lost along the way. Kat was fairly sure he wouldn't do anything to harm the ship, not when he needed the Commonwealth to rescue his family, but she didn't trust him. The Theocracy could have easily programmed him, perhaps without his knowledge, to serve as a triple agent. Or he might have goals of his own that conflicted with hers.

And she didn't like him.

"He's not going to have a chance to harm the ship," Pat promised. "He'll be under constant supervision at all times."

"I hope so," Kat said. "As long as he stays in his quarters, I don't mind."

She shook her head as they strolled back towards the conference room. Junayd had been . . . impressive. She hadn't wanted to shake his hand, but he'd offered. She hadn't expected that, not from a Theocrat. Some of the refugees who'd made it out *still* had problems shaking hands with women. And yet, she didn't trust him. Junayd had been a loyal Theocrat for over sixty years, climbing the ranks until they'd put him in command of their most powerful formation. Surely, he couldn't have changed allegiances *that* quickly.

But they would have killed him for failure, she thought. Execution wasn't something that would happen to her, not unless she screwed up deliberately. She might be dismissed from the service, she might be cashiered, but she wouldn't be put to death. *He didn't have anywhere else to go.*

"The training is going well," Pat said. "I think the militiamen are getting better all the time."

Kat nodded as they sat down and waited. "Are they going to be good enough?"

"I think so," Pat said. "But we have had a couple of breakdowns. I'm just praying that the simulations are worse than the real thing."

"Naval simulations are," Kat said. She smiled, remembering the days when she'd had to fend off an infinite supply of missiles, their drive speeds set firmly on *impossible*. "Although the Theocracy may feel otherwise, once we get more of the new missiles online."

"If the war lasts long enough," Pat warned. "We'll be fighting the coming engagement with the older missiles."

Kat nodded. "I know."

Admiral Junayd was surprisingly quick, she decided, as the marines showed him into the conference room. He'd changed into a tunic that made him look like a common spacer, although the lack of any rank insignia was enough to reveal that he was a guest. He certainly wasn't wearing anything that might identify his origins. But then his handlers would have insisted on nondescript attire. There was a good chance that some of Kat's crew would have lost friends or family during the war. They'd want a little revenge.

And while beating up Junayd wouldn't get them anything more than a court-martial, she thought, *it would be very satisfying.*

"Admiral," she said, keying her terminal as soon as Junayd's handlers had joined them. A star chart appeared in front of her, hovering over the table. "Have you been briefed on Operation Hammer?"

"The outline," Junayd said. Kat had to suppress a flicker of annoyance at how casually he said it, as if he *should* have had access. "It is a bold plan. Yours?"

"Mine and Admiral Christian's," Kat said flatly. "What do you make of it?"

Junayd cocked his head. "You can afford to lose?"

"Yes," Kat said. "Is there even a *remote* chance they can take out the entire fleet?"

"I rather doubt it," Junayd said. "But they *were* throwing all sorts of resources at new weapons systems when I . . . left."

"If they've come up with something new," Kat said, "they haven't shown it to us."

"I imagine they wouldn't," Junayd said. "They'd want to keep it in reserve until they needed it."

◆ ◆ ◆

Junayd had to fight to keep his mind from reeling. Operation Hammer wasn't just daring, it was, by the standards of all pre-war planning, utterly insane. No one had fought a full-scale interstellar war, true, but all the simulations suggested that the attacker would advance slowly, system by system, while the defender struggled to cut supply lines while readying a defense. Driving straight at the enemy's homeworld was madness. If the offensive failed, a large chunk of the attacker's mobile firepower would be destroyed or cut off, unable to retreat. If the offensive failed badly enough, the defender might be able to take advantage of the disaster to strike back.

But the Commonwealth was so powerful that it *could* pull off such an offensive and come out ahead, even if the offensive failed completely. Losing 6th Fleet would be bad, but the Theocracy would take a horrendous beating. The Commonwealth would still be able to hold the line, still be able to churn out newer and better ships. The war might be prolonged, yet it wouldn't be lost. There was no way the Theocracy could win.

"They'll defend Ahura Mazda with everything they have," he said. "They won't run."

"I'm counting on it," Kat said. "A chance to crush their remaining fleets. It's worth taking."

"Getting down to the surface might be doable," Junayd continued. "But after that, crushing their forces on the ground will be hard."

"We know," Kat said. She looked up at him. Junayd realized, suddenly, just how bright her blue eyes were. "Can you assist us?"

Junayd took a moment to assemble his thoughts. "It's fairly safe to say," he said, "that the vast majority of civilians on the ground will do what they can to stay out of trouble. They know that doing anything other than keeping their heads down will probably get them killed, or worse. A number *do* resent and fear their rulers, but there's very little they can do in a society where literally *everyone* is watching."

He took a breath. "I did have allies," he said. "And as I am believed dead, I don't think they will have made any attempt to round them up. My family went into hiding with some of them. But I don't know how loyal they'll be in the aftermath of an invasion."

Kat frowned. "So you can't raise the masses to assist us?"

"You'll have to override their television and radio programming," Junayd said. "If you can overpower those, I will speak to the masses. But they may not listen."

"And even if they do," the man sitting next to Kat said, "they'll be unarmed."

"Yes," Junayd said. "I suspect, as their society breaks down, you'll get people willing to work with you. But many others will be too fearful of retaliation to show themselves."

He paused. "Clear evidence you are going to win would help," he added. "Even being there, despite all of their propaganda, would shatter the lies. But it isn't going to be easy."

Kat didn't look pleased, but she nodded. "Start working out a plan to approach your people." She paused. "How would this affect your family?"

"It depends," Junayd said. "I would have to make covert contact with my allies first. But I don't know what's happened on the ground since I left."

"I see," Kat said. "What *might* have happened?"

Junayd shrugged helplessly. "They may have been adopted and slid into other families," he said. "My wives and daughters might have been married off to men who can keep them safe. Or they might still be safe, hidden in a complex well away from the Tabernacle. Or they might have been caught and executed for daring to be related to me. I just don't know."

"I understand," Kat said. She leaned forward. "We will do our best to save them."

"I know," Junayd said. "And I will do as you ask."

"That's all we need, for the moment," Kat said. "Unless you think you can talk the starship crews into surrendering."

"I doubt it," Junayd said. He considered the problem for a long moment. There were so many watchers seeded through a starship's crew that *nothing* went unnoticed. "I only managed to defect because I was in command of the entire squadron. Anyone else . . . they'd need to plan a mutiny and that's nearly impossible to do without being detected."

"Gibson managed it," Kat muttered.

She looked up before Junayd could ask who Gibson was. "Work on your plan, Admiral," she said. "We'll be departing soon."

"Indeed," Junayd said. "And may God defend the right."

CHAPTER SEVENTEEN

"That's the last of the reporters in their cabins, Captain," Roach said. "I'm afraid they're unhappy about their living space."

William waved his hand, dismissively. Sixth Fleet was on the verge of departing McCaughey. The reporters, and everyone else, were under a strict communications blackout. Their complaints would go unheard until the fleet reached its destination, whereupon there would be too many other problems for the government to care about a bunch of spoiled-brat journalists. Didn't they *realize* there was a war on? Or that the cabins they'd been given were twice as large as a lieutenant's cabin?

Probably not, he thought dryly. *They're used to five-star hotels.*

He dismissed the issue as he turned back to the tactical display. Sixth Fleet was slowly altering position, assembling its squadrons for the jump into hyperspace. A handful of drones were already being emplaced to masquerade as the missing ships, hoping to convince any watching eyes that 6th Fleet was still orbiting McCaughey. William had no idea if the Theocracy had the system under observation or not, but there was no point in taking unnecessary chances. It was worth some effort to *try* to convince the enemy that 6th Fleet was staying put.

And it will be completely worthless if they have the system under real-time observation, he reminded himself. *They'll see the fleet leave and the ECM drones take its place.*

He glanced at Roach. "Ship's status?"

"*Thunderchild* is at full readiness, sir," Roach reported. "She's ready to depart on command."

William allowed himself a moment of relief as he sat back and waited for the signal from *Hammerhead*. A month of frantic preparations, all culminating in the single greatest offensive in human history—it would go down in the record books, whatever happened. It felt odd to operate as part of a vast fleet instead of a small squadron or a lone ship, but there was no denying the sheer firepower 6th Fleet possessed. Or just how unhappy the Theocracy would be to see it appear in their skies. The shock of discovering how badly the war was going might upset their entire system.

But it probably won't, he told himself. *Fanatics can always come up with excuses for not thinking.*

"Hold us in place until we get the order," he said.

He forced himself to relax. *Thunderchild* was at full readiness. Her decks had been scrubbed, her compartments washed thoroughly . . . and then every last section had been checked and rechecked during the frantic preparations for departure. He had no reason to worry, no reason to think that anything was wrong, yet he knew his ship was about to face her most dangerous test. The Theocracy would throw everything they had at her.

"Captain, we are picking up a signal from the flag," Lieutenant Richard Ball said. The communications officer looked grim. "The gateway is opening now. We are to proceed into hyperspace as planned."

William sucked in a breath as the gateway blossomed to life on the display, an immense funnel of energy leading straight into hyperspace. It was huge, large enough to take the entire squadron; others, blossoming nearby, would allow other squadrons to follow them. His ship lurched as the gravity waves struck her hull, a grim reminder that real-space didn't like being torn asunder. There were just too many gateways in too close proximity to each other.

"Take us through," he ordered.

Thunderchild shuddered as she slid through the portal and into hyperspace. William felt queasy, just for a second; he swallowed hard, concentrating on his mental discipline. He'd been feeling the passage into hyperspace more and more lately, something that bothered him more than he cared to admit. Some people could never stand hyperspace, not even for a second. They needed to remain in stasis pods for the entire duration of the voyage.

And if I lost the ability to work in hyperspace, he thought morbidly, *would that make me a groundhog after all these years?*

"Transit complete, Captain," Gross reported.

"Tactical datanet up and running, Captain," Ball added. "The fleet command network is fully engaged. Repeater nodes are relaying test messages now."

William nodded, stiffly. No one had tried to fly such a fleet through hyperspace, not in all recorded history. Merely coordinating five hundred ships was a nightmare, a nightmare made worse by the ebb and flow of hyperspace energies. Signals could be lost or garbled, entire squadrons could lose touch with the remainder of the fleet. Contingency plans had been thought up, of course, but William knew all too well that the *real* problems would come from issues they *hadn't* foreseen.

And if we are attacked, he thought, *an energy storm might really ruin our day.*

"Signal from the flag," Ball said. "The fleet is to proceed along the planned vector to the first waypoint."

"Acknowledge," William ordered. The message would be repeated a dozen times, *Thunderchild* forwarding the signal to every other ship just to make sure they all got the message. "Helm, keep us in formation."

"Aye, Captain," Gross said.

"Local hyperspace appears to be clear," Cecelia put in. "Captain, there's a *lot* of distortion."

"Keep a wary eye on it," William ordered. Five hundred ships in such close proximity . . . he'd be surprised if there *weren't* any distortion. He'd actually proposed breaking up the fleet and having each squadron proceed to the first waypoint by a different route, but Admiral Christian had vetoed the idea. He preferred to keep his fleet together. "And watch for any raiders."

"Aye, Captain," Cecelia said.

William sat back in his command chair and waited. It was a week, as the starship flew, to the Gap, but Admiral Christian had decided on an oblique approach. William understood the logic *and* the importance of avoiding contact with enemy ships as much as possible, yet it also introduced a degree of slippage into the schedule. Who knew what would happen if too much time was wasted?

Perhaps nothing, he thought. *We'll have a clear path once we're through the minefield.*

He glanced at Roach. "Continue running tactical simulations," he ordered. "When the time comes to cross the minefield, we have to be ready."

"Aye, Captain," Roach said.

♦ ♦ ♦

Observation blisters were very rare on a Theocratic starship. Junayd himself, for all of his rank, had never been in a place where he could sit and gaze at the shimmering lights of hyperspace. He'd never been quite sure why observation blisters weren't included, even though he'd heard all the official and unofficial excuses. Perhaps his former masters merely wished to avoid reminding the spacers that there was an entire universe outside their hulls.

Wishful thinking, if that was what they had in mind, he thought, clasping his hands behind his back as he stared out at the fleet. *Spacers know too much about the hard realities of life.*

He sucked in his breath as a superdreadnought suddenly seemed to loom towards him, only to flicker out of existence when he blinked. Hyperspace played odd tricks on the Mark-I Eyeball as well as humanity's most advanced sensors; the more he stared at the fleet, the odder it looked. Destroyers larger than superdreadnoughts, assault carriers elongating in a manner that should have torn them apart, flickering lights that seemed to follow the fleet, then vanish in directions his mind wasn't designed to follow. Perhaps the old story about the spacer who'd seen God in hyperspace was true after all, he reflected. There were certainly plenty of strange stories that were completely unverifiable yet passed from spacer to spacer as if they were unquestionable truth.

The hatch hissed open behind him. He glanced back just in time to see Kat Falcone step into the compartment. Her lips thinned with quickly hidden disapproval, an expression none of his female relatives would have dared permit themselves. It wasn't their place to disapprove of anything.

"Commodore," he said, turning back to the blister.

"Admiral," she answered. She stepped up next to him. "Does this bring back memories?"

Junayd half turned his head to look at Kat. Her arms were crossed, striking a defiant pose even though she was looking at the fleet rather than him. It couldn't be easy for her to have him on her ship, he suspected. *He* wouldn't have found it very easy if their positions were reversed. She'd be lucky if she wasn't kept permanently confined to quarters under heavy supervision.

"I never commanded such a powerful fleet," he said. Admiral Christian was a lucky man. But, at the same time, coordinating such a force had to be a nightmare. "The largest fleet I ever commanded had only *five* squadrons of superdreadnoughts."

Kat glanced at him. "Do you miss it?"

"I miss being in command of my own ship," Junayd said honestly. "But I never enjoyed the freedom you did, not when there was a cleric on my ship. My orders could be overruled at any moment."

"My sympathies," Kat said. Her lips twisted with distaste. "Why did you leave?"

Junayd frowned, turning back to the blister. "I knew I no longer had a future," he said. "If I'd stayed, I would have been made to pay for my failures."

"And so you fled to us," Kat said. "You had no other aim in mind?"

"I wanted to survive," Junayd said. "And I wanted my family to survive. The only way I could do both was to defect, after leaving enough evidence to suggest that I died on my ship."

"You destroyed a superdreadnought and killed her entire crew just to escape," Kat pointed out.

Her voice was surprisingly mild. And yet, there was an edge to her tone.

Junayd looked at her again. He could tell she didn't approve. "Would you rather face that ship in battle? Again?" He shook his head. "I had no grand scheme, no plan to turn the defeat into a victory," he confessed. "I merely wanted to survive."

Kat looked doubtful. "And you gave no thought to the future?"

She pressed on before he could answer. "What do you think will happen, after we win?"

"Chaos," Junayd said. "The Theocracy will tear itself apart. All the little cracks within our society . . . they'll tear themselves open, bringing chaos and anarchy in their wake. Too many people want revenge for everything the government has done."

"And where do you see yourself?" Kat asked. "A returning leader, ready to unite your planet?"

Junayd laughed humorlessly. "If I can do something to mitigate the chaos, I will," he said. "But I doubt many of the people on the ground will listen to me."

He closed his eyes in bitter pain. He'd been famous back on Ahura Mazda. The population had thrilled to the tales of Admiral Junayd, God's righteous warrior. But he'd known he could be broken just as easily if his masters saw him as a threat. His family had been held hostage to guarantee his good behavior. And even after he'd started making contingency plans of his own, he'd known there were no guarantees. His wives and children might already be dead.

"Tell me something," Kat said. "Do you feel any guilt?"

Junayd cocked his head. "For what?"

"You commanded the battle fleet that captured Cadiz and five other worlds," Kat said, bluntly. "Millions of spacers and civilians died in the fighting or afterwards, during the occupation. One of those worlds has practically been swept clean of life. Do you feel any guilt?"

"I do not know," Junayd said, after a moment.

Kat lifted her eyebrows. "You do not *know*?"

Junayd stared back at her, evenly. "I believed it was my duty to serve my religion in any way I could," he said. "What I did . . . I did in its name."

"Millions are dead," Kat said.

"I believed," Junayd said.

He sighed. "I was at the heart of the Theocracy for a very long time, Commodore," he added reluctantly. "I saw corruption on a truly staggering scale. The laws enforced so harshly, against the common men and women, simply don't apply to their leaders. Many of them were more interested in enriching themselves than they were in hunting down unbelievers and planning for war. Others . . . had lost touch with their people, believing them to be little more than sheep who needed to be kept in line with the whip. And yet I clung to my delusions about the way things worked.

"And then I lost a battle and suddenly—"

"You were put on the spot," Kat finished.

"I gave it my all," Junayd said. He couldn't keep a hint of bitterness from leaking out. "And yet, I was tried and condemned for losing an unwinnable battle. And then they gave me an impossible task, with a death sentence hanging over my head. I chose to leave when it was clear I couldn't win."

He met her eyes. "I want my family to live," he said. "I want my homeworld to be free. I want—it doesn't matter what I want. All that matters is stopping the Theocracy before it is too late."

Kat gave him a long look, then turned back to stare out into hyperspace. Junayd wondered idly, why she perplexed him so. She didn't act like a woman, at least nothing like the women he'd married, but at the same time she didn't quite act like a man. He reminded himself, again, not to underestimate her. She'd beaten him in two successive engagements and foiled him in a third, preventing his masterstroke from being decisive.

"Tell me something," he said. "If you'd failed like me, Commodore, what would have happened to you?"

"It would depend," Kat said. "A small mistake . . . I might have been allowed to recover from it. The Admiralty might chalk the mistake down to inexperience and allow me to move on. But a bigger mistake? That could easily have gotten me dismissed or put in front of a court-martial board."

"You would have been allowed a chance to learn from your mistakes," Junayd said. "But to us? Failure is a sign of God's displeasure. An admiral who lost a battle lost because he did something to offend God."

Kat glanced at him. "Why did you survive?"

"I like to think that there would have been questions about how the speakers have been handling the war," Junayd said. "They're the ones who appointed me, after all. But in truth, I just don't know."

"You kill your own commanding officers for minor screwups," Kat mused. She sounded torn between amusement and pity. "No *wonder* you're losing the war."

She nodded towards the giant fleet. "There are some odds that just can't be beaten," she added. "We might lose the coming battle; we might lose the entire fleet. And yet, it can be replaced within months. We can trade five superdreadnoughts for every enemy superdreadnought and we'd still come out ahead. Your leaders managed to get you into an unwinnable war."

"I know that," Junayd said. "Do *they*?"

Kat met his eyes. "Do they?"

Junayd twitched. "Some of the . . . call them the *realists* . . . will certainly see the writing on the wall," he said, "but some of the others will merely see it as a spur to fight harder."

"Purging themselves of sin," Kat said. She sounded oddly amused. "And terminating all of your halfway-competent commanding officers at the same time."

Junayd couldn't help a flicker of bitter frustration. He *knew* most of those commanding officers, and he knew enough about his former subordinates to make educated guesses about who would have been pushed into the upper ranks after his defection. They didn't deserve to die, certainly not at the hands of their masters. Searching for heresy was thoroughly pointless when the odds were so heavily stacked against them. Kat's amusement was entirely understandable. The Theocracy, already in a terrible mess, was making matters far worse for itself.

"There are some decent men in the Theocracy," he said. He'd met quite a few men who had been unable to balance the demands of their posts with the reproaches of their consciences. "But none of them will have the chance to *act* decent if the Theocracy survives."

"It won't," Kat said. "And whatever takes its place, Admiral, will be very different."

"I know," Junayd said.

He'd dared to hope that he'd be able to parlay his defection into a position of political power once he returned home. But he knew it was a gamble, one he might well lose. It would be safer to take his family and return to Tyre, yet he needed power to survive. He didn't want to spend the rest of his life dependent on charity.

Someone will have to serve as the link between the occupation forces and the local population, he thought. *Why not me?*

Kat leaned back. "You've adapted well to our culture," she said. "What do you make of it?"

"Strange," Junayd said. He didn't even begin to claim to understand Tyre, let alone the rest of the Commonwealth. Tyre was just so *different*. "You should be in constant anarchy. But you're not."

"We compete for power and place," Kat said. She sounded almost as fervent as a cleric praising his religion. "Some of us start ahead of others, but we all compete. And we are judged by valid standards, not by devotion to a religion none of us believe in. Our competency is not judged by how well we can grovel."

"Point," Junayd agreed. He held up a hand. "But don't imagine, not for a moment, that the Theocracy doesn't believe in its religion. There are a *lot* of true believers, even in the upper ranks. Some of them will be very dangerous."

Kat nodded. "I know."

"And they're the ones you're going to have to kill," Junayd added. The Commonwealth had been oddly merciful towards its former enemies, but the fanatics were a very different kettle of fish. "Because if you let them live, they'll see it as a sign of weakness. Kill them all."

CHAPTER EIGHTEEN

Admiral Junayd's words hung in Kat's mind as the fleet followed its circular path towards the Gap, remaining well off the shipping lanes and taking evasive action at the slightest hint of an unidentified starship. Kat had been a spacer long enough to know that the odds of anyone getting a solid lock on their hulls, let alone an accurate ship count, were minimal, but she understood Admiral Christian's caution. The less warning the Theocracy had, the less time they'd have to muster a defense or devise contingency plans. She already knew a very hard fight was in store.

And we'll be killing innocents along with the fanatics, she thought. The enemy spacers had chosen to serve, but their civilians hadn't deliberately put themselves in a war zone. *And yet it can't be helped.*

"Commodore," Wheeler said, "the fleet is approaching the minefield. Admiral Christian is ordering the ships to heave to."

"Make it so," Kat ordered.

She sucked in her breath. On the display, the Gap and its attendant minefield were clearly visible. Long-range scans had picked up hundreds of mines, but ONI had warned that plenty of mines had been stealthed to make them nearly impossible to detect. The Theocracy presumably knew the paths through the mines, yet, if Junayd was to be believed, even *they* lost ships to their minefields. But, thanks to hyperspace, they probably wouldn't notice losing a few hundred mines. They were cheap and easy to manufacture.

They're probably running short of replacements, she thought. Hyperspace, as well as normal wear and tear, had probably destroyed quite a number of mines. *They had this minefield set up well before the war.*

"A couple of antimatter warheads would create an energy storm," Wheeler commented as if he were speaking to himself. "That would sweep the Gap clean."

"And the storm would take weeks to dissipate," Kat said. They'd discussed doing just that, back when the planning cell had been finalizing Operation Hammer. But hyperspace storms near the Gap had a tendency to last for weeks. There was just too much energy spewing around. "No, we have to clear the mines manually."

"Yes, Commodore," Wheeler said.

He paused. "Admiral Christian is ordering the carriers to begin launch sequence," he added, slowly. "The gunboats are being deployed."

"Good," Kat said. "And now we wait."

◆ ◆ ◆

Years had passed since Lieutenant Isabel Campbell had set foot on Hebrides, years since her parents had offered her the flat choice between marrying a pig farmer or the local schoolmaster. Isabel had taken a third option and fled to join the Royal Navy, refusing to even *consider* returning to her homeworld until her parents relented. And then the war had broken out and returning home had suddenly become impossible.

Cold hatred seethed in her soul as she steered the gunboat out of the launch bay and out into hyperspace. She'd *loved* her homeworld; she'd loved her family—she'd known they meant well, even though she couldn't accept their choices. And now they were all gone, her family and her would-be husbands alike, either killed by the nuclear blasts or dead of radiation poisoning. She'd volunteered for the mine-clearing mission purely because she wanted a chance to *hurt* the Theocracy, to make them pay for what they'd done. She would have happily carried a planet-buster all the way to their damned homeworld and fired it, if her superiors had let her. In her head, the Theocracy deserved total obliteration.

"Keep a constant sensor watch," she ordered as the squadron of gunboats neared the minefield. The techs swore blind that the gunboats were too tiny to interest the mines, but she wouldn't have cared to bet money on it. "I want every last mine zeroed before it's too late."

"You got it," Lieutenant Shawn Tombs said. Her copilot worked his console with practiced skill, isolating and targeting the mines. "Targeting . . . now."

Isabel nodded as the gunboat rocked, gravity waves slicing through hyperspace and lashing against her hull. Passage through the Gap had never been easy, even for superdreadnoughts and assault carriers. A lone gunboat could vanish in the blink of an eye, and no one would ever even *notice*. But it still beat trying to pass through the Seven Sisters.

"Weapons locked," Lieutenant Tombs said. "I have twenty-seven mines within my sights."

"Fire," Isabel ordered.

The gunboat shook slightly as the railguns opened fire. Her gunboat normally carried two shipkiller missiles and powerful plasma cannons for dogfights with enemy gunboats, but the shipboard techs had replaced them with tiny railguns that looked as though they belonged in a museum. The popguns wouldn't even *scratch* a starship if they happened to strike its hull, yet they should be more than enough to take out a mine. And the impact shouldn't be enough to *trigger* the mines.

Unless the techs are wrong and some of those mines are crammed with antimatter, Isabel thought as mines began to vanish. *A single detonation would really ruin our day.*

"Move to the next set of mines," she ordered. There was no time to waste. If *she* had been setting up the minefield, *she* would have put a ship or two in direct position to observe the mines and watch for anyone clearing the field. "Hurry."

"Of course, Most Gracious Empress," Lieutenant Tombs said.

Isabel gave him a one-fingered gesture, then returned to her console. Tombs had flirted with her ever since she'd entered the training program, something that flattered and appalled her in equal measure. She'd hoped to go home one day, not throw herself into a radically different culture and never look back. And yet, now there was no home to go to. The remainder of her people were refugees.

A dozen more mines died in quick succession, but the field was starting to wake up. Isabel cursed as a mine exploded, taking out two gunboats; a second detonated moments later, scattering a hail of shrapnel in all directions. The pilots hastily avoided the blasts, still firing burst after burst of railgun pellets to take out the surviving mines. Three more mines detonated, perhaps triggered by their comrades; Isabel pulled back, half hoping the mines would detonate in sequence, half fearing the potential results. Nuclear detonations might just cause an energy storm, particularly in the Gap.

"I've got five more mines targeted," Lieutenant Tombs said.

"Continue firing," Isabel said. A chain reaction of detonations would be very useful, *if* it didn't set off an energy storm. "I'll take us forward."

♦ ♦ ♦

"We used to think this minefield was impassable," Junayd observed.

Janice laughed, not unkindly. "It seems very passable to me."

"But then, we used to have a destroyer or two watching the mines from a safe distance," Junayd admitted. On the display, more and more icons were blinking out of existence as the gunboats ravaged the field. "I'm not sure if they have a guardship now."

"They should," Janice said.

"We only ever had a handful of escorts," Junayd said. The limited number of escorts had been a constant frustration, even before Kat Falcone had led her flotilla into Theocratic Space to attack a number of under-defended worlds. "They were always in short supply."

He stroked his beard in annoyance. His superiors had committed themselves to building up the largest battle fleet they could, and he had to admit that they'd worked miracles, but they'd concentrated on superdreadnoughts at the expense of everything else. The shortage of transports had been bad enough, yet the shortage of escorts and flankers had clearly taken its own toll. He didn't want to *think* about how many Theocratic superdreadnoughts had been lost because they hadn't had enough flankers. Superdreadnoughts were tough, but there was a limit to how much damage they could soak up on their own.

"A terrible oversight," Janice agreed. She tapped the display. "Do you have any further insights?"

"I'm afraid not," Junayd said. "None of those mines *should* be antimatter—"

"But you don't know," Janice finished.

"No," Junayd agreed. "Blocking the Gap permanently would have been a deadly mistake ten months ago. It would have cut the Theocracy off from its fleets. Now . . . now it might be a wise idea indeed."

◆ ◆ ◆

The mine seemed to loom up in front of Isabel, so close that there wasn't a hope of evading before it was too late. She gritted her teeth, ignoring the illusion. Her sensors insisted that the mine was well clear of her gunboat—and dead, as Tombs picked it off with a blast of pellets. The mine shattered, the debris flying in all directions. Another mine died a moment later, followed by five more. And then another exploded, taking out three more gunboats.

"Dave's dead," Tombs said.

Isabel nodded. There would be time to mourn later, assuming she survived. The minefield seemed to be getting thicker, layer upon layer of mines laid so close together that destroying one triggered several more. She was torn between admiring the sheer determination that had gone into assembling the minefield and laughing at the waste of resources the endeavor represented. The mastermind behind the plan *had* to have been a groundhog. A spacer would have understood that piling mines up so close together, even on an interplanetary scale, was just asking for trouble.

"Keep firing," she ordered. More and more mines were going active, trying to angle into position to damage or destroy passing ships. "Don't give them a chance to react."

She wondered, idly, just what the mines were programmed to do if they came under sustained attack. Their briefers hadn't known. The Commonwealth hadn't really experimented with mines, certainly not on such a large scale. The analysis had warned that the mines were possibly programmed to detonate in unison, yet their limited brains wouldn't be able to tell the difference between a deliberate attack and an energy storm. The Theocrats might have looked up one day to discover that their entire minefield had self-destructed.

And that would be a laugh, she thought nastily. *Their minefield wiped out by their own incompetence.*

"Twelve more mines down," Tombs reported. He paused. "That one looks *very* nasty."

"It does indeed," Isabel said. A mine was sending out sensor pulses in all directions without any regard for its own safety. "Kill it."

She braced herself, expecting an explosion. But the mine merely shattered into a thousand pieces. Its comrades went active a second later, sweeping space for targets. Isabel cursed, then launched a decoy drone as she yanked the gunboat back. The mines picked up the drone and detonated in sequence, obliterating the drone. But they'd also taken out a large chunk of the minefield.

"I see the light at the end of the tunnel," Tombs said. "Do you?"

"We're not out of this just yet," Isabel snapped. "Keep firing."

♦ ♦ ♦

"They've cleared a passage," Wheeler reported. "The flag is ordering us to advance."

Kat nodded. "Take us into the Gap," she ordered. "Point defense is to engage any surviving mines without waiting for orders."

She forced herself to watch as *Queen Elizabeth* crawled forward, advancing steadily into the space cleared by the gunboats. The debris posed no threat to the superdreadnought, but it was quite possible that one or more stealthed mines had remained undetected. She kept a sharp eye on the display, knowing that everything would depend on her electronic servants. No mere human, no matter how enhanced, could pick up an active mine and take it out before the damned thing detonated. And a nuclear blast so close to her ship might cause all sorts of problems.

"Seventeen mines killed by point defense," Wheeler said. "Long-range scans are clear."

Which proves nothing, Kat reminded herself. *The enemy could remain hidden from us even at very close range.*

The seconds ticked away as the entire fleet slowly made its way through the Gap and into Theocratic Space. Kat felt the tension rising on the flag deck, even though no enemy vessels appeared to menace or shadow the fleet. If *she'd* been in command of an enemy guardship, she would have hurried to report home. If she'd had *two* ships, one of them would have gone home and the other would have kept an eye on the fleet. But no enemy vessels materialized.

"Signal from the flag," Wheeler said. "Flanking units are to spread out."

"Pass the word," Kat ordered. If an enemy ship *was* lying doggo, the bastards had probably had more than enough time to get an accurate ship count before fleeing. "And keep watching the sensors."

"Local space is clear," Wheeler said.

Kat didn't feel any better, even as the flankers failed to pick up any enemy vessels. There was just too much distortion on the far side of the Gap, too many eddies that could conceal even an uncloaked ship from prying sensors. And yet, the enemy couldn't stay *too* close to the Gap. The chance of being blotted from existence by an energy surge was just too high.

She closed her eyes for a long moment, centering herself. Kat knew how to handle a battle, she knew what to do if she saw an enemy fleet, but sneaking around, unsure if she was being watched, was different. If Junayd was right, the Theocracy didn't have the resources to guard the shipping lanes, yet he could be wrong. He'd defected nine months ago. Everything Junayd knew was out of date.

And they might have gotten more ships from somewhere, she thought morbidly. *They've certainly been trying hard to purchase entire fleets.*

"Signal from the flag," Wheeler said. "Task Force Alpha is to proceed to primary target. All ships attached to Task Force Beta are to proceed to their waypoint, then scatter as planned."

"Acknowledge," Kat ordered. *Queen Elizabeth* and her squadron were attached to Task Force Alpha. In some ways, she wished she'd been allowed to take command of one of the Beta squadrons instead. "And then pass the word. We'll move out with the rest of the fleet."

"Aye, Commodore," Wheeler said.

Kat forced herself to relax as the fleet moved away from the Gap, deliberately selecting a course that would take it straight towards its target. It was a race now, if the enemy *had* been watching the Gap. Her vessels had to get to Ahura Mazda before any guardships could signal home. The tactical headache bothered her more than she cared to admit. Their desperate race to their final destination, following the shortest possible course, might alert the enemy to their presence. And yet, there was no choice.

"All sensor systems online," Wheeler reported. "No enemy ships detected."

We'll have to blow any freighters out of space, if we encounter them, Kat thought. *And run down any warships before they can blow the whistle.*

She rose. "Continue running combat simulations," she ordered. Admiral Junayd might as well make himself useful by playing the opposite side. No one was more qualified to say what the Theocracy would and wouldn't do when it saw a massive fleet bearing down on its homeworld. "I'll be in my office."

"Aye, Commodore," Wheeler said.

Kat strode through the hatch and into her office, silently noting the steaming coffeepot on the side table. Her steward seemed to have a form of ESP, somehow knowing whenever Kat needed a cup of coffee. She poured herself a mug, then sat down and keyed her terminal. A hundred messages sat in her inbox, all marked urgent. A quick glance at the headers told her that most of them were nothing of the sort.

And this will change, she thought as she studied the fleet display. The fleet train hung behind the warships, surrounded by a flotilla of flanking units. *Mobile StarComs will change everything.*

She made a face at the thought. The Royal Navy put out thousands of updates every day, most of which were completely irrelevant to her. Everyone knew that most of the updates would be discarded unread, even though someone had gone to all the trouble of sending them. It wasn't as if she could have replied instantly to each and every message. But now, with a mobile StarCom escorting the fleet, escape was impossible. Paperwork and micromanaging would follow her for the rest of her life.

And if I am micromanaged from home, she asked herself, *how much freedom will I have?*

She sighed as she tapped her terminal, deleting the messages. She'd liked the idea of being a captain because it would have given her an independent command, a command separated from her father and the rest of the family. But if mobile StarComs entered regular use, a captain might wind up with very little authority of her own. She'd have to call home for the slightest change in circumstances, rather than being allowed to use her own judgment. God alone knew what would happen if the StarCom was destroyed. An officer who wasn't used to thinking for herself wouldn't suddenly develop that skill when the shit hit the fan.

And the enemy will target the StarCom, once they realize what it is, she thought. *That's what I would do.*

She rose and started to pace the room, carrying her coffee in one hand. Her adult life had been defined by the war, first by the desperate bid to build up the navy before the shooting started, and then by the fight to survive long enough to take the offensive. She wasn't sure what she'd do afterwards, if she survived the coming battle. The Royal Navy was likely to start shedding officers left and right. She might manage to stay in, but if she didn't . . .

I don't know what I'll do, she thought. She finished her coffee and put the mug down on the table, resuming her pacing. *The end of the war won't bring an end to all our problems.*

CHAPTER NINETEEN

"I haven't seen anything of you for a week," Kat teased as Pat stepped into her suite. "What have you been doing?"

"Readying the landing force," Pat said. He gave her a tight hug, then kissed her. "Yourself?"

"Planning the engagement," Kat said. She'd spent most of the trip working with Admiral Christian and the rest of the planning cell, trying to game out everything the Theocracy could and would do. "I think we're going to be surprised when we finally reach our target."

Pat nodded. "Is there any sign we've been detected?"

"Not as far as we know," Kat said. "But we don't have any way to be sure."

She sighed as they walked into the admiral's mess and sat down. They wouldn't know if they'd been detected until they entered the Ahura Mazda system and began the operation. And even if they hadn't been detected in transit, enemy spies might have picked up a hint of what was in store or simply noted the disappearance of large numbers of starships from the front. If they had, the Theocracy might try to attack one of the naval bases or even raid Tyre itself.

"Then relax," Pat urged. "You won't know until you get there."

Kat nodded slowly. "Have you managed to refine your simulations?"

"Admiral Junayd has been making himself useful, but there are too many question marks," Pat said. "Hell, we don't even know where we're going to land."

"I dare say we'll find out when we try to take the high orbitals," Kat observed. "You'll have to make up your plan on the fly."

Pat grinned. "Best sort of plan."

Kat wasn't so sure. She understood the value of improvising, but she preferred having plenty of supplies to improvise *with*. Marines believed in "muddling through" and making the best of what they had, yet Kat knew just how easy it was to run short of something she desperately needed. Pat would have learned that lesson in boot camp.

"I've been working up the ladder," Pat added. "We've completed the first run of squad-level exercises. Now we're moving on to battalion and division-level simulations. It's a right pain, even in the machines."

"Pity we don't have a ship large enough for you to practice in," Kat said dryly. She was relieved to see Pat so enthusiastic again. "How is it going?"

"I wish I was back in the squad," Pat said. He laughed, ruefully. "We're going to be resting our hopes on the captains and lieutenants, I think. The campaign is likely to move too fast for orders from on high to be very effective."

"You've trained your people to deal with that," Kat reminded him. "Or have I missed something?"

"We have," Pat confirmed. "But you know how difficult it can be when one's subordinates go too far."

Kat nodded. "What do you make of Junayd?"

Pat met her eyes. "Should I be asking what *you* make of Junayd?"

"I asked first," Kat said.

"True," Pat agreed. He considered the problem as Lucy appeared, wheeling in the first course on a tray. "He's an interesting man, I think. He's clearly grown up in a very different culture from ours. Very odd set of reactions. He seems determined to treat you like a man."

Kat felt her cheeks heat. "Is that a good thing?"

"I don't think he was raised to respect women very much," Pat said. "I've tried to talk to him about his wives and family—that's *wives* plural—but he says very little. I had the odd impression that he wasn't *that* concerned about them."

"How nice," Kat said sarcastically.

"But he's also very practiced at keeping his emotions well hidden," Pat added. "He might be desperately worried for their safety, but not allowing us to see it."

Kat stroked her chin. "Why?"

"I suspect he feels helpless," Pat said after a moment. "He's here, surrounded by people who have plenty of reason to hate him. A command from you or Admiral Christian would be enough to get him shot. He has to make himself useful to us because it's the only way to get us to help him, but he's a proud man and he hates abasing himself in front of us."

"He spent enough time abasing himself in front of his bosses," Kat said tersely.

"I imagine the war would have gone differently if he'd had a completely free hand," Pat said flatly. "What do *you* think of him?"

"I wish I knew," Kat said reluctantly. "I don't like him. I don't think I will *ever* like him. I think he's planning something."

Pat lifted his eyebrows. "Like what?"

"I wish I knew," Kat said. She scowled down at her hands. There was something about Junayd that *definitely* rubbed her the wrong way. "He betrayed his people."

"I know," Pat said. "But do you blame him?"

"If I had been born on his homeworld," Kat pointed out, "I wouldn't be in a *position* to betray the Theocracy."

She gritted her teeth in frustration. She'd been profoundly shocked when she'd found out about Joel Gibson and his mutineers. Mutiny had been completely unknown in the Royal Navy before Gibson had smashed the taboo into thousands of little pieces. A military couldn't hope to survive if its officers and enlisted men couldn't trust one another. And yet, the Theocracy's leadership had often made it clear that they didn't give a damn about the men under their command.

And Junayd betrayed his own people, she thought. *How long will it be until he betrays us?*

"But imagine you were," Pat said seriously. Kat had to force herself to remember what he'd been saying. "What would you do?"

Kat sighed. If she'd been born in the Theocracy, she wouldn't have had any respect for its leaders. She wouldn't have had any compunctions about betraying them. But if she'd been born in the Theocracy, she probably would have been beaten or drugged into submission merely for being born a woman. She wouldn't even know that there *could* be anything else.

"He betrayed his crew," she said decisively. "I don't like him because he betrayed the men under his command."

She sipped her soup, her thoughts dark. She'd been raised to understand that her power and place came with obligations, obligations she could not put aside whenever the whim suited her. There were servants in the mansion she had to treat kindly because she was their employer, because they were bound together. Her mother had made that clear more than once. The servants might be subordinate, but they were still *people*. And Piker's Peak had drummed the lesson in, time and time again. Enlisted men were not puppets, any more than starships were toys. She owed it to her crews to treat them well.

And Junayd, damn the man, had deliberately sacrificed over a thousand lives to cover his escape.

Still, he had a point, she admitted freely. That superdreadnought would have returned to the war front, sooner or later. The ship would have killed Commonwealth spacers before being destroyed herself. Having the enemy superdreadnought destroyed by her own commander was far better, from the Commonwealth's point of view, than having to blow her out of space in honest battle. And yet, the whole affair rankled. Junayd had betrayed his own men to save his ass.

"That's a better answer," Pat said.

"If he'd said that he wanted to lead a resistance against the Theocrats, I would have understood that," Kat admitted. "But instead . . ."

She ran her hand through her hair. "He's just out to save himself."

"I doubt they gave him much of a choice," Pat said. "*Our* system doesn't kill people for making mistakes."

"He said as much," Kat agreed.

She glared down at the table. She'd studied men and women who felt they had been driven to treason, from Sulla and Julius Caesar to Benedict Arnold and Draco Trent . . . she hadn't really felt much sympathy for them, even though they'd thought they had good reason to turn against their former friends. Caesar, at least, had been at risk of his life; the others, perhaps, could have just withdrawn from public life if they found it unbearable. Whatever the rightness of their cause, they'd lost any claim to the moral high ground when they'd committed treason.

And does it make a difference, she asked herself, *if the treason is in our favor?*

"I don't think you have to like him," Pat said. "You just have to work with him if, of course, he can be useful."

Kat let out a breath. "I don't know," she said. "There are just too many unknowns."

She looked down at the table as Lucy removed the soup bowls and produced the next course, a steaming dish of curry, rice, and yogurt. If *Kat* had turned against the Commonwealth, for whatever reason, would she be comfortable plotting an attack on Tyre? She wouldn't be, she knew; she'd hate the thought of raining hell on her homeworld. And yet Junayd didn't seem to agree. He'd been happy to assist the planning cell before the fleet set out on its mission.

And he might have been programmed to do us harm when he has a chance, she reminded herself. *Or he might just have a crisis of conscience.*

"He *is* under close supervision," Pat reminded her. "There's no way he can damage the ship."

"He destroyed an entire superdreadnought," Kat commented.

"Only through careful planning," Pat said. "And even if he *did* take out this ship, Kat, it wouldn't disrupt the entire fleet."

Kat nodded reluctantly. She might be second-in-command of 6th Fleet, but there *was* a chain of command that ran all the way down to the lowliest midshipman in the fleet. If she died, Commodore Harper would assume command; if *he* died, Commodore Baker would take his place. There was no way Junayd could inflict enough damage to do more than annoy 6th Fleet. Hell, she couldn't imagine any way he could take out Admiral Christian himself.

And I wouldn't be in command, she reminded herself, *unless he dies or falls out of touch.*

Pat held up a hand. "Enough about Admiral Junayd," he said. "Too much of this talk will make me limp for a week."

"A disaster of galactic proportions," Kat said mischievously. "I'm sure they offer drugs for that now."

"I don't need them," Pat said complacently. He started to ladle curry and rice onto their plates. "Did you ask for extra chili?"

Kat smiled, remembering the shore leave they'd shared on Hindustan. "Lucy doesn't go in for the macho curries," she said. Kat had eaten something so hot on Hindustan that her stomach had rebelled after a single sniff. "She prefers ones that actually taste of something other than molten fire."

"It's a challenge," Pat said. "Do you know what you can do with a box of spices, sauces, and military rations?"

"Yes," Kat said. "And it never stops horrifying me."

Pat shrugged. "What *else* is bothering you?"

Kat looked back at him. "What do you think we'll do, after the war?"

"Good question," Pat said. "I don't really want to leave the Marine Corps. But if they don't want to keep me . . ."

He allowed his voice to trail off. Kat understood. The Marine Corps had expanded rapidly over the last eighteen months, with hundreds of thousands of new troops finally coming out of the various boot camps. Peace would bring rapid demobilization, sending countless marines back to their homeworlds with military skills and not much else. Pat was a war hero, with a stack of medals to his name, yet he might not be allowed to stay in the corps. God knew, he'd been a marine for over fifteen years.

"It depends," he said. "What do *you* want to do?"

Kat shrugged. "I don't want to go into politics," she said. "And while I *could* take a management position in the family business, I don't want it. I'd be bored stiff within a week."

"You could go far in politics," Pat pointed out. "You actually understand the military, which is more than can be said for many other politicians. And you'd know the danger of just sitting still and waiting to be attacked."

"I'd hate it," Kat said. "And besides, I'd never be my own woman. My father's shadow would always be hanging over me."

She shuddered at the thought. As her father's youngest child, she didn't have a hope of claiming a seat in the House of Lords. Nine other children were ahead of her in the line of succession. But if she resigned her family name and stood for election, she *might* win, only to find herself trapped in the House of Commons. She wouldn't find it easy to build coalitions and agree on compromises after being a captain and a commodore, an autocrat with unlimited power over her ship. And she really doubted she had the patience to learn the ropes, let alone the time. She'd fade from the public mind soon enough.

"If I have to leave the navy," she said, "I might just go into trading."

Pat blinked. "Seriously?"

"I have a trust fund," Kat said. She flushed. She never liked talking about money with him. "If I cash it in, I can purchase a modern freighter and start shipping goods from planet to planet."

"And then get snatched by pirates," Pat pointed out. "Unless you want to stay within the Commonwealth."

"I'd probably buy a few weapons," Kat mused. The idea of purchasing a surplus warship was tempting, although most warships made poor transports. "Besides, we'll have plenty of escort units to sweep pirates out of space after the war."

She grinned at the thought. The mission to Jorlem had been a personal disaster, with *Lightning* blown out of space and *Uncanny* damaged so badly that she'd been scrapped, but she had to admit it had been a political success. Her early contacts with a dozen worlds had led to new defense treaties centered around joint patrols and sharing intelligence. The Commonwealth might not find many new members in the Jorlem Sector, but it would have a chance to obliterate hundreds of pirate ships.

"Or I could buy a scout ship and go out surveying," she said. She looked up at him. "Want to go see what's beyond the edge of explored space?"

Pat smiled. "The ruins of an alien civilization? Or a living breathing alien race?"

Kat laughed. There was no shortage of hoaxes about extraterrestrials, ranging from the blatantly obvious to ones that had fooled some of academia's finest minds. And yet, none of them had ever led to *genuine* alien relics, let alone a living alien race. Humanity seemed to be alone, at least in this part of the universe. But was it likely that there was only one intelligent race in all the cosmos?

"You never know," she said. "But clear title to a star system with an inhabitable planet would be worth a mint."

"If we start expanding again," Pat warned.

"There's always someone ready to set out for a new world," Kat said. She sobered. "We might find a new home for William's people."

"Not in time," Pat said. "Was there any decision at all?"

"None," Kat said. "It isn't good."

They finished their dinner and walked through into the stateroom, leaving the plates and glasses behind for Lucy to clear up. Kat took Pat's hand and held it, gently, as she studied the star chart. The thought of going beyond the edges of explored space was tempting, very tempting. And exploring wasn't something she was going to be able to do if she stayed in the navy.

The UN Survey Service was disbanded when Earth was destroyed, she mused. *And no one was particularly interested in poking back out past the known borders.*

She looked up at Pat. Would he come with her if she *did* purchase a survey ship? Could they crew it on their own, between them, or would she need to hire others? And if he did, would their relationship survive? She loved him, but she was also a realist. Long-term relationships were relatively rare on Tyre. Might what they have endure past the pressures of war?

He won't want to leave the Marine Corps, she thought. *Any more than I want to leave the Royal Navy.*

"Two weeks," Pat mused. He nodded towards the star chart. Tiny units were moving on a course that led straight to Ahura Mazda. Others were heading off in all directions, their locations nothing more than best guesses. "We'll be ready."

Kat nodded, feeling suddenly downcast. Pat would have to transfer to one of the troop transports shortly before they reached Ahura Mazda. After that, she wouldn't see him again until the war was over. She knew him too well to think he would leave his station before he was no longer needed. He could die, down on the surface. *She* could die, in the omnipresent cold of space.

She pulled him to her and held him tightly. Candy had predicted, none too pleasantly, that she and Pat wouldn't last for long, if at all. They were just too different, she'd said; Pat was a commoner, from what was practically a whole new world. And yet, Kat thought he was talented enough to be brought into the family, wasn't he?

And you're being a soppy idiot, she told herself sternly. Candy was the boy-crazy one, not her. She'd long since given up trying to keep track of her sister's lovers. *Kat* preferred a single, steady relationship. *Worry about the future after the war is over.*

She slipped her hands into his waistband and pushed his trousers to his knees. His mouth found hers, his tongue flicking along the edge of her lips. She drew back, just for a brief second as he removed his trousers, to see him smile. Pat might not be classically handsome, but she found him attractive nonetheless.

"I took some care to make sure we had a few hours off duty," she said as he picked her up effortlessly and carried her towards the bed. "Let's not waste it, shall we?"

CHAPTER TWENTY

"This report is genuine?"

"It comes straight from Agent Joshua," Inquisitor Samuilu said. "His position gives him access to a great deal of enemy data."

Speaker Nehemiah studied the report for a long moment. Agent Joshua had never steered the Theocracy wrong before, although there were odd gaps in what he sent that worried his handlers back on Ahura Mazda. And yet, an all-out attack on Ahura Mazda itself? Such a venture seemed a little unlikely.

"I ordered a patrol ship from Croydon to check the minefield," Samuilu said. "A vast number of mines are missing, blown out of space in a pattern that suggests a large fleet passed through the Gap and into our territory. Assuming a least-time course between the Gap and Ahura Mazda, they could be here within two days at the most."

"And Joshua didn't tell us until now," Nehemiah mused.

"His sources are not always available," Samuilu reminded him. "But everything he's sent us has proven reliable."

Nehemiah looked up at the star chart, resisting the urge to say something blasphemous. The Battle of Hebrides had been a one-sided slaughter, suggesting worrying things about the next generation of enemy weapons, but the destruction of the entire planet had brought the Commonwealth's counteroffensive to a halt. Movement had frozen, giving him time to bombard the Commonwealth with messages promising peace, an end to war, as long as the enemy accepted the prewar *status quo*. And while the Commonwealth hadn't seemed receptive, they *had* stopped their offensive.

And yet, if Agent Joshua was correct, they'd merely picked a new target.

Two days, he thought.

But *was* it two days? Agent Joshua claimed the fleet had departed three weeks ago, but was he telling the truth? His contacts might have lied to him, even if he wasn't deliberately lying himself. By God, it was possible he'd been turned by the Commonwealth's counter-intelligence services. Too many other spies and sources had been eliminated in the first months of the war for Nehemiah to trust *anyone* completely. Feeding the Theocracy false intelligence would be worth almost anything to its enemies.

"A fleet definitely passed through the minefield," he mused.

"Correct," Samuilu said. "They could have triggered an energy storm if they'd merely wished to clear the mines."

Nehemiah thought fast. On one hand, Ahura Mazda was the most heavily defended world in the Theocracy. The planet had enough firepower in orbit to deal with almost any realistic threat. But on the other hand, an extended engagement in the system would almost certainly take out the shipyards and industrial nodes—even the cloudscoops would be targeted and destroyed. The Theocracy might win the engagement but lose the war as its fleets slowly became nonfunctional.

"This is our chance," Samuilu said. "Their morale is already sinking, sinking fast. We can mass our forces and deal them a crushing blow, one from which they will never recover. One final catastrophic battle would give the impetus to their peacemongers."

Nehemiah turned to look at him. "Are you sure?"

"The unbelievers are cowards," Samuilu insisted. His eyes were burning with fanatical determination. "And God has finally delivered them into our hands!"

He leaned forward. "Recall the fleets, Your Holiness," he said. "And ready them for one final battle."

Nehemiah studied Samuilu for a long moment, then turned and strode over to the window, peering down at the darkened city below. There were almost no visible lights, not outside the governing compound. Energy had always been carefully rationed, particularly to the lower classes, but now there were too many demands on the fraying infrastructure to keep the city alight. He knew just how many people were suffering in the darkness, unable to run an air conditioner in the sweltering heat. Their sacrifice was necessary, but reports from spies suggested that discontent was spreading rapidly. Public feeling was unfocused, so far, yet he knew that would change sooner or later.

And what will happen, he asked himself, *when the enemy finally lands?*

Samuilu believed that God had delivered the unbelievers into their hands. Nehemiah couldn't allow himself that luxury. God helped those who helped themselves, after all. Whatever happened, the engagement would be final in more ways than one. Either they would win decisively enough to convince the Commonwealth to back off or they would lose completely. There was no middle ground.

He straightened up as he gazed into the darkness. Hundreds of thousands of souls were trapped in the city below, struggling to survive another day as their homeworld fell apart. What would happen, Nehemiah asked himself grimly, when the water supplies failed? Or when contaminated food was accidentally delivered to the slums? The poor should learn to bear their burdens with pride, but would *they* see it that way?

Of course not, he thought. *If they snap, they'll lash out in all directions.*

"First Speaker," Samuilu said, "we have to start preparations."

Nehemiah closed his eyes for a long moment. Surrender wasn't an option. Even if he'd *wanted* to surrender, even if he'd thought he would survive the purges that would inevitably follow defeat, it wasn't an option. Samuilu and his fellow fanatics would take control of the government and order a fight to the finish, convinced that God was on their side. He considered options for purging the fanatics first, before they could purge him, but he knew such tactics would be tricky. Samuilu controlled too many loyalists for anyone to be certain of the final outcome.

And we would lose if we were having a civil war when the enemy arrived, he thought morbidly.

"Start preparing the defenses on the ground," Nehemiah ordered. "And recall the fleets. We need to mass our striking power before launching a counteroffensive."

"As you command," Samuilu said, bowing low. "And should we burn the occupied worlds?"

"No," Nehemiah said. He wasn't fooled by the sycophantic tone. Samuilu would obey orders as long as they were the orders he wanted to obey. "God will be angry with us. And we need His help for the coming battle."

"We are His chosen people," Samuilu protested. "Of course, He'll help us."

"And if we choose to defy His edicts," Nehemiah asked, "what does that make us?"

Samuilu looked unamused. Nehemiah didn't really blame him. Like most Inquisitors, Samuilu had risen to the top through a combination of zeal, fanaticism, sadism, and outright bullying. Anything he did, in his mind, was God's will. And nothing in his upbringing had taught him any better. The idea that he might lose God's blessing was alien to him.

"We will recover the occupied worlds soon," Nehemiah told him. "And then we will take the Theocracy to heights beyond imagining."

Nehemiah watched as Samuilu prostrated himself before backing out of the room, then the Speaker turned to stare out the window. Darkness hung over the city like a shroud, mocking him. The lights that would have turned his homeworld into a glittering jewel were gone. And yet, he knew what he would see in broad daylight: ramshackle apartment blocks, ugly barracks. The only truly spectacular buildings were the churches. But their presence wasn't enough to keep the city from falling apart.

It might be time to start considering other options, he thought. The Theocracy had always hung on a knife-edge between the different factions; now, with an enemy invasion on the way, that delicate balancing act was about to collapse. *And perhaps I should plan to flee the city for safer places.*

He shook his head reluctantly. There wouldn't be any safer places, not for him. If Samuilu and his ilk won the battle, if they won peace, they would hunt for Nehemiah relentlessly. But if the Commonwealth invaders won, they'd hunt for him too, intent on making him pay for the Theocracy's crimes. They wouldn't accept any excuses, not from him. They'd merely march him out into the broad sunlight, then hang him in front of the local populace. And most of the city's inhabitants would cheer.

"Bastards," he muttered.

He turned, striding towards the door. There was no escape, not now. He'd been riding a tiger most of his life. Getting off was impossible without being eaten alive. Samuilu might be right, damn him. A final decisive battle might just end the war. And even if it didn't, they'd go out in fire, a fate better than being hanged by the Commonwealth or tortured to death by the Inquisition.

Everything comes with a price, he thought as he walked down the corridor. His wives were waiting for him in the female quarters, waiting for him to favor one of them with his attentions. *And I have to pay the price too.*

◆ ◆ ◆

Ahura Mazda was the source of all evil, as far as the Commonwealth was concerned, but her primary star looked like any other star. Kat used her implants to pick it out of the star field, then studied the sun for a long, thoughtful moment. A dot of light, burning against the inky darkness of space. Nothing more. There was no sense of all-pervading evil, of the shadow that had reached out to draw dozens of worlds and millions of souls into its thrall.

She told herself, firmly, that she was being silly, yet she still felt a little disappointed. The distant star, five light-years away, was depressingly mundane.

"Our target," Pat said. They stood together in the observation blister. "It won't be long now."

Kat touched his hand. The fleet had dropped out of hyperspace once it had reached the final waypoint, allowing Admiral Christian and his command staff to check and recheck the entire command datanet before the fleet launched its offensive. Kat thought they were being paranoid, but she had to admit Admiral Christian had good reason to be careful. A single mistake in the wrong place would be disastrous.

She turned to look at Pat. "You're transferring to *Chesty Puller* this afternoon?"

"I'll be leading the first assault force," Pat said. "It's the challenge of a lifetime."

"And a very good way to get killed," Kat said. "You *will* be careful?"

Pat nodded, wordlessly. Kat knew what he was thinking. There was no way to guarantee survival, *anyone's* survival. A lone man, armor or no armor, could be swatted out of existence by a ground-based weapon, wiped out so completely that no one on the planetary surface would know they'd scored a hit. And even if he made it down safely, the enemy would throw everything they could at the spacehead, trying to obliterate it before reinforcements could be landed and brought into the battle. If something went badly wrong, Pat and his men would be trapped, unable to retreat the way they'd come.

And a single nuclear warhead would be enough to wipe out the entire landing force, she thought as she wrapped an arm around him. *They won't have any qualms about using nukes on their own homeworld.*

She leaned against him, wishing she could keep him safe. *He'd* accepted her putting herself at risk, if reluctantly; why did *she* find it harder to let him go into danger? But then, it was always easier to risk one's own life than send others to fight and perhaps die. She knew she couldn't have lived with herself if she'd sent someone else into the pirate lair.

"I'll come back," Pat promised. "You won't get rid of me this easily."

Kat elbowed him. "Prat."

Pat turned to face her, his face suddenly serious. "Kat . . . when the war is over . . . will you marry me?"

Kat stared, unable to speak as he reached into his jacket and produced a small black box, opening it to reveal an engagement ring. It was strikingly simple compared to some of the flamboyant rings she'd seen passed around high society, but that didn't matter to her. The starship etched into the gold fitted her better than diamonds, better than any gemstones.

Marriage would change her life, she knew. The navy might draw the line at allowing them to serve together. She was surprised no one had ever had a quiet word with her about their relationship, although her reputation had probably given them some protection. And Pat would have to grow used to being in high society. Her heartbeat was suddenly so loud she half suspected he could hear it. She loved him.

"I will," she said. It would work. They would *make* it work. "Yes, I *will* marry you."

She felt dazed, almost as if she was watching herself from a distance as Pat carefully removed the ring from the box and placed it on her finger. It fit perfectly, of course. Kat didn't wear rings, not on starships, but he wouldn't have had any trouble downloading her measurements from the ship's database. She studied the ring for a long moment, her eyes picking out a globe and anchor below the starship. He'd melted his commissioning coin to make the ring.

Standing on tiptoes, she kissed him. "Pat, I—"

"We'll have plenty of time during the voyage home," Pat said.

Kat groaned. Her family would want a big wedding. Her mother and sisters would want to make sure she walked down the aisle under the watching eyes of the entire planet. Their wedding would become the event of the century, everyone who was anyone invited to intrude on a private moment. She wondered, suddenly, if she could ask Admiral Christian to marry them. It would be perfectly legal.

"We'll have to endure a big wedding," she warned. They couldn't elope. She couldn't do that to her mother, even though she'd never wanted a big wedding. "And then we can go hide somewhere the media won't follow."

Pat lifted his eyebrows. "Ahura Mazda?"

Kat giggled. "Maybe," she said. "Pat—"

"I understand," Pat said. "I've stood in parades for hours. I can endure a big wedding."

"Just you wait," Kat said. She'd attended her eldest brother's wedding. Even as a guest, with no formal role in the ceremony, she'd found it tiring. And she still teased her brother about the excesses of his stag night. He'd probably want to take Pat out for a night, just to extract a little revenge. "You're going to hate it."

"I'll be with you," Pat said. "It's for a decent cause."

Kat stuck out her tongue. "Do you have any more banal romantic clichés?"

Pat grinned. "That's what I get for studying romantic movies to learn how to propose."

He met her eyes. "I love you," he said simply. "And I want to spend the rest of my life with you."

"I love you too," Kat said. She kissed him again, feeling her eyes beginning to water. "Be careful down there, all right?"

"I'm always careful," Pat said. He struck a dramatic pose, resting his hands on his hips. "I fight for the right so you may live."

Kat rolled her eyes. "And there I was thinking you watched that show for the girls."

"It's bad propaganda," Pat said. "The girls are the only things worth watching."

"True," Kat agreed.

She rolled her eyes. *I Fight for The Right* was an entertainment drama, produced and distributed shortly after the war had begun. The series followed the lives of five men and five women, the men going off to war while the women coped with life without them. Kat had thought the show stupid the first time she'd watched an episode. Endless sex scenes couldn't conceal the fact that Pat was right, it *was* poorly written propaganda. But she had to admit the series had a certain appeal too. What sort of man *wouldn't* put his life on the line to defend his home?

And yet, the producers don't seem to recognize the existence of female spacers, she thought wryly. There was a streak of sexism running through the series. *The show suggests they simply don't exist.*

Her terminal bleeped. "Commodore, Admiral Christian is requesting a private conference," Wheeler said. "Do you want me to put him through to your cabin?"

"I'll be on the flag deck in two minutes," Kat said. She hated long good-byes, but part of her wanted to stay with Pat. If she walked him to the shuttlebay—all of a sudden, the scenes where the girls had followed the men as far as they could made a great deal of sense. But she couldn't refuse Admiral Christian's call. "Have the call routed into my office."

She tapped her terminal, then looked at Pat. "Stay safe."

"I'll do my best," Pat promised. "And you too."

"I've got a superdreadnought wrapped around me and over a hundred more providing covering fire," Kat said. "I'll be safe."

"And so will I," Pat said. He gave her a kiss, then pulled back. "I wish—"

"Duty calls," Kat said. She smirked, looking down at the ring on her finger. "You should have given me the ring last night."

"We were busy," Pat said. "I love you."

He turned and headed towards the hatch. Kat fought the urge to call him back as the hatch opened. She turned and headed down to the flag deck. Wheeler was sitting at his console, watching the endless stream of updates flowing across the tactical display. Sixth Fleet, having spent the last three weeks simulating as many possible encounters as its tactical staff could imagine, was as ready as it would ever be.

"Admiral Christian has issued the last set of tactical orders," Wheeler said. "We'll be in the van."

"Good," Kat said.

She stepped through the hatch into her office, feeling oddly disconcerted as the portal closed behind her. The ring felt heavy on her finger. She understood, all of a sudden, why so many of her friends had enjoyed showing off their engagement rings. It was a sign of commitment, a sign that someone wanted to spend the rest of his life with you. And yet, what would they have endured? Pat and she had gone to war together.

Enough, she told herself firmly. *We'll be jumping in-system soon.*

She keyed her console. "Admiral," she said, "I'm here."

CHAPTER TWENTY-ONE

"Captain," Sonja Robertson whispered, "can they see us?"

William found himself torn between anger and amusement. Sonja was a reporter, a woman with long red hair and a heart-shaped face. He wasn't sure if she was as silly as she acted or not, but she had a positive gift for making people talk to her.

"I hope not," he said. "But we don't know for sure."

He smiled rather grimly. They'd slid out of hyperspace right on the edge of the system, carefully emerging on the opposite side of the sun from Ahura Mazda. And yet he wasn't sure if they'd escaped detection or not. Theocratic forces might not be able to afford the immense sensor arrays the Commonwealth used to cover its major systems, but they would definitely have rigged up a network to protect Ahura Mazda. Their homeworld could not be allowed to remain undefended.

"You could be wrong," Sonja whispered. "What then?"

William grinned. "You don't have to whisper," he said. "They can't *hear* you."

He leaned back in his command chair as the display began to fill with icons. "If they detected our arrival, they'll either wait for us to do something or dispatch a squadron out here to catch us," he added. "We can evade any hunters if they do come after us."

Sonja gave him a sharp look. "And how long will it take for them to react?"

"I have no idea," William said. "We'll know when their ships arrive."

He forced himself to relax as *Thunderchild* crawled forward, her passive sensors drinking in every last fragment of data. The Ahura Mazda system slowly began to take shape in front of him: a dozen cloudscoops, hundreds of asteroid mining stations, large settlements on a dozen planets and moons. Yet he still felt that there was something odd about the whole display. He mulled the problem over, time and time again, as his ship crept farther into the system, considering and discarding possibilities one by one. The Theocracy had apparently worked hard to center everything on Ahura Mazda.

Perhaps they did, he thought. *They want to keep everything under their direct control.*

That made sense, he reasoned. The pre-space powers had lost control of dozens of asteroid settlements during the march into space, as the interests of the spacers diverged from their former masters. Quite a few of the early out-system colonies had been founded by men and women who wanted to get away from Earth. The UN had certainly found it impossible to keep control of hundreds of colonies, despite being far more powerful than all the colonies put together. Clearly, the Theocracy had learned a few lessons from the past.

"Captain, I think the cloudscoops are pushing their systems to the limit," Cecelia said. "I'm not sure how long they can sustain this tempo."

William rose and paced over to her console. "Why do you think that?"

"Here," Cecelia said. "They're pushing out HE3 containers at a staggering rate, better than *we* can do. I think they're pushing themselves too hard."

"Oh, what a shame," William said. He looked up at the system display, silently estimating just how much raw material was being mined and shipped to the industrial nodes orbiting Ahura Mazda. "You may be right."

Sonja looked at him. "Does that mean that their system will collapse under its own weight?"

"I don't know," William said. He returned to his command chair and sat down. "But it would be unwise to *count* on it happening."

The hours ticked away slowly as the starship slid into the system, heading straight for Ahura Mazda itself. William forced himself to take a break, leaving Roach in command, even though sleep was impossible when they were so close to the enemy homeworld. He could practically *feel* the Theocrats watching for his ship, even though he *knew* such sensations were nothing more than his imagination. No wonder Sonja and everyone else spoke in whispers. The sense they were being watched, that the slightest sound would give them away, was impossible to ignore. Cold logic said otherwise, but what was cold logic now?

His terminal bleeped. "Captain to the bridge; I say again, captain to the bridge."

He strode back onto the bridge. "Report!"

"The enemy sensor network surrounding Ahura Mazda is good," Roach reported. "Too good."

William scowled. The Theocracy had deployed everything from simple radar to laser cages and active sensor beams. Getting through the sensor haze without being detected would be almost impossible, unless the Commonwealth ships were *very* lucky. Perhaps they could sneak through posing as a sensor malfunction, but he doubted they'd survive the attempt. It didn't look as though the network had been overstressed and was on the verge of breaking down. The Theocracy certainly wouldn't ignore an alarm so close to their homeworld.

"Hold us here," he said. "We'll see how much we can pick up without going any closer."

Ahura Mazda unfolded in front of them, a planet ringed by industrial nodes, shipyards, orbital battlestations, and asteroid habitats.

William had seen long-range sensor scans before, but seeing the planet in person brought it home to him just how much firepower the Theocrats had assembled to protect their homeworld. Six squadrons of superdreadnoughts and hundreds of smaller starships were merely the icing on the cake. Layer after layer of defenses would make breaking through incredibly costly.

He sucked in his breath. Hundreds of freighters held position near the industrial nodes, more transport than he'd thought remained in the Theocracy. It was hard to be sure, thanks to the sensor haze, but the freighters didn't *look* non-functional. Perhaps the Theocracy had been unable to crew the ships, or perhaps they were fearful of losing them to deep-strike raiders. Or perhaps—he shook his head. The answer, he was sure, would only make sense to the Theocrats.

They have enough escorts covering their homeworld to get a convoy safely through the Gap, he mused. *And yet they're holding them here.*

"I'm picking up over a thousand orbital weapons platforms and missile pods," Cecelia said. "They've been improving their defenses since the last time the system was probed."

Roach scowled. "Do they know we're coming?"

"Unknown," Cecelia said.

William let out a breath. The Theocracy could have deduced the Commonwealth's plan. Or they might simply have been reluctant to uncover their homeworld, even though the ships tied down guarding Ahura Mazda would have tipped the balance in any one of a dozen battles. For all he knew, someone had discovered the wrecked minefield and sounded the alert.

"Leave it for the moment," he ordered. "Can you get any solid visuals on the ground?"

"Some," Cecelia said. "But the detail isn't great."

"Show me," William ordered.

He shuddered as Ahura Mazda took on shape and form. Admiral Junayd had warned them that Ahura Mazda was densely populated, but he'd been understating the case. The largest city on Hebrides would have vanished without a trace on Ahura Mazda. The largest city on Tyre was still only a quarter of the size of the megacities on Ahura Mazda. Even from this distance, the cities were clearly overpopulated. He couldn't help wondering why the Theocrats hadn't expanded their metropolises or even established new ones. But he had a feeling that it would make social control difficult if they tried.

Bastards, he thought.

"I'm picking up over fifty PDCs," Cecelia said. "Their interlocking force fields will cover their capital and much of the surrounding countryside."

William glanced at her. "Is there a place for the marines to land?"

"I think so," Cecelia said. "But getting down is going to be hellish."

"Yes," William agreed. "*That* is fairly clear."

He studied the display for a long moment. Sixth Fleet *should* have enough firepower to sweep the planet's orbit clear of threats, but the engagement was going to be costly. And risky too, if a warhead accidentally struck the planet's surface. The possibility of accidentally committing mass slaughter could not be ignored.

But there was no way to avoid it. "Do you have solid locks on their defenses?"

"Yes, Captain," Cecelia said. "The superdreadnoughts may change position, of course."

"Of course," William agreed. He wished, suddenly, for the long-range missiles they'd used at Hebrides. But there just weren't enough left to make an impact. "I don't believe there is anything to be gained from trying to sneak closer."

Roach looked up. "Captain, our orders say we need to probe the system."

"And avoid detection," William pointed out. "If we slip any closer, Mr. XO, there is a very real chance of being detected and killed. And then the mission will be compromised."

"True, sir," Roach agreed reluctantly.

William didn't blame him for being concerned. It was *important* to have solid data on the defenses. Nothing they'd gleaned from previous recon flights could be trusted, not when the Theocracy had plenty of time to reposition its battlestations and emplace more automatic weapons. But there was always a point of diminishing returns. Getting closer would give them harder data, yet it would also raise the specter of being detected and destroyed. And then *none* of the data they collected would survive.

He glanced at Cecelia. "Do you have a solid lock on their StarCom?"

"Here," Cecelia said. She tapped an icon on the display. "It seems to be a modified Type-III, Captain. I doubt they have the ability for real-time conversations between star systems."

"It doesn't matter," William said. "A simple email will be more than enough to carry orders from place to place."

Sonja glanced at him. "Like a command to destroy every last occupied world?"

"Yes," William agreed. "They could send such a command, if they wanted."

He looked at Cecelia. "Can you determine what other targets need investigating?"

"They have several shipyards and a smaller web of defenses around their moon," Cecelia said slowly. "And a large facility that doesn't seem to have any purpose."

"That's an antimatter production facility," Roach said. William glanced at him, surprised and alarmed. "What *else* could it be?"

He might be right, William realized. The facility looked like a giant fuel storage dump, yet he saw no sign of a mining station on the lunar surface. And it *was* holding station on the far side of the moon, with all its mass between the facility and Ahura Mazda. The Commonwealth preferred to keep its antimatter production stations on the far side of the sun, but the Theocracy was too paranoid to let the antimatter out of its sight. *William* wouldn't have cared to take the risk—the threat of losing control of the antimatter outweighed the security risk if the facility were located on the far side of the sun—yet the Theocracy seemed to feel differently.

"Mark it down for attention when we hit the system," he ordered. A simple missile would be more than enough to take out the facility, knocking out the containment systems and detonating the antimatter. Done properly, parts of the Theocracy's defenses would be badly damaged. "What about the rest of the system?"

"There's very little worth inspecting, sir," Cecelia said. "Just cloudscoops and mining stations."

"Unless they're hiding an entire fleet in stealth," Roach put in. "They *could*."

"Let us hope not," William said. He didn't think an entire stealthed fleet was particularly likely. If the Theocracy had a few extra superdreadnought squadrons, it would have sent them to the war. The ships might have made a real difference if they'd been deployed six months ago. "Helm, pull us back carefully."

"Aye, sir," Gross said.

William sat back down, bracing himself. Crawling out of the system would be just as nerve-wracking as sneaking into the system, although the odds of being detected would go down sharply as soon as they were away from Ahura Mazda. It would take a stroke of very bad luck to be detected. And yet . . . he pushed the thought aside as he studied the live feed from the tactical department. Admiral Christian's staff would draw the final conclusions, of course, but *his* staff was telling him things he didn't want to know about the planet's defenses. Getting through them was going to be incredibly costly.

"Captain," Sonja said, "can we take the system?"

"Yes," William said. He rose. "But it won't be painless."

He passed command to Roach and motioned for the reporter to follow him into his office. The coming battle *wouldn't* be painless.

Hundreds of ships would be destroyed, perhaps including *Thunderchild*. But it had to be done.

"There's a lot of ships out there," Sonja said. "Are you sure we weren't detected?"

"There's no way to be entirely sure," William said. "But the odds of us having been detected are very low. Coffee?"

Sonja shook her head. She looked tired, he noticed, despite using her implants to keep awake. He didn't really blame her, even though experienced naval officers knew the odds of anything happening in interplanetary space were very low. Her bosses would be furious if she was asleep when something newsworthy happened.

She sat down on his sofa. "What happens if they *do* detect us?"

"We run," William said. "There's no point in trying to break contact."

He sat down in his chair, sipping his coffee. "You have to understand the scale of interplanetary space," he said. "A planet, even one as developed as Ahura Mazda, is very small. A starship is so tiny, it's really no more evident than a grain of dust floating in the air back home. They are not likely to detect us so long as we don't do anything stupid."

"So I've been told," Sonja said.

She leaned back, curling up her legs. "Do you *want* to see Ahura Mazda burn, Captain?"

"I want the war to end," William said firmly. "And I want it to end in a manner that ensures the Theocracy won't rise again."

Sonja met his eyes. "Do you want revenge for your homeworld?"

William took a moment to formulate his reply. "Burning their homeworld to ash would merely pile one crime on top of another," he said. On or off the record, the question needed to be answered carefully. "The vast majority of the folks down there have absolutely no control over their lives, let alone what their government does. It is not right that they should suffer or die. Revenge would be satisfying, but it would get us nothing."

He paused. "Does that answer your question?"

"I thought your people prided themselves on being hot-blooded," Sonja said.

"A common misunderstanding," William said. He wondered absently just who'd been filling her head with such crap. Sociologists were about as trustworthy as psychologists and only marginally more useful. "My people pride themselves on standing *up* for themselves, in handling certain matters themselves. If a person crosses the line, we are expected to deal with it ourselves, not go whining to higher authority."

He took a breath. "But a fistfight with a man doesn't oblige you to pick a fight with his wife and children too," he added. "How could our society have survived?"

"And yet you've lost everything," Sonja said. "Aren't you *angry*?"

William met her eyes. "If I thought that destroying Ahura Mazda would bring back the dead civilians and rebuild the smashed cities, I would destroy that cursed world without a second thought," he said. "But it won't. No amount of revenge and bloody slaughter will bring life back to the dead. I am angry, yes. I am angry at the bastards down there who have plunged their own people into a futile war and killed millions, perhaps billions, of innocents in a desperate bid to impose their will on the universe. I want them dead and gone.

"But I will do my duty, because that's all I have left. Do you understand me?"

Sonja leaned back, as if he was looming over her. William allowed himself a tight smile at her reaction. She might have been born on Tyre, one of the most cosmopolitan worlds in the galaxy, but she hadn't had much experience dealing with people from other cultures. It wasn't easy sometimes to understand, *truly* understand, that some people just thought differently than others. He wondered absently how she would handle herself on Ahura Mazda. She'd need protection at all times just to keep her safe from the crowds.

"Yes, Captain," she said. "I think I do."

"Good," William said. He yawned suddenly. "I'd suggest you take a nap. Nothing is going to happen for several hours at least."

Sonja lifted her eyebrows. "And if it does?"

"The crew has standing orders to hop into hyperspace at the merest hint we've been detected," William said, "then deploy jammers to hide our retreat. Any excitement won't last very long."

He yawned again. "I'm taking a nap too," he added. "It will be fine."

"I hope you're right," Sonja said. She didn't sound convinced. Perhaps she thought he was meant to be on the bridge, striking dramatic poses, until they were well away from Ahura Mazda. "And I hope we will have the chance to talk again."

She rose and headed for the hatch, her hips flowing in a natural rhythm. William caught himself staring at her backside, very clearly outlined by her shipsuit, and looked away, cursing himself under his breath. He was too tired to talk to a reporter, or anyone really. And yet, the sight of this woman reminded him just how much he'd put aside since he'd joined the Royal Navy. Save for a few sessions with spaceport sex workers, he'd never found a woman. He'd always put marriage off, assuming he would one day return home and find a wife. Now it was too late.

Maybe I should have taken Morag up on her offer, he thought as he lay down on the sofa and closed his eyes. *But I couldn't have lived with myself afterwards.*

CHAPTER TWENTY-TWO

"Ladies and gentlemen," Admiral Christian said. "The face of the enemy."

Kat sucked in her breath as Ahura Mazda appeared in front of her, ringed by row after row of defenses. Superdreadnoughts, orbital battlestations, so many automated weapons platforms that the analysts had practically lost count. Their best guesses about gunboats, armed shuttles, and other surprises were flowing up at the bottom of the display, warning that Ahura Mazda could potentially be defended by over a hundred thousand gunboats. Kat rather suspected that was a gross exaggeration, but she had no way of being sure. The Theocracy might have decided to plow vast resources into producing gunboats as the war swung against them.

"Our principal target remains Ahura Mazda," Admiral Christian continued. "Should we lose the engagement, for whatever reason, our flanking units will obliterate the cloudscoops as we retreat. Starving the system of HE3 will certainly do a great deal of harm to their economy, whatever else happens. We will, of course, attempt to ravage their system as thoroughly as possible."

He paused, his holographic image moving around the display. "We will aim to drop out of hyperspace here," he added, tapping a location near the planet. "Ideally, we will have plenty of room to deploy the fleet before they have a chance to muster a counterattack. We will, however, proceed on the assumption that they will throw everything they have at us before we reach orbital engagement range. They'll be very edgy about warheads flying around near their shipyards."

Kat nodded. It made sense. Any rational defender would prefer to keep the engagement as far from his shipyards as possible. But the Theocracy might not have that option. Their orbital space was so crammed that any detonation would probably damage *something*. Who could tell for sure?

"Once we clear orbital space, we will continue with the plan and attempt to land the marines," Admiral Christian said. "Should we be unable to isolate a suitable landing site, we will clear space to *make* them a landing site and establish a spacehead. At the same time, we will destroy the remainder of the system's infrastructure. One way or another, the Theocracy will lose the war today."

He paused. "Any questions?"

Captain Rogers loomed into view. "Shouldn't we attempt to *capture* their facilities?"

"Ideally, yes," Admiral Christian said. "We don't know how many of their industrial workers are volunteers and how many are slaves. We do know that the Theocracy has been rounding up anyone with industrial skills and shipping them to their homeworld. But we have to face the fact that they're unlikely to just *let* us take the shipyards. They might try to destroy them first."

"The crews might have a plan to rebel," Kat mused.

"We can't count on it," Admiral Christian said. "And mutiny isn't easy when your enemies hold all the cards."

He went on. "We leave our current position and advance in two hours," he said. "If there are any problems, I want to know about them before we leave."

"Just one," Captain Dawlish said. "Do they know we're coming?"

"Unknown," Admiral Christian said. "The analysts *think* they haven't been overloading their sensor systems, but they have enough sensors that they might be able to cycle them regularly, keeping up a basic maintenance routine while scouring space for any sign of threats. Or they may have discovered our passage through the minefield and drawn the right conclusions."

"Or they might have blown up the other worlds already," Dawlish pointed out.

"Mind on the job, Captain," Admiral Christian said tartly. "Right now, we have one task—get in there, blow the hell out of the defenses, and capture that damned world. They don't have enough firepower to stop us, and that, my friends, is all that matters."

And if we're wrong about that, Kat thought, *we can still devastate their system as we leave.*

"Assemble your formations," Admiral Christian ordered. "We leave in two hours."

His image flickered out of existence. Kat took a long breath, studying the planet's image thoughtfully. She'd commanded the attack on Hebrides, but Hebrides's defenses had been flimsy compared to the solid wall of firepower surrounding Ahura Mazda. The Theocracy had pushed everything it could into securing its homeworld, wasting resources she hadn't thought the government had. And yet, the gamble might have paid off for them. The Commonwealth was going to take significant losses even if it won.

We will win, she told herself firmly. *Even if they know we're coming, we will still win.*

She took a moment to gather herself, then rose and strode onto the flag bridge. Her squadron was already assembled, ready to open a gateway and slip into hyperspace at a moment's notice. Five light-years. It wouldn't take more than a few hours to reach their target, even if they were careful not to charge straight at Ahura Mazda. But they would. The longer they took to get there, the greater the chance of being detected. A handful of antimatter warheads would scatter the fleet and buy the Theocracy time to mount a defense.

"Commodore," Wheeler said, "fleet-level datanet engaged, repeaters on. Squadron-level datanet engaged, repeaters on. Tactical-combat datanet engaged, repeaters on."

He paused. "Squadron is currently at yellow alert," he added. "Should we go to red alert?"

"Negative," Kat said.

She sank into her command chair, her eyes flickering down the readiness reports. Commanding officers had been known to do a little fiddling, to suggest that their ships were in a better state than they were, but it didn't look as though any of her officers had decided to be dishonest. She couldn't blame them for wanting to stand up and fight, yet a damaged superdreadnought might be more trouble than it was worth. But it didn't matter.

"We depart in two hours," she said, glancing at the fleet-wide datanet. The fleet would spread out for the remainder of the journey, then bunch up again before emerging at Ahura Mazda. "Let the crews have their rest. They'll need it."

Kat closed her eyes for a long moment, feeling the superdreadnought's drives thrumming around her. She and Captain Higgins knew what was going on, but the ship's crew knew almost nothing. They were trapped inside an immense metal hull, rattling around inside her like peas in a pod, utterly unaware of their surroundings. They'd never see the warhead that punched through the shields and destroyed the ship, killing them before they had a chance to escape.

For some of them, she knew, the coming engagement would be their first taste of combat. Fran had argued against it, but they'd had to take on new crewmen during their layover at McCaughey. Some of the newcomers would be nervous, wondering how they would perform under fire; others would be waiting impatiently, relishing the challenge. She had no doubt that some of them were silently relieved that the war wasn't over yet, that their training hadn't gone to waste, that they'd have a chance to win glory. But glory came with a steep price. Kat knew all too well just how many men and women had died under her command. How many others would join them before the end of the war?

Wheeler cleared his throat. "Commodore, we have the final deployment orders from *Hammerhead*," he said. "We're ready to go."

Kat nodded. "Pass the word," she said. "We depart when the admiral gives the command."

◆ ◆ ◆

"It looks nasty," General Winters said.

"Yes, sir," Pat agreed. *Thunderchild* hadn't managed to get very good images of the potential landing sites, but he'd already spotted several possibilities. "I think our greatest advantage is going with Site Beta."

"It's a little close to a city," General Winters pointed out. "And *far* too close to the outer edge of the force shield."

"There aren't many other options unless we can bring down one of the shields," Pat pointed out. "And there's no certainty of finding help down there."

"Perhaps there's a tribe of cute and cuddly teddy bears willing to help," General Winters said mischievously. "No way to pick out any other ground-based defenses, Pat."

"Yes, sir," Pat said. "But that's likely to be true of almost everywhere."

General Winters nodded. "We'll be launching drones towards the planet as soon as the fleet deploys," he said. "Hopefully, we'll get some harder data before it's too late."

"And if we do run into trouble," Pat added, "we'll be able to stem the flow of reinforcements."

"Yes," General Winters agreed. He stuck out a hand. "Good luck, Pat."

Pat tersely took Winters's hand. Compared to offering Kat an engagement ring, dropping onto a heavily armed planet was peanuts. But he knew he would soon come to regret that glib analysis. Kat wouldn't have tried to kill him, whatever happened. The fanatics down on Ahura Mazda certainly would, if they got the chance. And no matter how many wildly optimistic assumptions they'd fed into the simulators, getting cut off from orbit would be absolutely disastrous. He wouldn't bet a single forced credit note from Jorlem that they'd be taken prisoner and treated well.

We'll be killed out of hand, he thought. *And we know it.*

He turned and strode into the next compartment. His company, one hundred marines, were sleeping on the racks, resting before being thrown into combat. Marines had all sorts of enhancements, but even the best of them couldn't keep someone alert indefinitely. Pat had been told that he could remain awake for over five days with a carefully tailored cocktail of stimulants, yet he didn't believe such exaggerations. His mind had always started to wander badly after four days without sleep.

Sergeant Bones sat up. She was one of the very few women in the Marine Corps, a native of a high-gravity world. The genetic engineering that had prepared her family for their new world had left her with a powerful form. Her muscles rippled under her shirt as she moved. The Theocracy probably wouldn't recognize her as a woman at all.

"Colonel," she said, "the company is ready to drop."

Pat nodded, glancing at his terminal. "We have seven hours, at least, before we drop."

"Yeah," Bones said. "Get some sleep."

"I will," Pat promised. "Is there anything I should be aware of?"

"Colin and Chad are hooked up with a pair of pretty young midshipwomen," Bones said stiffly. She was, Pat knew, a traditionalist at heart. Marines were not, in her worldview, supposed to socialize with the crew. "Duke's currently bonking Lieutenant George or being bonked by him, I don't know. I've told all three of them that they'll be thumped if they're not back here by 0900 to get a nap."

"A soldier who won't fuck won't fight," Pat pointed out.

"Yeah, but rest will do them more good than fucking," Bones said. "We're going to be depending on those three sluts when we drop."

"And we can depend on them," Pat assured her. In truth, he was surprised that only *three* marines had sought company for what could easily be their final night. *Chesty Puller* wasn't a superdreadnought, but her crew was large enough to include plenty of eligible young men and women. "Let them have their fun."

Bones sniffed in disapproval but said nothing as Pat undressed and clambered into his rack for a quick nap. They'd be woken, if they weren't already awake, an hour before the fleet zoomed out of hyperspace and encountered . . . what? Pat had seen enough of Ahura Mazda's defenses to know his marines were going to have a hard fight. He closed his eyes and tried to force himself to relax. He'd never found it easy to rest before an opposed landing.

She said yes, he thought. It still astonished him. *She said yes!*

The thought made him smile. He loved her, he *knew* he loved her, but he'd been unsure quite how she would react to his proposal. She loved him, he thought, yet . . . she'd said yes. He pushed his doubts aside, firmly. She'd said yes.

And then sleep reached up and overcame him.

◆ ◆ ◆

"It's a very heavily defended world," Grivets said. "Can we take it?"

"There's no such thing as an invulnerable world," Junayd said. He felt tense as the fleet rocketed towards its destination. The *last* time he'd been on a fleet heading for its target, he'd been sitting in the command chair. Now, he was just a helpless spectator. "It will be costly, yes. But it can be taken."

Janice frowned as she walked around the giant hologram. "Have the defenses been improved since you left?"

"There appear to be more automated platforms," Junayd said. "But they haven't installed any more battlestations."

"That adds weight to your claims about their economic infrastructure," Janice pointed out. "I don't think they can *afford* to build any more battlestations."

"Losses during the first phase of the war were higher than predicted," Junayd reminded her dryly. "Right now, they're trying to rebuild their superdreadnought fleets before it's too late."

It *was* too late, he knew. Passive sensors hadn't been able to pick up enough detail, but he could tell that there were seven superdreadnoughts in the shipyards, in varying stages of construction. Building had been slowing down even before he'd defected as the weaknesses in the Theocracy's industrial machine began to bite; now, he would be surprised if the Theocracy could produce a new superdreadnought in less than a year. And enemy warheads striking the shipyards would put their building program far behind schedule.

And their time is up, he thought grimly. *Nemesis is approaching.*

He surveyed the display for a long moment. The battlestations might not have been modified in the months since the war began. He'd certainly urged that the most advanced technology in the Theocracy— begged, bought, or stolen from the other interstellar powers—be deployed straight to the war front, where victory or defeat would be decided. And if that was the case, the battlestations would have weak fire-control systems and weaker point defense. The war had taught the Theocracy a number of very hard lessons.

"The crews might not be ready too," he mused.

Janice looked up. "Say what?"

"The battlestations are often crewed by relatives of various power-ful men," Junayd explained simply. "It keeps them away from the war front."

Grivets laughed humorlessly. "A powerful aristocracy keeping its family out of danger? How very much like home."

"That isn't true," Janice said sharply. "Lots of aristocrats put their lives in danger."

Junayd didn't bother to dispute it. "The point, young man, is that the battlestations might not be trained and drilled for war," he added. "Your people will have a chance to strike them before they're ready to meet you."

Janice looked doubtful. "If each of those battlestations has a thou-sand crewmen," she commented, "would they all be . . . well, *aristocrats*?"

"You might be surprised," Junayd told her. "I have seven brothers, thirty-seven cousins, and over a hundred nephews."

Grivets sneered. "No sisters or nieces?"

"In the Theocracy," Junayd reminded him, "only *men* can wield power."

"Yes," Grivets said. "And you brain-burn any woman smart enough to question why that is so. You'd probably have tried engineering women for dumbness if it wouldn't come back to bite you."

Junayd bowed his head ruefully. He wouldn't have put it past the more extreme fanatics to try, even though human history suggested that letting that particular genie out of the bottle would be disas-trous. Several asteroid habitats had attempted to create a slave race, for all intents and purposes, only to discover that their modified genes spread into the masters too. They'd effectively enslaved themselves. The Theocracy preferred to use the tried and tested methods of poor educa-tion, intimidation, violence, and if all else failed, brainwashing.

Any woman smart enough to realize what will happen to her if she opens her mouth, he thought coldly, *is smart enough to keep her mouth shut.*

Janice looked at him. "Your society disgusts me."

"Yes," Junayd agreed. "And that is why it has to change."

◆ ◆ ◆

"Signal from the flag," Wheeler said as Kat stepped back onto the flag bridge. "We're to exit hyperspace in thirty minutes."

Kat nodded as she took her chair. *Queen Elizabeth* was preparing for war, the low drumbeat of action stations echoing through the ship as her crew rushed to their duty posts. Captain Higgins had been running plenty of drills over the last week, everything from missile replenishment to damage control; soon, Kat knew, they'd have a chance to see just how well they would perform under fire.

"Check and recheck all combat systems," she ordered. Admiral Christian was doing the same, testing the combat datanet as the fleet bunched up again. "Did we pick up any enemy traffic?"

"Negative, Commodore," Wheeler said.

Kat pursed her lips, suspicious. The Theocracy *was* having shipping troubles, yet if they couldn't move supplies from place to place, they didn't have a Theocracy. Sixth Fleet wasn't flying through the middle of nowhere, well off the shipping lanes; they were approaching a capital world, the heart of a major interstellar power. The fleet *should* have picked up something heading towards Ahura Mazda, save for themselves.

Her unease grew as the timer ticked down remorselessly. The fleet was ready, its missile launchers and point defense systems primed to engage targets as soon as Admiral Christian gave the order. And yet, she was sure something was wrong. But no matter how she tried, she couldn't put her finger on it.

"Commodore," Wheeler said, "five minutes to emergence."

Kat braced herself. "Bring the squadron to red alert," she ordered. "Stand by for combat maneuvers."

"Aye, Commodore," Wheeler said. Sirens howled through the massive ship. "Three minutes to emergence."

Here we go, Kat thought. Her eyes sought out and found *Chesty Puller*, shadowing the superdreadnoughts, then *Thunderchild*, holding position with the rest of the flankers. *Ten seconds . . .*

"Gateways opening now," Wheeler said. Kat leaned forward as the display rapidly began to update itself. "We are entering the Ahura Mazda system."

CHAPTER TWENTY-THREE

Admiral Zaskar was not a very happy man.

To be told that a major enemy fleet was bearing down on Ahura Mazda, a world he was charged to defend, was quite bad enough. He'd drawn up a number of contingency plans for enemy attack, but none of them had actually been *tested*. And yet, to be given some very specific orders from the council was worse. He didn't *want* to carry out his orders, not given the likely danger to his homeworld, but he had no choice. The Inquisition had already taken his wives and children into protective custody. He had no doubt that one of his own crew would stick a knife in him if he disobeyed orders while his family would bear the brunt of the Inquisition's displeasure.

He paced his command deck, taking bitter satisfaction in watching the operators do their level best to avoid his notice. They might bow and scrape in front of him, but they knew as well as Zaskar did that he wasn't the ultimate authority on his flagship. *That* rested in the hands of a dozen red-robed Inquisitors and a company of elite soldiers, armed to the teeth and occupying strategic positions throughout the giant superdreadnought. Zaskar could issue orders, but if the Inquisitors saw fit to overrule him, they would.

He ground his teeth in frustration. Zaskar was convinced that ultimate victory would soon be theirs, but even *he* had to admit that the war was going badly. The demands of home defense prevented him from cutting loose a few squadrons of escort ships, ensuring that the freighters orbiting Ahura Mazda couldn't be sent out to resupply the fleets. Ahura Mazda had plenty of supplies, but getting them to where they were needed was impossible. And the infidel crews who had been hired at such high costs were growing restive, even though the camps where they were being held were practically luxury resorts. They would have to be purged soon, just for asking one too many questions.

And now the enemy fleet is closing in on us, he thought. He'd run the calculations a dozen times, but he didn't have the data to make more than educated guesses about the transit time between the Gap and Ahura Mazda. *When will they arrive?*

He paced backwards and forwards, glaring at the display. There was a truly staggering amount of firepower surrounding Ahura Mazda, yet it might not be enough to stave off the enemy attack, *particularly* if he carried out his orders. But he had no choice. As much as it galled him, he knew he had to obey. His life depended on submission.

An alarm sounded. "Admiral," one of his operators said, "a gateway is opening . . . correction, *multiple* gateways opening."

"Bring the fleet to full alert," Zaskar ordered. God, how he'd had to argue just to convince the watchdogs that there was nothing suspicious in not calling a full alert before the enemy actually arrived! Such a move would have just put wear and tear on his equipment and personnel he couldn't afford. "Ready the planetary defenses and then pass the word to the commanding officers. They are to open their sealed orders now."

"Aye, Admiral," the operator said.

Zaskar heard a muttered curse from the rear of the compartment as the enemy ships kept streaming out of hyperspace. Fifty superdreadnoughts . . . seventy superdreadnoughts . . . ninety superdreadnoughts . . . a hundred and *thirty* superdreadnoughts. He wanted to believe that most of them were decoys, sensor drones masquerading as superdreadnoughts, but his memories of the highly classified briefings on the Commonwealth's building programs suggested otherwise. And nearly a thousand smaller ships. They'd come out of hyperspace farther away from Ahura Mazda than he'd expected, but the deployment made a certain kind of sense. If coordinating four or five squadrons of superdreadnoughts and smaller ships was a headache, coordinating over a thousand ships had to be an absolute nightmare.

They'll need time to get into formation and ready their weapons, he thought. *And we're not going to let them have the time.*

"Signal the fleet," he ordered. Thankfully, the defenders had been given just enough time to prepare. "Task Force One will advance and engage the enemy. Task Force Two will prepare to execute Operation Night."

He sat down, grimly anticipating confusion and panic in the ranks. The sealed orders had been handed over with all the verification they could possibly need, but they were so strange compared to the normal run of orders, he knew too many of his men were going to question them. It was quite possible that the various watchdogs would react badly to an attempt to put the orders into practice, though the chief Inquisitors had been briefed on the plan. The enemy commanders just didn't know how lucky they were. Zaskar would have happily sold his soul for a chance to command without a minder watching over his shoulder.

A low quiver ran through the superdreadnought as her engineers brought her drives up to full power. Zaskar let out a breath he hadn't realized he'd been holding. Ahura Mazda's defenders had the best of everything, including repair crews, but he was all too aware that maintenance issues were a serious problem. Too many components coming off the production lines had been faulty for him to trust the engineers completely, even though the Inquisition had publicly executed a number of workers for poor work habits. And yet, his fleet appeared to be responding normally.

"Combat datanet engaged," an operator said. "Fleet online, missile batteries primed and ready to fire; point defense primed, ready to fire."

Zaskar smiled. One way or the other, the enemy was in for a nasty surprise.

"Deploy combat drones," he ordered. "And then prepare to fire on my command."

♦ ♦ ♦

"Launch drones," Kat ordered as Ahura Mazda appeared in front of her on the display, glowing blue against the inky darkness of space. "Ready all point defense systems."

"All systems online," Wheeler said. "Command datanet verified, point defense datanet and subnets online."

Kat nodded as more and more icons flickered into life on the display. She'd seen the raw data, of course, and read the assessments from ONI, but there was something about seeing Ahura Mazda in person that gave her chills. The planet was surrounded with enough icons to make up a small galaxy, ranging from tiny automated weapons platforms to giant asteroid habitats that would have to be watched carefully. Her drones, speeding away from the fleet, provided a constant stream of data, telling her things she hadn't wanted to know about the sheer level of firepower surrounding the cursed world. It didn't look as though 6th Fleet could count on the enemy defenses failing at a crucial moment.

"The enemy fleet is leaving orbit," Wheeler said. He paused, as if he couldn't quite believe what he was seeing. "The *entire* enemy fleet is leaving orbit."

Kat blinked. "The *entire* fleet?"

"Yes, Commodore," Wheeler said. "Every last starship, military or civilian, is leaving orbit and coming right at us."

The display updated, again. Hundreds of warships, ranging from superdreadnoughts to destroyers and corvettes; hundreds of freighters, ranging from tiny shuttles and light freighters to giant bulk freighters and colonist-carriers, all heading directly towards 6th Fleet. She'd expected the enemy to try to engage her forces as far from Ahura Mazda as possible, just to limit the risk to the planet's orbital installations, but she hadn't expected them to throw *everything* at 6th Fleet. And yet, the Theocrats *were* heavily outgunned. Perhaps they assumed that the freighters would soak up missiles that would otherwise take out superdreadnoughts.

And wrecking the remainder of their transport capability isn't exactly going to hurt, Kat thought snidely. *Even if we did nothing else, taking it out would practically guarantee that the remainder of their bases would wither on the vine.*

"Signal from the flag," Wheeler reported. "Admiral Christian is ordering us to reduce speed."

Letting them come to us, Kat thought. She doubted the fixed defenses could engage her fleet, not until the range closed sharply, but she saw no point in taking chances. Engaging the mobile units, and *then* the fixed defenses, would be a great deal easier than trying to tackle both at once. *Smart move.*

Kat sucked in her breath as the wall of icons advanced towards her fleet; gunboats and shuttles in the lead, freighters following, warships bringing up the rear. Admiral Christian deployed his own gunboats, ordering them to engage the enemy ships as they closed in with terrifying speed. Surely they couldn't have armed the freighters, could they? Freighters rarely carried anything more dangerous than point defense weapons, nothing more than popguns compared to military-grade armaments. But even if they had, the freighters wouldn't make good warships. Their only advantage lay in their size, and *that* wasn't enough to save them from antimatter warheads.

A thought struck her.

"Signal the flag," she said sharply. "Those shuttles are suicide runners!"

She cursed as a gunboat fired on a shuttle, only to be blotted out of existence by a colossal explosion. Kat didn't need the hasty report from the tactical department to *know* the shuttle had been crammed with antimatter, more than enough to devastate any target it actually happened to hit. The display fuzzed a second later as enemy ECM came into play, trying to confuse or blind her fleet's sensors. Theocratic ECM was inferior to Commonwealth technology, but there was an awful lot of it. The shuttles picked up speed, their gunboat escorts concentrating on engaging the Commonwealth's gunboats. A moment later, a shuttle slammed into a destroyer and both ships vanished in a terrible explosion.

"HMS *Buckley* is gone," Wheeler reported. "Point defense is engaging now."

Kat gritted her teeth, then keyed her console. "Get me an analysis," she ordered the tactical department. "Are those freighters crammed with antimatter too?"

◆ ◆ ◆

"The enemy has realized the danger," Zaskar mused as three more shuttles were blotted from existence. Antimatter was very much a two-edged sword. It couldn't be taken out before it could be detonated, unlike nuclear warheads, but its explosion could be dangerous to both sides. "They're concentrating on taking down the shuttles."

Taking out the shuttles *was* a good tactic, he had to admit. Indeed, it was the *only* workable tactic. A lone shuttle posed no threat to a mighty superdreadnought, but a lone shuttle crammed with antimatter could be catastrophic. And the shuttle crews were fanatics, primed to get their craft to their targets or die trying. Each successive blast, combined with the ECM, weakened the enemy point defense network, making it easier for the next shuttle to get through. Four enemy starships had already been destroyed.

But he had more cards to play.

"Signal the freighters," he ordered. "They are authorized to open fire."

♦ ♦ ♦

"Commodore, the freighters are volley-firing missiles," Wheeler reported.

"I see," Kat said.

She felt sweat trickling down her back as the new icons appeared on the display. The enemy missiles looked old, lacking the speed and probably the warheads of modern weapons, but that didn't stop them from being deadly. Her drones reported that the Theocrats had largely bolted missile pods to freighter hulls, turning them into one-shot weapons. And she *still* didn't know if the ships were crammed with antimatter or not.

"Signal from the flag," Wheeler said. "All enemy targets are to be engaged."

Kat silently saluted the enemy commander as *Queen Elizabeth* launched her first salvo, emptying her external racks as well as her missile tubes. The freighters *would* absorb most of her opening barrage, particularly with the enemy superdreadnoughts hanging back just out of missile range. But Admiral Christian had fourteen superdreadnought squadrons to four. The enemy might have scored a tiny win, yet odds like that couldn't be beaten. Sixth Fleet could shoot off two-thirds of its missiles and *still* have a decisive advantage.

She watched, grimly, as the barrage neared its targets. The freighters didn't seem to have any point defense, let alone modern ECM. Her missiles slammed into their hulls, obliterating the craft one by one. A number exploded violently, confirming her suspicion that they'd been loaded with antimatter; others, larger and bulkier, merely absorbed more of her missiles before they died. And yet their deaths hadn't been entirely in vain. Theocratic missiles were getting through point defense simply because the gunners were trying to take out the remaining shuttles.

"*Havoc* has taken heavy damage," Wheeler reported. "*Rodney* is . . ." He cursed. "*Rodney* is gone, Commodore."

"Remain focused," Kat ordered. The stream of enemy ships looked endless, but cold logic told her it was nothing of the sort. The invaders had been surprised, yet they had more than enough firepower to win the engagement. "Let them keep coming to us."

She cursed under her breath as a chunk of the fleet datanet dropped out entirely, smaller subnets hastily taking over its duties as the techs fought to reunite the fragmented sections. If the enemy was on the ball, they might *just* realize the opportunity. She allowed herself a moment of relief as the datanet popped back up again, before the enemy noticed the weakness. The Theocracy might have had a chance to give the isolated superdreadnought squadron a pounding.

They don't allow their people enough independence, she thought wryly. Her analysts were already picking apart the enemy formation, trying to isolate the flagship. *Orders have to come right from the top.*

"Enemy shuttles entering engagement range," Wheeler snapped.

"Order the point defense to open fire," Kat said. The enemy shuttles were surrounded by a haze of ECM, obscuring their exact positions. But all her point defense crews had to do was fire until they scored a hit. "Deploy an additional shell of sensor drones."

"Aye, Commodore," Wheeler said.

Kat frowned. Did the enemy know who they were shooting at? She knew, without false modesty, that the Theocracy considered her the most hated person in the galaxy. Even Admiral Christian didn't attract quite so much loathing. But she doubted Theocratic sensor crews could have picked *Queen Elizabeth* out of the squadron, even assuming they knew *Queen Elizabeth* was her flagship. *Did* they know? Her name had always been paired with *Lightning.*

And they gloated over my death after Lightning *was destroyed,* she thought. *They didn't stop until it was clear that I'd survived.*

A low rumble ran through the giant ship. "Direct hit," Wheeler reported. "Shields held."

A missile, Kat thought. *A shuttle crammed with antimatter would have crippled us.*

"Enemy ships are altering position," Wheeler added. "They're drawing back."

Kat nodded. The enemy superdreadnoughts presumably wanted to avoid a missile duel, one that could only end in their destruction. Admiral Christian's ships might have emptied their external racks, but they could still smother the enemy ships via missile tubes. And yet, she doubted Admiral Christian would *let* them escape so easily.

"Signal from the flag," Wheeler reported. "The battle line will advance."

"Make it so," Kat ordered.

◆ ◆ ◆

"Admiral," an operator said. He sounded nervous, as if he expected to be blamed for bringing bad news. "The enemy fleet is advancing."

And clearing the remainder of the freighters, Zaskar thought. On the display, the last of the freighters were being systematically wiped out. *But I didn't expect anything else.*

He allowed himself a moment of annoyance. Hundreds of expensive and effectively irreplaceable ships and shuttles had been thrown away, for what? They'd done more damage than he'd expected, if he was honest with himself, yet the ploy hadn't been enough. The enemy fleet had absorbed the damage and kept moving. Soon they would be in position to engage his ships directly. Operation Night would have to come into play before then.

And there was still one final card to play.

"Signal Task Force Three," he ordered. The whole tactic was a gamble, but it might just pay off. If nothing else, it would give the enemy a fright. "They are to engage the enemy at once."

♦ ♦ ♦

"Commodore!" Wheeler snapped. "I'm picking up another wave of shuttles!"

Kat frowned, puzzled. The enemy ships had lurked behind the warships, keeping their drives and weapons offline to ensure they weren't detected. And yet, the situation was still odd. They *had* to know that nothing short of overwhelming numbers would be enough to get the shuttles through the point defense, so why had they held a third of their number back? Did they have something clever in mind?

They weakened our datanet, she thought coldly. *But it wasn't weakened enough.*

"They're blasting out ECM pulses," Wheeler added. The wave of red icons doubled and then tripled, question marks hanging over a number of the returns. Some of the shuttles had been targeted before the ECM came online; others were now lost in the haze. "They're trying to confuse us."

"They're succeeding," Kat muttered.

"The flag is ordering the point defense to engage," Wheeler reported. The display updated again as the point defense opened fire. "All enemy contacts are to be targeted."

Kat winced. The enemy had just upped their chances of scoring a significant hit. If *every* target had to be engaged, a great deal of time was about to be wasted. But the fleet had plenty of point defense.

She cursed under her breath as hundreds of shuttles roared down on the fleet, a dozen vanishing from existence in colossal explosions even as their comrades kept moving. A destroyer was hit and wiped out in a giant blast, a heavy cruiser staggered out of formation, lifepods spewing from her hull; a superdreadnought was hit twice and blown into flaming plasma.

"Commodore!" Wheeler yelled. "They're targeting *Hammerhead*!"

Kat opened her mouth, but it was too late. There were no orders she could give, not when the fleet's point defense was aware of the danger. Five suicide shuttles made their final run . . . and HMS *Hammerhead* vanished from the display.

CHAPTER TWENTY-FOUR

"Commodore, *Hammerhead* has been destroyed," Wheeler said. "I'm not picking up any lifepods."

Kat swallowed, hard. Had the enemy gotten lucky? Very lucky? Or had they somehow picked the flagship out of the fleet and marked her down for special attention? But it didn't matter, not now. Her superior was dead . . . and she had to assume command.

"Priority signal to the fleet," she ordered. "Admiral Christian is missing, presumed dead. I am assuming command as of this moment."

She doubted that *anything* could have survived the explosion. Admiral Christian wouldn't have been able to escape, even if he'd run for an escape pod the moment he realized that five shuttles were closing in on his ship. But she couldn't unilaterally declare him dead, not yet. All that mattered was that he was unable to serve as the fleet's commanding officer.

Mourn later, she told herself savagely. *The battle is not over yet.*

"Fleet datanet refocusing on *Queen Elizabeth*," Wheeler reported. "It's accepted you as the new commanding officer."

For the moment, Kat thought. *Someone may try to challenge me after the battle is over.*

She pushed the thought aside and leaned forward. "Clear the remaining shuttles, then accelerate to engage the superdreadnoughts," she ordered. The enemy ships were holding position, just out of firing range. She had a feeling they would try to lure her onto the fixed defenses if she wasn't careful. "All starships are to engage as soon as we enter range."

"Aye, Commodore," Wheeler said.

Kat nodded, taking a second to survey the situation. Nineteen ships had been destroyed, seven more badly damaged. They would have to be withdrawn from the fleet, although she wasn't ready to send them back yet. There was just too great a chance of running into enemy patrols as they tried to slip home. Even getting them to the mobile shipyards at the rendezvous point would be chancy.

But we still have the advantage, she thought. *And we will use it.*

"Entering missile range in twenty seconds," Wheeler reported. "The enemy fleet is still holding position."

Kat's eyes narrowed. Four squadrons of superdreadnoughts couldn't *hope* to stand up to her fleet, with or without their external racks. The only viable tactic was to fall back on the planetary defenses, linking the orbiting firepower to theirs. But the enemy ships were just sitting there, as if they were trying to lead her on. Her eyes flicked over the sensor readings, looking for cloaked ships, stealthed mines, or other surprises but found nothing. The enemy practically seemed to be *inviting* her to destroy them.

"Entering missile range," Wheeler reported.

Kat bared her teeth. "Fire at will."

♦ ♦ ♦

"Admiral," the operator said, "the enemy ships have opened fire."

"I can see that, idiot," Zaskar snarled.

He couldn't help feeling a surge of dismay at the raw power roaring towards his ships. The missile swarm—his mind raced, trying to quantify it. If each superdreadnought could fire a hundred missiles in one salvo and if there were over a hundred superdreadnoughts . . . he shook his head, angrily dismissing the thought. There were enough missiles on their way to overwhelm his defenses and smash his entire fleet, even if a third of them somehow self-destructed along the way.

"Return fire," he ordered. "And then execute Operation Night."

He tensed. If one of his watchdogs, perhaps a crewman he'd least suspect of being tied to his overseers, hadn't gotten the word, he was probably about to be shot. But he had no choice, not any longer. The Commonwealth ships were out for revenge.

"Gateway generators online," an operator said.

Zaskar shivered. He'd sworn his life and his soul to the defense of his homeworld. The thought of abandoning her to the unbelievers was horrifying, even if there *was* a plan. But he had his orders.

"Open the gateways," he ordered. The enemy missiles were getting closer. Time was of the essence. "Get us out of here."

♦ ♦ ♦

"Commodore, the enemy ships are escaping into hyperspace," Wheeler reported. "They're deploying antimatter mines as they leave."

Kat cursed. Chasing an enemy fleet into hyperspace was asking for trouble, but the damned antimatter mines made sure of it. There was no hope of escaping an energy storm, let alone an engagement where the odds would be even. The enemy ships had made a clean getaway for the moment. She'd honestly never expected the Theocracy to break and run. They'd rarely retreated and never surrendered, regardless of the odds.

"Put the missiles on a ballistic trajectory and angle them towards the planet," she ordered finally. "And set us on a course to follow them."

She keyed her console, checking the live feed from the stealthed drones. The enemy had picked off several of them, but a number remained intact, broadcasting back from the very heart of the enemy defenses. There was plenty of data now, allowing the tactical staff to isolate the ground-based PDCs and select potential landing sites. The marines on the *Chesty Puller*—she couldn't help glancing at the ring on her finger—would have plenty of time to pick their landing site and establish a spacehead.

"A handful of enemy gunboats are returning to the planet," Wheeler reported. "They don't seem to have many more ships in orbit."

"Good," Kat said. "Prepare to engage."

♦ ♦ ♦

Speaker Nehemiah had never liked the pit, the command bunker buried deep beneath the Tabernacle. It was as luxurious as any other part of the building, but there was something about the bunker that bothered him. Mankind wasn't meant to live so far below the ground, so far below the sun and moon. But the pit was also the safest place on the planet. Nothing short of a planet-buster would crack the solid armor over their heads, while there were a dozen escape tunnels leading in all directions.

The command chamber was dominated by a massive hologram, showing hundreds of red icons slowly advancing towards the planet. Nehemiah was no military expert, but even *he* knew that was bad news. The enemy fleet had been hurt and hurt badly, yet it hadn't been hurt *enough*. They were still advancing towards the orbital defenses.

"Picking up a message," an operator said. "It's aimed directly at the orbital battlestations."

Nehemiah had no interest in talking to an unbeliever, but he had to know what his subordinates might be hearing. The last two days had been spent emplacing enforcers at all levels, a measure that would annoy commanders and military officers who'd clung with grim determination to what little independence they had. Some of them might *just* see value in listening to the unbelievers.

"Put it through," he ordered.

". . . is the Commonwealth Navy 6th Fleet," a male voice said. "Your superdreadnoughts have fled, your orbital defenses are at our mercy. The war is over. Surrender now and we promise you your lives . . ."

Nehemiah clenched his teeth. If he trusted the Commonwealth . . . but he didn't trust the Commonwealth. And even if he *did* try to surrender, he knew the fanatics would oppose him with all their might. He wasn't blind to the infiltration of new Inquisitors into the bunker or the upper levels of the building. The speakers might have already lost control over the Theocracy.

"No reply," he ordered when the message finally started to repeat itself. "We will continue to fight."

♦ ♦ ♦

"They haven't replied to our message," Wheeler said. "There's no sign they're considering a surrender."

Kat nodded. The fleet was slowing as it approached firing range, careful to give the antimatter storage depot and the shipyards a wide berth. She had a feeling the former was probably empty, but there was no point in taking chances. Below her, the enemy defenses were coming to life, probing space and systematically targeting her ships. They were ready to give a good account of themselves.

"Send in the gunboats," she ordered.

"Aye, Commodore," Wheeler said.

♦ ♦ ♦

"Now this," Lieutenant Tombs said, "is what I call a target-rich environment."

Isabel couldn't disagree. There were so many automated weapons platforms holding position over Ahura Mazda that she had the feeling she could have gotten out of the gunboat and practically *walked* around the planet. And, below them, the giant battlestations were just *waiting* for the fleet to come into range before opening fire. But they hadn't bargained on the gunboats.

"Fire at will," she ordered.

The gunboats zoomed down into the planet's orbital space, their crews jinking from side to side to avoid a hail of point defense fire. Tombs fired time and time again, blasting automated platforms out of space with wild abandon. Below them, other squadrons ducked through the defenses and launched giant shipkillers towards the battlestations. A number of gunboats blinked out of existence, but the survivors were more than enough to inflict real damage on the stations. And the stations had no opportunity to target their *real* tormentors.

"We're going to run out of space on the hull," Tombs observed as he killed yet another automated weapons platform. Its partner swung around and opened fire, forcing Isabel to dodge before the attack killed her and her partner. "There just isn't room for each and every platform I've killed."

"They'll probably decide they don't count," Isabel said. She yanked the gunboat to one side as a missile shot past her, its targeting sensors locking onto the nearest battlestation. "Or we'll just have to paint a number on the hull instead."

She caught sight of the planet and felt a surge of hatred. Ahura Mazda was the homeworld of a nightmarish religion, a monster that would kill unless it was killed. Part of her wanted to rain antimatter bombs on the surface until it cracked, the entire planet shattering into an asteroid cluster that would eventually fall into the local star. She'd been told there were innocents down there, innocents trapped and made helpless, yet those innocents had chosen not to question, not to resist.

"Fuckers," she snarled. Two more automated platforms died in fire. "Damn them to hell."

♦ ♦ ♦

"The battlestations are taking damage," Wheeler reported. "But they're still holding the line."

Kat nodded. "Launch the ballistic missiles," she ordered. "And prime them for engagement at close range."

She leaned back in her command chair and watched, grimly, as the missiles fell towards the planet below. There was one great weakness in wrapping so many defenses around a planet, she knew. The defenses were at the bottom of a gravity well. She could keep firing missiles down towards the battlestations, secure in the knowledge they couldn't fire back at her. And with the gunboats tearing through the orbital sensor nodes, the Theocrats would have real problems defending themselves.

"Squadrons Seven and Eight are requesting permission to target the enemy industrial nodes," Wheeler reported. "Orders?"

"Denied," Kat said. "Concentrate fire on the orbital battlestations."

"Aye, Commodore," Wheeler said.

Kat smiled as the first battlestation shattered, explosions ripping it apart. Great clouds of debris flew in all directions, a multitude heading down towards the planet below. The enemy PDCs opened fire, breaking the debris up into smaller chunks before the detritus could make it through the atmosphere and do real damage. She allowed herself a moment of pure relief, then cursed under her breath as a stray missile struck an asteroid habitat. The structure disintegrated, raining *more* debris on Ahura Mazda.

"The other battlestations are launching missiles," Wheeler reported.

They're desperate, Kat thought. The battlestations could not hit her ships with powered missiles, not at their current range. But if they threw enough missiles, they might just score a hit when the missiles went ballistic. *They know they're losing.*

"Repeat the message," she ordered. "And continue firing."

No response came as the planet's orbital defenses were slowly hacked apart, chunk after chunk of debris falling into the planet's atmosphere. Kat had a feeling that introducing so much material into the biosphere wouldn't do the planet any good at all, although she found it hard to care. Her sensors tracked a number of smaller pieces dropping down and striking the surface, some landing in the ocean and setting off tidal waves. She hoped the locals had enough sense to head inland, but she doubted the Theocracy would bother to warn them, let alone give them permission to flee. They'd be nothing more than useless mouths, draining their resources.

"Picking up additional targeting sensors," Wheeler said. He blinked in surprise. "They're moving a superdreadnought out of the shipyard!"

Kat glanced at him. "Show me."

The display altered, showing her one of the enemy shipyards. A half-finished superdreadnought was slowly inching out of the docking slip, its tactical sensors already coming online. She stared in utter disbelief. The ship didn't seem to have shields. Did it even have any weapons? She was torn between admiration for the crew's determination not to give up and grim horror. Didn't they *know* their ship was a sitting duck?

"Her drives are at quarter-power," Wheeler reported. "I don't think she *has* shields."

"Target her," Kat ordered. "Fire."

She mentally saluted the enemy officers as her missiles plummeted towards the superdreadnought, even though she had no idea what they'd hoped to accomplish before their deaths. Soak up a few more of her missiles? Or just give their ship a better sendoff than being killed in her docking slip? Or keep her from being captured? Explosions blasted through the incomplete ship, wiping her out of existence. Kat closed her eyes for a long moment, then dismissed the matter. There would be time to sweep up the debris later.

"Target destroyed," Wheeler stated.

"Continue sweeping orbital space," Kat ordered. "Do you have solid locks on their PDCs?"

"Yes, Commodore," Wheeler said. "There's a *lot* of them."

"And they're all heavily shielded," Kat mused as she studied the display. The Theocracy hadn't stinted on ground-based defenses either. "We can't take them out without doing vast damage to the planet."

She scowled. Most of the PDCs were easy to spot, but she was sure there were other ground-based stations that were carefully hidden. Picking off the military bases would be easy enough, yet she drew the line at dropping KEWs within a heavily populated city. She might have to make that choice, eventually, but not now.

"Pass the updated information to *Chesty Puller*," she ordered. "Inform them they can move as soon as the last orbital battlestation is gone."

"Aye, Commodore," Wheeler said.

Kat felt nothing, nothing at all, as the last battlestation writhed under her fire. The enemy had to know their position was hopeless, they had to know their world was naked and defenseless, yet they insisted on sacrificing the lives of thousands of their loyal defenders. She understood defiance, she understood determination, and yet, there were limits. Hundreds of thousands of men had died for nothing. Cold logic told her that their deaths would serve a greater purpose, that they wouldn't be around to resist the Commonwealth after the war, but she didn't want to embrace such thinking. The men had been sacrificed for nothing.

And then the final battlestation vanished from the display.

"Target destroyed," Wheeler said. "All observed enemy defenses have been destroyed."

"Load targeting patterns for ground-based defenses," Kat ordered. If nothing else, watching military bases be smashed from orbit might push the Theocracy's population to rebel. "And fire on my command."

♦ ♦ ♦

"Keep firing," Nehemiah ordered.

"They're out of range of ground-based weapons," an operator said. "The orbital defenses have been destroyed."

Nehemiah turned to glare at Inquisitor Samuilu. "What now?"

"They can't bring their starships into orbit because that will expose them to our fire," Samuilu said calmly. "They'll start attempting to land their marines. And we will be ready for them."

"Our men have been primed with the zeal to fight for us," Lord Cleric Eliseus proclaimed, loudly. His booming voice echoed through the giant chamber. "And even the unarmed have been told to give their lives to kill unbelievers."

"We should start issuing weapons," Samuilu ordered. "As soon as we know where they're landing, we *must* move at once to crush them."

"Of course," Nehemiah agreed. He didn't like the idea of distributing weapons, knowing they might end up being pointed at him, but there was no choice. Unarmed civilians would be slaughtered like bugs if they were told to charge enemy positions. "Order your forces to move as soon as possible."

"Of course, Your Holiness," Samuilu said.

♦ ♦ ♦

"Commodore," General Winters said. His face appeared in front of her. "We have picked out a suitable landing site to turn into a spacehead."

And Pat will be in the lead, Kat thought. Bitter guilt tore at her. She shouldn't have pressed for him to get the job. *If he lands in the first wave he will either win or die.*

"Understood," she said. She pushed her feelings into a compartment at the back of her mind and locked the door. "I'll have the fleet move into position to support you."

"Deploy additional waves of drones," General Winters urged. The display updated, showing how the landing force intended to slip through the atmosphere and reach the ground. Kat couldn't help feeling that the maneuver seemed excessively risky. "I think we're going to need them."

Kat nodded. "I will, General," she said. She wished she knew him better. Admiral Christian and General Winters had been old friends, she recalled from a formal dinner. The general wouldn't be quite so impressed with her, even though ironclad regulations named her as the operation's commanding officer. "They have a lot of firepower down there."

"We can take it," General Winters said. He sounded assured. Kat rather envied him. "Even if those ships come back, we can take it."

"Yes, General," Kat said. She took a breath. The missing enemy ships might be a serious problem if they were plotting a counteroffensive or even intending to head out into unexplored space and set up a whole new Theocracy. "The word is given. Land the landing force!"

CHAPTER TWENTY-FIVE

So tell me, Pat's thoughts urged. *Whose bright idea was this?*

Yours, his thoughts answered.

He gritted his teeth as the suit rocketed on its ballistic trajectory towards Ahura Mazda, tiny gas jets steering him towards the optimal reentry point. Hundreds of other marines were floating near him, he knew, but he found that hard to believe when they were keeping strict radio silence. They didn't even dare risk using lasers to communicate, despite knowing that the odds of being detected were ridiculously low. It was chillingly easy to believe that he was all alone in the vastness of space, utterly dwarfed by the giant planet looming above him.

And yet, his suit's passive sensors kept picking up signs of life, flashing up warnings about chunks of space debris falling into the planet's atmosphere. It was highly unlikely that he or any of the marines would actually collide with a piece of debris, but the problem could not be entirely dismissed. A large number of marines were heading through a relatively small region of space, a region crammed with the plummeting wreckage of a heated battle. And if they did hit something, the odds of survival were very low indeed.

Pat forced himself to wait, counting sheep under his breath as the planet grew closer and closer. The enemy would be looking for them, he knew; they had to assume an invasion was on the way. And they knew enough about Commonwealth doctrine to have a reasonable idea what form it would take, even if flying assault shuttles through low orbit was asking for trouble. They'd be looking for suited marines dropping from orbit.

A low tremor ran through the suit as it touched the uppermost edges of the planet's atmosphere. Pat closed his eyes as the suit spun him around, trying to keep a firm grasp on his surroundings as the planet shifted from distant orb to the ground far below him. His perspective was altered, time and time again; he reminded himself, firmly, that he was still perfectly safe. The enemy didn't seem to have noticed their arrival.

Too much debris entering the planet's atmosphere, he thought. His suit was tracking countless pieces of debris burning up below him, a handful of scattered fragments remaining intact long enough to hit the ground. *We're too small to be noticed.*

He opened his eyes. The ground was below him, growing steadily larger as he fell towards the planet. He'd done high-altitude, low-opening deployments before, of course, as well as space-based insertions, but this was different. He was staring down at an enemy target—no, *the* enemy target. The coming battle would determine the end of the war. His suit's HUD kept updating, picking out cities and matching them to the maps they'd obtained from Admiral Junayd. The enemy force shields were clearly visible, hanging in the air over the larger cities and PDCs.

And then the enemy opened fire.

Pat cursed as missiles and energy pulses flashed past him, the decoys going active seconds later and soaking up the barrage. *Something* had tipped the enemy off, something that had convinced them that the marines were finally on their way. A puzzle . . . he pushed it aside. The ground came up towards him, his eyes seeking out prospective landing sites as his suit's antigravity generators powered up. A series of explosions blasted out above him as the enemy continued firing, aiming at the second wave of marines. His suit flipped around as the antigravity field cut in the instant before he hit the ground. He touched down, already having deployed his weapons and equipment.

"A field," Sergeant Bones said. The remaining marines touched down and spread out, hunting for prospective targets. "Nothing more than a muddy field."

Pat was inclined to agree. He was no expert, but the cornfield looked as if it were lying fallow; in the distance, he could see sheep munching contentedly on green grass, utterly unmoved by the battle above them. A small farmhouse lay at the edge of the field, two young boys staring at the marines in complete disbelief. One of them turned and hurried inside as the marines spread out, the other continuing to stare. And then an older man appeared, barked orders at the remaining boy and dragged him into their home.

"Colonel," Sergeant Bones said, "should we let them go?"

"They know we're here," Pat said. The spacehead was small, but it would grow. And the enemy knew it. "Let them go."

He glanced up as his HUD reported incoming targets. Five aircraft, sweeping low as they closed in on the marines. His suit automatically tracked them and opened fire, blowing the lead aircraft out of the sky. The other marines opened fire a second later, taking down the remaining four. Within moments, the next wave of marines and their supplies landed. Pat barked orders, directing them to set up defense systems and then start preparing the spacehead to receive shuttles.

"Picking up an alert from the stealthed recon probes," Corporal Wallace said. "We have crowds massing in the nearby settlement."

"Understood," Pat said. "Armed crowds?"

"Unsure," Corporal Wallace said. "But there's a lot of them." He paused. "And long-range shellfire has just been detected."

Pat nodded as the point defense systems started to engage, sweeping the shells out of the air before they could reach their targets. The enemy might decide to use nukes to clear the way to the spacehead, he thought, but anything less would have real problems reaching the marines. Even if a spy was on the *Chesty Puller*, he wouldn't have been able to tell the Theocrats where the marines were going to land when the marines didn't know themselves.

He snapped out orders as more and more marines landed, taking a platoon himself to sweep the farmhouse. It was an odd design, he noted as they pushed down the door and walked inside; a third of the house seemed to be isolated from the rest of the structure. He couldn't help wondering, as they searched the remainder of the building, just who or what had been kept in the run-down third. There wasn't much luxury in the farmhouse, but clearly the isolated section was very basic indeed. The inhabitants had completely vanished.

"They would have kept the women here," Bones said. She sounded deeply shocked—and angry. "This place is practically a prison."

She was right, Pat decided, as they poked through piles of clothes. The only garments to be found in the isolated section of the building were long shapeless robes and veils, the latter meant to hide the wearer's face. There were no bras, no cosmetics—nothing he would have expected to find in a woman's room. There was nothing to do but wait—it *was* like being in a prison. He shuddered at the thought of Kat, or any of her sisters, growing up in such a nightmare, and then he turned and walked out of the building. The farmhouse, already badly damaged by so many armored men tramping in and out, didn't look as though it would survive for long. It would merely be the first of many destroyed buildings.

"Got more incoming fire," Captain Jackson snapped. Another wave of marines landed, hard on the heels of a hail of shellfire. "They've set up guns to the west as well as to the east."

"Understood," Pat said. "Keep defending the spacehead, Captain. I'll—"

"Incoming," Sergeant Bones said sharply. "A large crowd, marching down the road towards us."

"On my way," Pat said.

The road was really nothing more than a muddy track, Pat noted. That puzzled him. Hebrides had been a poorer world in many ways, yet the roads had been better; but then, the Theocracy probably didn't want its people to move from place to place easily. No doubt they would all have ID cards, and somewhere they would have stored complete records of the entire planet's population.

He pushed the thought aside as the crowd came into view, a mob of men carrying primitive weapons and chanting loudly as they marched. He had no idea if the chant was a prayer or cry of defiance.

"That man in the back is urging them on," Bones commented.

Pat nodded. A man in red robes was standing at the rear, his gaze flickering constantly between the marines and the advancing crowd. Pat had no trouble recognizing a rabble-rouser, someone who would happily whip up a mob and then vanish, leaving said mob to be brutally crushed or killed. Even relatively gentle ways of dealing with an impromptu gang tended to be thoroughly unpleasant for its members.

"They don't have any heavy weapons," he said softly. "There's no need to crush them."

"Yes, sir," Bones said reluctantly.

The marines lined up in formation as the crowd closed in. It would have been suicide against an armed enemy, but not against an unarmed and unarmored mob. Pat felt a sudden surge of hatred for the red-robed man, the man who'd sent hundreds of farmers to be killed, bashing their heads against an immoveable object. He lifted his rifle, targeted the man, and put an explosive bullet through his head. His body exploded into flame as it dropped to the ground.

"THIS REGION IS NOW UNDER OCCUPATION," he said, using the suit to amplify his words. The sound was so loud that anyone without ear protection recoiled in horror. "GO BACK TO YOUR HOMES. STAY THERE."

The crowd seemed to hesitate, a number slipping back now that the red-robe was dead. But others kept coming, howling as they broke into a run. Pat cursed under his breath, then gave the order to prepare the stunners as rocks, knives, and improvised weapons rained down around the marines. The crowd clearly hadn't had any real time to prepare for the brief encounter.

"Stun them," he ordered.

Blue sparks flared from body to body, sending the maddened crowd falling to the ground like ninepins. Pat felt a flicker of remorse, then led the marines forward as more alerts popped up in front of him. The enemy was sending actual troops forward now, staging them through the nearby village. He knew the marines should sweep up the stunned crowd and dump them in a POW camp, but there was no time to set one up. The enemy was clearly doing everything they could to get reinforcements into position to attack.

A shuttle roared overhead, followed by five more. Pat allowed himself a moment of relief that the spacehead was growing stronger, then led the marines down towards the town. He wasn't sure what he'd expected, but he had to admit the scene looked odd. Red brick buildings dominated, all seemingly deserted. The church at the far end of the town looked open, as if it was waiting for him. Pat glanced up sharply as a bullet bounced off his helmet. He directed a stream of plasma pulses towards the sniper. The entire building disintegrated into rubble, the sniper falling to his death somewhere within the debris. Thankfully, the local defenders didn't seem to be equipped with anything more dangerous than small arms.

That will change, he thought grimly.

"Colonel," Bones said, "here they come."

Pat glanced up abruptly as a second howling mob appeared from the side streets and charged towards the marines, followed by men who were clearly soldiers or militia. He braced himself as Molotov cocktails started to smash into the combat armor, then relaxed as it became clear that they weren't strong enough to do real damage. But the mob kept coming, bare hands tearing at his armor as if they thought they could break through by sheer force of will. Pat rapidly found himself buried in swarming bodies, his suit rocking backwards as they pressed down on him. His servomotors whined as he fought to stay upright.

Gritting his teeth, he triggered the stunner and spun around, shocking everyone within reach until he could see again. The soldiers were hurling grenades, utterly heedless of the mass of civilians around the marines. Pat cursed as he realized the grenades *could* harm his marines. They were stronger than the ones the Theocracy normally used, as if the enemy leaders had anticipated their landing.

He lifted his weapon and fired, blowing the soldiers away as the rest of his men freed themselves. Hundreds of civilians were dead or wounded, but there was no time to worry about them. More and more updates were popping up in front of him, cautioning him that the enemy was deploying additional troops to crush the spacehead. The Theocratic soldiers fell back, some trying to hold their ground while others turned and fled. Pat took a peculiarly savage delight in shooting the latter in the back. They'd gotten hundreds of innocent civilians killed for nothing.

"Two suits lightly damaged," Bones reported. "No injuries."

"Sweep the rest of the town," Pat ordered. More shuttles were landing, unloading hundreds of marines. General Winters would take command soon. "Hunt down the rest of the bastards before they get away."

The town was almost deserted, they discovered, save for a handful of men who either tried to attack the marines or simply ran in the opposite direction. Pat felt that something was missing as they searched a house, but it took him several moments to realize that they hadn't seen any women or girls at all. Come to think of it, they hadn't seen any children in the town, female or male. The youngest man they'd seen had been at least fourteen.

"You'd expect a town this size to have at least an equal number of women," he mused as they searched a house. Like all the others, there was a female section, bare and barren compared to the male side of the house. But it was deserted. "Where *are* they?"

"Maybe they all fled," Bones suggested. "The Theocracy's forces have a habit of raping every woman they see. Maybe they think we'll do the same."

Pat felt sick. Accidents happened in war—he'd been a soldier long enough to know that accidents happened—but rape was no accident. A Commonwealth soldier or spacer who was convicted of rape would be escorted to the nearest airlock and kicked out if he or she didn't beg for a firing squad or the hangman instead. His troops would not rape a local girl, no matter how much they hated their surroundings. But he was sure the Theocrats would have told their people that the marines were all rapists. What better way to encourage them to resist?

He walked out of the house and checked the stream of status reports. The spacehead was growing, despite the constant rain of shells. A couple of shuttles had been blown out of the air and three more had been damaged while they were on the ground, but the attacks hadn't been enough to stop the marines from reinforcing. More companies were forming up, spreading out around the spacehead. He sent orders to one company to establish a POW camp, then followed Bones into the next house. She stopped dead as she peered into the kitchen.

"Interesting," she said. "What do you make of this, sir?"

Pat looked past her. A man lay on the ground, his throat cut. Pat was no expert, but he figured the man hadn't been dead for more than an hour. The blood didn't seem to have congealed, which puzzled him. Had the knife been primed with something designed to stop the blood from clotting? Or had the victim died only a few minutes ago?

"I don't know," he said. A mystery, one he doubted they'd ever be able to solve. One more death amidst hundreds of thousands—no one would care enough to try to find out. "Sweep the rest of the house."

Pat's contingent worked their way through the town, slowly closing in on the church. He had expected fanatical resistance around the building, but instead the area was as dark and silent as the grave. Pat inched forward, half expecting to encounter a booby trap. The door opened as soon as he touched it, silently beckoning him inside. His suit's sensors revealed nothing to worry about, save for the darkness. He opened the inner door and jumped back as warnings flashed up in front of him.

"Nerve gas," he said. Sweat prickled on his forehead, even though he knew the gas couldn't get into the suit. Gas had always scared the pants off him, ever since entering the gas chamber during boot camp. Hardened marines still cringed when they remembered those minutes of pure terror. "Lethal shit."

"Shine a light in there," Bones suggested. She sounded uneasy. "Sir?"

Pat flicked his suit's flashlight on and peered inside. Bodies. Lots of bodies, lying on the stone floor. Most of the corpses wore veils, but enough of them were bareheaded for him to see that they were women and children. Boys and girls, murdered alongside their older sisters and their mothers.

He stumbled backwards, feeling his gorge rise. He wanted, he *needed*, to be sick. He'd thought himself used to horror, but this . . . this was beyond belief.

"They killed them all," he breathed. Nerve gas. It didn't look as though any of the women and children had died peacefully. Judging by their expressions, they'd died in screaming agony. "Why?"

He gathered himself. "Get a recording team down here," he ordered sharply. "I want everything recorded, everything. Pictures of the bodies, cause of death reports . . . the works."

Bones sounded bitter. "Why?"

"Because some asshole is going to make excuses for these bastards in the future," Pat snarled, his voice full of anger and fury. "Some stupid know-it-all who doesn't know a thing is going to question the whole story, then say it was somehow all our fault."

He *knew* it would happen. Humans were always making excuses for other humans. "And when they do, I want to rub his face in what these bastards did!"

CHAPTER TWENTY-SIX

"Why did they do this?"

Junayd studied the images on the display, feeling sick. He'd known it was a possibility, he'd even tried to discuss it with his handlers, but he hadn't really believed anyone would do it, not really. And yet, he'd never been one of the little people, one of the men who knew nothing but radio propaganda. The men in the town had probably feared for the future of their wives and children if the Commonwealth won; they had probably believed that the women would be raped while the boys were taken away and turned into good little unbelievers. Killing the women and children would have seemed the better course.

Kat glared at him. "Why?"

"Because they feel they have no choice," Junayd said tiredly. He had no idea what the common folk had been told in the time since his defection, but he could guess. "They think the women will be dishonored."

"They could just have run," Kat snapped. "We have plenty of images of people fleeing their homes."

"But that would expose their women to other dangers," Junayd told her. "They'd see death as the better option."

"*Their* women," Kat snarled. "Women don't *belong* to them."

Junayd looked up at her. "The vast majority of men and women on the planet below feel differently," he said curtly. "And convincing them otherwise will take time."

He studied the images for a long moment. Kat was right, it *was* sickening. But not, perhaps, for *her* reasons. The Theocracy was literally eating itself, destroying its women and children in a desperate bid to preserve them from the future. He had no doubt, as word spread, that there would be riots and uprisings, but there would also be chaos. Social breakdown would be followed by looting, rape, and mass slaughter as old grudges were paid off. And the Commonwealth, for all its power, couldn't do anything about it.

"I need to find my family," he said. "You *did* pass the word to the scouts?"

Janice cleared her throat. "We did as you instructed," she said. "But you know the risks."

"I know," Junayd said. "Everything I told you could easily be out of date."

He looked back at Kat. "They're planning something," he said. "And you have to be wary."

Kat scowled. "*What* are they planning?"

"They allowed four squadrons of superdreadnoughts and their escorts to retreat, rather than fighting to the last," Junayd said. "That shows a degree of contingency planning."

"Or someone deciding that trying to fight and getting squashed would be nothing more than suicide," Kat pointed out.

Junayd felt a flicker of envy. Kat Falcone had definitely enjoyed a measure of independence—as a woman, as a starship commander—that he had never shared, despite his rank and family background. She didn't understand the limitations facing her Theocratic counterparts. How could she? They were completely alien to her.

"Every commanding officer on our ships has an official minder, an overseer, if you will," he said softly. "And there will be a number of unofficial minders too, sleeper agents who will take steps if the commanding officer steps out of line. If the admiral in charge decided to take his ships out of the battle without prior agreement, he'd probably be shot in the back."

"*You* managed a mutiny," Kat snapped.

"I had a plan," Junayd countered. "And it wasn't a mutiny, but an individual escape. *And* I barely got away with it."

He nodded towards the projector, which was showing the records from the battle. "Even if *that* admiral managed to get control of his ship, the other commanding officers would hesitate to follow an order to retreat," he added. "And *their* minders would certainly take steps too. They couldn't be subverted in a hurry."

"Really," Kat said.

"Oh, yes," Junayd said. He laughed bitterly. "There are times when commanding officers are too afraid to cough for fear that someone will take it as a sign to start something violent. No, there was a contingency plan for a retreat. And I assume that means they have an idea in mind for the fleet."

Janice caught his eye. "A bargaining chip?"

"I doubt it," Junayd told her. "Surely the time to bargain was *before* hostile troops landed on their soil."

He took a moment to contemplate the possibilities. Four squadrons of superdreadnoughts could do a great deal of damage, but where? The Commonwealth's closest system was a month away, on the other side of the Gap. *And* it was heavily defended. Four squadrons of superdreadnoughts would be torn to ribbons if they tried to attack. They *could* try to head farther into Commonwealth space, he supposed, but there weren't many targets they could take. And basic maintenance issues would rapidly reduce their squadron to irrelevance if they didn't manage to obtain more supplies.

They might have a plan to reestablish the Theocracy somewhere beyond the edge of explored space, he thought. *But they won't have any of the* resources the original founders had, back when we were kicked off Earth. Unless . . .

He looked up. "They're planning to counterattack your fleet," he said bluntly. "*That's* what they have in mind."

Kat didn't look surprised. Any halfway competent commanding officer would have already considered the possibility. Her fleet wasn't exactly *weak*, but it *was* over a month from the closest naval base and at risk of running out of supplies. Junayd had seen and admired the Commonwealth fleet train, yet he knew expenditure had already been higher than predicted.

"Four squadrons of superdreadnoughts will not be enough to defeat us," Kat said flatly.

"It might not *stay* four squadrons of superdreadnoughts," Junayd said. He rose and started to pace the compartment. "They'll tell themselves, I think, that they have a chance to win a final decisive battle, that if they crush your fleet, they can force the Commonwealth to back off. I think they'll call in everything they have for the final engagement."

"It won't force us to back off," Kat said. "Even if we lose the entire fleet, we'll take one hell of a bite out of their remaining forces *and* obliterate their shipyards."

"You don't understand how these people think," Junayd said. "They'll justify the tactical retreat to themselves by plotting a counterattack. And then they'll throw everything at you because they think it's the only way to win. They won't give a damn about anything else, Commodore. They simply cannot imagine losing."

"Even with our troops on the ground," Kat said.

"They're already throwing everything they have at the spacehead," Janice put in.

"Yes," Junayd said. He straightened. "With your permission, Commodore, I would like to go down to the surface. I may be able to do some good there."

"Once we know the spacehead can be held," Janice said quickly.

Kat's lips thinned with distaste. Junayd had the feeling she wouldn't have hesitated to let him go, despite the risk. She had tried to hide the fact that she didn't like him, but she hadn't managed to keep her true emotions from him. If he happened to be killed on the surface, she wouldn't shed a tear. And, truthfully, that didn't bother him.

"Once we have finished landing and securing the spacehead," she said. "We have yet to solidify our grip on the system."

"As you wish," Junayd said.

He turned his attention back to the endless stream of images. The horror in the church wasn't the only one, he noted; the marines were stumbling over dozens of bodies, all killed to keep them from falling into Commonwealth hands. Women, children . . . and men, men who'd refused to join the mobs or leave their homes. Perhaps, just perhaps, they'd even tried to *defend* their families from the clerics. Junayd liked to think that *he* would have done that, if he'd had a chance.

And I did send my family away, he thought. *But did I send them far enough?*

◆ ◆ ◆

"Local space is clear, Captain," Cecelia said. "The enemy technicians don't seem to be doing anything."

William hoped she was right. Small marine landing parties were heading to the nearest surviving enemy shipyard, even though the shipyards could easily be blown out of space by fire from the ground. Admiral Christian, may he rest in peace, had hoped they could capture enemy techs and interrogate them, particularly the ones who had been hired from outside the Theocracy. ONI had suspected, perhaps with good reason, that *someone* was bankrolling the Theocracy, although they hadn't come up with any proof. Admiral Christian had hoped to find the proof before it was destroyed.

"Continue to monitor the situation," he ordered. The Theocracy might well have moved the techs elsewhere, if they'd expected an attack, but the shipyards had to be checked. "And watch for trouble heading our way."

He glanced at the main display. The fleet was holding station near the planet, launching an endless stream of shuttles, ECM drones, and sensor decoys towards the high orbitals. Without their network of orbital sensors, the PDCs on the ground were having problems distinguishing the real shuttles from the fakes, which hadn't stopped them picking off a number of shuttles as they made the transit down to the surface. The spacehead was only three hours old and already several hundred men had died.

Once we start clearing the PDCs, we can land more troops, he told himself. He'd seen the assault plans, although he'd been warned that they would have to be updated to fit the situation on the ground. *And then we can advance on the Tabernacle.*

"Captain," Lieutenant Richard Ball said, "I have a priority signal for you from the flag. It's marked for your ears only."

William rose. Kat Falcone had assumed command in the aftermath of Admiral Christian's death, although he had a nasty feeling that some of her commodores would seek to oppose or undermine her command once the spacehead was securely established. She *was* young, even if she was one of the most experienced officers in the fleet. And yet, her experience of fleet command was very limited.

"I'll take it in my office," he said. He glanced at Roach. "You have the conn."

"Aye, Captain," Roach said.

Kat's image was already floating in front of his chair as he entered his office and closed the hatch. "William," she said grimly. "Have you heard the news?"

William frowned. "About what?"

"Two separate problems," Kat said. "Pat uncovered an . . . atrocity on the ground, several atrocities. And our Theocratic friend thinks the enemy is preparing a counterattack."

"I wish I was surprised about the atrocity," William said. "And a counterattack . . ."

He scowled, stroking his chin. After what the Theocracy had done to his homeworld, he was prepared to believe that there simply weren't any taboos the Theocracy wasn't prepared to break. Rendering an entire world lifeless was horrifying, with good reason. It would unite the entire galaxy against them.

"It isn't like them to just give up, is it?"

"No," Kat agreed. "And we can't give up either."

William nodded, turning his attention to the near-space display. ONI's best guesses at the surviving enemy fleet strength suggested the enemy might be down to a mere thirteen superdreadnought squadrons at most, but several of them would be on the far side of the Gap. They'd need at least five to six weeks to get into position to challenge 6th Fleet, even if they were recalled immediately.

Unless they were recalled earlier, he thought. *We wouldn't know.*

It was a bitter thought. The Theocracy could have withdrawn the remainder of their fleet from the occupied systems, perhaps wrecking the planets as they departed, and 6th Fleet wouldn't know anything about it until they got the mobile StarCom set up. A fleet that could give Commonwealth vessels a run for their money might be closing in at this very moment—and they wouldn't have any warning until the ships dropped out of hyperspace. Hell, the enemy might copy *his* tactic of returning to realspace at the edge of the system and crawling towards the planet under cloak. But coordinating such an operation would be an absolute nightmare.

"All we can really do is prepare ourselves for the challenge, when it comes," he said. "And start raiding the rest of the system."

"You'll be taking control of the cloudscoops in the next two days," Kat said. "And as many asteroid colonies as possible."

"If they're not blown up first," William said pessimistically.

The Theocracy had never struck him as the kind of government that was inclined to leave something intact for its replacement. Losing the cloudscoops would eventually plunge the entire planet into darkness as fusion plants ran out of fuel. They could be replaced, of course, but that would take time. He had a nasty feeling the Theocracy wasn't going to give 6th Fleet that time.

"We have to do the best we can with what we have on hand," Kat said. She took a breath, running her hand through her hair. "I'll have to call a council of war once the spacehead is firmly established."

"Ouch," William said. His eyes narrowed. Was that a *ring* on her finger? "Shouldn't we get the StarCom set up first?"

"The techs are working on it," Kat said. She didn't sound entirely pleased. "We'll have to warn the Commonwealth that the enemy might be sending ships in their direction."

"Agreed," William said. He met her eyes. "Is that a new ring?"

Kat flushed. "Yes. Pat gave it to me."

"Congratulations are in order then," William said. "I hope the two of you will be very happy together."

He wondered, absently, just how many others had noticed. Kat wouldn't have been face to face with anyone, apart from her tactical aides. It wouldn't matter. Her marriage wasn't a major issue, not when the fleet was invading the enemy homeworld. He had no doubt that Duke Falcone would eventually turn the engagement *into* a major issue after the war.

"Thank you," Kat said. She still looked flushed. "I hope you'll do us the honor of attending."

"I will," William said.

The nasty part of his mind was tempted to suggest that she take the ring off, at least during the council of war. He could name three or four commodores who would be happy to make sarcastic remarks about allowing one's partner to go into danger, then ask pointed questions about just how badly Kat would be distracted by worrying about her fiancé. There were *reasons* why intimate relationships between officers were discouraged, even when they weren't technically illegal. But he trusted Kat. She'd sent Pat into danger dozens of times in the years he'd known her, and if she'd had qualms, she'd hidden them well.

Of course, she put herself in danger too, he thought. *And she has a right to wear his ring.*

"We'll be adding KEWs to the bombardment, I think," Kat added. "The enemy needs to be shaken up before the marines get to them."

"As long as they're not under the force shields," William pointed out. Accurately targeting KEWs at such a distance wasn't going to be easy. "Or do you want to risk sending the fleet closer?"

"We need a couple of monitors," Kat said tersely. "Even superdreadnoughts can't cut it."

William nodded. Naval monitors were supposed to be designed for bombarding targets on the ground while soaking up the enemy's response, but the concept had never gotten off the drawing board. A superdreadnought could do everything *they* could do against an unshielded target, without needing a specialized ship, while a monitor wouldn't be *that* much more effective against a shielded and defended target. There was just too great a chance of having the monitor blown out of space by the enemy's ground-based defenses.

But they would have come in handy now.

"The marines can cope," he assured her. "We're moving reinforcements down as fast as possible, aren't we?"

"Yes," Kat said. "But are we moving fast *enough?*"

"I think so," William said.

Kat still looked grave. "Concentrate on taking the shipyards," she said. "I'll be watching my back very carefully."

"Good idea," William agreed. "The threats don't just come from the enemy fleet, these days."

◆ ◆ ◆

Kat sat back in her office, feeling old, as William's image vanished from the display.

She'd thought herself immune to horror. She'd seen the aftermath of too many pirate raids to feel anything but a stark desire to hunt down and slaughter the perpetrators. She'd avoided many of the horrible disadvantages facing commoners, those who hadn't been born into aristocratic families, yet she thought she understood them. She understood the limits they'd faced, even if they hadn't existed for her.

But she'd underestimated the Theocracy's capability for sheer unending horror.

Kat could understand stiff resistance, even fanatical resistance. It was the only logical response to being attacked by something like the Theocracy, where survival meant humiliation, shame, or helpless collaboration. And yet, the Commonwealth wasn't going to slaughter or rape its way through the planet's population. There was no *need* to kill women and children instead of letting them fall into enemy hands.

They're using our own compassion against us, she thought. The Theocrats had succeeded in preventing the Commonwealth from liberating the other occupied worlds simply by threatening to destroy them. Now they were killing their own people in the hopes of dissuading the Commonwealth from advancing further. *And yet we cannot stop. We cannot even pull back and abandon the spacehead.*

She closed her eyes, trying to banish the images from her mind. Women and children, herded into a church and gassed. Why had the gas even been prepared? Had the Theocrats planned to slaughter their entire population if there was a risk of losing control? Or . . . or what? A pirate attack might be more savage, yet there was something unrelentingly horrible about what the Theocracy had done.

But we have to push on, she told herself as she rose. The Theocrats could not be allowed to hold their own population hostage. *There's no going back now.*

CHAPTER TWENTY-SEVEN

"Duck!"

Pat dropped to his knees as the hovertank came into view, firing burst after burst of plasma towards the marines. Bolts of brilliant light flashed over his head as he crawled backwards, careful not to attract the tank's attention. The rifles and machine guns the militia were armed with couldn't harm the marines, but the tank certainly could. And so could the armored men behind it.

One advantage of hovertanks, he thought. *They can be moved to any location at speed.*

"I have a shot," Corporal Jackson said.

"Take it," Pat ordered.

Jackson stood up on his knees, just long enough to fire a missile towards the tank. The craft jerked backwards, but the missile had a solid lock and plowed into its forward armor plating. Pat's visor darkened automatically as the plasma warhead detonated, burning brightly as it melted its way through armor. A moment later, the tank lurched to a halt. Any crewmen inside would have been killed the moment the plasma fire burned through the armored shell.

He lifted his own weapon as the enemy soldiers moved forward, firing a burst of plasma bolts at the nearest target. *These* soldiers were well trained, he noted, certainly better trained than the militiamen who'd wasted their lives on a desperate and utterly futile bid to stop the marines. They were bounding overwatch, one soldier covering his comrades as they advanced forward. Behind them, four more hovertanks crawled forward, firing.

Lucky they want to get to us before it's too late, Pat thought as he snapped out a string of orders. The mortars opened fire, raining shells on the advancing enemy. It would take a direct hit to smash an enemy battlesuit, but even a near miss would shake them up while stripping their cover away. *If they tried to dig in, life would get a great deal harder.*

He hit an enemy soldier, the plasma pulse burning through his target's armor and incinerating the victim inside. Other enemy soldiers returned fire, lobbing grenades and sweeping stunners towards their position. Pat puzzled over the latter for a moment, then dismissed the thought as two of his marines were killed. The best personal armor the Commonwealth had been able to produce *still* couldn't stand up to a plasma pulse.

"The tanks are charging," Bones snapped. "Missile teams, front and center!"

Pat watched as the tanks thrust forward. *Their* armor could stand up to his plasma rifles, although not to the plasma cannons his men were hastily deploying behind the front line. The battle was rapidly turning into a free-for-all, both sides advancing and retreating depending on the situation. He had to admit that the enemy tactics, as wasteful as they were, were well considered. If they punched through to the rapidly expanding spacehead, they could cut the marines off from their reinforcements and wipe them out to the last man. It was worth any cost, as far as the planet's leadership was concerned, to exterminate the landing force. They had to know the Commonwealth wouldn't be too keen on sending another.

He sucked in his breath as the lead tank died, but two more moved around it and kept coming, their weapons sweeping through the thin layers of cover protecting his troops. The marines crawled backwards, abandoning their lines; the hovertanks charged forward, only to impale themselves on the plasma cannons. Pat was silently relieved the enemy didn't seem to realize the potential of their own long-range guns. They were firing thousands of shells into the spacehead, wasting artillery in hopes of scoring a single hit, but trying to use them to clear the way for their ground forces would have been far more effective.

They don't trust their own people to call down fire, he thought as he picked off another armored soldier. *They're not allowed to be flexible, even when their own homeworld is under attack.*

The ground shook violently. He feared a nuke, just for a second, before a note popped up in his HUD. The fleet was firing KEWs towards targets on the ground, even though their accuracy was appallingly bad. Pat had authority to call for "danger close" strikes if he had no other choice, but he wouldn't care to risk such moves if they could be avoided. There was too great a chance of accidentally bombing his own people.

"Orbital images say the KEW took out four tanks," Major Harold said over the datanet. "But they're still coming."

Pat nodded and concentrated on holding the line as the enemy threw in attack after attack while shellfire rained down on the spacehead and KEWs struck targets to the west. The Theocrats seemed to have realized the futility of sending in aircraft, after losing several dozen to ground-based fire, but they were still aiming missiles and drones into the spacehead. Pat picked off a drone with a plasma shot, then inched forward as the enemy attack started to lose its momentum. Had they run out of men, he asked himself, or were they simply regrouping for another assault?

He glanced at the nearest tank, silently comparing it to the Commonwealth's vehicles. It hadn't shown any obvious inferiority, although there was a crudeness about the design that suggested it might have a few hidden weaknesses. But then, the Commonwealth had been able to afford a certain elegance the Theocracy had disdained. Pat recalled reading broadsides in various military journals arguing over the strengths and weaknesses of the latest designs. Some older military officers claimed that the elegance was a mistake in a weapon of war.

"The enemy are regrouping in the nearby town," Major Harold added. "General Winters requests you scatter them."

Pat nodded tersely. They'd overrun a number of towns before the enemy had mustered a major counterattack, discovering scene after scene of horror as they pushed through the settlements and out the far side. A number of women *had* survived, he'd been surprised to discover, but they were so fearful of the marines that they kept trying to hide, despite announcements inviting them to come into the light. He was just relieved that the Theocracy hadn't managed to brainwash everyone.

"Sergeant," he said, "status report?"

"Seven dead, nine wounded," Bones said. "I recommend sending the wounded back as soon as the reinforcements arrive."

"Leave Charlie Company to guard the lines," Pat ordered. "Alpha and Beta Companies will take the offensive."

The sound of shellfire grew louder as he led the marines through the field, heading straight towards the town. It was three or four times as large as the previous settlement, but there was something about its design that made the locale look cramped. He checked the live feed from the stealth drones as they orbited the town, picking out defenses and potential ambush sites while hiding from enemy gunners. A trained sniper with a plasma rifle could easily bring a drone down if he could see it.

"The enemy is mustering their forces at a road junction," Major Harold stated. "KEW strikes are inbound."

Idiots, Pat thought. The Theocrats simply weren't used to operating without top cover, certainly not on their own homeworld. They needed to keep most of their forces either close to the spacehead or buried under their force shields. *Putting them out like that is asking for trouble.*

He gritted his teeth as the marines advanced towards the town, moving from cover to cover as they closed in on their target. The buildings in front of them looked like large warehouses, but someone had been cutting makeshift murder holes in the walls . . . despite them, it didn't *look* as though the enemy had been expecting trouble in advance. But then, merely getting the planet ready to resist an invasion would have been an admission that the war wasn't going their way. Radio intercepts suggested that the Theocrats were ordering their people to stay put, but not telling them exactly what was going on. Rumors, if he was any judge, would be spreading wildly.

"Incoming," Bones snapped.

Pat nodded, ducking low as the defenders opened fire. No plasma weapons, just machine guns and rifles. His marines returned fire, putting a dozen plasma bursts into the building before it collapsed into a pile of flaming debris. Pat barked a command, then rose and ran towards the ruins, hoping to get into a firing position before the enemy could do something.

He threw himself down again as a bolt of plasma fire scorched his armor. Two red icons flared up in front of him—two men dead—as he hit the ground, cursing under his breath. The enemy had tricked him, luring his men into an ambush. He lifted his arm, launching a pair of grenades towards the enemy position as their fire intensified. Moments later, a thunderous explosion shook the ground and the enemy fire abruptly stopped. But his suit's audio sensors could pick up howling in the distance.

"Another mob," Bones warned as the dust cleared. "Here they come."

Pat couldn't be sure, but it looked very much as though the mob was hopped up on something. Their eyes were wild, even as they charged towards the marines waving makeshift weapons in the air. Behind them, using their own people as human shields, he could see armed and armored soldiers. And, depending on what they'd been drugged with, stunners might not be any use against the crowd.

Bastards, he thought as he snapped orders. *How many of their own people are going to die?*

◆ ◆ ◆

"Another mob riot, sir," Lieutenant Fletcher said.

General Winters nodded, chewing his unlit cigar thoughtfully as the latest stream of reports came in from the front. The enemy was definitely falling back, although they were taking care to set traps and destroy as much of the surrounding infrastructure as they could before retreating. *And* they were carelessly sacrificing their own civilian population, using them as human shields and mob rioters to wear down the marines.

The mobs can't hurt us, he thought. *But they can wear down our souls.*

"Send reinforcements to the town," he ordered. The enemy was getting better at separating the real shuttles from the sensor decoys, damn them. "And then expand the POW camps again."

He made a face as another report popped up in front of him. The enemy might be falling back, but his advance units weren't moving forward as fast as he'd hoped. He'd known that nothing could be guaranteed, yet taking out the nearest PDC was vitally important. His units *had* to disable the structure or the campaign would be drawn out for months, if not years.

"Major Harold reports more enemy units retreating behind the force shields," Fletcher added. "KEW strikes are of limited value."

"Ask the spacers to keep dropping them anyway," Winters snapped. That far from the front lines, the odds of striking a friendly target were minimal. Besides, KEWs were cheap. His marines were not. "As soon as the 45th is on the ground, start feeding it into the front lines."

He cursed under his breath as a shell landed right on top of the spacehead, the blast taking out two shuttles and damaging a third. The enemy had been crafty enough to place their guns *just* under cover, ensuring that there was nothing he could do to stop them from firing shell after shell into his defenses. And one or two getting through would be enough to do real damage.

But they have to run out of ammunition sooner or later, he thought. *And when they do, we will be ready.*

"Signal from the flag," Fletcher added. She sounded puzzled. "Commodore Falcone would like to know if we can receive Eagle Eye."

Junayd, Winters thought sourly. *He must really want to return home.*

To be fair, he admitted to himself, Admiral Junayd hadn't made any promises, unlike some of the other defectors he'd had to work with during his long career. He still boiled with rage whenever he thought about just how many politicians on Cadiz had made promises of vast popular support, none of which had actually worked out in practice. Junayd hadn't done that, not yet. But there was no role for him on the surface. His seat could be taken by a marine or a medic or someone else who was actually *useful.*

"Tell them that we don't have room for him yet," he said. "We barely have enough room to bury our dead."

◆ ◆ ◆

"Their spacehead appears to be holding," Speaker Mosul said. "I thought it was going to be destroyed!"

"They are being worn down," Inquisitor Samuilu said. "Our men are fighting bravely to kill as many of the unbelievers as they can."

"Indeed," Lord Cleric Eliseus said. "And clerics are driving the civilians out to fight!"

"And killing everyone who tries to flee," Mosul said. "There are reports of guns being turned on Inquisitors, are there not?"

Speaker Nehemiah kept his face impassive, even though Mosul had put his finger on a very sore spot. No one in their right mind wanted to issue plasma weapons, let alone suits of armor, to men who might rebel against the government, but that meant that the weapons they *did* have were largely ineffectual against enemy troops. Grenades and explosives did have some effect, and they certainly slowed the enemy down, yet those types of attacks came with a very high cost. Even the stupidest civilian had to realize that he and his friends were being expended for nothing.

"Lies," Eliseus snarled. "Foul lies spread by our enemies!"

"I have proof," Mosul said. "Reports from people I trust!"

He waved a hand at the display. "The enemy has landed," he snapped. "And they are already securing their spacehead. Our attacks have proven ineffectual."

"Our attacks have bled the enemy," Eliseus snapped back.

"But they have not *stopped* the enemy," Mosul snarled. "They're only a few days' march from the Tabernacle itself, are they not?"

"The Commonwealth does not have the stomach to keep fighting," Eliseus said. "Our warriors are primed to fight! We can trade ten of our lives for every one of theirs and still win. How many of their lives are they prepared to throw away?"

He rose, his flashing eyes sweeping the room. "Victory in this war will go to the side willing to fight for what it believes in," he hissed. "And I believe that God will grant us victory if we do not surrender our faith in Him!"

"God will not thank us for wasting thousands, hundreds of thousands, *millions* of lives," Mosul said. "The enemy has landed. Our entire civilization stands at the cusp of ultimate destruction."

"We have a plan," Inquisitor Samuilu said. "Victory remains within our grasp."

"Yes," Mosul said. "But at what cost?"

He tapped his fingers on the table as he spoke. "Most of the ship-yards are gone," he said wearily. "The remainder will be destroyed when the enemy boards them. There is no way we can replenish our losses before the Commonwealth launches a second invasion. Even if we win the coming battle, we will lose the war."

"The Commonwealth will not press the offensive after their fleet is destroyed," Eliseus snapped. "This is our darkest hour, but God will grant us victory!"

"The Commonwealth has more fleets," Mosul said. "Lord Cleric, the war is lost."

"Blasphemy," Eliseus thundered.

He strode around the room, glaring at the speakers. "God is testing us," he said. "There will be hard times. There will be hard times for all of us. But we will hold firm, never giving up no matter what they pile on us. God's chosen people will survive."

Mosul stared at him. "And if they destroy every last world in the Theocracy? We've already lost contact with the outside universe. Who *knows* what's happening out there?" He looked at Nehemiah. "They can destroy us," he said. "And they *will* destroy us."

"God will preserve us," Eliseus said. "They will not be permitted to destroy us."

Mosul sagged. "We believed we could win the war," he said. "But our plan went off the rails. Now . . . now we are on the verge of losing."

He sighed. "I beseech you," he said. "End this war now, before it is too late."

"Out of the question," Samuilu said.

Nehemiah glanced up. A dozen armed men had sneaked into the chamber. He tensed, knowing that resistance was futile. Eliseus and Samuilu controlled everything.

"These are our darkest hours," Samuilu said. "But with God's grace, we will survive and march into paradise."

Mosul opened his mouth. Nehemiah had no idea what he thought he could say, what might get him out of trouble, but it was too late. Samuilu snapped his fingers. His men grabbed Mosul, yanked him out of his chair, and threw him to the floor. The other four moderates were swiftly arrested too. Nehemiah knew, all too well, that none of them would survive the next few hours. Their families would be purged too, just in case. No trace of heresy could be allowed to survive.

"Very well done," he said coolly. He didn't dare let them see his own doubts, not now. His family was at risk too. "You allowed him to condemn himself out of his own mouth."

"Thank you, Your Holiness," Eliseus beamed.

He's mad, Nehemiah thought. He'd kept an eye on the Inquisitors, but he'd missed the Lord Cleric. *He's mad . . . and there's nothing I can do about it.*

"We will fight a delaying action," Samuilu said. His voice rose as he spoke. "Once the fleets are ready, we will hit them in space as well as on the ground. They will be crushed! And God will finally grant us the victory we deserve."

"Of course," Nehemiah agreed. His mind raced, trying to find a way out. But there was none. He doubted it would be long before he was taken into protective custody. The madmen wouldn't tolerate even the merest hint of disagreement. "God will always defend the right."

CHAPTER TWENTY-EIGHT

"I am truly sorry about the delay," Janice said as the hovertank made its way towards their destination. "It should have happened sooner."

"It is of no matter," Junayd assured her. "General Winters was right to be concerned."

He sat back in the tank and forced himself to relax. A week of hard fighting had given the marines a chance to clear an ever-expanding spacehead, ending with the destruction of a PDC near a large city. Now, wave after wave of reinforcements could be landed, allowing the marines to prepare themselves for the final thrust towards the Tabernacle. Junayd hoped there might be a way to avoid the devastation such a campaign would leave in its wake.

The thought made him shudder, despite himself. Starship combat was clean. He'd never seen enemy spacers gasping for breath as they were swept out of gashes in starship hulls and thrown into space, nor watched the wounded struggling to survive. A starship might die in agony, her last moments an eternity of pure horror for her crew, but all he saw was icons vanishing from the display. Crews might be blotted out of existence without him ever emotionally grasping what had happened. They were just . . . statistics.

But the world around him was *real*. The small convoy had passed through countless wrecked farms and villages, towns that had been fought over so savagely that they'd been reduced to rubble. Dead bodies had been collected and dumped into mass graves, the survivors, often wounded, left staring in horror at the wreckage of their world. And the insurgents, men who feared there would be no life for them if they were captured, were still sniping at everything that moved. An entire world was dying in front of him.

This is what we brought to other worlds, he thought. *And now it's come back to haunt us.*

He sighed inwardly. Civil Affairs teams were *trying* to organize the local population, but thousands of people were too scared to come out of hiding or be seen helping the invaders. The government had *finally* admitted that their world had been invaded, yet their messages had come tinged with bombastic promises about crushing the invasion force and pledging dire punishment for anyone seen collaborating. Junayd believed them. He knew *precisely* what the government would do if it drove the invaders back into space.

The tank hummed to a halt. Junayd braced himself as the hatch opened—he hadn't been given any armor, let alone a weapon—and then stepped out into the bright sunlight. The air smelled of home, he realized, the indefinable scent that belonged to Ahura Mazda and Ahura Mazda alone. A large mansion was right in front of him, surrounded by a trio of tanks and a dozen men in heavy armor. He and his escort were several miles from the nearest settlement, but Junayd knew they were right to be careful. Their passage might have been noticed.

He looked west. Smoke and flames rose from the front lines, reminding him that the battle was still underway. The marines were being challenged constantly, their defenses probed to keep them on the alert. No military force could hope to stay at full readiness indefinitely, not even the marines. Junayd knew his former masters were hoping to weaken the ground-based Commonwealth forces before they began their *real* counteroffensive.

Janice clambered out of the tank, her uniform looking rumpled. She'd dressed down as much as possible, trying to pose as a man, but it was hard to miss the swell of her breasts despite the ill-fitting jacket. And yet, he *knew* she was a woman. Someone who wasn't used to women in male clothes might mistake her for a man.

We will see, he thought.

"So," Janice said, "this is how the other half lives, right?"

"Yes," Junayd said. The mansion was tiny compared to some of the buildings he'd seen on Tyre, but immense compared to the tiny apartments allocated to the majority of the population on Ahura Mazda. It had been passed down from one of the first settlers, a man whose family had lost much of their power since the first landings. "Most people down there"—he nodded towards the plumes of smoke—"don't even know this place exists."

"The marines say he's inside," Janice said. "He's waiting for you."

"That's a good sign," Junayd said. "I hope."

He took a breath as he walked towards the doors, feeling sweat trickling down his back. If his old friend had been subverted, if he'd been forced to betray Junayd, there was a very good chance that both he and Janice were about to die. And yet, surely his confidante would have done more if he *had* been subverted. The mansion might be half hidden in the hills, but it wasn't concealed from orbital observation. There were plenty of reasons to assume the invasion force would pay it a visit.

The doors were already open, revealing a wood-lined corridor leading into a sitting room, the scent of wood bringing back memories, some good and some bad. A gray-haired man stood by the bookcase, holding a copy of a forbidden tome in one hand. His connections might not have been enough to save him, if the Inquisition had realized he owned so many banned books, but he'd never seemed to care. Junayd had never seen him as a potential threat.

"Nestor," he said. "It's good to see you again."

"Junayd," Nestor breathed. "I always knew you would return." He nodded to Janice. "And who is your companion?"

"Commander Wilson, Commonwealth Office of Naval Intelligence," Junayd said before Janice could say a word. Nestor was one of the most liberal-minded Theocrats, but even *he* had his limits. Better to let him think Janice was male. "A friend."

"More like a handler," Nestor said. He waved a hand at the comfortable sofas. "Would you care for something to drink? I'll have to make it myself, of course. The servants have been taken into custody by your new friends."

"I'm sorry about that," Junayd said. The question hovered on the tip of his tongue for a long moment. He wasn't sure he wanted to know the answer. "My family?"

"Waiting for you," Nestor said. "I had them brought here when I heard about the landings."

Junayd leaned forward. "Take me to them."

Nestor nodded and led him through a side door and down a concealed passageway Junayd didn't recall seeing during his last visit. Nestor's family had always been uncomfortably paranoid, not always without reason. The Inquisition had tried to have them all arrested more than once. Junayd was surprised Nestor hadn't been purged after his defection, after the Theocracy thought Junayd had died in the line of duty. Surely, his former protection hadn't been enough to save Nestor's life.

"There's news from the city," Nestor said. Junayd didn't have to ask to know which city he meant. There were hundreds of cities on Ahura Mazda, but only one of them was actually important. "The council has been purged. Nehemiah is still in control, it seems, yet Samuilu and Eliseus are pulling the strings. Everyone else is either dead or imprisoned."

"Shit," Junayd muttered. Beside him, Janice looked just as alarmed. "Are you sure?"

"Sure as I can be," Nestor assured him. "So far, there haven't been widespread purges, but hostages have been taken and everyone agrees it's just a matter of time."

Janice coughed. "How can a society *survive* like this?"

"They're not used to defeat, young man," Nestor said. "They certainly aren't used to a long war."

Junayd nodded, curtly. The longest campaign the Theocracy had fought, before launching the invasion of Commonwealth space, had been on Hobson's World, where the locals had resisted their new masters with fanatical determination. No one had doubted the outcome, not when the Theocrats controlled the high orbitals right from the start, but it had still cost thousands of lives to batter the planet into submission. The First Battle of Cadiz had cost more lives than the entire campaign on Hobson's World . . . and it had only been the start of the war.

"I kept them in a nearby homestead," Nestor said as they reached the female quarters. Some of the really old houses maintained a guard on the doors, but Nestor didn't seem inclined to honor the old traditions. "Officially, they were distant relatives of mine; poor, few close relatives, no strong marriage prospects. No one asked any questions."

"Good," Junayd said. He promised himself silently that he'd spend the rest of the night in prayer if he had the time. Nestor had come up with a good cover. No one would be interested in girls who were too wellborn to marry the lower classes, but too poor to interest the higher classes. "Can you wait here?"

"Of course," Nestor said. "And your companion can wait here too."

Junayd nodded his thanks, then stepped through the door. Nestor was being astonishingly kind under the circumstances. Strangers were *not* allowed in the female quarters, even if the rooms were empty. He still recalled the whipping his father had given him for sneaking into the female quarters back when he'd been a little boy. The old man had bloodied his back so badly that the scars had lingered for years.

He paused outside the inner door, feeling a sudden urge to turn back. Who knew *what* he would find? Bitter and resentful women? Or women who understood the blunt truth that he hadn't had a choice? He opened the door and stepped through, shaking his head at the surprising luxury that greeted his eyes. Female quarters rarely had any decoration, even though the women only left such spaces when they were summoned. Nestor, in so many ways, bucked tradition.

Junayd's three wives sat on the sofa, staring at him. He wondered, suddenly, just what they'd been told when they'd been hurried out of his house. The truth? Or something else? His senior wife smiled at him while his junior wives looked nervous. They knew their positions were uncertain as long as they failed to give him sons. And *none* of them had given him a son.

"Junayd," his senior wife said. She sounded relieved. "It's good to see you again."

A man didn't cry. A man *never* cried. But Junayd had to blink hard to keep the tears out of his eyes as he hurried forward. He'd changed, part of him realized. He'd never really appreciated just how *dependent* his wives had been on him, not until he'd seen how women lived elsewhere. Their very *safety* depended upon him. They couldn't speak for themselves, let alone own property and live independently. If he'd died, they would have been dumped on his nearest relatives.

"Our children," he said, hugging her. "Where are they?"

"Waiting for you," his youngest wife said. She'd been a beauty when he'd married her, purchasing her from her parents for a tidy sum. Now she looked stressed and worn. "They missed you."

"I missed them too," Junayd admitted. They might only be girls, but he loved them anyway. "I need to see them, then we will leave this place."

◆ ◆ ◆

"I'm very glad you found your family," General Winters said four hours later. "Are they well?"

"They're malnourished," Junayd said. Janice had insisted on taking the women to the medics, even though his wives had been reluctant. "But they survived."

"I see," General Winters said. "And did you learn anything useful?"

"Much of my old network remains intact," Junayd said. *That* had been a relief. He simply hadn't had much to bargain with on Tyre. "However, the government is now led by extremists and fanatics."

General Winters grunted in disapproval. "Was there ever anything else?"

Junayd shrugged expressively. "They told everyone I died," he said. "If I start making broadcasts now, I can try to convince people to rebel."

"Oh," General Winters said. "And do you think it will actually *work*?"

"It's the best shot we'll have of taking the planet without marching on the Tabernacle," Junayd pointed out. "If vast numbers of people rebel, the government and military will simply come apart."

"A lot of your people will die," General Winters said.

Junayd took a breath. "They'll die anyway, General," he said. "Or have you forgotten the mobs aimed at your troops?" He went on before Winters could say a word. "This is the best chance we'll have of convincing the troops to overthrow the government," he said. "And if it fails, you can *still* march on the Tabernacle."

"He's right, General," Janice said stiffly. Junayd glanced at her. She seemed preoccupied with a greater thought. "Junayd's name is well respected among the Theocrats."

"And that leads to a different question," General Winters said. "Would any of them recognize your voice? Or your image?"

"They'd certainly recognize my image," Junayd said.

"Images can be faked," General Winters said. "It wouldn't be hard to put images of you and Nehemiah fucking like little bunny rabbits on the air."

Junayd kept his anger under tight control. "Do you have a better idea?"

He understood the general's concerns. Chaos on the streets would either lead to mass slaughter, forcing his men to intervene before they were ready, or give the Theocrats an opportunity to purge enemies before the Commonwealth could move to assist the rebels. But the opportunity was already slipping away. Junayd *knew* Samuilu, knew just how much the Inquisitor wanted supreme control. Anyone who might aid the Commonwealth, anyone who might want to stop the war before everyone was killed, was on the verge of being purged. Time was running out.

Maybe we should put black propaganda on the air, he thought. *The people might believe it.*

"No," General Winters said after a pause. "But I expect you to run the crap you intend to put on the air past me first."

"Of course, General," Junayd said.

He allowed Janice to lead him out of the makeshift office and into the open air. The spacehead seemed to be expanding by leaps and bounds, dozens of prefabricated buildings springing up out of nowhere as more and more terrain was cleared by the landing parties. A dozen point defense weapons were in clear view, their sensors constantly sweeping the skies for incoming threats; a long stream of hovertanks was checked and rechecked before being sent down to the front lines. Junayd found the whole display a little terrifying, even though they were on the same side. The sheer level of resources the Commonwealth had deployed so casually was thoroughly intimidating. It seemed impossible to believe that there was anything capable of standing in their way.

Janice said nothing until they stepped into the intelligence compound and walked into her office. It was a barren room, barely large enough to swing a cat, but Junayd had been assured that it was completely soundproofed. He couldn't imagine *precisely* how the Theocracy might have managed to get a spy into ONI, yet ONI was still taking precautions. Junayd approved. Even paranoids had enemies.

"I read the doctor's report on your wives and daughters," Janice said. Her voice had an odd hint of . . . *something*. "Do you know what it said?"

"Malnourished," Junayd said.

"It said more than that," Janice said. Her voice hardened. "There was a strong suggestion that your wives are mentally ill."

Junayd blinked. "They're not."

"They were on the verge of going mad from the isolation," Janice snapped. "And your daughters aren't much better. Your two oldest daughters had to be practically dragged out of the doctor's office after spending nearly an hour talking to her. They were *that* desperate for someone new to talk to. *And* your wives have agoraphobia as well . . . they needed to be shut up in a small room just so they could sleep comfortably. Didn't you ever let them out of the house?"

"Not where someone else could see," Junayd said. He'd taken his wives and daughters on vacations, of course, secluded from public notice. But even that had been difficult when getting there posed a major logistics challenge. And later, as he'd spent more and more time away from home, he'd been content to leave them there. "It was—"

"They're not the only ones," Janice said. Her voice softened, but only slightly. "The women in the POW camps are . . . weird. Half of them seem terrified of men; the other half seem terrified of everyone. A couple panicked when they realized one of the marines was female. Most refused to let a medic, male or female, examine them. Why?"

"Doctors are rarely allowed to examine female patients," Junayd said curtly. He had spent a vast amount in bribes to arrange for his youngest daughter to be treated after she'd fallen badly ill. The greedy swine of a doctor had demanded enough money to buy a practice of his own. "The doctors have to ask the women's husbands or fathers to describe their symptoms."

Janice stared at him. "Are you mad? Is your entire population mad?"

"It's the way they were raised," Junayd said sharply. He would have been outraged, a few years ago, at being questioned so blatantly. Ahura Mazda was *his* world. But he'd learned hard lessons over the last two years. "They never thought to question it."

"It will change," Janice said. "Do you understand me? It will change!"

"Yes, it will," Junayd agreed. "The cracks are already starting to show. My broadcasts will make them worse. And then . . ."

He shook his head. It would be *years* before Ahura Mazda recovered from the Theocracy, if it ever recovered at all. And while he hoped to build a new power base for himself, he saw now it would be built on a rotting foundation. The population might reject him as thoroughly as they'd reject the speakers. God alone knew what would happen in the future.

"All we can do is press on," he said. "If Samuilu and Eliseus are running the government now, they won't surrender. They'll keep looking for ways to hurt you, whatever the cost."

CHAPTER TWENTY-NINE

". . . is Admiral Junayd," Junayd's voice said. "Reports of my death were falsified."

Kat watched as the speech went on, Junayd calling out his former masters for starting a hopeless war, throwing away so many lives, and finally allowing an invading force to set foot on Ahura Mazda itself. He spoke of a future without war, a future without the clerics, a future where life was free and uncontrolled. And he called on his people to rise up against their oppressors.

"A pretty speech," Commodore Daniel Hawkins said. His image floated in front of Kat, surrounded by the other commodores. The captains hadn't been invited to the high-level command meeting. "But is it going to be enough?"

"Preliminary reports suggest that a number of enemy units *have* mutinied," General Winters said. His image looked stern. He'd been reluctant to take part in the conference, pointing out that the situation on the ground needed to be closely monitored. "However, the enemy will soon start claiming that Junayd is dead and his voice a fake. It's the logical countermove."

"But that would convince their people that *other* news could be faked too," Commodore Nathan Romanov pointed out. "Like their claims to be driving on Tyre."

Kat nodded. She'd seen some of the propaganda broadcasts, although they'd cut out shortly after the marines had landed on Ahura Mazda. The Theocracy was driving on Tyre . . . the Theocracy had been driving on Tyre for the last eighteen months. Surely someone would have thought to question why the fleets hadn't *reached* Tyre. And the reports of hundreds of superdreadnoughts destroyed were pure fiction. The entire Royal Navy would have been wiped out several times over if they were true.

"Everything that hurts the enemy helps us," Commodore Stuart snapped. "An uprising on the far side of Ahura Mazda will hurt them, even if the rebels have no ties to us."

"There will be a brutal slaughter," Commodore Romanov countered. "We've already seen countless reports of men crucified for deserting their posts—"

"Which doesn't hurt us," Stuart said. "The well-being of the planet's population is secondary to ending the war. Our *priority* is ending the war."

He looked at Kat. "And that means selecting a new admiral."

Kat kept her face impassive. She'd expected a challenge to her authority sooner or later. She *did* have a great deal of military experience, but not in fleet or squadron command. Admiral Christian had chosen her, she suspected, because of the fear her name inspired among the Theocracy, not because of her experience. Now that the first engagement had come to an end, her position could be challenged.

General Winters cleared his throat, loudly. "The issue is not up for debate," he said. He stared at Stuart, daring him to object. "Admiral Christian selected Commodore Falcone as his second. Barring countermanding orders from Tyre, she is the legitimate commanding officer of the fleet."

"Her fleet command experience is quite limited," Stuart protested.

"A fact that Admiral Christian no doubt took into consideration," General Winters said coldly. "If you wish to register a protest, you may send one home via the StarCom. But until Tyre sees fit to overrule Admiral Christian's instructions, you will accept her position."

Kat winced inwardly. General Winters and Admiral Christian had been old friends, working together for decades. He'd want to honor his friend's final orders, even if they caused problems for his successor. And they would, Kat knew. She could be judged by time in grade or experience, but either way she'd lose. There were other officers in the fleet with more of both.

"The StarCom is being set up now," she stated bluntly. "Tyre may see fit to remove me from command. Until then . . ." She tapped her console, displaying a star chart. "As far as can be determined, the operations against the Theocracy's StarComs were successful," she said. "We won't know for sure, of course, until the various squadrons return to the RV point, but it certainly *looks* as though the Theocracy's command and control network has fragmented. Any orders from Ahura Mazda will have to be sent via courier boat, rather than StarCom. We are in a good position to block any such transmissions.

"However," she added, "there is good reason to believe that the enemy intends to mount a counterattack with its remaining ships."

"They shouldn't be able to crush us," Romanov said. "Most of their ships are in very poor condition."

"We practically shot ourselves dry," Stuart commented. "Reloading the missile tubes is still underway. *And* we are putting significant wear and tear on our equipment."

Kat nodded. "We will hold position here and stand them off when they arrive," she said, adjusting the star chart. "I've already deployed pickets in hopes of getting some early warning, but unfortunately we cannot count on them being so obliging. We must assume that the attack will come at any moment."

"They'll have to mass their ships first," Hawkins said. "Even if they got the orders out before we destroyed their StarCom, it will still take them weeks—at best."

"Yes," Kat said. "But some of their squadrons were stationed a great deal closer to Ahura Mazda."

She pushed the star chart aside, calling up an image of the local system. "Our smaller squadrons will be deployed to seize or destroy all remaining infrastructure within the system," she continued. "This may lure any enemy stay-behind units out of hiding, giving us a chance to pick them off before the main body of their fleet returns. Regardless of the final outcome, Ahura Mazda's industrial base will be largely destroyed. The war will end, one way or the other."

"At a horrendous cost," Romanov said.

General Winters snorted rudely. "Any *sane* government would be looking for ways to surrender by now," he said. "I shudder to imagine just how many millions of their own people have died in the last week alone, either through human wave attacks or merely being used as shields by their so-called defenders. The locals are just too scared of us to come over in large numbers."

"That may change," Kat said.

"Yeah," General Winters said. "But right now, the important thing is readying ourselves for the march on the Tabernacle."

"Which will take your forces under the PDC's shield," Romanov observed.

"And they know it," General Winters said. "We've picked up plenty of evidence of them digging in and preparing to fight to the last. Hovertanks, armored soldiers, unarmored infantry units . . . probably millions of drugged-up civilians too."

"Bastards," Kat said. Pat was down there. She'd seen a couple of his reports. "They're mad."

"Oh, there's a method to their bastardry," General Winters said. "I've had to withdraw a number of soldiers from the battlefield after they cracked under the strain of dealing with the fuckers. Mainly militiamen, I will admit, but even marines are affected. We're going to be dealing with the aftereffects for a very long time to come."

"They have to be stopped," Stuart said. "Can't you threaten their leaders or something?"

"I think they don't give much of a damn about their own lives," General Winters said. "If our friend is to be believed, half of them are fanatics and the other half see no way out. And the fanatics are firmly in control. Oh, we *could* offer concessions, but people like these would see any concessions as an admission of weakness. *They* wouldn't hesitate to grind our faces in the mud if they won. They can't see how *we* would be any different."

"Fuck," Kat said.

She closed her eyes for a long moment. Hebrides had been horrific, but the vast majority of the victims had been locals. Enemies, as far as the Theocracy was concerned. She could never condone the extermination of millions of helpless civilians, yet she could understand why the Theocracy considered them expendable. But the people on Ahura Mazda were the Theocracy's *own* civilians, their chosen people. How could the rulers slaughter their own citizens, or arrange for them to be slaughtered, just to gain a minute tactical advantage?

The coming engagement was going to be bad, she knew. General Winters couldn't delay the offensive indefinitely, even if he'd *wanted* to. They had to take the Tabernacle and destroy the enemy government before its fleet returned. Ideally, the Commonwealth had to force the government to surrender so it could tell the fleet to stand down. Pat and his men would have to fight their way through a fanatical enemy, wading through blood, just to get to their target. And taking it would be an utter nightmare. Stealth drones had told her things she didn't want to know about the Tabernacle's defenses.

"We *could* fake surrender orders," she mused. "Put out a signal purporting to be from their government, ordering a surrender?"

"I doubt it," General Winters said. "Their civilian broadcasting stations might be primitive as fuck, but they've got some pretty sophisticated mil-grade communications gear. The techs have had a look at it.

They think it may have come from Kennedy or perhaps Clarke, rather than something homegrown. It's certainly a few light-years ahead of anything else we've seen the Theocracy use. Getting false orders onto that network will be tricky."

"Did they steal it," Stuart asked, "or did they buy it?"

"We don't know," General Winters said. "They might have stolen the designs and then built their own."

He shrugged. "I don't think there's any way to avoid launching a major offensive, once everything is in place. Oh, it's *possible* that some kindly soul will blow up the Tabernacle and try to surrender, but we're not counting on it."

"We can't," Kat agreed. She glanced from face to face. "The bombardment squadron will remain in position to provide fire support to the groundpounders, while the main body of the fleet will withdraw to open space. I want this entire system *seeded* with recon platforms and drones. That fleet is *not* to get anywhere near us without being detected."

"They may try to retake the high orbitals," Stuart warned.

"I doubt it," Kat said. "If they're looking for a final decisive battle, they'll need to engage us and do it before we have a chance to react. They'll try to crush us against the planet's remaining defenses."

She shook her head in disbelief. The Theocracy had lost the war, yet it still had a handful of bargaining chips left. It *could* use them to get a better deal, but it seemed more intent on throwing them away in a desperate bid to hurt the Commonwealth as much as possible. She would have happily agreed to send the Theocracy's leaders into exile if they surrendered at once. Such a move wouldn't have won her any plaudits, but it would have ended the war.

And yet they're staking everything on a final battle, she thought. Even if she lost, even if every last ship in 6th Fleet was blasted into atoms, the Theocracy would be in no state to continue the war. *It's madness.*

"We'll start running simulations once we take up our new positions," she added. "By the time they arrive, I want a contingency plan for everything. Dismissed."

She leaned back in her chair as the images vanished, one by one. General Winters, thankfully, had short-circuited any challenge to her authority, although she knew that wasn't going to last. Tyre would have to rule on it, probably after a long political debate over who should be in command and who should carry the can if everything went south. Her father's last message had suggested that the politicians had already declared victory and were currently arguing over the division of the spoils. The political coalition that had fought the war was on the verge of breaking up.

But we haven't won yet, she thought. *And until we do, we cannot count the Theocracy out.*

◆ ◆ ◆

"It is a trick," Lord Cleric Eliseus snarled. "Admiral Junayd is *dead!*"

"They have faked his voice," Inquisitor Samuilu agreed. "But how?"

That, Speaker Nehemiah agreed, was a very good question. Junayd's voice was *very* familiar on Ahura Mazda, where he'd often addressed the population on the need to make sacrifices to build up the war fleet, but he doubted any of those broadcasts had ever made it to the Commonwealth. How could they? Surely, if the Commonwealth wanted to produce a believable fake, they would have needed something to *copy*. Otherwise, they might as well just produce a random speaker and claim he was Admiral Junayd.

And that meant . . . what?

Admiral Junayd had died in the line of duty. Disgraced or not, he'd died bravely. He'd been honored by his government, an empty casket buried under the Tabernacle itself. But they'd never found a body. *That* was no surprise, not when Junayd had been on a superdreadnought in hyperspace when he'd died, yet it was suggestive . . . suggestive of what? Junayd had been ambitious as well as clever and *very* capable. Could he have faked his death? Or could he have taken an entire superdreadnought over to the Commonwealth?

Such a feat seemed improbable. No one knew better than Junayd just how many minders were scattered through superdreadnought crews, a good third of them completely unknown to their nominal superiors. Plotting a mutiny without alerting one of them would be impossible; launching a mutiny without a great deal of prior planning and careful preparation would end badly. Junayd was good, but was he *that* good? Or had he simply faked his death?

The broadcast continued, scattered with references that subtly confirmed Junayd's identity beyond dispute. *No one,* not even the Inquisition, could have put them *all* together. Junayd was alive! And that meant he'd gone over to the enemy. He'd known he was going to be betrayed, that he was going to be forced to pay for his second set of failures . . . and so he'd chosen to betray his own people first. And that meant—

"Something has to be done," Eliseus snapped. "This . . . this *fake* could convince people to turn away from us."

"He's already had an effect," Nehemiah pointed out. There was something to be said for no longer being in charge. He might be killed horribly at any moment, but he could troll them mercilessly until they finally snapped. "Our society is breaking down under the impact of the invasion. We cannot deny that it is happening any longer."

He looked at the map. A number of towns *should* have been defended, but their commanders had refused to believe that there *was* an invasion. They hadn't changed their minds until the enemy troops had actually arrived, by which time it had been too late to mount a defense. He *had* tried to convince his new masters to be honest with the population, but they'd seen sharing the truth as a very bad idea. But that decision only undermined the people's faith in them when reality clashed with the news.

Of course it does, he thought sourly. *We tell them the enemy is nowhere near a town, but when the enemy actually arrives the population realizes we lied to them.*

"We will make new broadcasts," Samuilu said. "And we will prepare our population for a campaign of enemy lies."

Nehemiah suspected the horse had firmly bolted on *that* one. *None* of the broadcasts over the last eighteen months had suggested that the Theocracy was losing the war, let alone that Ahura Mazda itself might be attacked. The handful of preparations they'd made before the invasion had undermined their lies *before* the enemy had actually landed. Now, only a complete idiot would believe a word they said. No one had missed seeing the debris falling into the planet's atmosphere, even if they lived well away from the enemy spacehead.

"They *are* offering to talk with us," he pointed out. "Perhaps we should see what they offer."

"Impossible," Eliseus belted. "It is a trick to weaken us before the final offensive!"

"God will turn his back on us if we listen to them," Samuilu agreed.

Nehemiah nodded, reluctantly. How had it come to this? How had he fallen from planetary leader to court jester? And how many of his people were going to die when the enemy started their final offensive? He wanted to believe that God *would* save them, yet why did they deserve His help? Hundreds of thousands, perhaps millions, of their own people had died in the last week alone. And they'd all been thrown into the fire by their leaders.

But they are assured of a place in paradise, he thought. He'd once believed it implicitly, even though he'd been in no hurry to sacrifice himself. Government had been his duty, he'd told himself. But in truth, he hadn't wanted to die. *I just wanted to send others to die in my place.*

He rose, leaving the others to their plotting as he strode through the underground bunker and back to his quarters. He was lucky, he supposed. Mosul and his allies were only alive because Eliseus and Samuilu wanted to give them a show trial, *after* the Commonwealth spacehead was crushed and its troops brutally slaughtered. God alone knew where they were sent after they'd been removed from the bunker. There were plenty of secret bolt-holes scattered around the countryside where important prisoners could be kept, if necessary.

And Junayd is alive, he thought. He wasn't sure what to make of it. Could Junayd be a potential ally? Or was he too close to the Commonwealth now? *What does it mean?*

He walked through his door and sat down on the bed. His quarters were luxurious, but they were nothing more than a gilded cage. He had no way to get a message out, no way to signal his political allies, if any of them were alive. Eliseus and Samuilu could have purged half of them and cowed the rest, if they wished. He didn't know and probably never would. Maybe he'd be put on trial beside Mosul and his allies. The planet's new rulers wouldn't want to keep him around.

And all he could do, until then, was watch helplessly as his planet died.

CHAPTER THIRTY

"This," Sergeant Bones muttered, "is a very weird city."

Pat was inclined to agree. He'd landed on dozens of worlds, from Tyre and Jorlem to a couple of Theocratic worlds, but Samarian was easily the strangest city he'd visited. And perhaps the darkest. The streets were dominated by towering apartment blocks, each one built so poorly that a small explosion might be enough to bring it down. Pat had no love for bureaucrats, but he had a feeling that Samarian would come to regret the lack of building inspectors and quality control. Hell, a strong wind might *also* do real damage to the city.

And you volunteered to lead a patrol to make sure you had a feel for the local environment, his thoughts whispered. *Do you like what you see?*

He shuddered as he saw the piles of rubbish surrounding each of the apartment blocks. The city's basic services, already primitive, had been cut off entirely in the wake of the invasion, leaving garbage to pile up. A couple of bodies, both wearing red robes, lay on top of one of the piles, Inquisitors or clerics killed by their former parishioners. Surprisingly, the bodies looked intact. The last set of bodies they'd found had been savagely mutilated, their arms and legs hacked off before their throats had been mercifully cut. Pat didn't blame the locals for hating the Theocrats, but their rage was a problem. No one was transporting rotting corpses out of the city. The more assholes the locals killed, the greater the health problems.

If we weren't wearing light armor, he thought, *the stench would probably drive us out on its own.*

The population itself, he noted as they walked past a water station, looked apathetic, even though they were trying to return to normal. Pat had seen hatred on Cadiz and bitter helplessness on Verdean, but this was different. Men shuffled down a long queue, heads lowered, to collect bottles of water, then carried them back to their homes. Only a handful of women were in evidence, wearing veils that concealed every inch of their bodies, stripping them of all humanity. It was no surprise, Pat thought, that the marines had had to break up a number of savage sexual assaults. When women were considered less than human, their thoughts and opinions simply didn't matter.

"You'd think they would be glad of the chance for a change," Bones commented. They walked past a food station, then a registry station. The Civil Affairs teams were already going to work, registering the population and trying to assign them to work teams. "This place is a nightmare."

"Some of them feel the occupation isn't going to last," Pat said. "And others are probably unable to do anything without permission."

He scowled at the thought. One of his old drill instructors had instructed his boot camp platoon that the vast majority of the population on any planet wouldn't do anything unless they were told what to do. They simply lacked the ability to think and take action for themselves, relying on the government to do all the work. Pat had harbored his doubts, given how many rewards there were on Tyre for citizens who found newer and better ways to do things, but on Ahura Mazda, the civilians seemed unwilling to do *anything* without permission.

At least they're not shooting at us, he thought. The marines had made it clear, as they took the town, that anyone carrying a weapon would be arrested and detained, but he wasn't foolish enough to think his crew had rounded up *all* the weapons. *That might change if their former masters start inciting trouble.*

"Stay alert," he warned. "Things could turn violent at any moment."

He shook his head in bitter disbelief as they probed through an alleyway, silently noting several more bodies lying on the ground. How could anyone *live* like this? No wonder they were so apathetic. They'd been stripped of everything that made life worth living, denied freedom and human dignity . . . was *this* what the Theocracy had to offer the universe? He glanced up sharply as he saw something moving high overhead, then relaxed as he realized it was a bird.

A red icon flashed up on his HUD. "Got a contact report," the dispatcher said. "A mob of civilians, moving down Street Bravo-Sierra."

Pat sucked in his breath as the squad started to run. The Theocracy had named its streets, of course, but half of them were completely unpronounceable to his team. Naturally, the dispatchers had started assigning names and numbers to the streets as Samarian was rapidly brought under control, their constant flow of updates ensuring that the people on the ground all spoke the same language. Small groups of civilians scattered in panic as the marines ran past, clearly expecting the shooting to start again at any moment. Pat had a feeling they were right.

"On our way," he said. "Got any top cover on call?"

"Three drones," the dispatcher said. "But not armed with anything beyond missiles."

Pat ground his teeth in frustration. The stealth drones were about the only air support they could rely on when patrolling a city, given the dangers of dropping KEWs from orbit into populated zones, but their missiles tended to produce a great deal of collateral damage. Samarian was simply too poorly designed for the missiles to be trusted, not when several city blocks had collapsed because shells had landed too close to them. The marines would be on their own, at least until reinforcements were dispatched.

Should be able to fly helicopters over the city, he thought. *But they're bound to have a few HVMs hidden away.*

He turned the corner and cursed under his breath as he saw a pair of clerics running for their lives. Behind them, an angry mob was moving in hot pursuit, screaming their hatred at their former masters. Pat couldn't help thinking that the clerics looked surprisingly stout compared to the other civilians he'd seen. No doubt they'd been given a great deal of food while the rest of the population had been nearly starved. Rank had its privileges, as always.

"Damn it, sir," Bones said. She sounded grim. "What do we do?"

Pat thought fast. If they'd been wearing heavy armor, they could just have waited for the mob to grow tired of trying to batter through the suit or simply stun them. But instead they were wearing light armor, armor that *could* be broken if it was battered enough.

"Warning shots," he snapped, lifting his rifle. He doubted it would be enough to stop the mob, if only because the ones at the back would keep pushing the ones at the front forward, but they had to try. "Over their heads."

He squeezed his trigger, firing two shots. "Stop!" he ordered. He was tempted to just *let* the mob have the fleeing duo, but he had orders to arrest any clerics he encountered. If anyone was in control of the remaining enemy forces within the city, it would be the clerics. "STOP NOW OR WE WILL USE DEADLY FORCE!"

The mob didn't stop. Pat gritted his teeth. He didn't dare let the mob engage his men, but he didn't want to run either. Flipping his stunner out, he played it over the crowd, watching as the first row tumbled to the ground. The second and third rows trampled over their stunned comrades, only to be pushed onwards by those at the rear. Pat and the marines kept stunning the crowd, grabbing the clerics as soon as they came within reach. The two men were swiftly thrown to the ground, tied, and searched. Pat wasn't too surprised to discover that they'd both been carrying weapons under their cassocks.

They didn't try to fight, he thought, puzzled. *Why not?*

He sucked in his breath as the mob disintegrated, the remaining members turning to their heels and fleeing, leaving countless dead and wounded behind as they ran up alleyways, running as if the devil himself were after them. They might have thought the devil *was* after them, Pat knew. He'd listened to a handful of enemy broadcasts as the marines were securing the city, and they'd *all* insisted that the Commonwealth would kill the men, rape the women, and enslave the children. There was a dreadful monotony about the announcements that chilled him to the bone. A lie somehow became more and more believable the more it was heard.

"The mob has been dispersed," he told the dispatcher after a brief incident report. "We have the clerics safe and well."

"Oh, *goody*," the dispatcher said. "Reinforcements are on the way. The prisoners will be taken for processing."

Pat shook his head, looking down at the twitching mob. Stunners weren't always reliable, not when their targets were stunned repeatedly or simply in poor health. Some of the men in front of him would never awaken, dying or remaining in a coma indefinitely. Some might survive with proper medical treatment, but such treatment was unavailable. The medics were already working day and night trying to cope with civilians who brought their wounded and ill for treatment. No one would have time to cope with a mob.

"We'll resume patrol once they take the prisoners off our hands," he said. "And we'll see what else we find."

He shook his head slowly. Samarian had died a long time ago, the population reduced to husks that might as well be zombies. The mob was the exception, not the rule. And if the rest of the planet was no better off, rebuilding Ahura Mazda would take vast amounts of money and time. Would the Commonwealth agree to fund reconstruction?

Not our problem, he thought numbly. His head jerked up as he heard a trio of explosions in the distance. *We just need to finish the war.*

◆ ◆ ◆

"So tell me, Admiral," General Winters said, "how goes recruitment?"

"We have quite a few government workers coming over to us," Junayd said with little emotion. He looked down at the latest set of interrogation reports. "No one from the higher ranks as yet, but that isn't a surprise."

He grinned, despite his tiredness. No one was more desperate to keep his position than a middle-ranking civil servant, a man who despised the commoners below him but lacked the security of his betters. The men who'd run Samarian and the other cities for the Theocracy *knew* they were screwed unless they came over to Junayd. They'd be killed merely for being close to the invading unbelievers. It would be months before local services could be resumed, but he was already putting together work gangs to deal with the most immediate problems.

Paying the men for working will probably help too, he thought. *There's hardly any food or drink in the shops.*

"I didn't realize how bad the situation had become over the last few months," Junayd admitted. He'd been completely isolated from the commoners, even when he'd been expecting a quick show trial and quicker execution. "But it does give us an opportunity to win hearts and minds."

General Winters shrugged. "The civilians are largely meaningless," he said. "What about the military?"

"We *have* picked up a number of defectors," Junayd reminded him. He was surprised at Winters's attitude. A very *Theocratic* attitude. "But many of the senior officers will be closely watched. They'll need to plan their mutinies carefully."

He rubbed his forehead. He'd been spending half his time making propaganda broadcasts, then encouraging other defectors to do the same. They didn't have to promise much, not really. A hot meal, a warm drink, an end to the fighting . . . no wonder the entire front line was wavering, on the verge of disintegrating. He'd been isolated from the groundpounders too, he knew now. The men on the front lines were even worse supplied than the fleet!

"And then they have to be vetted," General Winters said. "Are you *sure* of them?"

"Of course not," Junayd said bluntly. "How can I be?"

"Defectors are prone to having second thoughts, General," Janice put in. "They may well think better of their choice after getting a hot meal and some proper sleep."

General Winters snorted. "Are *all* your people so untrustworthy?"

Junayd bit down the hot flash of anger that threatened to overwhelm him. The men on the front lines weren't the only ones who hadn't had enough sleep. Watching the interrogations, then making his pitch to the higher-ranking defectors had drained him more than he cared to admit. Even with several defectors taking over the broadcasts, he was still working himself to the bone.

"I don't think you understand us very well," he said. "General, there is *no* trust on Ahura Mazda. None at all. Everyone does his best to screw everyone below him while trying to avoid being screwed by everyone above him. The blame is dumped on the shoulders least able to handle it, General. Civil servants take bribes, military officers cheat their men, the government fucks its own population. Everyone who can't get onto the bottom rung . . . they literally have nowhere to go."

"And so they take it out on their wives," Janice said quietly.

"Shit rolls downhill," Junayd said.

He'd hoped to put together a provisional government, ready to take control when the Tabernacle was finally taken or destroyed, but he was starting to suspect the Commonwealth would demand far-reaching social change. The reporters had filed hundreds of human interest stories, topics ranging from starved populations and human shields to child brides and wives who'd been repeatedly beaten to within an inch of their lives. Junayd couldn't *blame* the Commonwealth for wanting to change Ahura Mazda after it won the war, but he knew global transformation wouldn't be remotely easy. He hadn't lied to General Winters. Corruption was deeply engrained in the planet's society.

"So we can't trust your folks," General Winters said. He smiled, rather unpleasantly. "Can the Tabernacle trust its own commanders?"

Junayd shook his head. "Of course not," he said. "Any officer on the ground who reported the actual truth would be executed. I would be astonished if they knew just how *much* territory you control."

"They did keep lying about the number of superdreadnoughts blown out of space," Janice agreed. "And about everything else too."

"They can't possibly fight a war like that," General Winters said. "They *need* accurate information."

"But subordinates will be punished for providing it," Junayd reminded him. "So they lie, either to make themselves look good or simply to keep their heads on their shoulders. If they can say they've taken out a hundred of your tanks, who's going to believe otherwise? They think God is on their side. Of *course* they're going to win."

General Winters eyed him. "Did *you* ever act like that when you were in command?"

"I like to think I didn't," Junayd said. "But then, I saw myself as a military officer, first and foremost. God rewarded those who worked hard for His cause. I couldn't allow myself to cling to delusions."

"But you believed the Commonwealth was weaker than it was," Janice pointed out snidely.

"If 6th Fleet hadn't been in position to reinforce 5th Fleet," Junayd said, "things would have been different."

He pushed his frustration aside. Mistakes and miscalculations happened. There was no point in going over and over what could have been different, what should have been different, when the past was impossible to change. Mistakes needed to be acknowledged, then learned from. He'd learned that lesson the hard way, but his former masters had not. They'd preferred to blame their failures on him.

"And what would have happened if you *had* won?" Janice asked. She waved a hand towards the nearest wall, indicating the world outside. "Would you have imposed *this* on all of us?"

Junayd didn't bother to deny it. But, in a sense, an invasion and occupation of Tyre would have been a great deal worse than anything on Ahura Mazda. Tyre's population hadn't been ground down by decades of oppression, nor had they been kept largely ignorant of the outside universe. The high orbitals could have been taken, he was sure, but suppressing the entire planet would have cost millions of lives and more treasure than the Theocracy could afford. They might have decided to merely burn the entire planet to ash rather than try to convert the population. It would have been sinful, but they'd justified other sins to themselves in the past.

He dismissed the thought. "We are also building up a better picture of the enemy's tactical deployments," Junayd added. "And looking for a way into the Tabernacle that doesn't include a forced landing."

"If they know you're alive," General Winters said, "will they not start purging your allies?"

"It depends," Junayd said. Nestor had confirmed that there had been no general purge, although many of his former clients had found new patrons. "They may not believe it's me, for a start. I've done everything to convince them otherwise, but I may not have been successful. If they do, they'll tear their own command network apart if they launch a new set of purges. It might trigger a civil war."

"Which you're counting on," Janice said. "A civil war might just give us a chance to put an end to the *real* war."

"Yes," Junayd said. "But nothing is truly guaranteed."

"Of course not," General Winters said. "And you cannot even guarantee the loyalty of the men coming over to us."

"The higher their rank," Junayd said, "the more focused they'll be on their own position and power. You can trust them to uphold their own interests. It's the common soldiers you have to watch. They're the ones who might switch sides for a second time."

General Winters looked oddly pleased. "So we have to rely on our cold steel," he said. "For all your cleverness"—he shot an unreadable look at Janice—"we still depend on the marines."

"Yes," Janice said. "I think that was always true."

CHAPTER THIRTY-ONE

"The cloudscoops are coming into range, Captain," Cecelia said. "Missiles locked."

William nodded as the enemy stations appeared on the display. They didn't look *that* different from Commonwealth designs, although they were bunched up rather than dispersed around the gas giant. The concept struck him as poor planning, if only because a storm below could disrupt *all* the cloudscoops, instead of just one. But he had to admit that the positioning *did* make it easier to keep the engineers under control. The skimming he'd seen in facilities elsewhere probably wouldn't be a problem here.

"Communications," he said. "Send the surrender demand."

"Aye, Captain," Lieutenant Ball said.

William tensed. The attempts to board the enemy shipyards had largely failed, the Theocrats blowing up the facilities rather than allowing them to fall into Commonwealth hands. Thirty-seven marines had been lost before Kat Falcone had vetoed any further attempts to capture the shipyards, choosing instead to blow them up from a safe distance. It was frustrating, William felt, but there was no choice. If nothing else, the shipyards and industrial nodes could no longer turn out a stream of weapons to be turned against the Commonwealth.

The Theocracy is dead, he thought. *But it refuses to die.*

"No response, Captain," Ball said. "I don't even know if they *heard* the message."

"Understood," William said.

He felt a bitter surge of hatred mingled with disgust over the wastefulness. Didn't the Theocrats realize that whoever controlled Ahura Mazda after the war would *need* fuel? But they seemed determined to make sure that any survivors on the planet's surface suffered as much as possible. The marines had reported everything from water contamination to jammed sewers and destroyed pumping stations. The doctors had warned that diseases unseen since the human race had learned how to improve their immune systems were going to make a reappearance. The entire population might be doomed to a lingering death.

"Tactical, take out one of the cloudscoops," he ordered. *Thunderchild* was alone, the rest of the fleet preparing for the final confrontation, but no other ships should be needed. "Communications, repeat the message after the missile hits. And make it clear that we won't be trying to board the structures."

"Aye, Captain," Cecelia said.

William gritted his teeth as the missile roared towards a target with no point defense, no shields.

The missile struck home, obliterating the cloudscoop in a flash of nuclear fire. It didn't look as though the occupants had evacuated either, although there was no way to be sure. The engineers might have fled during the confusion of the Commonwealth invasion and hidden themselves somewhere in the inky vastness of space, waiting to see who won.

"Target destroyed," Cecelia said.

"Message sent," Ball added. "There's still no proof that they can even *hear* it."

Cecelia's console bleeped. "Captain, we have a hint of turbulence on the starboard bow," she said. "It *may* be a cloaked ship."

"Show me," William ordered. Thankfully, *Thunderchild*'s shields were already raised, her weapons already charged. Their visitor, if it *was* a visitor, wouldn't be scared off. "Do you have a track?"

"Not as yet," Cecelia said. A single icon appeared on the display, blinking rapidly. "I don't have a solid lock either. The dispersal pattern is too great."

William leaned forward, feeling his heart beginning to race. No cloaking device ever built could hide *everything*, but spotting the turbulence—the tiny flickers of energy caused by the passage of a cloaked ship—was tricky, more of an art form than a science. A *good* cloaking device randomized everything, denying automated sensors the chance to pick up a repetitive pattern. But Cecelia *had* spotted something.

It might be a false alarm, he reminded himself. *But it's far too close for comfort.*

"Hold us here," he ordered. "Bring up an automated firing circuit, primed to fire the moment he launches his missiles."

"Aye, Captain," Cecelia said.

William nodded, never taking his eyes off the display. The contact was inching closer, trying to get into point-blank range. Detection would soon be inevitable, when the cloaked ship would have to fire or give up the advantage of surprise. William silently calculated the vectors in his head, trying to deduce when the enemy CO would open fire. They'd know their own systems, of course, but what did they know about his sensors? If they didn't know, they'd be careful not to get *too* close.

"She *could* be friendly," Roach said.

"I hope not," William said. He'd heard horror stories about two cloaked ships accidentally firing on each other despite being on the same side. *Uncanny* had done it twice during her checkered career. "No one should be *trying* to sneak up on us in a war zone."

He glanced at Cecelia. "Can you identify the power dispersal pattern?"

"Negative, sir," Cecelia said. "I'd say she's a cruiser, perhaps an assault cruiser, but without a solid lock it's impossible to say for sure. She *might* be another bastard design."

"I hope not," William said. They'd encountered a handful of bastardized ships during the war. All of them had provided nasty and unpredictable surprises. "Keep passive sensors locked on her."

"Aye, sir," Cecelia said.

William allowed himself a tight smile. If the cloaked ship had remained undetected until she got into firing range, she would have crippled or destroyed *Thunderchild* with her first barrage. But she *had* been detected, giving him the chance to do unto her as she'd planned to do unto him. And yet, he faced the same problem as his opponent. If he fired too soon, the enemy would have a chance to raise shields and fire back; if he held his fire too long, his enemy might get the first blow in anyway.

Let her come just a little closer, he thought.

"Mr. Ball," William said, "has there been no reply at all?"

"No, Captain," Ball said. "There has been no response."

William considered it. The Theocrats were certainly ruthless enough to use the cloudscoops to bait a trap, knowing that Kat wouldn't send superdreadnought squadrons to smash cloudscoops. But they'd left the ambush too late. He could take out the remaining cloudscoops before the cloaked ship could react and they had to know it.

He took a breath. "Destroy the remaining cloudscoops," he ordered. "And prepare to fire on our new friend."

Thunderchild shuddered as she flushed her forward tubes. William braced himself, expecting to see point defense weapons spring to life or an undetected cloaked ship materializing between their position and the cloudscoops but saw nothing. The missiles slammed home, the warheads wiping the cloudscoops out of existence. Ahura Mazda was going to go dark soon, William knew. They didn't seem to have built up a fuel stockpile or contingency plans for alternate fuels. But then, the Theocrats really didn't seem to care about their population

"Energy flux," Cecelia snapped. "She's powering up her weapons."

"Fire," William ordered.

The display changed rapidly as the enemy ship fired its missiles at almost the same instant, her missiles aimed right at his hull. Her CO had messed up the timing slightly, William noted; he'd been unable to resist the urge to get as close as possible. But he'd failed to save the cloudscoops. He'd have to blow *Thunderchild* out of space if he wanted to keep his command . . . and his life.

"Point defense online," Cecelia said. "Missiles inbound, twenty-two seconds to impact."

"Enemy ship reads out as a modified light cruiser," Roach added. "They buckled additional missile pods to her hull."

That explains the odd power dispersal pattern, William thought. *But that's not going to do her hull any good.*

"Bring us about," he ordered. "Missile tubes to rapid fire."

"Aye, Captain," Cecelia said. "Rapid fire . . . now!"

Thunderchild shuddered as seven missiles made it through the cruiser's point defense and slammed into her shields. Roach barked orders to the damage control teams as red icons started to flash up on the display; William allowed himself a moment of relief once he saw that none of the damage was serious, not when a trained and experienced crew could perform repairs under fire. The enemy ship, her shields not yet solidified, staggered under his blows, but kept coming, firing as she came. Her missile throw weight seemed to be equal to his.

"Prepare to take evasive action," William ordered as the two ships converged. "Do *not* give her a chance to ram us."

Gross swallowed. "Aye, sir."

William didn't blame him for being concerned. It was difficult to ram another ship by accident, but the move could be done deliberately. Both starships would almost certainly be destroyed. His ship shuddered, again and again, as she took direct hits, but kept going, pounding away at the enemy vessel until her shields failed. A second later, she exploded into an expanding cloud of debris.

"Target destroyed," Cecelia reported. "No lifepods detected."

They didn't have time to get to the lifepods, William thought. *But even if they had, would they have tried to abandon ship?*

"Deploy sensor drones," he ordered. "Helm, prepare to—"

An alert sounded. "Two more ships detected," Cecelia said. "They're decloaking nearby."

William swore. The brief but intense battle had attracted more starships. Another light cruiser and a destroyer. Normally, he would have gambled on *Thunderchild* being able to take on another light cruiser, but his ship was in no state for a fight. And they were too close for him to hop into hyperspace before they entered firing range.

"Alter course," he ordered. There was nothing keeping them near the gas giant. "And send an emergency signal to Ahura Mazda."

"Aye, Captain," Ball said. He hesitated. "Captain, it will take at least thirty-seven minutes for the signal to reach Commodore Falcone."

We could do with a miniature StarCom now, William thought. *There aren't many ships close enough to help.*

"Send the signal anyway," he ordered. "Helm, keep us heading away from them. Tactical, deploy two passive sensor drones along our course."

"Aye, Captain," Gross said.

Roach peered down at his console. "They'll follow us into hyperspace if we try to open a gateway," he said.

"It looks that way," William agreed. *Thunderchild* could probably outrace her foes unless a *third* starship was lying doggo along their current route. The enemy didn't need precognition to guess what he'd do if he saw himself outgunned. "Tactical, stand by forward missiles."

"Aye, Captain," Cecelia said. Her console started to bleep an alarm. "Target Two and Target Three are locking weapons on our hull."

"Stand by point defense," William said. *Thunderchild* had a higher rate of acceleration than the enemy cruiser, unless ONI had dropped the ball again, but it would take time for her to get out of engagement range. "Keep monitoring the drones."

"Aye, Captain," Cecelia said.

The display flickered, then updated again. "Targets Two and Three have opened fire."

"Return fire," William ordered. "Drop mines, then deploy ECM drones."

"Aye, Captain," Cecelia said.

William forced himself to appear calm as the enemy missiles raced towards his ship. There were some advantages to being the target in a stern chase. If nothing else, the enemy missiles had to catch up with his ship while the enemy ships were racing towards his missiles. But the enemy had enough missile tubes to give his point defense units a run for their money. If he brought the ship about, they'd just smother him with missiles.

"Enemy ships are launching a second barrage," Cecelia reported.

Roach laughed, humorlessly. "Their superiors are going to have a fit."

"Only if their first barrage kills us," William commented. "Launch a second barrage, targeted to cripple their ships."

"Aye, Captain," Cecelia said.

William kept a wary eye on the display as the enemy missiles closed in on *Thunderchild*. A dozen fell to his point defense, a dozen more were lured away, expending themselves uselessly on the ECM drones, but five survived long enough to slam into his rear shields. *Thunderchild* bucked sharply, her hull *screaming* in pain. William clung to his command chair, praying desperately that they'd survive long enough to escape the enemy ships. The enemy couldn't keep up such a bombardment, could they?

"Major damage, rear section," Roach reported. "Fusion Two is down; Fusion Three is showing signs of imminent collapse. Drive field intact, but Engineering reports that we've lost two nodes and three more are iffy."

"Enemy destroyer has taken heavy damage," Cecelia put in. "She's dropping out of the race."

"Redirect all missiles to the cruiser," William snapped. Losing one fusion plant was a problem, losing two was a disaster. His ship wouldn't be able to maintain her current speed if she lost power or more drive nodes. "And divert all nonessential power to shields."

"Aye, Captain," Cecelia said.

"Nonessential power being redirected now," Roach said. "We're down two shield generators."

And that means the others could burn out at any moment, William thought. *And that would leave the hull bare.*

"Continue firing," he ordered. "And ready—"

"Captain," Cecelia interrupted, "the probes are reporting turbulence directly ahead of us!"

"Lock forward missiles on the center of the distortion and then fire," William snapped. There was no time to waste. The enemy was trying to drive him into a trap, but he'd seen through it before the jaws had slammed closed. "Now!"

"Aye, Captain," Cecelia said. Her voice wavered. "She's another cruiser—"

"She's a dead cruiser," William said. The enemy ship was decloaking, but unless she had some technology he'd never heard of, she wouldn't be able to get her shields up in time to save herself. The vessel's point defense was badly unprepared, only taking out four of his missiles before the remainder slammed into her hull and obliterated her. "Good shooting."

Cecelia flushed. "Thank you, sir."

Thunderchild rocked again. "Direct hits, rear section," Roach snapped. "Rear shields are down. Fusion Three is *gone!*"

"Try to push as much power to the drives as you can," William ordered, although he knew the maneuver was futile. The drive nodes needed more power than his ship could now supply. "Helm, bring us around. Keep our shields between us and them."

"Aye, sir," Gross said.

Another shockwave ran through the ship. William gritted his teeth. He'd lost one ship, now he was going to lose another. And there was no way he'd be given a third command. Hell, mere *survival* was unlikely. The Theocrats wouldn't stop to pick up lifepods. They'd either use them for target practice or leave them to drift helplessly in space. But *someone* should be along soon enough to pick them up.

A thought occurred to him. "Tactical, switch the drones to active," he ordered. "Have them project images of two decloaking cruisers."

"Aye, Captain," Cecelia said.

William gripped his command chair, thinking fast. The enemy ship was damaged too. If her CO *thought* that more enemy ships were closing in, what would he do? Flee? Or take the opportunity to blow *Thunderchild* out of space first? But he had to know that the Theocracy couldn't afford to lose more ships. The Commonwealth could produce an entire squadron of light cruisers in the time it would take the Theocracy to produce *one*.

Not any longer, William thought as he eyed the display. *We've smashed their industry beyond repair.*

The enemy ship hung there for a long moment, then opened a gateway and slipped into hyperspace. William let out a long breath as he realized he and his crew were going to live. The enemy had fallen for his bluff. He felt an urge to laugh as he realized the retreat suggested a moment of rational thinking among a very irrational society.

"They're gone," Cecelia said. "There's no hint of any other cloaked ships in the vicinity."

"They might be calling for reinforcements," William reminded her. "Mr. Ball, send a distress call to Ahura Mazda. Tell them we need a tow back to the planet."

"Aye, Captain," Ball said.

William looked down at his ship's status display. The damage control teams could not repair *Thunderchild*, not without a shipyard. Her entire rear section had been torn to ribbons. She'd need months in a shipyard, if the navy didn't decide to simply scrap her. *Thunderchild* wasn't worth keeping when the Commonwealth would be trying to build down after the end of the war.

But at least she wasn't entirely wrecked, he thought numbly. *They'll just decide to scrap her or sell her for whatever they can get.*

"Get the remainder of the crew out of the damaged sections, then seal them off," he added, taking control of the situation. He was the commanding officer. He couldn't wallow in guilt. "Once the sections are sealed, ready the crew for evacuation following Level Two protocols."

"Aye, sir," Roach said.

William took a moment to gather himself. The crewmembers were lucky. They would have a chance to collect their personal belongings before abandoning the ship. Hell, he could do it too. He had items in his cabin he didn't want to lose. But saving them wouldn't bring back what he'd lost. His ship had been his life. And with his homeworld a barren wasteland, he had no idea where he'd go.

Scott did offer to take me, he thought. *But why would I want to join a smuggler band?*

"Twenty-two crew are confirmed dead," Roach reported. He sounded grim. "Nine are still missing. Damage control teams are sifting through the wrecked sections now."

"Understood," William said. It wasn't the first time he'd lost people under his command, but it never got any easier. And yet . . . he compartmentalized his feelings. There would be time to mourn later, once the living were safe. "Bring the bodies back. We'll take them with us and bury them before we leave the system."

"Aye, sir," Roach said.

"Captain," Cecelia said, "two battlecruisers just dropped out of hyperspace. They're hailing us."

"Tell them we need accommodation for my crew, then a tow back to Ahura Mazda," William ordered bluntly. "And ask them to come alongside ASAP."

CHAPTER THIRTY-TWO

"So one of your clients lost *another* ship," Israel Harrison said as Lucas sat down at the conference table. "To lose one ship may be regarded as a misfortune, but to lose two seems more like carelessness."

"A line your speechwriter gleefully stole from Oscar Wilde," Lucas snapped. His implants had flagged the quote at once. "But he didn't get it *quite* right."

"He's having an off day," Harrison said. His eyes narrowed. "I trust you came prepared for the meeting?"

Lucas kept his face impassive. The governmental coalition was definitely falling apart as politicians readied themselves for the future. Whoever could make a credible claim to have won the war would have an excellent chance in the next set of elections, assuming the aftermath didn't wind up costing the crown millions. And yet, the war was not over. Declaring victory ahead of time struck him as dangerously premature.

He studied Harrison for a long moment as the Leader of the Opposition turned his attention to another attendee. Harrison had clashed before, repeatedly, with both King Hadrian and his father. The political strife had been buried when the war broke out, but none of the issues behind it had been resolved. Harrison, no doubt, wanted to make sure that certain issues were addressed before the war finally came to an end, either to secure his own position or put the Commonwealth on a steadier keel.

And he can't stand for reelection, Lucas thought. *He's desperate to make an impact before he loses power.*

It was, he thought, a problem. Tyre was *meant* to be balanced between aristocrats, who took the long view, and elected politicians who represented the will of the people. The best of the former were often raised to the peerage, where they became single-minded defenders of the aristocratic system. But the politicians, who were limited to ten years in office, always wanted to move forward fast, the only way they could make an impact.

"All rise," the prime minister said. "All rise for His Majesty King Hadrian."

Lucas rose. The king looked tired but surprisingly determined. Beside him, the prime minister looked concerned. Very little of the agenda for the meeting had been disclosed, which suggested that the king was determined not to give opposition time to materialize. He would pay a political price for that, of course, but he'd clearly deemed it acceptable. And that meant . . . trouble. Lucas rather doubted he was going to like what he was about to hear.

"Be seated, please," King Hadrian said.

He waited until everyone had sat down and coffee had been distributed before he spoke again. "First, I have good news," he informed them. "After careful negotiation, the Revered Elders of New Pennsylvania have agreed to hand over two of the three main continents on their home-world to the refugees from Hebrides. They are insistent on maintaining the third continent, the only one they settled, for themselves. The refugees have accepted this condition."

Lucas nodded slowly. New Pennsylvania had been settled by Amish farmers from Earth, expelled, like so many others, by the UN. Their population was small, their Commonwealth membership little more than nominal. But they had plenty of unused land, more than enough for the surviving refugees to rebuild their society. Who knew? Maybe the two societies would meet and flow into one.

Or maybe they would start fighting, Lucas thought. *They're very different at heart.*

"The Royal Estate will make a major commitment to fund the early settlements," the king continued. "We will also be attempting to pass a bill through Parliament, requesting additional funds from the public purse."

Harrison looked irked but said nothing. Lucas could guess at his feelings. Settling a world was expensive, yet helping the refugees to build a new home would be popular, and opposing the bill would be political suicide. He couldn't even make a *show* of resistance to satisfy his zealots and then quietly switch to supporting the bill. The king had scored a political point at the opposition's expense.

"The Amish do not have food reserves to spare," the king added. "Thankfully, we can and we will supply enough food to keep the refugees alive until they can start farming the land."

Lucas nodded, hastily reviewing the files in his implant. New Pennsylvania didn't have any facilities outside her atmosphere, save for a handful of satellites the Commonwealth had provided. The refugees were not going to have an easy time of it, no matter how much funding they received, but there was plenty of room for development. A gas giant, plenty of asteroids . . . given time, New Pennsylvania could be turned into an industrial powerhouse. He was marginally surprised no one had taken the system already.

But we are the closest power in the region, he thought as he made a mental note to get in on the ground floor himself. Colony development projects were long-term investments, but they were almost always solid. Only four colonies had failed in all of human history. *No one else was in a position to just take the system.*

"That's the good news," the king said. His face twisted. "The bad news is that the war on Ahura Mazda is not yet over."

"The war as a whole is not yet over," Lucas said. "All these declarations of victory are premature."

"Our victory is certain," the First Space Lord said stiffly.

"It isn't certain until we win," Lucas countered.

The king acknowledged his contribution with a nod. "The report from Ahura Mazda makes it clear that Admiral Christian is dead," he said. "Commodore Falcone has assumed command of the fleet, as per Admiral Christian's orders. However, several of her subordinates have filed official protests. Commodore Falcone lacks seniority as well as experience, they say."

Lucas cursed under his breath as new reports downloaded themselves into his implants. He'd known that the first reports had arrived, but he hadn't fully reviewed their content. He was already overwhelmed by his duties. Given what was at stake, he'd prepared himself for everything from the Theocracy surrendering to Ahura Mazda being blown up by its own masters. Stalemate . . . he hadn't expected a stalemate. But the final messages from Kat and General Winters made it clear that the stalemate wouldn't be prolonged indefinitely. The groundpounders were already massing for the final campaign.

"A number of noses will be put out of joint if she remains in command," the First Space Lord noted. "However, she *was* Admiral Christian's choice as successor. General Winters has spoken firmly in favor of her."

"Then we should honor Admiral Christian's last request," the king said. "Commodore Falcone can be given a brevet promotion to admiral, if necessary."

"Which will put many more noses out of joint," the First Space Lord said. "Commodore Hoskins has both command experience and seniority."

Lucas gritted his teeth. Kat hadn't included a personal message to him in the data dump, but he could guess at her feelings. She wouldn't back down from the responsibility, even if she feared she wasn't up to it. The Royal Navy had taught her that, cautioning her that an officer who refused a promotion or a command would never be offered another one. And yet, moving from squadron command to fleet command was a huge jump forward. He wouldn't have blamed her for having qualms.

"What sort of message does it send to our fighting men," Harrison asked, "if someone can be jumped ahead of them just like *that*?"

He snapped his fingers. "Admiral Christian was a good man," he added. "But we shouldn't honor his request purely because it was his *last* request."

"There's also the issue of changing command in the middle of a war zone," the king pointed out coolly. "The enemy fleet is still out there, no doubt massing for a final battle."

"Unless the fleet has set out to wreck as many of our worlds as it can," Harrison countered.

"We have enough firepower around our worlds to tear them to ribbons, if they try," the First Space Lord said. "Even *c*-fractional strikes are unlikely to make an impact."

Lucas wasn't so sure. Intercepting a projectile traveling at a goodly fraction of the speed of light was difficult, particularly if it wasn't being propelled by a drive field. He had a great deal of faith in the electronic defenses surrounding Tyre and the other worlds, but he also understood their limitations. And the Theocracy had already demonstrated its willingness to commit mass slaughter if necessary.

The king cleared his throat. "Kat Falcone enjoys my full support and that of the Admiralty," he said firmly. "Admiral Christian saw fit to put her in command. I see no reason to overrule him now."

Really, Lucas thought. *And what are you playing at, Your Majesty?*

He contemplated possibilities for a long moment. Kat *was* famous, no matter how much she tried to avoid the limelight. The king might hope that some of her fame would rub off on him. It had to be frustrating, Lucas admitted privately, not to have had a chance to gain experience and fame of his own. But it was also possible that he was defending the aristocratic prerogative, even though his techniques were clumsy. The prerogative had to be upheld, but not at the price of undermining the entire system.

But I can say nothing, he thought. *I can't undermine Kat myself.*

The First Space Lord didn't look happy, he noted. Harrison *definitely* didn't look happy. And the prime minister seemed concerned. But none of them were prepared to oppose the king, not on *this* matter. Lucas suspected their silence boded ill for the future.

"We can leave the battle and the conclusion of the war in her hands," the king said bluntly. "We must turn, now, to more important matters."

Lucas's implants popped up a notification. A new file had just been downloaded from the room's processor.

"The war may be coming to an end," the king added, "but the aftereffects will linger for years, perhaps decades, to come. The bill we intend to propose will hopefully alleviate those effects before they can prove fatal to our Commonwealth."

The file opened. It was strikingly short for a bill, Lucas noted. That would change, he was sure, when lobbyists started adding various levels of pork to the final version. But he skimmed through it quickly, feeling his stomach twisting uncomfortably. The bill wasn't a bad idea, he had to admit. And yet, he had a sneaking feeling it would never even get past the first reading.

Harrison put his doubts into words. "You have *got* to be joking."

The king looked back at him evenly. "Do *you* find this amusing?"

Lucas reread the bill. "You are talking about making a major investment in every Commonwealth world, as well as the former Theocratic worlds," he said. "You plan to install shipyards and industrial nodes, found training colleges and—Your Majesty, do you have any idea how much this will *cost*?"

"Yes," the king said. "But I believe it is an investment we need to make."

"I believe that very few MPs will support it," Harrison said. "Even the Crown Loyalists will hesitate."

"We have to reach out to the colonials," the king said. "All our prewar plans for integrating them into our society were smashed by the war. Right now, we have to make it clear that we are *not* going to exploit them."

Lucas wished, suddenly, that he had seen the bill ahead of time. His analysts would have been able to provide a comprehensive list of the bill's weaknesses, then offer suggestions on possible amendments that would make it more palatable. But he wasn't entirely dependent upon his staff. The more he looked at the document, the more apparent the weaknesses became.

"I understand your feelings, Your Majesty," he said. "But this level of investment is not only unprecedented, it is dangerous."

He went on before anyone could object. "Building new cloudscoops and opening training colleges are daunting alone," he said. "Investing in tools and supplies is a workable way to kick-start more local industries, but building entire shipyards and industrial nodes—Your Majesty, the market for so much product simply doesn't exist."

"We have a shortage of freighters," the king pointed out.

"That's because of the war," Lucas countered. "We committed over half of our entire Merchant Marine to support the Royal Navy. Much of the remainder was committed to evacuating Hebrides before the planet died. And yet thousands of new freighters are already coming out of the shipyards. More will be coming when we start downgrading warship production. By the time these shipyards are up and running, the freighter shortage will be a distant memory."

"They will be producing other ships," the king said.

"No, they won't," Lucas said. "They won't have a market."

He tapped the table. "Building up local industries will take time and careful investment," he said. "*Not* splashing vast amounts of money around."

The king showed a flicker of anger. "You do not feel that we should assist the colonials?"

"I feel that our assistance should be carefully measured," Lucas said. "*Nothing*, Your Majesty, breeds resentment like charity."

"And you are talking about a major percentage of our GNP," Harrison added. "Your Majesty, I do not believe that the population will cheerfully accept such a commitment."

He was right, Lucas knew. Plenty of spending bills had failed because of the demands of the war. But that would change, once the war was over. The demand to invest money domestically would become irresistible. Parliament didn't control *all* the purse strings, but the king would need Parliament's support to pass the bill . . . and Harrison was right. Parliament was more likely to kill the bill stone dead.

He's inexperienced, Lucas thought. He glanced at the prime minister. Surely, that wily old bird had cautioned the king against overcommitting himself. *And he's too used to getting what he wants on a silver platter.*

The problem was worse, he suspected, than any of them had realized. Tyre's population wouldn't welcome competition from off-world. If the king's plan failed, a vast amount of money would have been wasted; if it succeeded, the market would be flooded with cheap goods that would undermine local production. And that meant . . . what? Trouble, almost certainly. Parliament *and* the aristocracy would unite against off-world competition.

"Your Majesty," he said, "this bill will never pass. Let it die, now, before you waste political capital trying to get it through Parliament."

The king met his eyes. "Are you saying that you refuse to support it?"

"Very few people will support it," Lucas told him. "I suggest you let it die, here and now. It does not have to become public."

"I would rather give everyone a chance to consider it," the king said stiffly. "We'll meet again, a week from now. By then, perhaps we can make the bill more workable. Until then, please keep the details to yourselves."

Lucas rather suspected that the only way to make the bill workable was to tear it up and start again, but he kept that thought to himself as he rose and strode out of the room. Sandra met him outside, looking brisk and efficient as always. She fell into step beside him as they walked back to the aircar.

"I have an update from the Janus Plant," she said. "The fault in the production line was a glitched computer matrix. They've replaced it and pulled out the rest of the components for testing before deciding what to do with them."

"Good," Lucas said. His mind was elsewhere. Technically, he should call a ducal conference and tell them about the planned bill, but the king *had* asked him to keep it a secret. If it could be dropped without further ado, there was no reason to spread the news any further. The king's life was hard enough already. "Tell the managers that I want a full update once the checking process is complete."

"Yes, sir," Sandra said. They climbed into the aircar and took off. "Back to the mansion?"

"Please," Lucas said. Where *else* would he go? He had to consider the bill even if he couldn't share it with anyone else. "I have a great deal of work to do."

He looked down at the city below him as the aircar rocketed away from the palace. The cosmetic damage had been cleared within months of the terrorist attacks, but the city still felt on edge. Tyre had been safe for so long, its competition kept within the rules, that being physically attacked had come as a nasty shock. Lucas knew that the vast majority of the soldiers on guard were unnecessary, but woe betide any government that thought about removing them. The planet no longer felt safe.

I need a holiday, he thought. The thought of going to the beach and just forgetting who he was, if only for a week or two, was extremely attractive. *A long stay in the mountains, perhaps, or a place in the sun.*

"Ashley requests a private meeting," Sandra added. She sounded oddly amused. "She wouldn't say what it was about."

Lucas nodded. Ashley, his eldest daughter, had taken a position within the Falcone Corporation rather than trying to make her own way in the world. And yet she'd done a good job. Lucas might favor his children, but he wouldn't have let Ashley *keep* the post if she'd been bad at it. She was—

The threat receiver shrilled. "Shit!"

"Hang on," Sandra snapped. The aircar lurched. Lucas glanced at the display and swore as the aircar twisted, the autopilot taking evasive action. They'd just been targeted by a ground-to-air weapons system. A sleeper team? He'd relaxed, more than he *should* have relaxed. Or a terrible accident. Had the local defenses locked on to them? "Sir, I'm going to—"

There was a flicker, right at the corner of Lucas's eye. He didn't have time to process it, to realize what it meant, before the high-velocity missile slammed into the aircar, blowing the vehicle into a colossal fireball.

No one survived.

CHAPTER THIRTY-THREE

"I have the latest report, Admiral," the operator said. "The 34th Superdreadnought Squadron is only at seventy percent effectiveness."

Admiral Zaskar nodded without turning his attention from the display. The Commonwealth might have taken out the StarComs, but the orders to muster every remaining warship in the Theocracy had been sent before the network had been destroyed. It was taking time, more time than he cared to admit, to rally the troops, yet the fleet was slowly coming together. They could carry out their mission. And they *had* to succeed. The entire Theocracy was depending on them.

"Have engineers sent to assist the crews," he said. He'd declared that no one would be punished if their ships had problems they couldn't fix, but he knew from bitter experience that most of his officers probably wouldn't believe such words. And why should they? Too many officers had previously blamed their subordinates rather than face up to problems caused by their superiors. "And make sure they get a full complement of missiles."

"Aye, Admiral," the operator said.

Zaskar turned his head to watch the operator scurry away, then looked back at the tactical display. The fleet was lurking five light-years from Ahura Mazda, well out of detection range . . . or so he hoped. He'd read too many intelligence reports that were, that had to be, wildly exaggerated to put too much faith in anything. If the Commonwealth was truly as advanced as some of the reports suggested, the Theocracy had been beaten long before it had actually gone to war.

They can't know we're here, he told himself. *They'd have crushed us before turning their attention to the planet.*

He tapped the display, bringing up the latest intelligence report from Ahura Mazda. The majority of the enemy fleet was holding position near the planet, well clear of the defenses on the ground. They *had* managed to clear a couple of the PDCs, according to his long-range sensors, but not enough to let them bombard the planet into submission. And yet, he knew that would change. The enemy seemed to be massing its forces for the final drive on the Tabernacle. His fleet needed to be ready to intervene before that happened.

"Admiral," another operator said, "the supply officers report that they are running out of missiles."

"Have them distribute what they have," Zaskar ordered impatiently. "And remind the crews that missiles are *not* to be wasted."

God is testing us, he reminded himself. *And we will not let Him down.*

But despair hovered at the back of his mind, threatening to overwhelm him. Ahura Mazda had been savaged, even if the Tabernacle still held out. The enemy had utterly wrecked the system's industrial base, crushed it beyond repair. There would be no more missiles, no more gunboats . . . no more superdreadnoughts. The remaining fragments of the Theocracy's industrial base couldn't even *begin* to meet the fleet's requirements. And that meant?

The end, he thought.

He'd always prided himself on looking unpleasant truths in the face. His patrons had never approved, even though they'd found his honesty useful. And the unpleasant truth was that the Theocracy was doomed. Even if he won the coming battle, which wasn't going to be easy, they would be naked and helpless when the Commonwealth mustered another offensive. The enemy would put a second fleet through the Gap and smash the remainder of his ships before the Theocracy had a chance to rebuild.

And yet, what choice did he have?

His family was down on the surface, held hostage. He knew, beyond a shadow of a doubt, what would happen to them if he disobeyed orders. Better to throw his fleet into the fire than risk losing his family. And who knew? Maybe the Lord Cleric was right. God would grant them victory if they proved themselves worthy.

He keyed the display, flicking through long-term plans outlined by the tactical officers belowdecks. The Theocracy would return to the offensive, crush the Commonwealth, and occupy its worlds. Red arrows led all the way to Tyre and beyond, showing how the Theocracy would stamp its will on the entire universe. But he knew they were nothing more than fantasy, nothing more than sheer wishful thinking. The Theocracy would be lucky if it managed to preserve Ahura Mazda, let alone the other worlds under its sway.

It had been a mistake to launch the war, he thought.

His minders would kill him, he knew, if he dared express such a thought out loud. The Theocracy had a manifest destiny, they would say, to reshape the entire universe. Everyone had *known* the war was inevitable, that the Commonwealth could not be allowed a chance to influence and subvert the occupied worlds. But the decision to go to war had doomed the Theocracy. They'd finally picked a fight with someone bigger than themselves, after decades of easy victories. His superiors had learned nothing from invading worlds that lacked even a single weapons platform to defend themselves.

Zaskar closed his eyes for a long moment, then switched the tactical display back to the fleet setting. The ships hung in the darkness, worker bees and fleet tenders moving from superdreadnought to superdreadnought, parceling out missile supplies and spare parts to where they were most needed. The armada was, in many ways, the most powerful fleet the Theocracy had ever assembled, yet it was barely a match for its enemy. And too many of its ships were in poor condition. His government had also made a major error, perhaps, in not training more engineers.

Definitely another mistake, he thought numbly.

He had grown up a child of privilege. He'd long since come to terms with the Theocracy's decision to keep its population in ignorance. A thinking population might imagine all sorts of things, like questioning the Theocracy's right to rule. But such governance ensured that there was only a limited supply of trained engineers. The Theocrats were even short of men who could do little more than remove a faulty component and replace it with a new one. And when they'd needed to expand, they'd discovered that they simply didn't have the manpower. His fleet was suffering for sheer lack of maintenance.

And we will never have the chance to correct our mistake, he thought. *And even if we do . . .*

He shook his head slowly. The Theocracy was too rigid to survive. If it wanted to survive, it would have to change . . . and change would eventually bring the whole system tumbling down. And who knew what would happen then?

"Admiral, a courier boat just arrived from Ahura Mazda," a third operator said. "The Tabernacle wants us to be ready to move in five days."

"Understood," Zaskar said. He saw no point in expressing his doubts. Five days wouldn't give him time to even *begin* to tackle his problems. "I'm sure we can move on command."

◆ ◆ ◆

"The latest reports from the front are clear," Inquisitor Samuilu said. He nodded towards the display. "The enemy is massing for a drive on us."

"It looks that way," Speaker Nehemiah agreed dryly. He had a feeling that the situation was worse than Samuilu knew. There was a mindless optimism to some of the reports that amused him. *Thousands* of unbelievers killed? Really? "They'll be plunging straight into your defense line."

"Yes," Lord Cleric Eliseus agreed. "And our soldiers stand ready to resist them."

There won't be much of a planet left, afterwards, Nehemiah thought. The Inquisitors had granted permission for the defenders to use nuclear, chemical, and biological weapons. He'd tried to talk them out of using the latter two, if only because the defenders were ill prepared to cope with them, but he'd failed to convince Samuilu not to deploy everything in his arsenal. *And the invaders will start using their own nukes if they decide it's the only way to get to us.*

"And the fleet is bracing itself for the final battle," Samuilu said. "But it is clear that we are losing the war."

Nehemiah's head jerked up sharply. Samuilu had never admitted that the Theocracy was losing the war—*had* lost the war, to all intents and purposes. He'd remained optimistic, utterly convinced that God would grant them victory, even after Commonwealth boots had landed on Ahura Mazda itself. But now . . . he'd changed his mind. Somehow, Nehemiah didn't find that very reassuring.

"Too many of our people have betrayed us," Lord Cleric Eliseus rumbled. "They will need to be purged."

"They're behind enemy lines," Nehemiah reminded him. Junayd, damn him, had proved alarmingly effective. Too many soldiers had deserted to the enemy; too many officers and civil servants had crossed the lines, no doubt seeking further employment in the postwar universe. And the Inquisition's purges had only made matters worse. "We can't get to them."

"Yes, we can," Samuilu said. "We can get the remainder of the true believers out, then destroy the entire planet after we leave. The unbelievers will burn with the traitors."

Nehemiah felt his mouth drop open. "Are you—?"

He swallowed hard. Samuilu *was* mad. Somehow, he'd come up with a way to rationalize his flight from Ahura Mazda—*and* blow up the entire planet in a final gesture of spite. Lord Cleric Eliseus couldn't have come up with it, Nehemiah thought. But whoever had worked out the plan didn't matter. All that mattered was that the planet was doomed.

Along with everyone on it, he thought.

He opened his suddenly dry mouth. "How?"

"We have the last of the antimatter," Samuilu reminded him. "When the Tabernacle is on the verge of falling, we will send a signal to the storage depot. The explosion will shatter the entire planet."

Nehemiah wasn't sure if there was enough antimatter left to shatter an entire planet, but it hardly mattered. A chunk of antimatter no larger than his fist would be enough to do *real* damage to Ahura Mazda. The civilians who weren't killed in the blast would die soon afterwards, as clouds of radiation swept across their homeworld. Hebrides, but on a much larger scale. And no one, absolutely no one, was going to come to their rescue. The entire population would perish.

He looked from one to the other, trying to see a *hint* of doubt about the plan. But neither Samuilu nor Eliseus showed any hint of concern. They were *both* mad, both determined to lash out even as they died. The Theocracy would die with them too. There was no way Admiral Zaskar's fleet would be allowed to escape, not after the final atrocity. The Commonwealth would search the entire galaxy for them. No colony world would survive long enough to rebuild its fleets and go on the offensive.

And I used to be in charge, he thought. *If I had chosen otherwise . . .*

But he knew he'd had no choice. The Theocrats' very ethos demanded expansion. They couldn't allow themselves to be confined by the Commonwealth, their borders weakening as news sneaked through the blockade and into civilian ears. He'd supported the war, but even if he'd had his doubts he couldn't have *stopped* it. He would have been removed from power if he'd tried to keep the Theocracy from going to war.

And now he was trapped in the Tabernacle, under the control of a pair of madmen, waiting helplessly for the end of the world.

They won't take me with them, he told himself. *And it won't be long before they kill me anyway.*

He turned his gaze to the monitors. Men, dozens of men, hanging from ropes, convicted of attempted desertion or treason; two women, caught outside their homes, flogged so hard that their backs were covered in bloody scars. And children, male children, being given guns and taught how to use them. They'd be killed in their first battle, but they might just slow the Commonwealth down for a few minutes. Or so he'd been told. *The Theocracy*, he thought grimly, *was steadily eating its own.*

"They're closing in on a POW camp," Samuilu commented. "The prisoners cannot be allowed to survive."

Nehemiah looked up. He'd lost track of the conversation. But it didn't matter. "Will they survive if they are rescued?"

"It doesn't matter," Samuilu said. "All that matters is that they never see home again."

Nehemiah rose. "You can handle it," he said. "I have to go."

He half expected to be yanked back as he walked towards the door, or to be grabbed by the guards outside, but nothing happened as he made his way back towards his quarters. There were no guards on duty outside his door, not even an Inquisitor. An unsubtle insult, a way of telling him that his life was no longer worth protecting . . . his life and those of his wives and children.

They already took my sons, he thought as he opened the door and stepped inside. *And soon they will take my wives and daughters, too.*

He was surprised, in all honesty, that they hadn't taken his daughters already. Drusilla had managed to steal an entire freighter, although *that* had largely been blamed on her bodyguards. A woman? Steal a freighter? She shouldn't even have *known* there was a world outside the female quarters. But Nehemiah couldn't help feeling an odd flicker of pride in his daughter. *He* had no doubt, whatever he had said in public, that Drusilla had planned it herself. She'd had a better education, thanks to him, than most of her male counterparts.

Shaking his head, he rose and walked towards the female quarters. If all he could do was prepare himself for death, he could start by saying good-bye to his family. And then, perhaps, find a way to get a message out. But, in truth, he had no idea how to proceed. He had never had to do anything for himself since he'd grown to adulthood. And now he was as helpless as a newborn.

Of course they don't have guards on my door, he thought sourly. *Where would I go?*

♦ ♦ ♦

If there was one thing Aeliana had learned from her mothers and father, it was that it was better not to ask questions. Her father and his sister-wives reacted badly to *any* show of female intelligence, particularly after Drusilla had managed to somehow escape their quarters and vanish completely. Aeliana envied her half sister for her escape, even though her father had made it clear that Drusilla had gone beyond his protection. But she'd had no choice. Drusilla had been on the verge of being married when she'd fled.

Aeliana loved her father, but she had no illusions about him. She'd been sneaking into the male quarters—and beyond—for years. His terminal didn't have a password, but it *did* have a dozen programs to help her learn how to use it. She'd discovered the awful fate that lay in wait for Drusilla simply by reading her father's files. Her rebellious half sister would be brain-burned if she didn't learn to bow her head and accept her place in life. After that, Aeliana had started planning her own escape.

She'd discovered more than once that she could easily sneak around the Tabernacle as long as she wore male clothes and a cap. No one looked twice at a young boy who might easily be the son of a powerful man. Drusilla had been too well developed to pass for a young man, but Aeliana was more boyish. A couple of pieces of paperwork and a willingness to lie when necessary completed the disguise. Indeed, she'd seriously considered sneaking all the way out and simply vanishing into the streets. As long as she looked like a man, no one would be trying to rape her or force her back into her home. But now . . .

She watched her father finally go to sleep, then hurried to her room to don her clothes. Getting the first set had been hard—she'd resorted to bribing her brother—but afterwards, it had been simple to get newer clothes as time went by. Her father had been unable to figure out how to get a message to the enemy lines, but she had a plan. And she was damned if she was staying in the Tabernacle any longer. Rumor had it that Eliseus wanted her for his bride, and she had no intention of marrying an old man. Eliseus had been around for decades, if not centuries.

But father can no longer say no, she thought as she strode through the door. She'd practiced walking like a man until there was nothing about her stride that said *woman*. *The old wretch can have me whenever he wants me.*

The thought made her shudder as she walked down the corridor, careful to keep her head up high. Drusilla had been threatened with being brain-burned; Aeliana had no doubt that she, too, would get the same treatment if she refused to behave. And there was no way to avoid it if she stayed home. Either she played the obedient wife or she would be warped and twisted into a brainless animal who couldn't even string two words together.

And if father is right, she told herself, *we all might be about to die.*

The guards at the gates barely glanced at her papers before waving her out, nodding towards the streets outside the Tabernacle. Darkness was already falling, but her papers gave her clearance to be out after curfew. The patrollers should check her papers and then let her go without delay. However, if they tried to search her, they'd discover the truth. A woman in male clothing would be whipped, if she were lucky.

God will provide, she thought as she heard gunshots and explosions in the distance. Her father had told her the streets were safe, but she knew he'd been lying. She'd read too many of his reports. *And if it is His will I get through, I'll get through.*

CHAPTER THIRTY-FOUR

"Commodore," Lucy said, "Commodore McElney has arrived."

Captain McElney, Kat translated mentally. William had been given a courtesy promotion as soon as he'd boarded *Queen Elizabeth*. There could only ever be one captain on a ship. *And I don't want to see him.*

She closed her eyes in bitter pain. Her father was dead. The man who'd sired her, who'd given her a life well above the ordinary, who'd helped her and taught her and disciplined her, was dead. Her father was dead. She couldn't quite believe it. He'd always been there for her, even when she'd been determined to stand on her own two feet. And now he was gone.

He shouldn't have died, she thought numbly, unable to move. Duke Lucas should have lived for decades more, thanks to his genetic enhancements. *They killed him.*

She stared up at the display, shaking her head. Her father was dead. The preliminary reports had claimed that a team of sleeper agents, armed with a MANPAD, had managed to down his aircar with an HVM. How had they known where he was going? How had they managed to get into place to take the shot? Where had the damn gunships been? The Theocracy had killed her father. She knew it. They'd managed to keep a sleeper team under cover long enough to take the perfect shot.

"Commodore," Lucy repeated. "Commodore—"

"I know," Kat said harshly. She forced herself to sit upright. She wasn't the only one mourning a loss. "Show him in, then bring us both coffee."

She rose and glared at her face in the mirror. Her expression looked so dark that the nasty part of her mind wondered why the mirror hadn't cracked. She heard the hatch open, but kept her eyes on the mirror, trying to control herself. There was no way she could mourn her father properly until after the war.

"Kat," William said quietly. "I am truly sorry."

"I'm sorry too," Kat said. She wasn't sure if she was sorry about her father, or *Thunderchild*, or both. Losing a second ship so quickly after the first wouldn't look good on William's record. "I should have sent you out with an entire squadron."

She cursed herself. The enemy was watching her. Her long-range sensors had picked up enough proof that cloaked enemy ships were still watching the system to make her paranoid. She'd sent *Thunderchild* out alone because she hadn't suspected the ship would be ambushed, not when the Theocracy desperately needed to preserve its strength. But she'd made a mistake. Cold logic suggested otherwise, suggested that the trade had been squarely in the Commonwealth's favor, yet her emotions told her she'd screwed up. Losing William would have been an absolute disaster.

"It wasn't your fault," William said. He sat down on the sofa and took the mug of coffee Lucy offered him. "And your father's death wasn't your fault either."

"I know that," Kat said. She sipped her own coffee. Lucy must have warned him before he'd walked into her cabin. "But I don't believe it."

She looked down at her cup for a long moment. "What did the techs say about *Thunderchild*?"

"Scrapyard," William said. He sounded unhappy. Kat didn't blame him. *Thunderchild* could be repaired, *if* the navy was prepared to make the investment. "The crew is already being broken up."

"They may be needed elsewhere," Kat said. She understood his concerns, but there was no choice. "You're being assigned to my tactical staff until further notice."

William nodded, seemingly drained. "Thank you," he said. "Do I get a chance to shower first?"

"Yeah," Kat said. She felt . . . tired. Tired and worn. But she had her duty. "Unless the enemy shows up in the next few minutes, that is."

She tapped the display, switching to the ground map. Pat's last message had been terse, but General Winters had briefed her that the invasion force was ready to begin the final offensive against the Tabernacle. The operation was going to be nightmarish, he'd warned, even though thousands of enemy soldiers and civilians had deserted. The fanatics would dig in and fight to the last, sacrificing hundreds of men just to slow down the offensive. And recon probes had shown *children* being prepped to fight. There would be nothing of Ahura Mazda left by the time the fighting was over.

"They'll almost certainly launch their attack when we move," she said. "Unless they've snuck off somewhere, I suppose."

"Don't count on it," William warned. "A lone officer couldn't organize a retreat without permission from Ahura Mazda."

"Junayd made that clear," Kat muttered. "But even a fanatic can see the writing on the wall, sometimes."

She scowled as she altered the display, studying the operational plans. The reports from the surface concerning Admiral Junayd were a mixed bag. On one hand, he was putting together the framework of a postwar government; on the other hand, his wives and daughters had been kept in a terrible state. And they'd been the lucky ones. Some of the women who'd stumbled into the camps had been fantastically lucky just to be alive.

"Perhaps," William said, "but if they were *rational*, they would have surrendered long ago."

"True," Kat agreed. The enemy government remained intact, despite the invasion and the bombardment. It would collapse soon, she thought, but the entire planet was likely to follow the government into hell, unless Junayd actually did manage to patch together a *working* government. "And they haven't responded to any of our offers to discuss surrender."

She ground her teeth together in frustration. The personal message she'd received from the king had warned her that the news channels had been carrying reports from Ahura Mazda ever since they'd been released from the buffers. Public opinion was swinging against the mere *suggestion* of offering better terms than unconditional surrender, even though members of the former government wouldn't be offered anything more than their lives. The public wanted to see the bastards swinging on ropes, not dropped onto a hellish penal world. And the king had ended his message by warning her that offering decent terms might end her career too.

"They're going to lose their fleet," William pointed out. "And even if they try to hold out indefinitely, it isn't going to work."

"I know," Kat said. Sooner or later, the PDC fusion cores would run out of power. If the Theocrats refused to surrender, the PDCs would be smashed from orbit. "But what are they going to come up with first?"

"I don't know," William said. "They killed everyone in the POW camp."

Kat shook her head in frustration. *That* hadn't been made public, not yet. But the news blackout wouldn't last. The Theocrats had murdered detainees in a POW camp just to keep them from being rescued. Thousands of men and women, almost all of them from the Commonwealth, lying dead. The public would go wild. Kat was privately surprised she hadn't received orders to withdraw her forces and toast the entire planet. Three-quarters of the Commonwealth would cheer.

But we would have to live in such a universe afterwards, she thought. *And then?*

Her intercom bleeped. "Commodore, this is Wheeler," it said. "General Winters requests an urgent conference."

Kat exchanged glances with William. "Put him through," she ordered. "And inform him that Commodore McElney is with me."

General Winters appeared in front of her. "Commodore," he said, "I'm afraid we have a problem."

Kat felt her heart sink. "What now?"

"We had a rather unusual walk-in," General Winters said. "She has a worrying story."

William frowned. "She?"

Kat shared his confusion. A number of women had been taken into the refugee camps, but almost all of them had been swept up in the advance. A *woman* rarely crossed the lines, as if none of them could bring themselves to leave their homes. Given how brutally the Theocracy enforced the rules of gender segregation, she found it hard to blame them. *She* would have hesitated to go outside if she'd known the decision meant savage punishment if she was caught.

"Yes," General Winters said, "a young woman who claims to be the daughter of Speaker Nehemiah, Princess Drusilla's half sister. We checked her DNA against the records and it matches. Both women clearly share a father."

"Her sister also had the nerve to flee," Kat mused. She'd never quite grasped how hard it must have been for Drusilla to leave, at least until her forces had come face to face with the realities of Ahura Mazda. "What did she say?"

"It's not good news," General Winters said. "Apparently, there's a stockpile of antimatter somewhere on the world's surface. If it looks like they are going to lose, they'll get their leadership out and then blow up the entire planet."

Kat blanched. "Is she telling the truth?"

"She certainly *thinks* she's telling the truth," General Winters said. "But she could easily be repeating a lie she was told."

"Shit," William breathed. "Enough antimatter to crack an entire planet—"

"It wouldn't have to be *that* much," Kat said. Her mind started to race. Where *was* the antimatter? If they dropped a KEW in the wrong place, they could detonate it by accident and destroy the entirety of Ahura Mazda. Pat was down there. So were billions of innocent civilians, many of whom were already suffering. "What do they want?"

"Princess Aeliana insists that they merely intend to blow up the planet when it becomes clear that they've lost," General Winters said. "Her father told her that they didn't have the antimatter at the Tabernacle, but they'll send a signal to the storage depot when the time comes. And that will be that."

Kat sagged, fighting the urge to bury her head in her hands. There was no way she could recover the landing force before the Theocrats blew up their own planet. The bastards would probably be watching for signs of an evacuation. And even if she could, she couldn't recover more than a handful of civilians. The entire planet's population was being held hostage by their masters. What the hell could she *do* about it?

"They plan to send the signal from the Tabernacle, right?" William asked. "If we were to nuke the Tabernacle ourselves—"

"That would kill millions of innocents," Kat pointed out.

"But save billions," William countered.

He was right, Kat knew. A penetrator warhead would do a great deal of damage to the city, but it would utterly destroy the Tabernacle. Or would it? Admiral Junayd had told them that there were bunkers deep below the city, bunkers that might be untouched by a nuclear blast. They could still get their message out if they remained connected to the planetary datanet.

She took a long breath. What could she do? Try to negotiate? But the fanatics *wouldn't* negotiate. Or try to win the battle before the signal could be sent? She could blanket the airwaves with jamming, if necessary. And yet, would that tactic be enough to keep the signal from going through? What if there was a landline to the antimatter depot? She could go mad trying to figure out all the possibilities.

"We can't get to the bunker," she mused. "Or could we? Could we dig a tunnel ourselves?"

"I don't think we could without being detected," General Winters said. "We *do* have some Moles with us, but getting that far down would be tricky. Even a complete idiot would know to listen for drilling sounds."

Kat nodded ruefully. She'd gone through a stage of being interested in building while her family's mansion had been undergoing repairs. Building a bunker deep under the surface was a remarkable engineering challenge. The Theocracy wouldn't have stinted on the defenses, either. Getting down to the bunker without being detected would be almost impossible.

Father would say to pick the least dangerous option and cope with it, she thought. *But what is the least dangerous option here?*

"General," she said, "do you have a recommendation?"

"Not as yet," General Winters admitted. "I have teams interrogating Junayd and the other high-level defectors, hoping one of them knows something we can use. Otherwise, we may have to throw in an offensive and hope we can break through to the bunker before it's too late."

"Wishful thinking," William said.

Kat nodded in stoic agreement. She knew how stealthy Pat could be, but there was no way he could get a platoon through the enemy defenses, into the Tabernacle, and down to the bunker before the enemy pushed the button. And yet, there might be no other choice. Everyone she'd landed on the surface had just become a hostage. They would die when the enemy leadership decided to kill everyone, including themselves.

"See what you can find out," she said finally. She paused as a thought struck her. "They want to get their leadership out?"

"That's what she said," General Winters reminded her.

Kat studied the display, her mind racing. If Aeliana was right about there being enough antimatter to shatter the entire planet, there was literally nowhere for the enemy leadership to go . . . unless they planned to link up with the remains of their fleet. The enemy might be skulking around the system, but they'd never manage to get a cloaked ship close enough to the planet to pick up a shuttle. No, they'd have to evacuate their leadership during a major offensive. And that meant she might just be able to bar the way.

"They'll send in their fleet to cover the escape," she said. "And as long as we can fend off the fleet, they won't detonate the bombs."

"Unless they think they're trapped," General Winters commented.

"True," Kat agreed. "But if they're willing to try to preserve themselves, perhaps they'll accept the next offer of surrender."

"Perhaps," William mused.

Kat sighed. "I'll discuss the issue with my fleet commanders," she said. "General, send Aeliana up to the fleet, then draw up a plan to assault the Tabernacle. We may have no other option."

"Understood," General Winters said.

His image vanished. "Shit," William breathed. "Why didn't we anticipate this?"

"Because we didn't realize just how mad they have become," Kat said. The Theocracy seemed to delight in finding worse and worse ways to commit atrocities. "And we didn't realize just how far they were prepared to go."

She had no doubt the Theocrats *would* detonate the antimatter stockpile. The threat could be an elaborate bluff, but for that to be true, it would have relied on too many things going right. They couldn't have predicted Aeliana, could they? Drusilla herself had admitted she probably wouldn't have gotten away with escape if her family hadn't thought of her as a *mere* woman, too silly to tie her own shoelaces without help. No, the antimatter depot was real.

If we could find it first, Kat thought, *we could capture the antimatter.*

"Go get a shower and some rest," she ordered. The clock was ticking. Who knew when the enemy fleet would arrive? Soon, she suspected. The enemy wouldn't want to try to fly a shuttle out through a war zone. The craft might be picked off in the confusion. "I don't think we have long before the final engagement."

William nodded. "Aye, Commodore."

Kat watched him go, then looked back at the map. An entire world, billions of people, all held hostage by madmen. And no matter what she did, there was just too great a chance of the enemy detonating their makeshift bomb. Some parts of the Commonwealth would cheer the bloodbath, others would blame her for the nightmare. They'd be sure, from the comfort of their armchairs, that there was something she could have done to prevent the disaster. But what?

Pat was down there, she knew. Pat and General Winters and countless men and women she didn't know, men and women she would *never* know if the bomb detonated. The fear of losing them was so strong it almost held her paralyzed. What did it say about her, she wondered, that she feared more for her own people than the enemy civilians? But then, the enemy civilians were just faceless masses, their deaths nothing more than an incomprehensible number. She knew they had lives and loves, hopes and fears, but she didn't quite believe it.

And yet, she knew her duty. She had to do everything within her power to stop the bomb from being detonated, even at the cost of thousands of lives. William was right. If she destroyed the Tabernacle, if she took out the surrounding city, that might just save the rest of Ahura Mazda. And yet, she would have to live with mass slaughter on her conscience for a long time. Telling herself that millions had died to save billions would be cold comfort, and she knew her reputation would not survive.

And if it did, she thought, *would I want it?*

She took a moment to compose herself, then bottled up her feelings as she rose to her feet and headed for the hatch. The enemy ships might be on top of the fleet at any moment. Hell, she knew it was all too likely they might slip out of hyperspace at the edge of the system and try to sneak up on her. Why not? She didn't have vast sensor arrays covering the entire system.

"Mr. Wheeler," she said, as she stepped onto the Combat Information Centre. Bobby Wheeler looked up at her, expectantly. "Call a fleet conference. Immediately."

"Aye, Commodore," Wheeler said. "Is the enemy coming?"

"It looks that way," Kat said. The near-space display was clear, but that proved nothing. "And we have very little time to prepare."

CHAPTER THIRTY-FIVE

"Transit completed, Admiral," the operator said. "No enemy ships within detection range."

Zaskar nodded, although he knew the absence of visible ships was largely meaningless. The Commonwealth's cloaking devices were very good. If there *was* a prowling enemy ship within sensor range, word of his arrival was already winging its way to Ahura Mazda. But the odds were staggeringly against early detection. He'd brought the fleet out of hyperspace so far from the planet—and on the other side of the star—to minimize the odds of being detected.

They haven't had a chance to set up long-range sensor arrays, he thought as his fleet settled down into combat formation. *And if they didn't need them, they would have tracked down our spies long ago.*

He kept his face impassive despite the growing tension on the bridge. The clerics had been busy preaching to members of the crew, promising them that this would be the final battle, promising them that God was on their side. And yet, even the clerics had been unable to keep rumors from spreading, rumors that suggested that Ahura Mazda had already fallen, that God had turned His face from His chosen people. The fleet's spacers had expected to die in defense of their homeworld, not flee as freighter crews fought and lost the battle for the high orbit-als. It was hard to believe, deep inside, that victory was truly assured.

We should be able to catch them by surprise, Zaskar told himself. *And if we can push them against the planetary defenses, the firepower advantage will be on our side.*

"Admiral," the operator said, "the fleet is ready to advance."

"Make sure the cloaking devices are fully operational," Zaskar ordered. "If a ship is at risk of a glitch, they are to cut power and fall out of formation."

The cleric glanced at him. "Is that wise?"

"We dare not alert the enemy to our presence," Zaskar said bluntly. He was sick of clerics questioning his judgment. "They could easily break orbit and escape if they have advance warning of our arrival."

Or head out to challenge us in interplanetary space, he added silently. It was normally fairly straightforward for a fleet to refuse battle. But now, with almost every last warship in the Theocracy bearing down on them, the Commonwealth vessels had ample incentive to accept the challenge. Even if they lost, they'd still tear his fleet to ribbons. *We're gambling everything on a single battle.*

He glanced down at the stream of updates from his ships. His crews had worked frantically over the last few weeks, but they couldn't come to grips with the shortage of supplies and spare parts. He knew, all too well, that his missile loads were very low and his point defense datanet badly flawed. He'd given orders to reroute the datanet through a dozen ships, even though doctrine argued against devolving the system. But he had no choice. Breaking the datanet into subnets might make the difference between survival and certain death.

"They will not escape us," the cleric snapped.

"I don't intend to give them the chance, Your Holiness," Zaskar said. He cleared his throat. "Order the fleet to advance as planned."

"Aye, Admiral," the operator said.

"And order the Alpha and Beta crews to get some sleep," Zaskar added. "They are to report back to their stations one hour before estimated arrival time, unless summoned."

Unless we are detected earlier, he thought. The Commonwealth would have scattered hundreds of remote sensor platforms around Ahura Mazda. They'd have a fair chance of picking up his fleet, even if the odds *did* favor him. *At that point, all of our tactical planning goes out the airlock.*

"The crew should spend the next few hours in prayer," the cleric insisted. "God needs to be beseeched for his help."

"They need to be rested when we engage the enemy," Zaskar said, quietly. He'd spent hours in prayer himself. He knew the time spent wasn't particularly restful. "God will know His own."

He settled back in his command chair. He'd have to go for a rest himself, once the fleet was firmly underway. The cleric might try to interfere, despite Zaskar's warnings. The Inquisitor genuinely believed that four years studying various holy writings and then serving as a fleet cleric gave him the understanding he needed to issue orders. And yet, he was wrong. No one knew for sure, but rumors claimed that clerics had gotten thousands of men killed because they'd issued bad orders at the worst possible times.

And no one will dare say no, he thought. *Even I take my life in my hands every time I oppose him.*

The cleric turned away, his beady eyes scanning the operators at their consoles. Zaskar wanted to glare at the cleric's back, but he didn't quite dare. Who knew *who* was watching, even in the Combat Information Centre? A show of disrespect would not go unnoticed. He felt another flash of envy for his Commonwealth counterparts. *They* didn't have interfering busybodies telling them what to do, did they? A Commonwealth captain was in sole command of his ship; a Commonwealth admiral was in sole command of his fleet. And while he knew that system hadn't always worked out for the Commonwealth, he knew it worked better than the Theocracy's.

Honestly, he thought. *The war would have gone much better if the clerics had stuck to merely tending souls and encouraging the crews.*

He glanced at the time, silently weighing up the distances. Thirty-seven hours to Ahura Mazda, unless they were detected first. And then, an engagement designed to hammer the enemy long enough for the speakers to flee Ahura Mazda. He wasn't sure how he felt about that, not after the clerics had promised the crew a final decisive battle. Cold logic told him that the war was lost and Ahura Mazda was doomed, yet emotion told him that the fleet and the speakers should die in defense of their homeworld.

But we might survive, he told himself. *We were kicked off Earth and still survived.*

◆ ◆ ◆

"Is this serious?"

"I'm afraid so," General Winters said. "There's a bomb on the planet that could destroy everything."

Pat stared at the map, unable to quite process what he was hearing. Enough antimatter to wreck an entire planet? He felt cold ice running down his spine, the same pure terror he felt when he knew he was inching his way through a minefield. The slightest misstep could easily set off a mine. A number of wounded soldiers in the stasis pods had stood on IEDs and had their legs blown off.

But they can have their legs regenerated, he thought. *There's no way we can regenerate an entire planet.*

He shook his head slowly as the full impact of the news sank in. There was no way the landing force could be evacuated before the enemy realized they were leaving and triggered the bomb. Unless they thought the threat was enough to convince the Commonwealth to leave. No, if that was the case, the Theocrats would have made the threat public. They couldn't have *counted* on someone sneaking out of the Tabernacle and making it through the front lines to safety.

And there was *definitely* no way the entire planet could be evacuated.

"We have to stop them," he breathed. "If we take out the Tabernacle first, they won't be able to send the detonation command."

"Precisely my thought," General Winters said.

He keyed the display, throwing up a map of the Tabernacle and the surrounding city. Pat scowled as more and more tactical icons blinked up, warning of everything from emplaced guns to heavy armor held in reserve. Protected by the PDC's force shield, the defenders would have to be cleared man by man, giving the enemy plenty of time to trigger the bomb. Pat would have hated to throw himself into the teeth of enemy defenses even without the threat of planetary annihilation, but there was no choice. There was, quite simply, no room to maneuver.

"Getting a force to the Tabernacle and then down into the bunker before they hit the switch will be tricky," General Winters said. "We have, however, identified a secret escape tunnel leading directly *to* the bunker. The bastards clearly figured they'd need a way to get out someday before their own people tore them apart."

Pat wasn't surprised. He'd seen Cadiz and a dozen other worlds that were either poor or ravaged by war, but nothing had prepared him for the sheer level of horror on Ahura Mazda. The population was so degraded that only a relative handful seemed willing to either join or oppose the Commonwealth. He'd seen grown men flinch from marines and Civil Affairs officers. And the women seemed to truly believe that they were nothing more than property.

General Winters keyed the map. "We'll be launching a major armored thrust here, at Town #46. Logically, the speakers will be unwilling to detonate the bomb unless they feel themselves to be in direct danger. Town #46 is an excellent choice for biting off a chunk of their defenses without opening a throughway to the Tabernacle."

"And as long as they still think they can escape," Pat said, "they won't detonate the bomb."

"Precisely," General Winters said. "The spacers have the high orbitals securely blockaded. I don't think the bastards have a hope in hell of making it out unless their fleet covers their escape. But they won't see themselves to be in *direct* danger."

He looked up at Pat. "The attack is a diversion," he added. "You'll be taking your company and securing the outer tunnel, then striking directly into the Tabernacle. You are *not* to hesitate, whatever the cost. Kill everyone in the bunker, if necessary. But that signal is not to be sent."

Pat swallowed hard as the general's words sank in. Sneaking through the tunnels and attacking . . . hundreds of things could go wrong, each convincing the enemy that their time was up. His troops wouldn't be able to stop for anything. They'd need to take suicide nukes of their own, as a very last resort. He couldn't think of an alternative. The Theocrats couldn't be talked into surrendering while their fleet might already be on the way. They *had* to be stopped.

"It'll take us four hours to reach the tunnel entrance, sir," he said, studying the map. Orbital observation showed a small farmhouse, surrounded by miles upon miles of forest. The maps they'd obtained from the enemy defenses stated that the entire area was reserved for Theocratic leadership. "We could make a jump onto the target, but that would be too revealing."

"Your call," General Winters said. He smiled humorlessly. "But for what it's worth, I agree with you."

Pat nodded. No one had paid much attention to the entire region, save for a pair of recon flights during the early stages of the invasion. The enemy hadn't mounted any defenses in the area, although intelligence suggested that a number of surviving enemy soldiers had established base camps within the forest. Pat wasn't too surprised. A skilled team of soldiers would have no trouble harvesting enough to eat, either by trapping small animals or gathering roots and other edible flora.

And rooting them out will be an absolute nightmare, he thought. *But right now it isn't a real concern.*

"I'll gather the team," he said.

He considered the problems for a long moment. The operation was not going to be easy. Marines were used to jumping into situations without proper preparation, but such missions were always risky. And this was the worst of all. They might well be detected as they made their way down the tunnel. Admiral Junayd and his fellows had plotted out the interior of the bunker as best as they could, but they knew nothing about its internal security systems. Pat would be astonished if there weren't any. A regime as paranoid as the Theocracy would fear coups more than a populist uprising.

And a single mistake could get them to trigger the bomb, he thought. *Even if we jam the enemy radio networks, they might use a landline.*

He looked up. "When do you intend to launch the diversionary assault?"

"When your team is in position," General Winters said. "Give them a few moments to realize they're under attack before you move."

"Aye, sir," Pat said.

The largest attack might seem the most dangerous, he knew, but it was often the unseen threat that was truly lethal. If the marines were lucky, if everything went according to plan, the Theocracy would be paying more attention to the attack on Town #46 than to their own defenses. But if they were wrong . . .

He shook his head. There was no choice. They'd been committed from the moment they'd learned about the bomb. It *had* to be disabled.

"I'll gather the team, sir," he said. "We'll leave as soon as possible."

"You have top priority," General Winters said. "Draw everything you need from stores. And good luck."

"Thank you, sir," Pat said.

He felt sweaty as he turned and walked out of the office. He'd expected to join the attack on the enemy defenses, not be charged with a mission that could only end in total victory or mass slaughter on an incomprehensible scale. He wished, as he keyed his terminal to assemble his marines, that he had time to call Kat, but he knew he didn't. His call would be unfair, hellishly unfair, to the men who couldn't call their partners before embarking on the mission.

The final mission, he thought morbidly. *Either we win or die.*

♦ ♦ ♦

"You're going to wear the deck out," William said.

Kat barely heard him as she paced forwards and backwards in the CIC. Local space was clear, yet she couldn't shake the feeling that the enemy was out there, watching her. The Theocrats did not seem to realize that Aeliana had fled the Tabernacle. They were busy making their plans to escape. They had to make their bid for freedom before the end came.

And the only way they can break through our lines is through a diversion, she thought numbly. She wasn't blind to the irony. Both sides in the war were staking everything on a diversionary tactic.

She shook her head, slowly. The Theocrats were merely planning to escape. *She* was gambling everything on her marines being able to capture or kill everyone in the Tabernacle before the Theocrats blew up the entire planet. Sure, they probably didn't have enough antimatter to reduce Ahura Mazda to an asteroid cluster, but it wouldn't make much difference to the population if all that happened was that their world was turned into a radioactive hellhole. Kat had seen the images from ruined Earth. Even now, there was no hope of resettling humanity's former homeworld.

And if we get this wrong, she thought, *the entire galaxy will blame us.*

She'd sent a message to Tyre, outlining the situation and what she was doing to counter it, but there had been no response. The War Cabinet, already shocked by her father's death, seemed inclined to leave matters in her hands. She felt a little betrayed, but she understood the sentiment. They wouldn't want to complicate matters when *she* could take the blame if things went wrong.

"You've done everything you can," William said.

"I hope so," Kat said. She'd repositioned the fleet and covertly brought up as many people as she could from the surface, but the evacuation was only a drop in the bucket. Evacuating Ahura Mazda in full was utterly impossible. Her entire fleet train couldn't hope to move more than a couple of million people at a time. "But what if I've missed something?"

"Then everyone else has missed it too," William said. He lowered his voice. "You've done everything you can, Kat."

Kat folded her arms. She felt . . . nervous. No, *worse* than nervous. She'd known the risks when she put her own life on the line, but now she was gambling with an entire planet. She knew, of course, that *she* hadn't transported a few hundred tons of antimatter to the planet's surface, any more than she'd built the detonation system—small consolation.

We should have considered the possibility, she thought.

She felt sick, despite herself, as the hours ticked away.

And Pat was down there, leading his men on a do-or-die mission. His ring felt heavy on her finger, mocking her. She wanted to call him back, even though she knew he'd never forgive her if she did. Yet, the thought of him being safe was almost worth it. He'd be alive to hate her.

A console chimed. "Commodore," Wheeler said. "Long-range sensors are picking up turbulence. Tactical analysis calls it a cloaked fleet."

Kat sucked in her breath. "Red alert," she ordered. New icons appeared on the display, heading straight for her fleet. The enemy clearly wasn't trying to be subtle. She rather suspected they'd decloak before they entered firing range. "All hands to battlestations!"

CHAPTER THIRTY-SIX

"Admiral," the operator said, "the enemy fleet has detected us."

Zaskar ignored the cleric's sharp intake of breath. He'd *hoped* to get into firing range without being detected, but he hadn't *counted* on it. The Commonwealth's sensors were just too good. And now the enemy fleet was bringing up its shields and slipping into combat formation. They were ready for him.

Did they know we were coming, he asked himself, *or were they just being paranoid?*

He pushed the thought aside and leaned forward. "Decloak the fleet," he ordered, concentrating on projecting an impression of calm confidence. "Raise shields, bring up the tactical datanet and prepare to engage."

"Aye, sir," the operator said.

Zaskar nodded, studying the enemy fleet as it moved slowly into position. The first battle had proven costly, but the enemy clearly hadn't suffered too badly. Their crews were trained to reestablish their datanets and realign their formations on the go without waiting for orders from higher authority. They'd probably broken up a couple of squadrons and plugged the surviving ships into other formations—not something he would have wanted to try with Theocratic craft, but it seemed to work for the Commonwealth.

Because we train our crewmen to follow orders and nothing else, he thought. *And they train their crewmen to use their brains.*

"Enemy missile range in seven minutes," the operator said. "They're bringing up their ECM now."

"Interesting," Zaskar mused. Was there a *reason* for that? He couldn't open fire until the enemy ships entered missile range. There was no need to establish hard locks on their ships, not yet. Were they just trying to confuse his sensor crews? They'd certainly want to hide their full strength from him. "Launch sensor probes, then establish a shell of recon drones surrounding the fleet."

He ignored the cleric's astonishment. Recon drones were *expensive*, but there was no point in withholding them from the battle now. One way or the other, everything hinged on this final engagement.

"The enemy fleet is launching gunboats," the operator warned. "They're slipping into assault formation now."

"Launch our own gunboats," Zaskar ordered. "Deploy half of them to attack the enemy ships; hold back the other half for fleet defense."

"Aye, Admiral," the operator said.

Zaskar gritted his teeth. It was hard to be sure, but he seemed to have a slight edge in gunboats. And yet, *their* gunboats were superior to his. The odds might be more even than he cared to admit. But raw numbers *would* give him an edge, he was sure. He *needed* to weaken the enemy as much as possible before the missile engagement began.

"Enemy gunboats on attack vector," the operator stated. "Our gunboats are moving to intercept."

"The point defense is to engage as soon as the gunboats enter range," Zaskar ordered. "The crews are *not* to wait for orders."

The cleric gasped. Zaskar ignored him. There was no *time* to issue orders. The enemy gunboats would carry one or two shipkillers apiece, antimatter-tipped warheads that would do real damage to his vessels.

They *had* to be stopped before they got into firing range or his fleet would be crippled. His point defense crews *had* to engage the gunboats as soon as they could.

"Aye, Admiral," the operator said.

Zaskar nodded. The enemy fleet had smoothed itself out into a conical formation, its superdreadnoughts surrounded by destroyers and light cruisers while the battlecruisers held back. It was a reasonable enough formation, giving the enemy commanding officer the opportunity to absorb Zaskar's thrusts or go on the offensive himself, depending on what Zaskar did. Its only downside was that it would be harder for the enemy ships to scatter if the fighting didn't go their way, but *that* wasn't likely to be a problem.

"Hold us at the extreme edge of missile range," he ordered. "And fire as soon as we have solid locks on their hulls."

"Aye, Admiral," the operator said.

◆ ◆ ◆

"That's a lot of ships," William said quietly as the enemy fleet decloaked. "They must have brought every remaining ship in their fleet."

"It looks that way," Kat agreed. "We'll never have a better chance to end the war."

She smiled, pushing her doubts aside. Ten superdreadnought squadrons, flanked by over two hundred battlecruisers, cruisers, and destroyers . . . a formidable force, perhaps the most powerful armada the Theocracy had ever deployed. Tactical icons flashed up on her display as her analysts identified a number of superdreadnoughts. Four squadrons were clearly the ships that had escaped Ahura Mazda, seventeen other superdreadnoughts had been spied orbiting a dozen worlds within the Theocracy. Many of them were in poor condition.

"Commodore," Wheeler said. "The fleet has entered formation."

Kat nodded. Her gunboats were already en route to the enemy ships, but they wouldn't be enough. The enemy point defense would probably be able to keep the gunboats from doing real damage. No, she needed her superdreadnoughts to win the fight.

She glanced at Ahura Mazda, hanging in the display. She'd ringed the world with stealthed recon platforms, watching for a shuttlecraft trying to flee the Tabernacle. She doubted the enemy had managed to fit a gateway generator onto a shuttle—the Commonwealth hadn't managed to produce anything of the sort—which meant that the shuttlecraft would have to be picked up by a starship. Logically, the Theocrats would head straight into deep space, which was why she had an entire squadron of battlecruisers lurking under a cloaking field, ready to engage anyone fleeing the planet.

And the Theocratic leaders might just be stopped before they can send a signal, she thought. *But they may have set a timer.*

She pushed the thought aside. "General signal to the fleet," she ordered. "The battle line will advance to engage the enemy."

"Aye, Commodore," Wheeler said.

Kat sucked in her breath. "The fleet is to open fire the moment we enter missile range," she added. "I want their point defenses *swamped.*"

She shared a grin with William. The enemy ships seemed oddly hesitant to advance, even though their only real chance of scoring a major victory lay in closing the range as much as possible. But then, they'd be torn to ribbons by her energy weapons even as they savaged her fleet. *She* would have tried to use her remaining ships as a bargaining counter rather than risk everything on one final battle. And yet the Theocrats had nowhere to go. Why *not* place their fate in God's hands?

They won't have any support to build their new homeworld, she thought, as the range narrowed sharply. *This time, they'll be completely on their own.*

She felt an odd flicker of admiration for Ahura Mazda's founders. They'd clearly planned well, taking *years* to build up supplies even though they'd told their own people that they'd been chained up at gun-point and marched into the colony ships without even the clothes on their backs. She couldn't deny the magnitude of their accomplishment, even as she hated what they'd become. Perhaps the original Theocrats would be as horrified as Kat if they set foot on modern-day Ahura Mazda. Or perhaps they'd see it as their due, the holy society they'd wanted all along.

But their intentions no longer mattered.

"Entering missile range," Wheeler reported. "Missile batteries engaging . . . *now*."

Kat nodded as *Queen Elizabeth* shuddered, flushing her external racks and internal missile tubes. The display seemed to blur as thousands of missiles raced towards their targets, the enemy opening fire at the same moment. She winced at the sheer volume of missiles bearing down on her ships, then forced herself to relax. There were no freighters here loaded with antimatter, no unpleasant surprises . . . the battle would be conventional, fought and won by warships and missiles. And she had more advantages, she suspected, than the enemy realized.

"Our gunboats have taken out four ships," William reported, "but they've taken heavy losses."

"The tactical officers insist that the enemy has improved their point defense systems," Wheeler added. "They're no longer running a hierarchical command structure."

Kat nodded. She'd expected the Theocrats to make the switch months ago, after they realized the Commonwealth point defense systems were vastly superior to theirs. The change wouldn't have required much more than some reprogramming, except for a switch in mindset that the Theocrats would have found painful. She understood from her conversations with Junayd that the Theocrats flatly *refused* to grant autonomy to their junior officers, even at the cost of weakening their fleets.

But the lesson took them too long to learn, she told herself firmly. *They don't have time to learn the other lessons we might have taught them.*

"Our missiles will enter the enemy point defense range in ninety seconds," Wheeler reported. "Their missiles will enter our range in one hundred and ten seconds."

"The point defense is to engage at once," Kat ordered.

She braced herself. The enemy fleet was in poor condition. If she was lucky, she might just be able to cripple it with the first barrage.

And if I can't, she thought darkly, *I have plenty more missiles to fire.*

◆ ◆ ◆

Speaker Nehemiah jerked awake as his intercom bleeped. He pulled himself away from his junior wife and keyed a switch, accepting the call.

"Yes?"

"The fleet has arrived," Inquisitor Samuilu said. "You are ordered to make your way to the situation room."

Ordered, Nehemiah thought. The Inquisitor wasn't even *trying* to pretend any longer. Power had shifted. *And they may refuse to take me if they think I'm powerless.*

His junior wife opened her eyes as Nehemiah climbed out of bed, watching him as he hastily pulled on his ceremonial robes. Nehemiah opened his mouth to rebuke her for showing unseemly interest, then decided such talk wasn't worth the effort. Besides, he knew what was coming. It was unlikely that any of his wives would survive, even down in the bunker.

The thought cost him a pang of guilt. He had no sons any longer, thanks to the war and his political enemies. It wasn't *common* to love daughters, yet he did . . . even though he knew his daughters would go, one day, to another household. He didn't want to leave them behind to die, let alone fall into enemy hands. And yet he had no choice. The entire Theocracy hung in the balance.

He hurried down the corridor, noting just how few guards there were now. Inquisitor Samuilu and Lord Cleric Eliseus had been rearranging everything after a number of soldiers had turned on their masters in a brutal mutiny that ended badly. They didn't want to add more armed men to the mix, not when they were planning to flee. Nehemiah wished, suddenly, that he had a weapon, although he wasn't sure what he would do with it. Take the shuttle for himself? Or kill the fanatics before they killed him?

The main display was practically *glowing* with red and green icons. Nehemiah cast a practiced glance over it, silently noting the two fleets converging on one another. They were committed to a close-range engagement, he thought. He hoped he was wrong. The Theocracy needed to preserve *some* ships, if only to ensure the safety of their next homeworld.

"Speaker," Lord Cleric Eliseus said, "God has granted us an opportunity."

"Of course," Nehemiah said. He ignored the older man's babbling as he studied the ground-side display. The enemy had launched a major assault on a town, clearly trying to bring relief to a mutinous garrison. No doubt the traitors would surrender as soon as they could, giving the enemy a chance to plan an assault against the more solid defense lines further towards the Tabernacle. "I assume you intend to use it?"

"Of course," Inquisitor Samuilu said. "It's time to leave this sinful world."

♦ ♦ ♦

"Enemy missiles entering point defense range," the operator warned. "The point defense gunners are engaging now."

Zaskar kept his eyes firmly on the tactical display as red icons started to vanish. He'd underestimated the ability of the enemy forces to reload their external racks, he noted. Either that or the unbelievers had managed to cram more missile tubes into their superdreadnoughts. He wondered, absently, how they'd done it as the remaining missiles bunched up, picking their targets and thrusting forward.

But the decentralized point defense is working, he thought. Nearly half of the incoming missiles had been killed . . . and the remainder were being picked off, one by one. *We are holding our own.*

He gritted his teeth as the enemy missiles slammed against their targets. A dozen superdreadnoughts, their shield generators already in poor condition, were blown out of space, seventeen more taking heavy damage. He cursed, inwardly, as thirty-seven smaller ships were wiped out of existence. They'd absorbed missiles that would have damaged his larger ships, he knew, but they'd also mounted enough point defense to make a difference when the enemy launched their second barrage.

"Sir," the operator said, "the enemy is closing the range."

Zaskar bit off a venomous curse. He couldn't afford a close-range engagement, not when it would leave both sides in pieces. And yet he couldn't retreat either. The speakers were depending on him to keep the enemy distracted long enough for them to escape. Who knew what would happen if he retreated?

"Order the fleet to reverse course," he snapped. The move would confuse his people at the worst possible moment, but there was no choice. The enemy ships were already firing their second barrage. "And continue firing!"

"Aye, sir," the operator said.

Zaskar took a moment to study the enemy formation. Their point defense was damned good, but five of their superdreadnoughts and a dozen smaller ships had been destroyed. Seven more ships were clearly disabled, two of them leaking plasma as they staggered out of formation. Another was dead in space, lifepods spewing from her hull. A moment later, a stray missile struck her unshielded hull and vaporized her.

Wasteful, Zaskar thought. The missile's seeker head had probably gotten confused, but it was still annoying. *That missile could have damaged a live ship.*

"Pull the formation back together," he ordered after a moment. "And recall the remaining gunboats."

"Aye, sir," the operator said.

◆ ◆ ◆

Queen Elizabeth shook as an enemy missile slammed against her shields, then shuddered violently as she unleashed another spread of missiles. Kat hung on to her command chair and watched, keeping her expression under tight control, as the missiles raced towards their targets, their controllers seeking out weak points within the enemy's defenses. The Theocrats clearly weren't *used* to a devolved command system, she noted absently. Their firing groups seemed to be all over the place.

But they still have a chance of preserving their strength, she thought. *We're not damaging them enough to make a difference.*

"The enemy fleet is reversing course," Wheeler reported. "They're trying to head out into interplanetary space."

Drawing us out of position, Kat asked herself, *or trying to avoid a close-range engagement?*

"Pursuit course, best possible speed," she ordered. She was tempted to check the situation on the ground, but that would be nothing more than a pointless distraction. There was certainly nothing she could do about it, whatever was happening. "Continue firing."

She allowed herself a cold smile as the fleet slowly picked up speed. Coordinating hundreds of starships wasn't easy, but the enemy would have a difficult time reversing course before the range had narrowed sharply. And the closer the range, the harder it would be for their point defense to pick off her missiles. The same was true in reverse, of course, but she was confident her point defense crews had the advantage. She definitely had an advantage in missile tubes.

"The enemy fire is starting to slack," William commented. "They're not putting out as many missiles per barrage."

Kat nodded in agreement. The enemy hadn't lost *that* many ships. She had a feeling the Theocrats were finally running out of antimatter and nuclear-tipped missiles. And they had no hope of finding more, not after she'd devastated the industrial nodes orbiting Ahura Mazda. Their fleet wouldn't be able to threaten anyone, even if it escaped her.

She allowed her smile to widen as she watched her missiles sinking into the enemy armada, her tactical staff picking out firing groups and targeting their command ships. Brief confusion would ensue among *her* vessels if the enemy took out a command ship, but she'd drilled her crews extensively to set up a new hierarchical network if the original command ship was destroyed. The Theocracy, it seemed, hadn't realized they needed to train, if indeed they'd had the time. Every time *they* lost a command ship, their point defense network fragmented and needed to be rebuilt from scratch.

"Entering sprint mode range," Wheeler said.

"Signal all ships," Kat ordered. The enemy fleet was picking up speed, but it was too late to escape now. "Switch to rapid fire."

"Aye, Commodore," Wheeler said.

Kat watched as the enemy ships writhed under her assault. They seemed torn between trying to close the range and simply escaping, although she had to admit that their CO was doing an excellent job of holding the formation together. But their fire was slacking off badly.

Keep pushing, she told herself as another enemy ship vanished from the display. Two more fell out of formation, one apparently powerless. She'd try to board her later, if her crew didn't trigger the self-destruct. *Keep pushing and the entire formation will come apart.*

CHAPTER THIRTY-SEVEN

"I feel naked," Sergeant Bones commented.

Pat nodded in grim agreement as marine platoons surveyed the farmhouse from the forest. They couldn't bring their powered armor with them, not if they wanted to sneak up on the farmhouse without being detected. Instead, they'd donned camouflage rural combat uniforms, knowing the outfits wouldn't provide nearly enough protection if they were caught in an ambush. Pat had plenty of experience fighting with and without the armor, but he felt naked too. The enemy could have prepared all sorts of surprises for anyone who stumbled across the farmhouse.

But it didn't look as though they had, he noted. His marine team didn't have any active sensors, but passive sensors weren't picking up anything more than a pair of heat sources in the lower bedroom. The farmhouse itself looked more like a vacation home than any of the farms he'd seen elsewhere, like the country resort Kat had once taken him to, instead of a place where people lived and worked. But that was par for the course in authoritarian societies. The great and the good *always* had nice places they could relax.

"Two people in the lower bedroom," he muttered. The heat sources *looked* like people, although he couldn't be sure. "No others, as far as we can tell."

Pat glanced at the lead platoon. They knew as well as he did that the sensor results could be spoofed. A man wearing a set of BDUs would be almost invisible to a heat sensor, even without taking any additional precautions. But they couldn't wait in the forest indefinitely, not when the diversionary attack was already underway. And, worse, the enemy fleet had arrived.

We might run into the bastards coming the other way, he thought as he used hand signals to issue orders. *They won't try to fly straight out of the Tabernacle.*

Bracing himself, he slipped forward. Crossing the neatly mowed front lawn and sneaking up to the door was risky, offering the greatest chance of being spotted with the Mark-I Eyeball, but there was no choice. He tested the wooden walls—someone had placed wood over reinforced concrete, confirming that there was something very odd about the farmhouse—and then scrambled up the slats and through the open window. The guards would be watching for someone coming in the door, he suspected, but they wouldn't expect someone coming down from *above*. They already *knew* the upper floors were deserted.

Sergeant Bones followed him as he slipped forward. The interior of the bedroom was just as odd as the rest of the building, a giant bed that rested on a concrete floor. He tested his footing carefully as he inched forward, then glanced into the next bedroom. A man lay on the bed, fast asleep. Pat walked into the room, covered the man's mouth with one hand and pushed an injector tab against his neck. The man started, too late. The drug took effect seconds later.

He'll sleep for hours, Pat thought as they checked the rest of the upper level before heading to the stairs. *And by the time he wakes, it will all be over.*

He heard someone walking down the corridor and drew his knife just as the man came into view. The Theocrat's eyes opened wide with shock, but Pat threw the knife, watching it punch through the left eye and embed itself in his brain before the stranger could say a word. Pat hurried forward and straight into the next room, where two men were playing cards. Neither man had a chance to sound the alarm before they were both killed.

"The building is clear," Bones reported. "I'll bring in the rest of the platoon."

"We need to find the way to the bunker," Pat said. The reports had suggested the tunnel entrance would be in the basement, but he had a feeling it would be hard to find. "Get the sweep team in here."

He was almost disappointed, ten minutes later, when the hatch to the basement proved to be hidden under a carpet in the living room. The tech hacked it open within seconds, allowing Pat to drop down into the darkened compartment. Another door could be seen at the rear of the compartment, half-hidden within the shadows. He couldn't help thinking, as he sneaked up to it, that it looked like a banker's safe.

"It's designed to be easy to open," Corporal Nigel Rothschild reported. "But I have no idea what might be lurking on the far side."

Pat glanced at him. "You can open it from this side?"

"Technically, *no*," Rothschild said. He smirked. "But whoever designed this system never heard of the electron-tunneling effect. I can hack into the command system and open the hatch."

His smirk grew as he started to work. "Idiots really should have kept the entire system on manual," he added. "You just can't hack a manual hatch."

Pat nodded, his body heavy. There was no point in trying to see what was going on in space or over at Town #46. Everything depended on him. He resisted the urge to pace, barely, as Rothschild carefully unlocked the hatch. Kat was up there, fighting the largest space battle in recorded history.

"Done," Rothschild said.

The hatch hummed, then hissed open. Pat raised his weapon, but there was nothing on the far side save for a long concrete tunnel sloping downwards into the darkness. There were no lights, something that puzzled him more than he cared to admit. Was it a security measure or something more sinister? He slipped his night-vision goggles into place, then led the way forward. Time was definitely not on their side.

"There," Bones said.

Pat nodded. A small tram sat at the bottom of the tunnel, waiting for them. He'd hoped to find something like it, although he hadn't counted on such a discovery. The Tabernacle was nearly forty miles away, after all. The Theocrats weren't going to be *walking* that distance in a hurry.

"Get the first platoon into the tram," he ordered. "We'll send it back as soon as we reach the far end."

The tram hissed to life on command, an antigravity cushion powering up moments later. Pat braced himself as they started to move, picking up speed rapidly. He'd crept through darkened tunnels before, during basic training and later exercises, but this was different. He could hear a faint hum in the air as they glided towards the Tabernacle, followed by strange whispers and echoes that seemed to have no discernible source. His implants picked up flickers of electronic traffic, suggesting that the tunnel was part of a landline system as well as an escape hatch. They'd have to take the system apart to be sure.

"See if you can hack their system," he muttered to Rothschild. "Perhaps we can shut the bastards down completely."

"I'd need to get into the landline," Rothschild said. "Their insulation isn't very good, sir, but I'd probably set off an alarm if I cracked their wire."

"Primitive," Bones said.

"But effective," Rothschild said. "Landlines have always proven harder to hack than electronic communications."

Pat felt sweat trickling down his sides as they reached the end of the tunnel and disembarked. A giant hatch loomed up in front of them, easily large enough to take a tank. He puzzled over it for a long moment—a tank couldn't have fit through the tunnel—and then nodded to Rothschild to go to work. Unless the enemy was utterly incompetent, there would be a guard post stationed on the far side of the hatch. That was what *he* would do.

"They set up a neat little system," Rothschild said slowly. He set up his terminal beside the hatch and went to work, carefully isolating the locking mechanism. "I'd bet good money this place will survive the antimatter bomb."

"Depends where the bomb is," Pat muttered back. "If it's somewhere nearby, the bunker isn't going to have a hope."

He'd reviewed the problem during the frantic preparations for the mission, but no answers had been forthcoming. Some of the analysts had even wondered if the bomb was nothing more than a giant bluff. But too many things would have had to go flawlessly for *anyone* to place any faith in such a scheme.

No, he thought. Aeliana had been incredibly lucky to survive without being killed by a stray shot, captured by the prowling security forces, or raped by one of the mutinous soldiers. *They would have contacted us to make sure we got the message.*

"Shit," Rothschild said.

Pat jumped as the hatch clicked and started to rattle open. Rothschild had opened it too early, before they were ready. He cursed, then used his implants to bring up the chart Junayd had drawn of the bunker. They'd have to move now, without waiting for reinforcements. Gritting his teeth, he slipped forward as soon as he could.

Two guards, on the far side, gaped at him, then grabbed for their weapons. Pat shot them both down, silently relieved that neither of them had managed to sound the alert. The remainder of the company was already on the way, pressing through the hatch as Pat advanced into the barracks. A dozen men were getting dressed, clearly readying themselves for departure. Pat threw a gas grenade into the compartment and watched as the men tumbled to the ground. Anyone who hadn't been immunized to the gas would collapse the moment it touched them.

"Platoon One, with me," Pat ordered. The bunker's internal security systems might have missed them, but it was unlikely they would miss the gas. "Platoons Two through Seven, you know your targets. Go."

The interior of the bunker was strange, a bizarre mixture of luxury and austerity that puzzled him. Some walls were covered with paintings of famous scenes from history; others were completely barren. He couldn't help cracking a smile as he saw a painting of Admiral Junayd positioned on one wall, a caption proclaiming him a holy martyr. Under the circumstances, he was surprised it hadn't been taken down and desecrated. Maybe the Theocrats just hadn't had the time.

He turned the corner and ran into four men dressed in red uniforms. Pat shot them, too late to stop one of them from slapping a device at his belt. Alarms started to howl a moment later. Pat cursed and began to run, his platoon dogging his heels. The remainder of the company would secure the entrances and life support, hopefully gassing everyone in the bunker. He'd hoped to put everyone to sleep before they realized they were under attack, but their cover was blown. The bastards might just hit the switch before they fell asleep.

A checkpoint loomed up in front of him, manned by seven men with heavy weapons. Pat unhooked a plasma grenade from his belt as they opened fire, triggering the weapon as it reached its target. A wave of white heat blossomed down the corridor, so hot it scorched his skin as he pushed onwards. The checkpoint was melted instantly, its defenders vaporized. He unhooked another grenade and threw it ahead of him as his team encountered a second checkpoint, Sergeant Bones shoving Pat to one side as the defenders started shooting at him with plasma weapons. Pat barely had a moment to realize that Bones had been hit, then the grenade detonated, setting off the plasma confinement chambers and destroying the enemy position. He covered his eyes at the blaze, then looked at Bones. A plasma bolt had struck her above the chest, burning through her skin. The shock alone would have proved fatal.

"I'm sorry," Pat told her.

He had no time to mourn. He took one last look at her body, then resumed the race towards the bunker's command center. If he didn't get there shortly, everyone who had been killed would have died in vain.

◆ ◆ ◆

"That's the emergency alarm," Inquisitor Samuilu gasped. "They're here!"

Lord Cleric Eliseus stared at him. "How?"

Junayd, Nehemiah thought coldly. *And now they're on the verge of breaking through and ending the war.*

He didn't know if the treacherous admiral knew about the tunnels or not, but he'd had plenty of allies and clients. One of them might have known where to find the tunnel. Or maybe the Commonwealth had come up with some revolutionary new way to find an underground tunnel. But under the circumstances . . .

"It's over," he said quietly. They'd planned to take the escape tunnel, then hike down to the hidden shuttlecraft. That plan was useless now. "They've won."

"They won't win," Samuilu snarled. He turned to the console. "I'll burn the entire planet before I let them win."

"Don't," Nehemiah pleaded. He would have sold his soul for a weapon, if the devil had appeared and offered a bargain. "Samuilu . . . you'll kill everyone on the planet!"

"They deserve it!" Samuilu bellowed. "We wouldn't have lost if there hadn't been so much unbelief among us!"

Nehemiah struggled to find words, knowing the effort was futile. Samuilu was a fanatic. He believed every last word he was saying. Samuilu would sooner burn the world to ash than let the population succumb to heresy. By his damned standards, he was doing them a favor. God would know His own.

"This is madness," Nehemiah pleaded. "Samuilu . . . just stop. Think about it! The children . . . how do they deserve to die?"

"They'll be born again in paradise," Samuilu said. His hands were dancing over the console, typing in a series of commands. "Speaker, you failed. Let us show you the way."

"No," Nehemiah said.

He started forward, but Eliseus grabbed him. A second later, a shimmer appeared in the air between them and Samuilu. A force field . . . there was no way the two could get to the Inquisitor now, not without heavy weapons. And by the time they got them, it would all be over.

"Damn you," Nehemiah snarled. Eliseus was praying loudly, begging for God to accept his final sacrifice and shrive him of his sins. "Shut up, damn you."

Nehemiah felt a sudden sharpness and gasped in pain. Eliseus had drawn a knife and stabbed him. His mouth dropped open in complete shock as his arms and legs buckled, sending him falling to the floor. He'd never expected to be stabbed.

"Die," Eliseus said, "and face your fate like a man."

◆ ◆ ◆

Pat used his last grenade to burn down the inner hatch, then charged into the command center. A man lay on the floor, bleeding out; another man was standing over him, holding a bloody knife. He turned as Pat entered, lashing out as if he thought he could slash Pat's throat. Pat caught the knife on his sleeve, then knocked the man back against the force field. A surge of energy ran through him and he dropped to the ground, dead. The man standing on the far side of the force field turned to see what had happened, then resumed typing commands into his console. Pat didn't need to know the specifics to realize that he was preparing to trigger the bomb.

"You'll all die, all of you," the man cried out as the remainder of the platoon followed Pat into the chamber. Pat recognized him from Junayd's more detailed briefings. Inquisitor Samuilu, one of the fanatics. "This planet will burn."

Pat felt his blood run cold. His company had failed. He'd never doubted the bomb was real, yet he'd hoped . . . they'd failed. The bomb was about to be detonated. He checked the force field, but nothing short of a plasma grenade would break through—and he had none left. His plasma rifle wouldn't be enough. And the man was leering at them, practically rejoicing in his own death . . . and then Pat suddenly felt very calm.

I'm sorry, Kat, Pat thought as he pressed the terminal at his belt. The sensor within the terminal picked up his ID chip at once, arming the bomb. *I'm sorry.*

The world went white.

♦ ♦ ♦

"General," Colonel Washington said, "the enemy force field has collapsed!"

General Winters turned to look at him. "How?"

"Preliminary analysis suggests that the PDC's shield generator has been destroyed," Lieutenant Carter said. "Sir, it went up like a volcano."

The nukes, General Winters thought. *Shit.*

"Order the attacking force to pull back," he ordered. If the force shield was gone, there was no longer any need to risk his men. KEWs could eradicate the defenders if they refused to surrender. "And watch out for desperation attacks."

And we need to find that antimatter, he thought grimly. *If the bastards put it on a timer too, the war might not be over yet.*

♦ ♦ ♦

"Admiral," the operator said, "the Tabernacle has been destroyed."

Zaskar flinched. The heart of the Theocracy, built on the spot the first colony ship landed so long ago . . . gone? It couldn't be. But it was true. There was no hope of picking up the speakers now. The fleet was taking a beating. And if the enemy kept closing in, it wouldn't be long before they destroyed his entire fleet.

He was tempted to fight to the last. But there was no point.

"All ships capable of opening gateways are to retreat," he ordered. "The remainder are to fight long enough to hold the bastards off, then surrender."

The cleric stared at him. "Surrender?"

"The war is over," Zaskar snapped. "But we will survive."

◆ ◆ ◆

"The enemy fleet is breaking off," Wheeler reported. "They're attempting to retreat."

"Press the offensive," Kat snarled. The news from Ahura Mazda had hit her like a punch in the gut, but there was no time to mourn. "Don't let them get away!"

She scowled as the enemy fleet disintegrated, a good third of their surviving ships opening gateways and vanishing into hyperspace. The remainder were fighting, but without their missiles they couldn't hope to survive for long. She'd won the battle . . . but at a truly terrifying price.

"Commodore, the remaining enemy ships are trying to surrender," Wheeler reported. "Orders?"

Kat glared at the display. She wanted to kill them. She wanted to crush them like bugs, like the vermin they were. Pat was dead. He'd died saving Ahura Mazda from its masters. Who *cared* about anything else?

"Kat," William said quietly.

Kat gathered herself. "Accept their surrender, then dispatch marines to take the crews into custody," she ordered. "And then swing the fleet back to the planet."

"Aye, Commodore," Wheeler said.

We won, Kat thought numbly. She looked down at the golden ring on her finger. *But was it really worth it?*

CHAPTER THIRTY-EIGHT

Kat rose to her feet, two weeks later, as the marines escorted the five Theocrats into the conference room. She saw their faces stiffen, just slightly, as they saw her, their eyes tracking across her chest before fixing firmly on her face. They didn't seem to know *where* to look, she noted. She would have found their reactions amusing, she admitted to herself, if Pat had been there to share the joke. But he was gone. She still felt numb.

"Be seated," she ordered. She'd been tempted to have them stand, but that seemed mindlessly cruel. "Please."

She took a moment to survey them as they took their seats. Speaker Mosul, rescued from one of the Inquisition's jails; Speaker Farah, the sole survivor of the post-coup Theocratic government; Lord Cleric Rather, the senior surviving cleric. And behind them, Admiral Junayd and Administrator Nestor. Between them, they made up the closest thing Ahura Mazda had to a provisional government, their authority recognized, perhaps reluctantly, by the remainder of the planet's military. Kat rather doubted the provisional government would last very long, certainly not past the first election cycle. But for the moment they would suffice.

And Junayd is supposed to be on our side, she thought. *He'll keep them in line.*

She was tempted to wait, to drag the ceremony out, to rub their faces in their humiliation, but it would have been nothing more than pointless spite. They'd come to the superdreadnought to negotiate, instead of trying to stick the battle out and fight to the last. She knew they hated it, she knew they resented having to come to the negotiation table, but they'd come. They understood, more than their predecessors, just how hopeless their position was.

And watching as we disarmed and removed the antimatter stockpile probably helped, she told herself. *They know their former masters were preparing to kill the entire planet.*

"My government has authorized me to inform you of our terms of surrender," she said, keeping her voice firm. Junayd had advised her to act as stereotypically masculine as possible. "These terms are not negotiable. If you refuse to accept these terms, my fleet will take whatever steps are necessary to impose them. In that case, the final terms may be considerably steeper."

She took a moment to gauge their reactions, then went on. "First, all of your remaining warships, planetary garrisons, and occupation forces will surrender themselves into the custody of Commonwealth representatives," she said. "You will send orders via our courier boats to your garrison commanders to make sure they understand that they are to surrender, instead of destroying the occupied worlds.

"Second, Ahura Mazda and the other inner worlds will be under a general occupation until we can trust you to handle your own affairs without posing a threat to us or anyone else. All heavy weapons are to be surrendered to the occupation authorities. The outer worlds, the ones you occupied during your expansion, will be liberated; the remaining Theocratic populations will be repatriated to Ahura Mazda. We will provide transport to ensure that this is completed as fast as possible.

"Third, until proper elections are held, you will be recognized as the provisional government of Ahura Mazda. However, you will be required to govern in line with the principles laid down in the Commonwealth Charter, including religious freedom, sexual and gender equality, and emigration rights. The occupation forces will have the authority to over-rule or remove you from power if you transgress those limits."

She saw Rather wince. The Theocracy's claim to absolute power had been broken by the invasion and occupation. If the clerics were denied the right to *force* their views on their population, who knew *what* would happen? Kat knew, from the reports that had flooded in over the past two weeks, that large parts of the planet were in a state of upheaval. Churches had been burnt, clerics had been murdered. The entire planet was on the brink of civil war.

"Fourth, religious freedom specifically does not include the right to incite civil disobedience, violence, or any other form of harm against women, unbelievers, or the occupation force," Kat added. "You will be responsible for silencing clerics who incite violence. If you are unable or unwilling to do it, we will do it for you."

Rather definitely didn't look pleased, she noted. Farah didn't look pleased either, although Mosul seemed oddly amused. Junayd had suggested that he was definitely one of the moderates, someone who had good reason to dislike the clerics. Kat had a feeling that he'd be a raving fanatic by the Commonwealth's standards, but such musings hardly mattered. All that mattered was ending the war.

"Fifth, the Commonwealth will not seek general revenge against your soldiers, spacers, clerics, or civil servants. The vast majority of them will be repatriated to Ahura Mazda as soon as possible. However, we can and we will prosecute and punish those guilty of war crimes against both civilians and military personnel. We require your full cooperation in unearthing and trying the guilty. Those found guilty of committing atrocities will be punished."

Mosul looked as though he wanted to say something, but held his tongue. Kat waited for a moment, then continued.

"Sixth, the Commonwealth will *not* demand any form of compensation from the Theocracy for the damage inflicted on our worlds," she said. Mosul looked astonished, then relieved; he knew, even if the others didn't, that the Theocracy was in no state to pay anything. The economy had collapsed completely. "However, you *will* acknowledge, without any attempt to evade or mitigate the severity of your crime, that the Theocracy planned and launched a war of aggression that claimed the lives of upwards of two *billion* spacers, soldiers, and civilians. You will make no attempt to destroy your records, hide this truth from your civilians, or do anything else to obscure the question of war guilt. Your former masters started this war and lost it. No other interpretation will be permitted."

She took a long breath. "Finally, you will not be permitted warships, orbital battlestations, ground-based PDCs, or any other weapons until we determine that you no longer pose a threat to the rest of the galaxy. During that period, the Royal Navy will undertake to provide a minimal level of security for your planets. The Commonwealth will establish and operate naval bases throughout your territory to make this easier. Any other starships will be carefully inspected, repeatedly, while we hold responsibility for your security.

"The treaty has been prepared for your signatures," she concluded. "You have time to discuss it among yourselves, if you wish, but the Commonwealth has no intention of altering any of the terms. If you refuse to sign, we will take whatever steps we deem necessary to remove the threat you pose to the rest of the galaxy. There will be no further discussions."

She nodded to the marines, who escorted the five Theocrats out of the compartment. They looked stunned as they left, as if they were either unable to come to terms with the speed of their fall from power or unable to quite comprehend that a *woman* was dictating to them.

She had no doubt they would tell themselves that she was merely Tyre's mouthpiece, repeating the orders of her very masculine king.

And they would be right, she thought, looking down at her terminal. *This time, I am merely repeating orders from on high.*

Shaking her head, she rose and left the compartment.

◆ ◆ ◆

"They signed, eventually," Junayd said. "You do realize that their authority is very limited?"

"Of course," General Winters said. "And so is yours."

Junayd nodded. General Winters had been assigned to command the occupation force, although he seemed unsure if the appointment was a reward or a punishment. But there was no doubt that *he*, not the provisional government, would hold ultimate authority on Ahura Mazda. Junayd could and would build a power base of his own that would nonetheless be very limited. And yet the occupation would not last forever.

"We will start by trying to rebuild the economy," he said simply. "It should win us some friends."

He gritted his teeth. It wasn't going to be easy. Millions of people were starving on the planet below, millions more blaming the former government for their plight. And the food distribution network had collapsed completely. He had no idea how many people were going to die in the next few months, but he was sure it would be a terrifyingly high number.

And the farmers aren't helping, he thought. *The miscreants have armed themselves and are defending their fields against all comers.*

"If you can," General Winters observed. "What's going to happen when the first true elections are held?"

Junayd knew the voting process wasn't going to be easy. His home-world had no idea *how* to hold free elections. The planet had simply never had them, even back at the start. Ambitious people joined the military, the clergy, or the civil service and rose steadily in the ranks, occasionally by knifing the person above them in the back. The idea of holding elections, of asking the people to decide, was utterly alien. And the idea of giving everyone the vote, including women . . .

There's going to be trouble, he predicted silently. *What man is going to want his wife to have a vote?*

"I daresay we'll learn," he said instead. "It won't be easy, but we will do it."

He looked up at the holographic planet for a long moment, watching the tactical icons taking up position on the surface. There hadn't been any major resistance, thankfully. The remaining PDCs had surrendered without a fight once the provisional government started broadcasting orders. But that would change, he knew. The records were a mess, but it was clear that thousands of heavy weapons had vanished into the shadows. Clerics, former regime loyalists, and people with nowhere else to go would have plenty of tools and ammunition to mount an insurgency. The next few months were not going to be peaceful.

But we will rebuild, he told himself. *And we won't be spending half our GNP on warships any longer.*

That hurt, more than he cared to admit. He'd *loved* commanding his own ship, even if he *had* had a damned cleric looking over his shoulder. No matter what he did for the rest of his life, he would never command a warship again. The Theocracy wouldn't *have* any warships. Decades, perhaps centuries, would pass before the Commonwealth allowed his people to defend themselves. And by then he would be long dead.

But we were lucky, he thought. *The Commonwealth could have done a great deal worse.*

He looked down at the deck. He'd seen the postwar plans the Theocracy had drawn up, back in the first flush of victory. The Commonwealth would have been crushed without mercy, its societies turned into clones of the Theocracy or simply destroyed. Tyre would probably have been bombarded back to the Stone Age, just to keep it from posing a threat. And Kat Falcone, General Winters, and everyone else he'd met during his stay in the Commonwealth would have been killed. By comparison, the Commonwealth had been absurdly merciful.

General Winters snorted. "Be ready to leave in an hour," he said. "We'll be returning to the surface."

"Of course, General," Junayd said. "I understand."

◆ ◆ ◆

"There's been no sign of the remaining enemy ships," Kat said tiredly. She sat with William in her cabin, drinking coffee. "They seem to have vanished completely."

"We'll see them again," William predicted. "They won't have gone far."

Kat nodded. The Theocratic ships had been in poor condition, even without the final engagement. She doubted their crews could keep them operating for long, no matter what happened. They'd simply be unable to obtain the spare parts and expertise they needed to keep the ships going. Pirates faced the same problem, but they tended to use much smaller vessels.

The Theocrats might just sell the ships for ready cash, she thought. *Or they might have a secret bolt-hole somewhere within their former territory.*

She contemplated the star chart as she sipped her coffee. Theocratic Space was marginally smaller than the Commonwealth, but there were plenty of star systems that had been deemed useless and barely surveyed, even during the first great age of expansion. The Theocrats would have no problems turning a useless world into a hidden base, assuming they'd stockpiled colonization supplies somewhere. Or maybe they'd head out beyond the rim of explored space and then find an undiscovered world and cannibalize their ships to set up a hidden colony.

If they can, she thought. *Do they have any women on their ships at all?*

"We'll be surveying the nearest systems over the next three weeks," she said. "And then we'll be going home."

William lifted his eyebrows. "They're recalling the fleet?"

"They'll be leaving four squadrons of superdreadnoughts on duty here," Kat said, nodding towards the display. "And probably around a dozen other squadrons. But the main body of the fleet will be going home for the victory parade."

"It's not *quite* over," William reminded her.

Kat made a face. He was right. The remaining enemy garrisons had to be removed before their personnel decided they would sooner blow up their planets than surrender. She'd already sent courier boats to the nearest stars, each one carrying a high-ranking official who should be able to order a surrender. But it would take weeks, if not months, to ensure that every remaining garrison was no longer dangerous. And then their personnel would have to be repatriated before the locals slaughtered them. Once again, a nightmare.

But this is just the mopping up, she told herself firmly. *We won the war.*

A bitter grief overcame her as she looked down at the deck. Pat was dead. Her father was dead. Countless others were dead or would die before the mopping up was completed. It hardly seemed worth it. She and Pat had *planned* to spend the rest of their lives together, perhaps buying a freighter and heading out to trade. Those plans were now gone.

She glanced up as she felt a hand touch hers. "It's no consolation," William said, his brown eyes meeting hers. "But I am sorry for your loss."

"Thank you," Kat said, blinking away tears. "I wish . . ." She shook her head fiercely. "What are you going to do when we get home?"

"I don't think I'll be staying in the navy," William said quietly. "I've lost two ships. I doubt the Admiralty will give me a third command. And I would waste away behind a desk."

"You should stay," Kat said. She had no idea what *she* would be doing, but she was damned if she was leaving the navy. "You're a good man."

"Not everyone would agree," William said. He sighed. "And besides, I watched my homeworld die. I don't know where I should go."

Kat felt a flicker of betrayal, betrayal she swallowed hard. She didn't *own* him. She certainly didn't have any right to demand he stay with her, even though she had come to depend on his steady presence over the last two years. And yet, the thought of him leaving her . . .

"Your people are getting a new world," she said. "Are you planning to go there?"

"I don't know," William admitted. "My brother"—his face twisted—"is planning to go legitimate after the war. He offered me a place in his crew. But I also have a duty to my people. I should go and help them tame their new world."

"You could also help them by staying in the navy," Kat pointed out, calmly. "You're a good man."

"So you said," William countered. "I'm tired, Kat. I just want to rest."

"I understand," Kat said.

But she didn't, not really. Why would anyone want to give up the navy? But William had been in the navy longer than she'd been alive. He'd inched his way through the ranks, fighting desperately for recognition that had been granted freely to men and women with the right connections. As much as she hated to admit it, William had a point. Losing two ships would not endear him to the Admiralty, particularly as the fleet was being cut back to a peacetime establishment. William was unlikely to get a third command, even with Kat's family pulling strings on his behalf.

And now my father's dead, there will be a struggle to determine who inherits the Dukedom, Kat thought. *We won't be pulling any strings for a while.*

"You'll have plenty of time to make up your mind," she said, although she had a feeling that William had already made up his mind. He wasn't a very changeable person. "And you will be joining me for the victory parade, won't you?"

"Of course," William said. "How could I refuse?"

Kat surprised herself by leaning forward and giving him a hug. "It's been an honor," she said. And it had. She'd learned to respect him even as he'd learned to respect her. "And whatever happens, you will always be able to count on me."

"And me too," William said. He looked at her hand as she pulled back. "And I am truly sorry."

"I know," Kat said. She should take off the ring, she knew. It wasn't as if she could marry a dead man. But she couldn't bring herself to remove it. "General Winters thinks Pat triggered his nuke, sacrificing himself to save the entire planet. It was how he would have wanted to go."

She shook her head. "But it doesn't seem enough, does it?"

"No," William said. "But the pain will fade, in time."

He rose and headed for the hatch. "Take care of yourself," he said gently. The hatch hissed open. "Please."

"I'll try," Kat promised. She had to go on, somehow. Pat would have wanted her to go on, to live. But she didn't know how. "And thank you, once again."

CHAPTER THIRTY-NINE

"Welcome home, Commodore," the pilot said.

Kat nodded, shortly. Her brother Peter had insisted on sending one of the family's shuttles for her, rather than allowing her to use a military shuttle. She wasn't sure if he was being paranoid or not, but the enemy cell that had killed her father remained undiscovered. Who knew where they'd strike next? The war might be over and the occupied worlds now liberated, yet Tyre had not yet relaxed. It would be a long time before the Commonwealth lowered its guard again.

She rose and stepped out of the hatch. The scent of blossoming flowers greeted her, bringing back a wave of memories. She'd grown up on the estate, spending her days studying with her father's tutors or running and climbing around the gardens. The treehouse she'd built years ago was long gone, but the treehouse her father's staff had put together for the children was still visible, poking out of the trees. Her nieces and nephews were running around it, laughing and shouting as they scrambled up and down rope ladders. She couldn't help wishing, just for a moment, that she could be a kid again. In hindsight, it had been nice not to know anything about the realities of adult life.

But I always wanted to grow up, she thought.

She was tempted to join the children, but she pushed the thought aside and strode down towards the gates. Her brother was waiting for her, a tall handsome man with light blond hair, a muscular body, and a grim look on his face. Kat couldn't help thinking he looked tired, even though he'd had the best genetic enhancements money could buy. There was something saggy about him that worried her. Peter had gone into the family business almost as soon as he'd graduated, their father assigning him to tasks that had allowed him to learn the ropes, but he hadn't expected their father to die so soon.

None of us did, Kat told herself. *Father should have lived for decades to come.*

"Peter," she said.

"Katherine," Peter said. He sounded as if he had aged a couple of decades in the months since Kat had last seen him. "Welcome home."

Kat sighed as he turned to lead her into the mansion. She'd never had much of a relationship with her eldest brother. He'd already reached adulthood when she'd been born, spending as little time as possible at the mansion. And they'd had very little in common. He'd considered her a little brat; she'd considered him a stuffed shirt. He'd gotten married a couple of years after Kat's birth and his children weren't that much younger than Kat herself.

She followed him through the corridors, noting how many portraits of her father had been placed on display, a black rim indicating that the house was in mourning. The remainder of her family would be in their rooms, she was sure. She wondered, absently, just what they intended to do now their father was dead. Peter would have to fight if he wished to inherit the Dukedom, to say nothing of their father's vast patronage network. Their uncles and aunties were probably going to make their own bid for power.

Peter led her straight into their father's study—his study, she supposed now. The mansion belonged to their immediate family, not to the Falcone clan as a whole. She couldn't help feeling oddly ill at ease as she took a comfortable chair, remembering the few times she'd been summoned to her father's office as a child. It had been made clear, time and time again, that *none* of the children were to enter without their father, no matter the cause. Entering his study without him felt wrong.

She watched Peter pace around the desk, then sit down. "Katherine," he said. It looked odd too, to see him behind her father's desk. "You did well."

"Thank you," Kat said. She was sure Peter hadn't summoned her to the mansion to compliment her on winning the war. He could have sent a message while the fleet had been mopping up the remaining enemy garrisons. "I—"

Peter looked at her hand. "Are you sure you want to wear that?"

Kat held up her hand, allowing the ring to glint under the light. "Yes."

Her brother looked uncomfortable. "I believe our father would have approved the match," he said stiffly. His own marriage hadn't *exactly* been arranged, but his family had made it clear that they expected him to produce heirs. "And I am sorry about his death. But wearing his ring after his death is not healthy."

"I know," Kat said. She made no move to take the ring off. "But I will wear it anyway."

Peter met her eyes. "I believe you are in line for a promotion," he said. "After winning two major space battles, no one is going to question your position."

Kat found it hard to care. No promotion would bring back her lover. And no matter what she did, she would never escape her family's shadow. Part of her was just tempted to return to her rooms, lock the door, and hide. But she knew that wasn't an option.

"Good," she said sourly. "And what next?"

Peter cocked his head. "The family is in disarray," he said. "Uncle Fredrick and Uncle Richard are readying a challenge to my position. Can I count on your support?"

Kat shrugged. "What good would it do?"

"You're a famous officer," Peter pointed out. It struck her, suddenly, that he wasn't used to bargaining with her. "Your word counts for a great deal."

"Oh," Kat said.

She forced herself to consider the problem. Uncle Richard, her father's younger brother, had never struck her as being particularly interested in serving the family's interests. He'd been more of a playboy than anything else, back when she'd been a child. And while Uncle Fredrick was more competent, she simply didn't like him very much. He always had to get his way . . . and, when he didn't, he threw a fit. Everything had to be just so with him.

But could he win? Could either of them win?

She leaned forward. "Are there no other challengers?"

"Not yet," Peter said. "Ashley *may* try to throw her hat into the ring, but I should be able to come to an agreement with her. Auntie Darcy has potential, yet a good third of the family detests her."

Kat smiled. "I always liked her."

Peter stiffened. "And you would support her over me?"

"I never said she'd make a good duchess," Kat pointed out. Darcy had been fun, back when Kat had been a child, but Kat wouldn't have trusted her with anything serious. "Has she grown up?"

"Not really," Peter said.

Kat made up her mind. "Then yes, you can count on my support," she said. "But I'll want something in return, later."

Peter sighed. "If it is within my power to provide it, without threatening the family, I will," he said. "And I thank you."

"You are welcome," Kat said with equal formality. She'd never expected to be playing power broker. Hell, she *wasn't* playing unless the two uncles managed to band together and mount a joint challenge. "But I trust you will not be expecting me to attend the debate?"

"You may find it interesting," Peter said. He looked pained. "Your future will be affected too."

"I'd sooner have half my teeth removed," Kat said. She'd attended one family conclave in her time, shortly after she'd turned sixteen. It wasn't an experience she wanted to repeat in a hurry. "I'm sure you can handle it."

She allowed her voice to darken. "And if you can't handle it," she added, "how can you handle the family? And the clients?"

Peter looked irked. "We shall see," he said. "But the family's position has been weakened, Katherine. You need to bear that in mind."

"I shall," Kat said. She rose. "And, if you don't mind, I need to freshen up. I've been offered a place of honor in the review booth."

"So you have," Peter agreed. "Try not to let the media catch you falling asleep next to the king."

Kat flushed. "It was *one* time," she protested. She'd dozed off in the stands during an award ceremony at school. In hindsight, only her father's influence had saved her from being unceremoniously expelled. "And I was thirteen!"

"Yes," Peter said. He gave her a thin-lipped smirk. "And it will be much more embarrassing if you do it at twenty-nine."

◆ ◆ ◆

William had been surprised when he'd passed through the security checkpoints outside the parade grounds that the staff pointed him to the regal box. His knighthood assured him a decent seat, but right beside the king? And then he saw Kat Falcone settling into her seat and knew the answer. She, or the king, had invited him into the box.

He sat down next to her, feeling oddly exposed. The box was surrounded by a force field, with a platoon of armored marines within eyeshot, but he couldn't help wondering if an enemy sniper might be taking aim at them. He was surprised the security staff had agreed to allow the king to appear in public, especially in a place where thousands of civilians and military officials were mingling. And yet he had to admit the king *needed* to be seen. The public had to know that the head of state wasn't hiding in a bunker but sharing the danger.

Although his appearance isn't that dangerous, he thought. *The force field around this box could stand off a nuke.*

"Kat," he said, "did you invite me here?"

"The king did, I believe," Kat said. She sounded oddly distracted, as if she was worrying about some greater matter. "I don't know why."

The crowd cheered loudly. William glanced up, just in time to see King Hadrian himself appear at the top of the stairs. He rose hastily and bowed as the king made his way down to the regal chair, waving to the crowd. William couldn't shake his first impression of the king—that he was a junior officer out of his depth—but he had to admit that Hadrian had gotten better at playing to the audience. Behind him, Princess Drusilla and Princess Aeliana followed, both wearing dresses that seemed to glow under the light. The crowd cheered them loudly.

Everyone knows that the princesses risked their lives to save the Commonwealth, William thought as the king sat on his chair. The seat wasn't quite a throne but was large enough to make it clear who was in charge. *The media has been talking about their escape for months.*

He sat and watched, torn between excitement and boredom, as the spacers, soldiers, and marines marched across the parade ground. The crowd cheered itself hoarse, hooting and hollering. William couldn't escape the impression that most of the crowd didn't know what they were cheering, or why. The gaps in the formation where troops should be bore mute testament to the high cost of the war. No one would ever know how many people had died because of the war, directly or indirectly, but countless families were grieving their dead relatives. Kat was mourning her lover. It seemed wrong, somehow, to cheer.

And millions of people died on Hebrides, he thought bitterly. *The end of the war hasn't brought peace.*

His eyes swept the crowd, picking out those who didn't seem so pleased. Were they people who'd lost someone to the war? Or people who knew the price that had been paid? Or merely people who thought the war had been wasteful? There were already commentators asking pointed questions about the government's plans to finish the war, pointing out that there had been easier and cheaper ways to win. But all of their questions were driven by hindsight, by what had been discovered after the end of the conflict. The government of the time hadn't known enough about its enemies.

He frowned as he spotted Sandy McNeal, wearing black as he watched the parade. The representative for Hebrides looked grim, mourning his dead world even as he applauded the end of the war. Beside him, Rose MacDonald—his hatchet woman—looked worse. God alone knew what would happen, now that the survivors were *en route* to New Pennsylvania. Hebrides hadn't been a rich world, even before the war. Funding the growth and development of a whole new planet would be an absolute nightmare. He could easily imagine hundreds of thousands of youngsters choosing to leave rather than trying to rebuild a society they'd often found restrictive.

God help us, he thought.

It felt like hours before the parade finally came to an end. William was tired, unwilling to stay and yet unable to leave; beside him, Kat seemed to feel the same way. The king looked enthusiastic, as if he could have remained in the box for hours to come. But then, William thought, he'd been preparing for his role almost from birth. Beside him, Princess Drusilla glowed; Aeliana looked scared. *She* would never have seen so many people in one place back on her homeworld, not when she'd been cooped up from birth. William couldn't help feeling sorry for her. It would be a long time before she felt safe on Tyre.

And the rest of her family is dead, William thought. *A high price for her freedom.*

The king rose. The crowd fell silent.

"Two years ago, the storm broke," the king said. William had to admit the king had an excellent speaking voice. "The Theocracy of Ahura Mazda launched a sneak attack on our worlds, aiming to crush our fleets and shatter our unity before we could rally and take the fight to the enemy. Their ships attacked Cadiz and 5th Fleet, then hit and occupied five other worlds while raiding forces struck deep into our territory. It looked as though we might lose the war.

"But we held. Our spacers and soldiers refused to yield, fighting desperately to hold the line and find new ways to take the war to the enemy. Our people rallied to the cause, enlisting in the military or finding employment in our growing war industries. We stopped the enemy offensive and then struck deep into their space. And now, finally, we have won the war. The threat is gone."

The crowd cheered. The king stood there, drinking in their applause. William felt a stab of bitter resentment, despite himself. King Hadrian hadn't commanded any ships or served in a groundpounder unit. He hadn't done anything except chair the War Cabinet and make speeches. And yet, he was practically claiming the credit for himself.

"But this victory came at a very high cost," the king continued when the crowd had finally quieted down. "Hundreds of thousands of spacers, soldiers, and militiamen lost their lives in combat; millions of civilians were killed, either by enemy occupation forces or enemy strikes on our worlds. We do not even *begin* to know how many *enemy* servicemen and civilians were killed in the fighting. Their deaths, I pledge to you, will not be in vain.

"Years ago, we planned a slow and steady expansion of the Commonwealth. New member worlds would have assistance to develop their economies, while steadily integrating into our system. Those plans were destroyed by the war. The demands of the war industries had to come first. We could not waste resources on developing colonial worlds when we had to protect ourselves from the Theocracy and then go on the offensive.

"But now that the war is over, we have a serious problem. Countless worlds have suffered because of the war. Countless populations have experienced all manner of problems because of the war. Rebuilding the occupied worlds will be hard enough, but repairing the damage to the unoccupied worlds will be worse. The war exposed many of the cracks in our own societies. I swear that we will not let those cracks go untended.

"I pledge to you that the Commonwealth will work to rebuild, to repair the damage caused by the war, to heal worlds the enemy occupied for decades. I will commit the full resources of the monarchy to making it work. And, to seal my pledge, I tell you now that Princess Drusilla has accepted my offer of marriage."

William felt Kat start beside him. She hadn't known.

He fought hard to keep his face under control. Even *he* had been unable to hide from the tabloid speculations about who the king would marry, but Princess Drusilla? She might have been branded a heroine—and the crowds were already cheering her name—yet he doubted it would be long before the king's political enemies remembered just who had fathered her . . . and worry, perhaps, that she would exert undue influence over her husband.

The crowd seemed happy, judging by the racket, but here and there he could see shocked and unhappy faces: Israel Harrison, Leader of the Opposition; Duke Newport, perhaps the most powerful aristocrat save for the king himself; Peter Falcone, Kat's oldest brother and probably the next in line for the Dukedom. The king hadn't consulted anyone outside his privy council, William realized slowly. He might not have consulted anyone at all.

And who knows, he asked himself, *what will happen when the opposition gets organized?*

He shook his head, slowly. The king could marry whomever he wanted, if he recalled his civics lessons correctly, but if Parliament disliked the Royal Consort, they could force him to abdicate or simply impeach him. And then? The king didn't have any siblings. His closest relative was a cousin. But that cousin was married to a duke and technically barred from the throne. The entire affair was going to be one hell of a mess.

It may be a good thing I'm leaving, he thought, sourly. He'd promised Kat he'd stay for Pat's funeral, but not much longer. *This conflict could turn ugly in a hurry.*

CHAPTER FORTY

Kat couldn't help thinking, as the empty casket was placed into the ground by the marine honor guard, that Pat would not have appreciated the sheer number of reporters who'd turned up for his funeral, although he might have been amused by his former comrades flatly refusing to allow them into the cemetery. The hovering crowd of vultures was on the far side of a security fence, lying in wait for the handful of guests to leave. Someone, probably one of her uncles, had told them that Kat and Pat had been engaged before his death. The media had promptly turned the story into a love affair to rival *Romeo and Juliet*.

Bastards, she thought. *It isn't as if we killed ourselves because we were too stupid to wait and see what happens.*

She pushed the thought aside as the ceremony finally came to an end. Pat's will had specified a minimal service, with no more than a handful of his fellow marines and friends in attendance. His sole surviving relative, a sister, hadn't been able to return to Tyre for the funeral, although Kat had promised to visit her when she had a chance. The poor woman had found herself under siege by the media before she'd learned what had happened.

"I'm sorry, Pat," Kat said quietly. "You deserved better."

She pulled the ring from her finger as the marines started burying the casket, then walked over and dropped it into the earth. No one said anything as it was buried, respecting her unspoken wishes. She hated to admit that Peter was right. Keeping the ring was bad enough, but wearing it was definitely unhealthy. She turned to walk away from the grave, then stopped as she saw an aircar landing neatly on the far side of the graveyard. A hot flash of anger burned through her, only to fade when the hatch opened and the king stepped out. He looked as tired and worn as she felt.

"Your Majesty," she said stiffly. Two days had passed since the king had announced his marriage, two days since the entire planet had gone crazy. Half the population seemed to support the match; the other half appeared to detest the very idea. "Have you come to pay your last respects?"

"I believe he was a good man," the king said. He glanced past her, his eyes crossing the grave and the stone-faced marines guarding it. "And I am genuinely sorry for your loss."

"Thank you," Kat said.

She watched the king salute the grave, unsure how she should feel. The king had never been a close friend of Pat's, and he certainly hadn't been invited to the ceremony, but he'd taken the time to come anyway. And he *hadn't* turned it into a media circus. Kat was silently grateful for that, if nothing else. The media probably didn't know who'd been in the aircar until it had landed past the security fence.

"There are some matters I wish to discuss with you," the king said, when he had finished. He indicated the aircar. "Please will you join me?"

Kat hesitated, then nodded. Pat's friends were planning to hold a wake, but she didn't feel like drinking herself into a stupor. She waved to William, silently reminding him that he'd promised to join her for dinner before leaving Tyre, then followed the king into the aircar and sat down. She'd expected luxury, but the aircar was little more comfortable than a flying taxicab. And yet the king seemed quite happy with it.

"Your Majesty," she said. There were questions she wanted to ask him, but she didn't know how. "What can I do for you?"

"Your promotion to admiral is going through now," the king told her as the aircar rose into the air. A pair of gunships appeared from nowhere and fell into escort position. "You'll probably be placed in command of 6th Fleet. The Admiralty is looking at permanently establishing a full-scale fleet deployment within the Ahura Mazda Sector. If so, you'll be going back there as commanding officer."

"Again," Kat said. She never wanted to see Ahura Mazda again—technically, she'd never set foot on the blighted world—but it beat a desk job. "Is this confirmed?"

"Not as yet," the king said. "But there are few other candidates."

He paused. "It's been three months since the end of the war," he added. "Ahura Mazda is in pretty bad shape, and it isn't the only world staring starvation in the face. There are dozens of Theocratic garrisons that need to be shipped home, hundreds of little problems that need to be tackled before they turn into big problems. I'm trying to get some Relief and Recovery services out there, but it's not proving easy. Too many people think we should put our own planets first."

"We should," Kat said.

"But then the Theocracy will take root once again," the king reminded her. "We still haven't accounted for *all* of their remaining warships."

Kat made a face. ONI's best guess, which she took with the routine grain of salt, was that most of the surviving enemy ships would become nonfunctional very quickly. For once, she didn't disagree. But they hadn't been accounted for, and until they were, they *were* a prospective threat. Unless they *had* headed out beyond explored space, in which case, they wouldn't be a threat for generations, if at all.

"It is important," the king said. "And the longer we wait, the harder it will be to lay the groundwork for the former Theocratic worlds to join the Commonwealth."

"It will take years for them to be ready," Kat said, quietly.

"Then we'd better get started," the king said. "My father oversaw the creation of the Commonwealth. I wish to oversee its expansion."

He paused. "And there is a second point," he added. "Now the war is over, I am reformatting my privy council. A couple of my father's former advisors have requested permission to leave their duties, and I have granted it."

Kat glanced at him. "Was that before or after you announced your forthcoming marriage?"

"Before," the king told her. "They wanted to leave earlier, but I asked them to stay until the end of the war. I want you to take one of those vacant seats."

Kat stared at him. "Are you serious?"

"Yes," the king said. "And I need your answer soon."

Kat took a moment to consider the implications, but she knew she was already out of her depth. The king's privy council consisted of his most trusted advisors, men and women who were friends as well as allies, people who could be relied upon to tell him the truth. To be asked to take a seat on the privy council was a great honor. And yet, it had deeper implications. Her *father* hadn't been on the privy council. She'd always had the impression he'd refused a seat.

And if I take the seat, she thought, *what does it mean for my family?*

"I would have to check with my brother," she said, finally. "But I have no personal objection."

The king looked oddly disappointed. "Your father would have snapped out an answer at once," he said.

"My father was the Duke," Kat pointed out. "I am not."

"True," the king agreed. He pulled a small terminal out of his pocket and glanced at it. "I believe you will be given your next assignment by the end of the week. I need your answer by then. There's no formal investiture ceremony, thankfully, but you *will* have to be briefed on a number of issues before you leave. My staff will see to it."

"I understand," Kat said.

The king reached out and touched her hand, gently. "For what it's worth, I need your advice and support," he said. "There are too many old fogies on my privy council, men I inherited from my father. They lack vision."

"William was old enough to be my father," Kat pointed out.

"But he wasn't on the privy council," the king countered. He smiled, rather thinly. "Do you have any questions?"

"Just one," Kat said. "At the parade . . . why did you announce everything?"

For a long moment, she thought the king wasn't going to answer. And then he leaned forward, as if he were about to impart a secret.

"The Commonwealth has been sorely tested by the war," the king told her. "And now that the war is over, all the naysayers are trying to pull back, to abandon commitments that need to be honored. But this isn't the time to stop. For the sake of the entire Commonwealth, for the sake of the future, we cannot slow down now. We must *not* surrender the opportunity to expand the Commonwealth and bring prosperity to the galaxy. And I will not let that be buried beneath partisan politics."

He paused. "Does that answer your question?"

"I think so," Kat said. Should she talk his request over with Peter? Or William? Or should she keep it to herself? She had the feeling she'd been told something in confidence, even if the king hadn't *specifically* told her to keep it private. "And I'll let you know in a day or two."

The king nodded. "I'll watch for your message," he said. "And thank you."

Kat nodded. "Please drop me off at the Admiralty," she said wryly. "I can find my own way from there."

"Of course," the king said. "We wouldn't want more rumors, would we?"

♦ ♦ ♦

The palace, King Hadrian had often thought, was a gilded cage. He had been its prince, then its king, but he'd always been trapped within its walls. He'd never been allowed to leave, save for short periods where he'd always been closely supervised. His father, the most imposing man the young Hadrian had ever known, had never been willing to allow his son to endanger his life. There was only one heir, he'd said. Hadrian could not be risked.

He strode through the uppermost levels, feeling alone even though he knew there were servants only a call away. He'd never been friendly with them, not even the maids who'd flirted shamelessly with him as he'd grown into adulthood. His father had encouraged him to remember that he was the prince, the man who would be charged, one day, with ruling the Commonwealth. But he'd never had any *real* friends, let alone outside experience. He knew much, but it was all theoretical.

Kat would accept his offer, he was sure. No one could quibble over her qualifications or connections. And he could use her presence as a lever to winkle two or three of the other old fogies off the privy council. His father might have ensured the bastards would stay there, as long as they chose to remain, but Hadrian didn't have to fire them to get them out. And *then* it would become easier to set his own agenda.

And if there is one thing the lords and the commoners have both forgotten, he thought as he strode into his private chamber, *it is that my family built this kingdom.*

His father had been a great man, Hadrian admitted. It wasn't something he could dispute, even if he wanted to. King Travis had guided his homeworld through the aftermath of the Breakaway Wars and then had started building the Commonwealth. But Hadrian wanted to be great too, to have his name remembered along with his father's. And he would, he promised himself; he would be great, whatever the cost.

And the war had provided the perfect opportunity. His power—direct and indirect—had expanded with the Commonwealth, with the colossal growth in war production, and opportunities for patronage. With the war over, the gateway to greatness lay open, beckoning him. He was not going to waste the moment.

And whatever the cost, he was going to win.

End of the First Arc

Kat Falcone Will Return.